ILJA LEONARD PFEIJFFER, a classicist by training, made his literary debut with a poetry collection in 1999 that was an homage to the experimental poetry of his great models, Pindar and Lucebert. In the years that followed, in addition to poetry, he has written stage plays, essays, columns, travel accounts, stories, political satires, and four novels written in the spirit of Rabelais. In his other novels, including his debut he has toyed with the idea of world literature and divided the critics between those proclaiming him a genius and those who think him an antiquated stylist. He's a bit of both. *La Superba*, published in Dutch in 2013, is Pfeijffer's masterpiece of a novel, and was greeted with unanimous praise upon publication, including winning the Libris Literatuurprijs, the Netherlands' most prestigious literary award, and the Tzum Prize, awarded for "the most beautiful sentence of the year," which he has now won twice. His most recent poetry collection, *Idyllen*, published in 2015, became the first single work of poetry to ever win in the grand slam of the three major Dutch poetry awards— the VSB, Jan Campert, and Awater.

MICHELE HUTCHISON lives in Amsterdam and translates from Dutch and French. She has translated Ilja Leonard Pfeijffer, Joris Luyendijk, Simone van der Vlugt, Esther Gerritsen, and Pierre Bayard, alongside a number of children's books, graphic novels, and poems. She also works as an editor and blogger.

LA SUPERBA

—

Ilja Leonard Pfeijffer

TRANSLATED FROM THE DUTCH BY
MICHELE HUTCHISON

DEEP VELLUM PUBLISHING
DALLAS, TEXAS

Deep Vellum Publishing
3000 Commerce St., Dallas, Texas 75226
deepvellum.org · @deepvellum

Deep Vellum Publishing is a 501c3
nonprofit literary arts organization founded in 2013.

This book was published with the support
of the Dutch Foundation for Literature.

N **ederlands**
letterenfonds
dutch foundation
for literature

—

ISBN: 978-1-941920-22-0 (paperback) · 978-1-941920-23-7 (ebook)
LIBRARY OF CONGRESS: 2015960718

—

COVER DESIGN AND TYPESETTING
Anna Zylicz · annazylicz.com

Text set in Bembo, a typeface modeled on those cut by Francesco Griffo
for Aldo Manuzio's printing of *De Aetna* in 1495 in Venice.

DISTRIBUTED BY
Consortium Book Sales & Distribution · (800)-283-3572 · cbsd.com

Printed in the United States of America on acid-free paper.

Contents

—

A Zena a prende ma a non rende

PART ONE

The Most Beautiful Girl in Genoa

I.

The most beautiful girl in Genoa works in the Bar of Mirrors. She is neatly dressed like all the girls who work there. She also has a boyfriend who drops in on her from time to time at work. He uses hair gel and wears a sleeveless t-shirt with SOHO on it. He's an asshole. Sometimes I watch them in the mirrors, kissing secretly in the cubbyhole where she prepares the small dishes they serve free with the aperitif.

This morning on the Via della Maddelena I saw someone who'd been mugged. "*Al ladro!*" he shouted. "*Al ladro!*" Then a boy came running round the corner. The man chased after him. He was wearing a white vest and he had a fat face and a fat belly. He looked like an honest man who'd learned to work hard for paltry pay from a young age. The boy ran uphill, to the Via Garibaldi, past the sundial and then carried on climbing, up the steps of the Salita San Francesco. The fat man who had been mugged didn't stand a chance.

Later I sat drinking on the Piazza delle Erbe. It's an unusual kind of place, evening just happens there without me having to organize anything. The little orange tables belong to the Bar Berto,

4

the oldest pub on the square, famous for its aperitif. The white tables belong to the nameless trattoria where it's impossible to eat without a booking. The red and yellow tables belong to various cafés and behind them there's another terrace, a little lower down. I can look up the names if you're interested. I was sitting at a blue table on the upper part of the square, looking out onto Bar Berto's terrace. The blue tables belong to Threegaio, set up by three homosexuals who brainstormed for days on end and still couldn't come up with a better name than that. I was drinking Vermentino from the Golfo di Tigullio. An impressive looking she-man wearing very dark sunglasses was sitting on a bar stool in front of the building. It was a reassuring sight, she was always there. Street musicians. Rose sellers. And then she spoke to me, "There's something feminine about you." She ran her fingers through my hair like a man claiming something as his own. "What's your name?" Her voice was like a dockworker's. "Don't worry, I know. I'll call you Giulia."

That night there was a short but violent thunderstorm. I was on my way home when it started. I sheltered in an arcade. It had an official name I noticed later: Archivolto Mongiardino. The black sky lit up green. I'd never seen anything like it. The rain clattered down like two cast iron portcullises on either side of the vault. After a few minutes it stopped.

But the streetlights had gone out. In the alleys barely penetrated by daylight, a medieval darkness reigned. My house wasn't far. I could find it by feeling my way, I was sure. Yes, the street went upwards here. This had to be Vico Vegetti. To my left and right, I felt scaffolding. That was right. There were renovations here.

And then I almost tripped over something. A wooden beam or something similar. That's what it felt like. Dangerous leaving something like that lying around in the street. I bent down to move it to one side. But it didn't feel like wood. It was too cold and slippery for that. It was too rounded to be a beam. It felt strange, and a bit disgusting, too. I tried to use the light of my mobile phone as a torch, but it was too weak. I was almost home. I decided to push the thing behind the builders' dumpsters and come back the next day to examine it. I was curious. I really wanted to know what it was.

2.

Prostitutes are for lunch. They appear around eleven or half past eleven. They hang around in the labyrinth of alleyways in the sloping triangle between Via Garibaldi, Via San Luca, and Via Luccoli, on either side of the Via della Maddalena, in small dark streets with poetic names like Vico della Rosa, Vico dei Angeli, and Vico ai Quattro Canti di San Francisco. In these alleys the sun doesn't even shine at midday. They lean there casually against doorposts or sit in clusters on the street. They say things like "*amore*" to me. They say that they love me and they want me to come with them. They say they want to run their fingers through my hair. They are black. They are blacker than the anthracite shadows in this city's entrails. They give off the smell of night in the afternoon. They stand there on haughty, towering legs, a flickering glimmer of arrogance in their eyes. They sink their white teeth into men's pale white flesh. I don't know how I'd ever get out alive. Civil servants with leather briefcases dart away skittishly.

Later I see them again in the Galleria Mazzini: Genoa's magistrates in their shirtsleeves, dark blue jackets slung across their shoulders, their calf-leather briefcases filled with the few documents of any real importance in their sole charge. They like to walk on the marble floor, past the antiques on display, enjoying the lofty reverberations of their footsteps under the crystalline roof. Griffins with the Genoese coat of arms on their chests support the chandeliers, their beaks twisted with arrogance. If you walk through the Galleria from the Piazza Corvetto, you come out at the Opera. Where else?

I walked toward the sea. In the distance, a yellow airplane glided over the waves and scooped up water. There were forest fires in the mountains. I know people who can tell tomorrow's weather from the height at which the swallows soar. But the low flight of a fire plane is the most reliable indication of a blistering summer.

I've bought myself a new wardrobe so that I can slip into this elegant new world a new man. A couple of Italian summer suits, tailored shirts, an elegant pair of shoes, as soft as butter but as sharp as a knife, and a real panama hat. It cost me a fortune, but I considered it a necessary investment to give my assimilation a boost.

That evening, I spoke to Rashid. He sells roses. I usually bump into him a couple of times a night. I offered him a drink. He came to sit with me for a while. He was from Casablanca, he said, an engineer who specialized in air-conditioning and refrigeration. In Casablanca, he has a large house but no money. That's why he came to Genoa, but he can't get a job because he doesn't speak Italian. During the day, he tries to learn Italian from YouTube videos. In the evenings, he sells roses. Every evening he does the rounds of all the terraces to Nervi. Then he walks back. To Nervi and back is twenty-four kilometers. He lives with eleven other Moroccans in a two-room apartment. "Of course there are rats, but luckily they aren't that big. All Moroccans think you can get rich without even trying in Europe. Of course they won't go back until they've saved enough to rent a Mercedes for a fortnight and put on a show that they've become spectacularly rich and successful in Europe. It's a fairy tale that gets better with every retelling. But I've seen the reality, Ilja. I've seen the reality."

When I walked home, the flag was fluttering high on top of the Palazzo Ducale's towers. It wasn't the European flag, nor the Italian flag. It was a red cross on a white background: the Genoese flag. La Superba. Above the harbor and in the distance, above the black mountains of Liguria, I heard the griffins screeching.

And then it came back to me. The previous night I'd stumbled over an object in the dark on the Vico Vegetti. And I'd hidden the object behind a garbage can. Now the streetlights were working again and I was actually quite curious.

But the thing wasn't there anymore. There was all kinds of stuff near the garbage cans down on the corner of the Piazza San Bernardo, but nothing you could stumble over. Well, perhaps it wasn't that important. Besides, I realized that showing so much interest in garbage might look a bit funny to the few passersby. In any case, it wasn't the image I wanted to adopt as a proud, brand-new immigrant to the city. I went home.

But a little higher up in the alleyway, near the scaffolding, there was a dumpster full of builders' waste. I remembered clinging onto the scaffolding in the pitch dark when the power cut out. On the off chance, I looked to see whether the thing might be there. At first

I didn't see it, but then I did. I looked back over my shoulder to see if anyone was looking, picked it up, and got the fright of my life.

It was a leg—a woman's leg. Unmistakably a woman's leg. And when it had been in the right context, it had been attractive—slender and long, perfectly proportioned. It was no longer wearing a shoe, but it still had on a stocking, the long, old-fashioned kind that only models on the Internet still wore. To cut to the chase, there I was, in the middle of the night, in my new foreign city holding an amputated female leg, and, all things considered, this didn't seem to me the ideal start to my new life. Maybe I should call the police. But maybe I'd better not. I put the leg back and went off to bed.

But later I awoke with a start, bathed in sweat. How could I have been so stupid? Of course I could tell myself that I had my own reasons—which for that matter many would have found understandable—for not wanting to have anything to do with a chopped-off woman's leg I'd accidentally discovered in a public place—but I'd stood there holding it in my hands. What I'm saying is I'd stood there groping it twice with my callow, canicular paws. Hadn't I ever heard of fingerprints? Or DNA evidence? And when the leg attracted the attention of the *carabinieri*, which sooner or later it was likely to do, would they carelessly toss it to one side as yet another sawn-off woman's leg found in the alleyways, or wouldn't they possibly be curious as to whom it had belonged to, who had amputated it, and whether this had happened with the approval of its rightful owner? And wouldn't they, once that curiosity had taken root, carry out a simple search for clues? And wasn't an investigation of the neighborhood then quite an obvious next step? Wake up, you dope.

But I no longer needed to tell myself that. I was already wide awake. More than that, I was already getting dressed. It was still nighttime, dark, no one about. I had to act quickly. The leg was still there. I didn't have any kind of detailed plan, but removing the *corpus delicti* from the public arena seemed a sensible place to start. I took it home with me and leaned it against the back of the IKEA wardrobe in my bedroom.

3.

I want to be part of this world. When I woke up, I heard the city starting to chew the day between her ancient, rotten teeth. In different parts of the neighborhood, her crumbling ivories were being drilled. Neighbors swore at each other through open windows. On the wall of the palazzo my bedroom looked out on, someone had written that all smiles are mysterious. Someone else had written that he thinks the Genoa football club is better than the Sampdoria football club, but in terms much more explicit than that. Someone else had written that he loved a girl named Diana and that to him she was a dream become reality. Later on, he or somebody else had crossed out the confession. There was garbage on the street. Pigeons pecked around in their own shit.

Today ships will arrive with Dutch, German, and Danish tourists on their way back from Sardinia and Corsica. They arrive dozens of times a day, and the tourists cautiously and reluctantly lose themselves a bit inside the labyrinth for an afternoon. They seldom dare venture much further than the alleys a few meters from the Via San Lorenzo. Others walk along the Via Garibaldi to the Palazzo Rosso and the Palazzo Bianco, oblivious to the dark jungle lying at their feet.

I like tourists. I can watch them and follow them for hours. They are touching in their tired attempts to make something of the day. When I was a boy, school used to give us lists of all the things we shouldn't forget to take on our school trip. The last item on the list was always "a good mood." That's what tourists carry in their rucksacks when they trudge through the streets and look at the map on every corner to try to find out *where* on earth they are. And *why* was that again? Finding every building pretty, every square nice, and every little shop cute is a matter of survival. Sweat pours from their foreheads. They think they understand everything, but they're suspicious at the wrong moments, while not fearing the real dangers. In Genoa, they are more helpless than anywhere else. Incomprehension and insecurity are written all over their faces as they hesitantly wander around the labyrinth. I like them. They're my brothers. I feel connected to them.

But I want to be part of this world. I want to live in the labyrinth like a happy monster, along with thousands of other happy monsters. I want to nestle in the city's innards. I want to understand the grinding of its old buildings' teeth. I went outside and walked along the Vico Vegetti, the Via San Bernado, past the garbage cans and the Piazza Venerosa, down to the Via Canneto Il Lungo to do some shopping at Di per Di. I bought detergent, *grissini*, and a bottle of wine. Then I took the same route home. But I did happen to be walking along with a plastic bag from Di per Di. My bag was my green card, my residence permit, my asylum. Everyone could see that I'd been admitted. Everyone could see I lived here. I had spoken scarcely more Italian than the words "*prego*" and "*grazie*," but when they spotted my plastic bag from the supermarket, no one could consider me an outsider any longer. I stopped at a kiosk and bought *Il Secolo XIX*, Genoa's local paper. I had resolved to read it every day. I clamped it proudly under my arm, making sure it was folded in such a way that everyone could see that it was *Il Secolo*.

When I got home, I looked at the wall of my building. I live on the ground floor of a tall palazzo in a narrow alleyway that climbs steeply. "Ground floor" is a relative concept for an alley at such a steep gradient. To the right of my entrance, there must be a large area under my bedroom that is probably storage space for the restaurant at number one rosso, which has been closed since my first day here. The whole building is made of deeply-pitted, grayish chunks of rock, crumbling cement, and patches of old layers of plaster here and there. All in all, the entire thing is rotten, peeling, and decayed. But it has been for centuries. And proud of it. When this was built, there was no gas, electricity, running water, television, or Internet. All these amenities had been tacked onto the outside in a makeshift way over the years. There are wires running from the roof along the front wall, entering through holes drilled into the various apartments. The plumbing and sewage have been added to the outside too—a disordered tangle of lead piping. Next to my front door, I noticed a thick pipe entering my house through a hole. And then I saw the sticker again:

> *derattizzazione in corso*
> *non toccare le esche*

The same sticker I had spotted all over the city over the past days had been placed on the water pipes going through the wall into my house, too. I smiled contentedly. I didn't live in a hotel. I lived in a real building, a real Genoese building with the same sticker as so many other buildings in the city. I must look up what it means at some point, just for the fun of it.

4.

My waitress has had a nasty fall. Or something else happened. I hadn't seen her for a couple of days in the Bar of Mirrors. Then I saw her walking along the Salita Pollaiuoli in her own clothes. She said "Ciao" to me. She had a bandage around her left elbow and her left wrist was stained red with iodine disinfectant. There were red patches on her left leg and foot, too. Later I was relieved to see her serving in her neat waitress uniform. Her white shirt was short-sleeved so the bandage and the red patches on her arm were visible to all. The patches on her leg were concealed by her black trousers, but she'd rolled up the trouser leg to her ankle, probably because the seam irritated the wound on her foot too much otherwise. It was clearly visible because she was wearing open shoes. Closed-toe shoes would hurt too much, I was sure of that. I repeatedly ordered drinks from her, and each time I wanted to ask what had happened and whether she was alright. But I didn't dare. I was worried she'd take the question the wrong way. I was afraid that she'd think of her tall boyfriend with the gel in his hair, that bastard, even though I didn't see him that night.

I've noticed how good friends greeted each other. Imagine this: you're a fat man wearing a dark blue polo shirt. You're wearing your sunglasses on the top of your head. You heave yourself up onto the terrace, puffing and panting. With visible reluctance, you go and sit down at a free table as you remove your mobile phone from your trouser pocket all in a single, fluid movement. The waitress comes and asks you what you want to drink. The question is not unexpected but still it annoys you. You stare at the floor and in your mind's eye run through all the drinks in the world. Each one seems even more disgusting that the previous. Finally you order a Campari and soda with a dismissive gesture. You order it in such a way that it is clear to everyone on the terrace that you understand that you'll have to order something and you'll just order a fucking Campari and soda then. After that, you immediately continue messing with your mobile phone, causing you to puff and pant again, meaning: I'm an important man and that's why everyone's bothering me, but I hate this damn thing, this phone, if I designed one it would be so much better, but that doesn't interest me, and, what's more, that's how things always go in this country, no wonder the economy's doing so badly and that it's unbearably hot. It means: I just got a message from the prime minister but I don't know how this phone works and I wish he'd leave me alone for a moment and decide himself whether to invade Afghanistan or not, but he's incapable of it, he can't even hitch up his own trousers without me. Next the Campari and soda is served. You don't even glance at the drink, nor at the waitress who brings it. You're much too busy puffing and panting and not understanding how your own phone works, not understanding how anyone can invent a device that even you can't figure out. The waitress asks if you'd like anything to eat. You growl something incomprehensibly exotic like: just a small bowl of green, pitted olives with

Tabasco on the side. Or: gnocchi with chili sauce, hold the pesto, lemon on a stick. Or: peanuts. Then your friend turns up. He's happy to see you and particularly happy that he's not the first one to arrive today and that you're already there. He shouts, "Ciao!" even before he's walked onto the terrace and then "Ciao!" again, and then a third time "Ciao!" as he sits down at your table. All this time you don't look at him. You're much too busy.

A waitress comes over to him, too, and he orders a drink. You're just in the process of sending your message to the prime minister and you can't understand why the damn thing won't send. Your friend says "Cheers," but you try the prime minister's other number first. Doesn't work, either. You huff and puff. Things are like this all the time in Italy these days. You slap the phone onto the table dejectedly. Only then do you look at your friend and say something like, "If Milan bought Ronaldinho, I could have told you Abramovich would put down 150 million for Kaká. It's crazy they're not investing in a center back this season. Crazy!"

The Bar of Mirrors is like a porcelain grotto inside. People walk up and down the inclined street outside. The street goes up to the Piazza Matteotti before the Palazzo Ducale. You might also say that it goes to the Via San Lorenzo or the Piazza de Ferrari. It goes down, too. But not many people dare go that way. You get to the San Donato, the touristy bit, which is alright, but then it begins to rise up again. The Stradone Sant'Agostino is the least adventurous. It leads to the monastery and Genoa University's Faculty of Architecture and, behind that, the Piazza Sarzano. From Piazza Sarzano you can go back down again to the harbor, the sea. If you really have to. But it's not recommended. The medieval Barbarossa

Walls are in the way. And the small streets that do exist can't be found on any map. "Small streets" is not a good description, they're more like staircases or improvised temporary walkways over crumbling stones.

The street that ascends and descends is called Salita Pollaiuoli. If you dare turn right before San Donato, you come out on the Via San Bernardo. As the crow flies it is about another fifty meters or so to the Torre dei Embriaci where there's a good bar. But just try finding it. I'd be interested to know if I'd ever see you again.

Of course I'll see you again. I bump into the same people all day, even though the labyrinth stretches from Darsena to Foce, from the sea to the mountains, from the harbor to the highway, from Principe Station to Brignole Station. I've asked myself how that's possible. You'd expect a maze to have been built so that people would be out of sight of each other, so they wouldn't bump into each other all the time—a maze of this size ought to reduce the chances of bumping into the same people to zero. But now I understand that it's the exact opposite. People can avoid each other in a city of straight lines with clear boulevards and avenues between home and office, office and gym, gym and supermarket, supermarket and home, departure and destination. The person who knows where he's hurrying doesn't notice a thing and is no longer observed. In a city of straight lines, people are like electrons in a copper wire—fast, interchangeable, and invisible. The stream can be measured, but individuals cannot be observed with the naked eye. A labyrinth is precisely the place to encounter other people. You can never find the same place twice. But because no one can, everyone wanders around those same alleyways all day.

Some spend their whole lives wandering around here. Or longer. I'm sure I'll see you again, my friend. It's impossible to find the same piazza twice or walk along the same alleyway twice, unless you are trying not to.

5.

Today I thought about all the different kinds of girls in Genoa.

Some women don't fit into any category, that's true. Like the girl in the Bar of Mirrors. She's made of different fabric than other girls—the same stuff smiles are made of: pathos and summer days. Her mere existence makes me as happy as a small child, and I imagine myself sobbing against her soft shoulders. We'll leave her aside then. We're talking about girls, not the rare epiphany of a goddess.

I used to think were two kinds of girls: pretty and ugly. But in light of my most recent research findings, that dichotomy is no longer valid, although I fear the simplicity of the model will always retain its charm.

Of course there are pretty girls. That's not the problem. You'd like to sketch them carefully with a pencil. You'd like to skate over their smooth undulations with precise fingertips. You'd like to briefly taste the perfect balance of their curves, lines, forms, and volume with a connoisseur's tongue. Even more than that, you'd like them to take their clothes off and then not to have to do a thing. They might be like a photo you'd be all too happy to download—perfectly suggestive, or explicitly spotlighted.

Girls like that are the way Milo Manara draws them: hieroglyphs of promise. They're never not posing, though they don't even need to pose since they already fulfill every standard just standing there. You'd never actually be able to smell them, never be able to tease them by playing with a minuscule roll of fat, nor lick the sour sweat from their armpits, if only because they're imaginary, just drawn that way. There is something artificially innocent about them, something oo-la-la-ish. Of course they end up in army barracks without their panties, but that's just because they happened to be kidnapped by soldiers when they were in the middle of undressing. You get that a lot. But they'll never ring your doorbell without their panties asking if they can give you a handjob in the rain because they've never done that before. They'll never sit on your silver candelabra without further explanation, then lick your table clean before disappearing on home without saying a word.

Recently I got one of those celebrity magazines free with *Il Secolo XIX*, full of photos of real Manara girls in little more than bikinis. In the accompanying interviews, they say stuff like, "I love men who are honest"; "My daughter is the most important thing in my life"; "I'll never have sex if Love with a capital L isn't part of the picture"; and "I'll always have a special place in my heart for God." Seriously, just give me the ugly girls then. At least they understand they have to do their best. Or the pretty girls, but then without the interviews, for God's sake. Or just the bikini-less ones, preferably captured on film.

I saw a tourist girl at San Lorenzo with her tourist boyfriend. He had a camera, she had pink high heels, a yellow handbag, and a scandalous denim miniskirt. They were Russian, you could see that. I checked it for you just to make sure, my friend: they spoke Russian. He wanted to take a picture of her in front of the cathedral.

She protested. She wasn't looking her best today. But when he got ready to take a shot anyway, she put her middle finger to her bottom lip and her other hand to her crotch. They took dozens of photographs like that: next to one of the lions, then the other, in front of the big door, on the steps next to the tower, and so on and so on. She adopted a porno pose for every shot. She wasn't particularly good-looking, more shameless than refined. She was bored but not so listless to not realize she'd have to do something for a sexy result. I watched her, breathless. There wasn't a spark of humor or fun in her poses, no fiery lust in her eyes. She bent her body mechanically for the predictable desires of the photographer and all those future browsers who'd click the thumbnails into a cliché of lust. And that was exactly what was so irresistibly sexy.

You've also got women with spunk lighting up their eyes in anticipation. In a manner of speaking. They're usually too young for their age. Lacey nothings frame their gym-fed, well-baked muscles. Someone like that is dry and unpalatable. She dresses like an unwrapped mummy, like that woman of indeterminate age somewhere in her late forties, with short black hair and skirts that get shorter by the day—the one who pays a neighborly visit a couple of times a day, smiling mysteriously, to Laura Sciunnach's jewelry shop in the Salita Pollaiuoli, across from the Bar of Mirrors, because Bibi with all the tattoos works there, the perfect Don Juan, whose scorn for women causes them to swoon. She's ugly, but she walks along the street as though she'd inserted two vibrators before closing the door and stepping out onto the street. She never double-locks the door when she comes home drunk at night. She's like a hungry keyhole through which she wants to be spied. If only somebody would ravish her, for God's sake. Dripping with lust, she'd report it to the disbelieving *carabinieri* half her age in their shiny boots, their shiny, shiny boots. And she's not that ugly, really. I tried to make eye contact with her. I try to make eye contact with her several times a day from the terrace of the Bar of Mirrors.

On the terrace of the Doge Café on Piazza Matteotti, I saw a girl who had painted a girl on herself. She was Cleopatra behind her own death mask. Or maybe she was someone completely different behind Cleopatra's mask, the only people who know that are the ones who wake up beside her the next morning, rub the sleep from their eyes, full of disbelief, and begin the difficult process of reconstructing the night before in an attempt to figure out the identity of this pale, unknown lady who has so obviously nestled herself between their sheets. And it's not until she has restored her façade for hours in the bathroom that they remember. Women like that cost money. They don't just need lotions and potions but designer clothing for every hour of the day, in line with the fashion of the moment, and a lot of shoes, in particular, a lot of shoes. All of those clothes and shoes are only bought to take off again. But to achieve that goal, they have to be expensive, everyone knows that. Each morning she turns herself into the woman she thinks a woman should look like—as she thinks I want her to look. It doesn't matter whether she knows what I want or not. It's more important that she does her best to satisfy her image of my image of her.

The worst are fat American women who are under the misapprehension that intelligence is more important than looks. That's such a stupid concept. They talk about immigration laws in slow, clear English. She was on the terrace of the Doge Café in front of Palazzo Ducale, too, but she was a misunderstanding. With her tits like burst balloons in a comfy summer dress like a pre-war tent, she had no right to talk about any subject whatsoever. She should withdraw to a dark sitting room in Ohio and sit at her computer with shaking fingers and send messages to Internet forums for women with suicidal tendencies under the pseudonym FaTgIrL. She was eligible for a postnatal abortion. Her mere existence was bad enough. The fact she wasn't ashamed, that she marred, insulted the elegance of Genoa's, of Liguria's, of all of Italy's Piazza Matteotti with her pontifical presence, and the fact she also thought she had the right to be considered a human being rather than an ugly, fat woman, was repulsive.

Fat women as such aren't the problem, particularly when they're blonde. Don't get me wrong. I've been able to treat a few to breakfast in my time, I'll be damned if it isn't true. They're animals. You'll have the best sex of your life with fat girls, believe me, my friend. If they want to. If they don't want to, they're pointless and pathetic. But usually they do want to. They'll rule your bed like six porno films at the same time. They won't lie photogenically on their backs and wait for what you will or won't do with your automatic libido; they'll ride you until you bleed in the full realization that they have to make amends to be considered women.

There are only two kinds of women: those who understand and those who talk. Those who get the game and understand they'll first have to make a woman of themselves to be allowed to play, and those who knowingly disqualify themselves with the crazy idea that it's about something other than the game. That's the truth, my friend. That's the truth. And I discovered it. And the game is complicated enough, so don't come to me with your improvements or complications. You know I'm right. And I'm not a sexist or a racist. Exactly the same rules apply to black women as far as I'm concerned.

The ideal women are men. In their attempts to become desirable women, they have to exaggerate. As a parody of sexy women, they transform themselves into inflatable dolls of tits and erectile tissue, and that's exactly what's so sexy. They know exactly what they're there for—but women like that don't exist. Although I have seen them on occasion down by the harbor, on the roadside near the Soprealevata highway's exit ramp. And later I saw two more near the Palazzo Principe train station. But I've forgotten where and have never been able to find them there again, nor near the harbor. Maybe I keep going back at the wrong time.

6.

But in the meantime, the fact was that I had an amputated female leg in my house. Although I needed to come up with a solution as fast as possible, of course, in any case before it began to smell a bit funky, it was also exciting in a peculiar kind of a way. I went home earlier than usual. But I didn't take the leg out of the cupboard. I could spend hours thinking about not doing things like that. And then I thought of something. Was it true? Yes, it was true. Was I sure? I was sure. I'd only touched the stocking. I hadn't touched the sexy bit of naked thigh above the garter. I certainly would have remembered how that felt. I was immediately grabbed by an almost irrepressible urge to do it anyway. But that wasn't the point. I realized that I could get rid of all the fingerprints and traces of DNA by taking off the stocking.

It was a sensible plan. No, it wasn't exciting; it really was a sensible plan. The best plans are. Exciting and sensible. In inverse order, but in this case that didn't matter. It didn't matter in any single case, except for the fact that the question whether something was exciting or not almost always takes priority and the question whether it's sensible or not usually tends to get pushed to the background, at the most being claimed retrospectively, as a means of justification, which is not really that regrettable given that this all too human mechanism contributes significantly to the preservation of the human race.

I was raving, I know I was. I was nervous. I opened my bedroom wardrobe. As though I was removing an easily broken ivory artifact from a safe with white gloves to allow a scholar, who had traveled from afar, to study it, or as though I was scooping a delicate, fragile algae from the surface of a forgotten, glassy lake of unfathomable depths—that was the way I took the leg from the IKEA wardrobe and laid it on the table. In other words, slowly and carefully. The pompous comparisons are only intended to maintain the tension. Well, not only. With a bit of good will, they also evoke the reverent trembling of my hands.

I stroked the curves of her foot, her heel, instep, and ankle. I gently pinched each toe. "You have such tiny little toes," I said. She began to laugh. It tickled. The back of my hand slid along her shin. The jagged edge of a nail caught in her stocking for a moment. "Sorry." I followed the soft lines of the subtle contours of her knee with my index finger. I let my hand descend to the tender, vulnerable skin of the back of her knee, where I lingered a while so I could summon up the courage to take her whole calf in my hand. The bulging muscle filled my reverent hand like a breast. Shapely yet bashful, firm yet soft, sturdy yet cute, she was light in the palm of my hand, which she perfectly filled. We were made for each other. "You probably say that to all the ladies." I didn't reply. I moved my hand excruciatingly slowly up along the inside of her leg to her thigh. She began to moan. "What are you doing?" she whispered. But I wasn't doing anything. I teasingly tugged at her garter with little, absent-minded, detached movements. And then I climbed the sloping mound of her thigh muscle. I let my fingertips and my thumb rest in the shallow, barely noticeable hollows on both sides. I began to knead, gently and carefully. She liked it. She made growling noises like a purring cat. And as my hand crept farther and farther upwards, like a hungry animal, she began to moan more and more loudly.

I stopped abruptly where the stocking ended. With a surgeon's precision, I took the garter band between the thumb and index finger of each hand and, without touching the skin, peeled the stocking slowly from her increasingly bared leg. I denuded her copper thigh, her round, funny knee, her mirror-smooth shin and her cheekily rounded calf, her chiseled ankle, where I faltered for a moment to change direction and finish my work with an elegant maneuver by which I freed her heel, her curved instep, and her giggling toes. I laid the stocking next to her on the table. She shivered but not from the cold. The minuscule, scarcely visible blonde hairs were now standing on end. She sighed deeply and moved her leg to the side to allow me access. "Please," she whispered. I kissed her mouth and came.

7.

And that was how I ruined everything. Fuck, what a moron I was. A big blob of my sperm on an amputated woman's leg. That was exactly the kind of DNA the CIA folks liked best. With the certainty that a man was involved in the unsavory affair, and the bonus of quite a big hint as to the motive. And then to try coming up with the excuse, in the face of such persuasive evidence, that you'd just happened upon the leg in the street during a storm-induced power outage, and that that blob was only there thanks or no thanks to the fact that she had moved her leg aside with a sigh, after I'd carefully taken off her stocking, and had whispered that it was alright. "But you must believe me, your honor, I swear to you, that's what happened."

I live in my imagination too much. And look what comes of it. Problems come of it. Sperm on a ripped-off, rotting limb comes of it. What a fine mess I'd gotten myself into. How humiliating. How could I have let myself get carried away like that? Of course it's also part of my job to represent the thoughts and motivations of others as vividly as possible and if necessary, to create characters from nothing, characters onto whom I can project myself so vividly that they become flesh and blood, allowing me to set down a convincing portrait of them on paper. But that doesn't mean that when I'm not holding a pen, I should start believing in my own delusions and consider one leg sufficient to project the rest spread-eagled onto it, breathe life into a whole new willing mistress and throw myself, panting, upon her. That would get me into another fine mess. Worse, it already had.

I decided I had to get rid of the leg as quickly as possible. But first, of course, I had to give it a thorough cleaning. Naked skin is easy to wash, easier than skin clothed in nylon. That was what I told myself as I tried to apply some kind of logic to my actions and retrospectively give the stocking striptease a rational justification. I put the leg in the shower. It was a strange kind of automatism, if I can use that word for something I'd never done before and, with a probability bordering on certainty, would never do again. All things considered, it was an object and you washed objects in the sink, but clearly I thought legs belonged under the shower, as though there were still a woman attached to it.

And then I realized that I'd miss her. I undressed and got into the shower with her. But that was only intended as a sweet gesture, like having a shower together after sex. I washed her gently, carefully and attentively. It was our farewell. After that I got a garbage bag and pulled it over the leg without touching the freshly-washed skin or leaving any evidence. I tied the bag tightly shut, got dressed, went outside and threw the bag into the builders' dumpster. Sure enough, I felt a little sad.

8.

Come si deve. If there's a concept that characterizes and unifies Italy (in so much as that exists), it is this life philosophy that everything has to be the way it should be, *come si deve*. Of course everyone has different ideas about that— how things should be—but everyone does agree that it must be as it should be, not necessarily because that's good, but because it has always been that way. The most obvious example is food. Each region, each province, each city, each quarter has different ideas about how *spaghetti al ragù* should taste. They even call it different things. But everyone agrees that it should taste like it has always tasted. A chef's creativity is not appreciated. The chef should be a craftsman like a cobbler, not an artist. The chef, like the best cobbler, doesn't spring any surprises on you. That's why you always eat so well in Italy. And that's why they have such nice shoes.

But that's what all of life is like in Italy, from the cradle to the grave. You're born, grow up, get married and leave home, have children who leave home when they get married, and you die. You celebrate Christmas at Christmastime and eat roast lamb at Easter. You go to the seaside in August. All the shops will be closed. In Genoa, it's an entire month of scarcely being able to buy the bare necessities. There are only two tobacconists open in the whole city center, one newspaper kiosk, and one liquor store. If you're lucky. And just try to find them. Bewildered tourists wander around among the closed shutters. The mayor calls for legislative measures, and rightly so, but just try to do anything about it, because everyone goes to the seaside in August and not in June or July, which would be much more sensible since at least there'd be a place on the beach and everything would cost half what it costs in August. But that's not *come si deve*.

It is life according to a liturgical calendar of recurrent, annual family parties, family outings, birthdays, name days, home and away matches, qualifying rounds and finals. It's a spiral that ends after seventy or eighty rotations with a memorial plaque on the gray walls of a church, formulated and designed like all the other memorial plaques. We look back with pride and gratefulness at a rich and full life that progressed just like other lives, in the same streets, on the same squares, in the same houses, and on the same beaches, with breakfast at half past seven, *pranzo* at half past twelve, *cena* at nine o'clock, blessed with children and grandchildren who will do everything exactly the same. *Stanno tutti bene. Tutto a posto. Come si deve.*

I've seen a woman who was exactly like that. I see her all over the place because she's always at the right place at the right time. She has breakfast at Caffè del Duomo on San Lorenzo. She lunches at Capitan Baliano on Matteotti. At six on the dot she comes into the Bar of Mirrors for an aperitif. She has a glass of Prosecco and then, why not, another glass of Prosecco. She always says that as she orders it: "Oh, why not, another glass of Prosecco." As though it were an exception. And she'll never order a third glass of Prosecco. She always says that, too: "I never have three glasses of Prosecco as an aperitif. Two is enough for me." She's an exemplary Italian in every way. I couldn't imagine her in any country but Italy. She's so *come si deve* that outside of Italy she'd wither and die like a tree that had been transplanted out of the specific, precious microclimate of its natural habitat. On Saturdays she meets her friend on the square at exactly the right time on exactly the right day at exactly the right place to eat pizza. She is exactly fifteen minutes late for the meeting and her friend is exactly fifteen minutes later than she.

They then have a fixed ritual of apologies from the lady who's too late, resolutely waved off by the lady who was less late. It's a stainless steel routine that's repeated to the second, time after time, week after week, year in year out, generation after generation.

Two days a week, she has her granddaughter, a notorious red-headed diva of about three years old. She's called Viola. I know this because that's what everyone keeps calling her. Her, too. Each time the little girl does something, it doesn't matter what—climb up onto her lap, climb down off her lap, walk in circles around the parasol stand, stir the Prosecco with her finger—she says, "Viola, don't do that!" As an aperitif she gets an *acqua frizzante* with a straw and a bowl of *patattine*—what do you call those again? Fries? Then she says, "Look, Viola! Here's Viola's aperitif!"

The most beautiful girl in Genoa, who works at the Bar of Mirrors, is besotted by Viola. She kisses her, strokes her red curls, cuddles her, and babbles away endlessly to her about the fries, about her new shoes, about the color of the straw, pigeons, parasols, freckles, dancing, and the bandages on her cuts and scrapes that haven't healed yet. It's astonishing. It's a holy miracle to witness. The magic of the fairy-tale harmony between a little tyke and a good fairy. The most beautiful girl in Genoa should be as unap-proachable as a glimpse of an image you catch in a mirror, but before my very eyes she turns into the most endearing essence of approachability. The old lady watched with the smile of an Italian grandmother who found it only natural that her granddaughter should be adored by waitresses. I decided to speak to her.

I loved speaking Italian. I wasn't very good at it, but I liked to, which seems to me to perfectly fit the definition of an amateur.

Whenever I was on a roll, or at least thought I was, it felt like swimming in the waves of a warm sea. I could bob on the rhythm of the long and short syllables. I would stretch myself out on long, clear vowels and then make a playful, thrashing sprint across the staccato of consonants. I'd dive down into a daring construction, knowing I'd need a subjunctive sooner or later, but would come up spluttering. It didn't matter what it was about or whether it was about anything. It was a game. I didn't need to swim anywhere; it was enjoyable enough just to be in the water.

Although I loved Italian and tried my best to learn it, I didn't really take it seriously as a language. It's a language for children, a language that tastes of rice with butter and sugar. The language is perfectly suited to a month at the seaside in August with the whole family, when the world can be easily organized and divided into clear categories like *bello* and *brutto*, *buono* and *schifoso*, *libero* and *occupato*, *pranzo* and *cena*. The language is also exceptionally suited to shouting at children the whole damn day that they shouldn't do that, whatever it is they're doing, and to say that's enough. You can also say goodbye to each other the whole day in it. It's a language that makes a racket and that's the only thing that counts, like when children are happy, weeks-on-end happy, drive-you-crazy happy with a rattle.

But I was, too. I was happy. I wanted to make a racket. And the fact, the more than obvious fact, that I had to practice and improve my Italian gave me a wonderful excuse to address complete strangers on any random subject. I would never do that in my own language because those people don't interest me, let alone what they have to say, and because my own language isn't a toy.

And if I accidentally say something insulting in Italian, I can always add a few grammatical blunders and then sit there smiling naively like a screwball foreigner. I could get away with anything—that was what was so fun about it.

So that was how I spoke to Viola's grandmother. She was so Italian and so *come si deve* I thought she'd prove entertaining training material.

9.

"My name is Franca. But it's better that you call me Signora Mancinelli and use the formal mode of address because you have to practice your Italian and the formal modes are more difficult. And you? What? Giulia? Giulian? Gigia? Leonardo. That is a bit easier, indeed. Like Leonardo da Vinci. I can remember that. Or, if you asked today's youth, Leonardo DiCaprio. I'm an elderly lady of the upper class. They still had education in my days. I know who Leonardo da Vinci was. See that man over there? Look hard."

He sits on the terrace at the Bar of Mirrors almost every day, a bon vivant, suffering from some subsidence, who acts too young for his age. He has white hair and wears brightly colored Hawaiian shirts from the plastic boxes of remainders at the market. When he comes shuffling along with his plastic bags from the Di per Di, he looks like a tramp. But once he's sitting down he orders a mojito. Tramps don't drink cocktails. And he has plenty of chitchat. Everyone who says hello to him is treated to an undoubtedly priceless anecdote, freshly plucked from the riches of his daily life. He bares his teeth as he smiles and draws passersby and waitresses into his monologue. He wears glasses on his forehead, which are supposed to give him the air of an elderly intellectual. But I don't fall for that. He has holes in his shoes. His eyes are deep-set, his cheeks have caved in, and his stubble sticks to his chin like the frayed edges of an unwashed bathmat. He nods briefly at fellow tramps passing by over the gray paving stones.

"Watch out," the signora says. "He's a very important man. Bernardo is his name, Bernardo Massi. He's rich." She leaves a meaningful silence. "Very rich. Although they say his wife left him. But I know he still has a palazzo on the Piazza Corvetto." I nodded to show I'd understood how significant that was. I tried to get a better look at him but some tourists had sat down at the table between him and me. They were seriously blocking the view with an excess of cameras and sticky body parts, peering at a map. The waitress came and they ordered a beer and an iced tea. The waitress asked whether they wanted anything to eat. They have the charming habit here of serving a range of snacks with the aperitif, with the compliments of the establishment. But the tourists became acutely suspicious, suspecting it was a dirty trick to make them pay for more than the two drinks they'd ordered and which would certainly be too expensive, here right in the center, and you know, you have to be very careful in these southern countries because they'll rip you off right in front of your nose, and in any case we're never coming back here, it's much too expensive, but why am I fussing about it, are you fussing about it, we're on holiday, so we'd better enjoy it, otherwise you don't really have a life do you, that's what I always say, it's pretty important to enjoy yourself in life, even on holiday, so let's just drink our drinks.

I don't know whether it's shamelessness, indifference, or a cultural code. But why in God's name do tourists have to wear their dirty underwear as soon they sit down in a southern country and block my view? He was wearing a stained t-shirt from a German football club and shorts that had been washed to shreds; she was wearing comfy, baggy holiday shorts. They looked like intelligent, wealthy people to me. No doubt they had a house in Dortmund and a delectable DVD collection in their designer shelving unit, a car with fancy wheel trims in the garage, and evening wear for their work's New Year's reception in their recessed wardrobe.

In the Pré quarter, where Rashid lives along with the rest of Africa, every underprivileged illegal immigrant spends the first sixty euros he earns on a fake Rolex with imitation diamonds so that he can begin to fit in a little bit with the respectable Europeans, and those heirs of the *wirtschaftswunder* were just sitting there in their underwear. What kind of an impression do you think that made? And what do you think it means? What did they mean to say by this? If you're on the beach by the Deiva Marina or at a campsite in Pieve Ligure I can understand it. But this was right in front of my view, on the most precious terrace in the city, in the shadow of centuries, in the historical center of Genoa, La Superba, the heart of the heartless one that had allowed them to penetrate to the roots of her pride. Does it mean they don't understand or they don't want to understand? Or are they sending out a special message? Like: We just happen to be on holiday here, nice to get away from all the stress, and that's why we're doing what we want, just having a lovely nice time being ourselves for those three weeks a year, you know. Or: Those Italians don't know a thing, it's just one big hip-hip-hooray beach from the Costa Brava to Alanya. Or is it actually intended as a status symbol dressing like that, does it mean you can permit yourselves to go on holiday without caring about anything whatsoever?

"Don't be fooled by appearances," the signora said.

"My apologies, signora, I was distracted for a moment."

"He looks like an unmade bed. He dresses as though he has shares in the illegal sewing shops in the Pré. It wouldn't surprise me if he did. I must ask Ursula some time."

"Who are you talking about?"

"Ursula Smeraldo. She has a countess in her family. By marriage, though. And just between you and me, she's rather down on her luck, if you get my meaning. But we're practically neighbors on the Via Giustiniani, and it would be strange if I didn't greet her. What's more, she knows what's going on."

The tourists' shamelessness reached a new low. They'd unfolded their map and asked the waitress where something was. They had the goddamn guts to speak to her! Probably about something ridiculous like the aquarium. She stood bent over their table for minutes on end, giving them all kinds of explanations. My waitress. She was sacred. No one can ask her the way to the aquarium in their underpants. She's not allowed to reply, and certainly not so extensively and sweetly and prettily. Not so sweetly and prettily. Not so extensively. Not so bent over and so much in my line of vision it hurt.

"I know about her, too."

I gave the signora an irritated look.

"Ursula told me that Bernardo Massi broke up with his wife. But everyone knows that he's powerful and important, that he's rich, I mean, even though he dresses like a tramp. Don't be fooled by the exterior. Everything is hidden in Genoa. We don't have any squares with fountains, no palazzi with fancy façades. All the gold and art treasures are hidden away behind incredibly thick walls of common gray limestone. A true businessman stashes away his fortune in an old sock and goes out onto the street wearing tatters in the hope of receiving alms. In Milan and Rome, everyone wants to show off everything, *fare bella figura*, with a flamboyant display of good taste and excess. In Genoa everyone understands that it doesn't give you an advantage. To the contrary. The man who splashes his wealth about ostentatiously has far too many friends, as the saying goes. The saying is a bit different from that, but you understand what I'm saying. Do you understand what I'm saying? You have to learn how to behave in this city. It's a porcelain grotto."

"I think I can only see the exterior," I say. Only then did the waitress turn around. She asked us whether we might like something to eat. She asked it coolly, unapproachably, and proud, like someone with a countess in her family, like the marble duchess herself—La Superba.

10.

If I think about these notes, my friend, and think about how I'll turn them into a novel someday, a novel that needs to be carried along by a protagonist who will sing himself free from me and insist on the right to his or her own name, experiences, and downfall in exchange for my personal confrontation with my new city, which is more like a triumphal tour than a tragic course toward inevitable failure—and, on the grounds of that alone, is not suitable material for a great book—then I think about how crucial it will be to make tangible sense of the feeling of happiness that this city has given me time after time, even if only as a sparkling prelude to the punches of fate. Happiness, I say. I realize you could no longer repress a giggle when I said that. I realize that it's strange to hear such a weak and hackneyed word come out of my mouth. Happiness is something for lovers before they have their first fight, for girls in floral dresses at the seaside who don't see the jellyfish and the ptomaines, or for an old man with a photo album who can no longer really tell the difference between the past and the present. Happiness is basically a temporary illusion without any profundity, style, or class. The candy floss of emotions. And yet, for lack of a better word, I feel happy in Genoa, in a golden yellow, slow, permanent way. Not like candy floss, but like good glass. Not like a carnival, but like a primeval forest. Not like the clash of cymbals, but a symphony.

It is also remarkable, or I daresay unbelievable, that happiness is dependent upon location, on longitude and latitude, city limits, pavement, and street names. I've read enough philosophy, both Western and Eastern, to realize that wisdom dictates you should laugh at me and dismiss my sensation as an aberrance. So be it. That's the point. The more I think about it as I write these words, the more I become convinced of the importance of putting into words this impossible, undesirable, unbelievable feeling of happiness.

Street names and pavement. That's the way I formulated it. In the first instance as a stylistic device, of course, sketched with the rough *sprezzatura* that characterizes my writing. But in the second instance, it's true, too. I'll give you an example: Vico Amandorla can make me so happy. It's an insignificant alleyway that runs from Vico Vegetti to Stradone Sant'Agostino. It's a short stretch, and you don't encounter anything of any importance along the way. The alleyway isn't even pretty, at least not in the conventional manner. Normal, ugly old houses and normal, smelly old trash. But the alley curves up the hill like a snake. A little old lady struggles uphill in the opposite direction. The alley is actually too steep, built wrongly centuries and centuries ago or just sprung into existence in a very awkward manner. The alley is pointless, too. You come out too far down, below the Piazza Negri. If you want to be there, at San Donato, it's much better to just take Vico Vegetti downhill and then turn right along Via San Bernardo. That's faster and more convenient. And if you want to be in the higher part of the Stradone Sant'Agostino, at Piazza Sarzano, it's much quicker and more convenient to follow the same Vico Vegetti in the other direction, past the Facoltà di Architettura straight to Piazza Negri. All of this makes me very happy. And then the pavement. This alley isn't paved with the large blocks of gray granite you get every-where in Genoa, but with cobblestones as big as a fist. You can't walk on them. There's a strip of navigable road laid with narrow bricks on their sides. Half of them have sunk or come loose. There hasn't been any maintenance here since the early Middle Ages. And then that name. Who in the world wouldn't want to stroll along Vico Amandorla? It's a name that smells like a promise, as soft as marzipan, as mature as liquor in forgotten casks, in the cellar of a faraway monastery where the last monk died twenty years ago one afternoon with an innocent child's prayer on his lips in the cloister gardens, in the shadow of an almond tree, as happy as a man after a rich dinner with dear friends. Say the name quietly if you are afraid and you won't be afraid anymore: Vico Amandorla.

From Piazza Negri you can walk, during museum opening hours, through the cloister gardens of Sant'Agostino to Piazza Sarzano and the city walls. The passage through the cloister is triangular, undoubtedly as an architectonic compromise with exceptional topographical circumstances. The tip points toward the tower, which is sprinkled with colorful mosaics that clash with the strict and sober gray of the cloister. What's the statement? What must the monks who wore away the pavement of the cloister passage with their footsteps have thought at the sight of their own festive tower? That it was Mardi Gras outside? That the gray life in the cloister clashed with that path upwards to heaven, a path as garish and variegated as a rocket, ready to be fired so that it can burst out into a cascade of colors?

Piazza Sarzano is a square that I still don't really get, a square like a formless mollusk with a Metro station I never see anyone going into or coming out of. But just to the right of it, left of the church, is a secret passageway to another city—a medieval wormhole. With its profound and contented pavement, the street swings steeply up the hill to a forgotten and abandoned mountain village straight out of Umbria or Abruzzo. A handful of narrow, abandoned little streets that rise and fall around a shell-shaped village square that slumbers in the sunshine. But in the distance you don't see any mountaintops, no hills crosshatched with vines, no goatherds, but the docks of Genoa. This is a magical place you cannot be in without realizing that you actually can't be there because the place cannot exist. This is Campo Pisano, a perfect name euphonically, an ideal marriage between sound and rhythm. Its meter is the triumphant final chord of a heroic verse. The name fits perfectly after the bucolic diaeresis of the dactylic hexameter. The succession of a bi-syllabic and tri-syllabic obeys the *Gesetz der wachsenden Glieder* and creates a charming *auslaut* after the first unmarked element of the dactyl, by which an ideal alternation between a falling and a rising rhythm arises. The sound is carried by the open vowels that shine like the three primary colors on an abstract painting by Mondrian. The falling movement from the *a* to the *o* finds a playful counterpoint in the high *i* before it is repeated.

The cool hard consonants articulate the composition like the black lines on the same painting, with the racy repetition of the *p* right in the middle. It is a name like an incantation to evoke a magical abode. A spell of otherworldly sophistication is needed to bring to life an impossible place. If someone were to unscrew the street's nameplate from the wall, Campo Pisano would vanish into the mists of the docks, only to reappear when an ancient high priest remembered the name and it passed through his wrinkly lips between the Barbarossa walls and the sea. Campo Pisano. It's a happy place with a tragic past, in the same way that only people who have known pain can be happy because people who are painlessly happy like that blow away like a Sunday paper in the wind of an early day in spring. This place was once a kind of Abu Ghraib. Prisoners of war were locked up here after La Superba's army and navy had finally put down their archenemy Pisa for good. The curses of the defeated and humiliated Pisani still ring out to this day. Symbols of Genoa's power are worked into the pavement in mosaics made of uneven pebbles. I'm the only person about at this time of day. The green shutters on the houses are closed. The wine bar won't open until the evening. In the distance I can hear a goat bleating, or a ferry honking.

Vico Superiore del Campo Pisano is a dead end, but Vico Inferiore del Campo Pisano isn't. Or the other way round. It depends which day it is. One of the two of them is a new wormhole, not back to Genoa and the present, but to America and yesterday's future. The road curves gently downhill to the left and leads to a grotto. Dampness and vegetation seep from moldy walls. These are the vaults of the bridge that links Piazza Sarzano with the Carignano quarter. The high priest lives under the last arch. His skull is older than the city. High above him, the people of Genoa go in search of parking spots and bargains. Closer to the sea the fast traffic races along the Sopraelevata, the raised motorway along the coast.

The grotto opens out into a post-apocalyptic landscape, or to be more precise: this is the perfect location to film an old-fashioned science fiction film, preferably in black and white. Its official name is Giardini di Baltimora, but people know it as Giardini di Plastica, the plastic garden. It's a gigantic dog-walking spot that also serves as a shooting-up area for heroin addicts and a kissing zone for young couples without places of their own. It looks like a 1960s or '70s version of the twenty-first century. Desolate green with charmingly gray mega-office-blocks. Above-ground nuclear bunkers in a field of stinging nettles. Pre-war spaceships that have crashed in a forgotten hole in the city and gradually been reclaimed by nature.

All kinds of pathways go back up to the Middle Ages from here, or to Piazza Sarzano or Via Ravecca. But you can also walk under the supports of the rusty behemoths, across the underground car park beneath which the motorway runs to the sea, past peeling bars and clubs with unimaginative names, under the skyscraper, to Piazza Dante. The city will reveal itself to you there once again, with an ironic smile. Yes. After your epic journey, you're simply back on Piazza Dante. Thousands of Vespas, Porta Soprana, Columbus's house, the cloisters of Sant'Andrea, in the distance the fountain on Piazza de Ferrari and, on the other side, Via XX Settembre. You know every street here. It's just a three-minute walk to your favorite bars. You burst out laughing in surprise. But how am I ever going to write about this, my friend? How can I ever make people believe that a city makes me happy?

II.

Religion is the opiate of the masses. Although Italy has flirted more often and more intimately with Marxism than most other Western European countries, it is one of the most drugged up countries I've ever seen. The Holy See actively gets involved in politics. The pronouncements of the Holy Father are even widely reported in progressive and left-wing newspapers. Not a week goes by without a public debate that is only a debate in that the Vatican has regurgitated one of its anachronistic opinions in a press release. There are few politicians who have the courage to commit electoral kamikaze by distancing themselves from the dictates of the Holy Mother-Church or casting doubt on the authority of the old right-winger who believes himself Christ's terrestrial locum.

Genoa is a civilized, northern, and even explicitly left-wing city, where money is earned, where people can read and write, and where all the old people go to church. Or they take communion at home if they live on the seventh floor, with their fluid retention and their walker and the lift's out of order again. The tabloids scream outrage. In Genoa, a salesman's healthy skepticism is the norm, just as the pleasant shadow in the alleyways doesn't evaporate under any amount of sun. Jesus said that Peter wanted to build his church on a rock. Peter's church in Genoa is on Piazza Banchi and it is built on shops. The foundations of trade still lie under the church's foundations. But even here, the mayor only has to come up with the idea of organizing a Gay Pride parade for the archbishop to put a stop to it the next day.

Being a Catholic doesn't have to be a conscious choice, not like the existential struggles in Dutch Protestantism that go with being doubly, triply, quadruply Reformed or Restored Reformed. In the fatherland, conversion to Catholicism is for men of my profession worthy of a press release, guaranteed fodder for an endless series of discussion nights in community centers. In Italy, it's something you're born into, just like being born a supporter of Genoa or Sampdoria, and just as you're born someone who eats *trofie al pesto* and not egg foo young with noodles. God isn't someone you search for on a hopeless path with your hands cramped into a begging bowl, but someone like the coach of a football team or the chef in a restaurant: he'll be there, and no doubt he'll do his best, because that's how it's always been. So you get baptized and you marry in a church, not because you particularly want that, but because it makes Granny happy and because that's the way it's always been. Catholicism is the default, the standard setting, and too many complicated downloads and difficult processes are needed to deviate from it. Most people won't go to all that trouble.

But this wasn't what I intended to talk about at all. Religion is a bit of a woman's thing after all. The men in Italy celebrate their own holy high mass every Sunday at three o'clock on the dot. Since time immemorial the year has unfolded around the cycle of friendly duels and preliminary rounds that lead to the championship and the final position. The religion is called Serie A. Mass is each team's weekly match. At three o'clock on Sunday afternoons, millions of Italian men sit in their regular parish to be flagellated for ninety minutes by the live coverage on Skynet or some other subscription channel. Sampdoria's church is the Doge Café on Piazza Matteotti; Genoa's church is Capitan Baliano, diagonally opposite. At halftime during the service, everyone smokes a fraternal cigarette together on the same square before returning to their own temple at exactly four o'clock for the second half and another forty-five minutes of suffering, hell, and damnation.

Nobody enjoys it, as befits a religion. I've watched a football match in a bar a few times back home. You have to drink a lot of beer and do the cancan together, and by the second half getting beer down each other's throats becomes more important than watching the match. In Italy, on the other hand, it's a deadly serious matter. The men drink coffee and swear.

There isn't a single Italian male who doesn't know about food. He can't cook, his wife does that, but he knows better. It's his job to deliver negative comments about each course in an indignant manner. And there isn't a single Italian male who doesn't know about football. He's incapable of sprinting fifty meters, but he knows better. Each Sunday it's his job to give an indignant and scornful commentary of every move made by the top athletes in the stadium.

But Italians don't know a thing about football. They don't understand it and they don't even like it. Every time a player loses possession it's the referee's fault for not spotting a foul. Each goal conceded is proof of the scandalous inferiority and the appalling ignorance of the opponent who has gone and gotten it into his thick skull to score against their team. They cheer if a player on their team brings an adversary down with a violent tackle and jeer when the referee penalizes this action. And, in general, even with the best will in the world, no one can understand how, these days, the best-paid top players constantly make the most basic fuck-ups. The game is mostly unwatchable, because when Italian clubs compete with each other, they never take a single risk, and their lineups only have half a striker.

It's the same every Sunday. No one takes any pleasure in it. But they wouldn't miss it for the world. It's ritual. The week exists by the grace of Sunday afternoons. It wouldn't surprise me if the same match had different results in different parts of Italy. On the Genoese subscription channels, Genoa beat Palermo 4-0, after which an orgy of pretty things you can buy if you're happy explodes onto the screen. Palermo probably won the same match 4-0 on the Sicilian subscription channels.

Like every religion, Serie A has a gospel. But it's much better than those four books in rotten Greek the Vatican's had to make do with for centuries. It's printed on pink paper and appears daily with new messages of salvation every time: the *Gazzetta della Sport* makes it possible to lose yourself in fantasies about Sunday afternoon all week long, with retrospectives that are updated daily, prognoses, statistics, and charts. You don't need any other newspaper if you want to be an Italian among the Italians. *Tutto il rosa della vita* is its slogan—everything pink in life. The world's fucked, hundreds of thousands of poor bastards are landing on Lampedusa, the government has declared a state of emergency, there are soldiers in the streets, and people are dying of poverty, but if you read the *Gazzetta dello Sport*, none of that has to bother you. There, it's just about the things that are really important, like the percentage of risky passes from the left wing in comparison to the 1956–57 season.

Italy lives in its imagination. The opium of its people is pink.

12.

I often thought back to my short and confusing relationship with the leg, or rather with the girl I'd fantasized onto it. I was ashamed. But I had to get over that. In a certain way, it had been perfect love. Because I'd dreamed her up myself, she was the woman of my dreams. And yet she was concrete, material and physical enough to have me believe that I wasn't dreaming. I could actually touch her, stroke her, feel her, and she moved, sighed, and groaned exactly as I imagined in my loveliest fantasies.

The problem with complete women is that they can interfere with your fantasies. There's a good amount of body to grope, but in fact you do exactly the same thing as when there's only a single leg available to you. You quench yourself with her skin, while her melting thoughts become your thoughts. You moan sighs into her mouth. You create an image of her and expect her to live up to it. The more she manages to match your unspoken fantasy, the better she is.

Good sex is the illusion that the other finds your lovemaking good. Love is like a mirror. You see your own countenance in the delighted face of the other. You hope the other sees herself reflected in you, while you project your own longings onto the emptiness of her astonished eyes. I mean: everyone finds true love sooner or later. But there are at least six billion people on earth. How probable is it, statistically speaking, that the collection of limbs lying next to you in bed happens to be the one unique person who makes your existence complete? How likely is it that "The One" should drop onto your lap like a snow-white dove who has died in midflight right above your beseechingly outstretched hands? True love is the decision to start believing in the fantasy at hand, instead of fantasizing. My love for the leg was exactly like that. All things considered, it was exactly like that. Do you understand?

And unlike an un-fabricated girl with a mouth in a face on a head atop shoulders that has a mind of its own, my mistress could say nothing that impeded the illusion. She was perfectly identical to the image I'd made of her. And so she remained a concept, a work of art, the snow-white dove I could catch wherever I wanted her to fall. When I had sex with her, I had sex with my own fantasies, and so the sex was perfect. Because that's how things are. Because every encounter is accompanied with wild assumptions about what the other is thinking, with her trembling little shoulders and her eyes so brown in the headlights of your rampant lust. At night, the other looks like the unlit motorway to the embodiment of your unclear dreams, but you haven't realized that as you honk with your dimmed headlights, she is driving even faster toward an uncertain destination behind you. And after the head-on collision, once perfect limbs dangle off sharp edges of broken glass. I know you understand me. You're not like the others.

And after having spewed out all of my so-called wisdom, you'll also understand how stupid I was. It's all about the garbage bag, dummy. You can fantasize as much as you like and have a nice shower, but if you go and casually wrap an accommodating, pristine, gray piece of plastic around her leg with your desirous sweaty fingers, you'll leave impeccable fingerprints behind. She was still there. I carefully lifted her out of the garbage can and brought her back home with me.

13.

The butcher was a redheaded girl. She was wearing a white apron and sky-blue clogs as she pulled up the shutters. The metallic rattle spread like whooping cough through the neighborhood. The hours of the *pranzo* and siesta were over. The city went about its business, hawking and sighing. A street-cleaning vehicle from the sanitation department drove through the narrow streets with a noisy display of revolving brushes, sprayers, and vacuum cleaners, streets that were impossible to get clean after all those centuries. The vehicle was driven by a woman with a generous head of black curls and a formidable hook nose. Maybe she had an excellent sense of smell and that was why she'd been chosen for the job. She couldn't get through. A beggar was lying on the street, refusing to get up; of course it was the dirtiest place in the greatest need of a clean. She got out, swearing. She was small, wearing a baggy green uniform. And when the tramp still didn't react, she gave him a nasty kick. Yelping like a dog, he retreated under an *archivolto*.

"This is a city of women," the signora had said to me a few days previously. "You have to understand that." She'd appeared out of nowhere, as usual, around the San Bernardo in a long elegant dress and with a thin cigarette between her fingers. "A city whose menfolk are always at sea is ruled by women." I said it was better that way, but she disagreed with me in no uncertain terms.

The cleaning truck carried on, leaving behind a trail of slime made up of half-aspirated, wet trash. A drunk Moroccan smashed a beer bottle. Someone threw a garbage bag onto the street from the fourth floor. At night, the rats have the place to themselves, but they're not only around at night. This is Fabrizio De André's street, which he sung about as *la cattiva strada*, the shit street, Via del Campo. With bright red lipstick and eyes as gray as the street, she spends the entire night standing in the doorway, selling everyone the same rose. Via del Campo is a whore, and if you feel like loving her, all you have to do is take her by the hand.

"Maestro, how are things? Terrible as usual?" It was Salvatore, the one-legged beggar. He's from Romania, but he's become welded to this city. Everyone knows him because there's no escaping him. He knows how to find everybody. He speaks a kind of universal Romance language—a mixture of Romanian, Italian, Spanish, a couple of Rhaeto-Romance dialects, and a handful of Latin words.

"One-legged" is the wrong word. He has both his legs, but when he's begging, he rolls the left leg of his trousers up to his thigh to expose an impressive scar and then he struggles around with a crutch, as though that rolled-up leg no longer worked. I've seen him after work in the evening with both his trouser legs down and the crutch under his arm, running to catch the last bus. But from time to time I give him a coin. He's a street artist. He amuses me.

"I'm sorry, Salvatore. I don't have any change today."

He gave me a friendly pat on the shoulder. "Don't you worry, maestro. You're my customer. You can pay me tomorrow instead."

It's two hundred meters from Via del Campo to Africa. I walked through the Porta dei Vacca, crossed the road, and was all of a sudden in the Pré. Hundreds of Internet cafés and call shops of barely a door's width across were packed with Kenyans and Senegalese. In the meantime, their wives were earning the money selling tinkling gilt items on the street—phone cases, paper handkerchiefs, CDs, rubber plungers, and elephants hand-carved from tropical hardwood. They sat there majestically spread in traditional robes. Numerous greengrocers had squeezed themselves in between the phone centers like narrow, man-sized caverns. They had Arabic or Swahili lettering and price lists. And in some mysterious way, there was still space left for hairdresser's shops specializing in African hair, which is totally different from other hair. You can get your frizzy hair straightened and then buy Afro wigs in all the colors the Maker didn't dare think of. I suspect you could also get a spell cast on your husband's mistress in there. Why else would they be so full of excited, shabby-looking black women, not having anything hairdresser-y done to them?

In a corner behind the dryer hoods, the village elders gathered to discuss the situation that had arisen and the measures to be taken. Dotted around the place were a few people having their hair cut. Muslim brothers strolled sternly along the street. Prostitutes were conspicuously inconspicuous in the alleyways. Further down at the seafront, fishermen returned to sell their catch and mend their nets. High up on Via Balbi, tourists and Interrailers with rucksacks and bottles of Fanta were emerging from Palazzo Principe's train station to make their way bravely to their hotels.

I was drunk on the city, crazy and confused and much too happy for the circumstances. Or much too depressed. It changed by the minute. Everything spun around me with a commotion of noise, stench, and impressions that were poured out faster than I could swallow them. The streets were too slanted, too steep, too twisted, too crooked, and too uneven. I felt like I was about to fall.

14.

Rashid smiled when he saw me. But he looked terrible. He had lost weight. His eyes looked tired. It was relatively late in the evening, and he was still carting around an impressive number of roses. It would be difficult to sell them all before closing time.

"How's business?"

He responded with a helpless smile. I invited him to join me, and ordered a small beer for him. He put his bucket of roses down on the ground. He sighed.

"Why did you come here, Ilja?"

I took a sip of my Negroni and pondered the question.

"You come from the north, Ilja. There's so much rain there the fields are green and the roses flower on their bushes for free. There's free money for everyone who goes to the counter. You're given a clean house in a safe neighborhood bordered by grassy pastures and there are windmills, cheese farms, and pancake restaurants, and after a while you can pick up your Mercedes from Social Services. Am I right or am I right?"

I smiled.

"Well?"

I ordered another Negroni for myself and a small beer for him.

"You're an intelligent man, Rashid, you know you're talking bullshit."

"That's not what they think in Africa."

A beggar came to ask for money. I automatically waved him off. Rashid spat in his face.

"Well?"

"Well what?"

"Why did you come here, Ilja?"

"And you?"

"I asked you first."

"I came here to write a book."

"That's not an answer."

"Why shouldn't that be an answer?"

"Because you don't listen to a woman until you've looked her in the eye."

"Is that a well-known Arabic saying then?"

"No, I made it up myself."

"And what do you mean by it?"

"That you don't start writing about something until you're already fascinated by it, which implies that you already know it, and so you came here for other reasons at the start, and after that you decided to write a book about the city to give yourself an alibi."

"Do you really think that, Rashid?"

"Yes, I really do."

"You're too intelligent to be selling roses."

"I know that."

15.

"I'll tell you the truth, Rashid. That northern paradise of yours, where the grass is always green because it's always raining, that's where I was born and where I spent my whole life. In a way, it really is a paradise. It's a peaceful, multicolored country. The trains are blue and yellow and run on time through the tulip fields. The tax forms are blue or pink and easy to fill in. If you have to pay something, you don't have to try to be clever or come up with a plan because you won't get out of paying it, and when you get a rebate, you get it back that very same month. Blonde girls spray their stolen bikes pink. Policemen smile. They tell you to clip on a red backlight next time and hand out stickers against racism. The waste is separated and goes in containers of various bright colors. There are special offers at the supermarket that everyone can take advantage of and if you take advantage enough, they give you free little multicolored fluffy creatures that you can stick to your dashboard with their sticky feet, or to your windowsill, or wherever you want. But you know what the thing is, Rashid?"

"What?"

"Exactly that."

I ordered myself another Negroni and a small beer for him. We clinked glasses. "To looking women in the eye, then."

"But what exactly?"

"What do you mean?"

"You didn't finish your story."

"In a way, I did. In a way, I've said everything, Rashid. In my homeland, I had it easy all my life and lived well. But it was too easy and too good. I knew the way from my house to the station like the back of my hand, from the supermarket to my house and from one bar to the other. Do you have that expression in Arabic too? Like the back of your hand? I fell asleep even before I went to bed, in a manner of speaking, and didn't even wake up in the meantime. I knew everything already. I knew the story already. And at the end of the day, I'm an artist. I need input. Inspiration is what they call it, but I hate that word. The challenge to wake up in a new city where nothing is obvious and where I have the freedom to reinvent myself anew. The challenge of waking up. Got that?

"Maybe I should apologize for my choice of words. I wouldn't ever put words like 'input' and 'challenge' in my writing. I just wanted to say that a comfortable life also has its disadvantages. Comfort is like a lullaby, a drug, an antidepressant that numbs the emotions. You can see it on the faces of the people in my homeland. They have the limp expressionlessness of people who no longer have to fight for anything and aren't particularly pleased about it because it's become normal for everything to function perfectly. Or sometimes the sensation takes the form of a kind of unspoken complacency that looks down on the world pityingly from the top of a tall, gangly body with the expression of someone who doesn't have to have seen everything to fully grasp everything that's different and automatically consider it inferior. Although there are more poets than tax inspectors, my homeland isn't a very poetic country.

"Here in Italy nothing goes without saying and everything has to be continually re-fought. Because the system doesn't work. Because there is no system. And if there were one, nobody would believe in it. Or circumnavigate it for a joke. Out of habit. Or to gain some minute advantage. Or not even. In the perpetual *opera buffa* of daily life, the simplest of actions, like buying bread at the bakery, or picking up a parcel from the post office, can come complete with the most unexpected complications. This entire country called Italy depends on improvisation. That's why Italians are the most resourceful, resilient, and creative people I know. I enjoy that. It awakened me. That's why I'm here. Is that an answer, Rashid?"

He didn't say anything, but finished his beer and stood up. Salvatore walked past with his bad leg but ignored us.

"What is it, Rashid? Have I said something wrong?"

"Is there poverty in your country? Have you ever gone hungry there? Is there a fucking civil war? Are you being politically persecuted? And how did you get here—in an unreliable inflatable dinghy without any gas, or by EasyJet?"

"Sit down, Rashid, please. I only told you my story because you asked for it. Let's talk about your story now."

He went to the toilet, came back, picked up his bucket of roses and walked off without saying anything. Without even thanking me for the beers. But that was fine, I understood. Maybe he had just enough time to walk all the way to Nervi and sell part of the contents of his bucket. When I finished my Negroni and went inside to pay, it turned out he'd already paid the entire bill.

16.

Before disembarrassing myself of her for the second and final time, I wanted to see her again. I got the plastic bag out of the wardrobe and began to open it. It was difficult. I'd knotted it really well. And that turned out to be no bad thing because when I finally managed to open the bag such a foul smell wafted out I almost vomited. Holding my breath, I quickly re-knotted the bag even more tightly than before. And when I remembered that I'd stroked and caressed that dead, rotting piece of human offal, I really did throw up.

If I ever reworked these notes I'm sending to you regularly, of course I'll take out that shameful fumbling with the leg. That stays between us, my good friend, you'll understand that. But that would be a bit of a shame because I'd be leaving out an opportunity to exploit the affair as a striking metaphor for that misunderstanding we call love. You love a woman with the passion of a man who, against his better judgment, decides to believe in a forever—which, once you've realized that she only exists in your fantasies, is yet again surprisingly brief—upon which you dump her; and when you think back later to that umpteenth best time of your life and re-read the diary in which your sensitive caresses reverberate in the blistering blindness of your delusions, a smell of decay rises up that almost or actually does make you throw up at your own naive romanticism. Something like that. I'd put it less crudely so as not to scare off too many readers. And I'd invent an affair to breathe life into the metaphor. For example, I'd take a character like myself, too often disappointed and, more often than that, too disappointing in love to still believe in fairy tales, a cynic and an avowed bachelor who only ever has meaningless one-night stands these days, and not even that often, and put him in a position like mine: an immigrant in a new, sunny country; and against his wishes and against his better judgment, I'd let him fall completely, utterly, hopelessly in love again with a sizzling southern woman, the most beautiful girl in the city. And then of course I'd have it all go wrong. Something to do with cultural differences. Something about a fundamental lack of understanding. Something about his fantasies being quite different from hers. So that his deeply engrained cynicism is once again painfully justified, and when he looks in the mirror after that he feels sick. And then the metaphor of the leg. That might work, don't you think?

But no. It was a pity, but hey. I washed the outside of the garbage bag with a sponge scourer. The leg inside felt disgustingly soft. It was decaying. All of a sudden I could no longer take it. I had to get rid of it as quickly as possible. I decided washing would no longer be necessary if I just threw the bag in the water. Somewhere far away. And of course not in the sea. I wasn't that stupid. The package would be politely returned to sender by the languid summer waves. I needed fast flowing water. I needed the river. I walked toward the Bisagno.

17.

There wasn't much water in the Bisagno. It was summer. The river, which can swell in the autumn to present a serious threat to the area around Brignole Station, had shrunk to an impotent trickle in a bed of dried-up rocks. Traffic raced along behind me along Via Bobbio. I saw the Marassi football stadium in the distance. Behind it was the prison, and behind that the graveyard.

There I stood with a garbage bag containing a rotting woman's leg. Yep. Well done, Leonardo. It would take an Olympian throw to even reach the water. A police car with siren and flashing light raced past. I could go to the bridge. And then I could drop it from the middle…Do you believe this yourself? The package would get stuck in a stupid little bush at the second bend, if it didn't immediately get stranded on the stones. And then what? Climb down. I could picture the whole thing. Mr. Poet descending corpulently from the embankment to pick up a garbage bag from the riverbed. And what do you think you're doing, Sir? Do the contents of said garbage bag look familiar to you? And might you find it a good idea to accompany us to the nearby station so you can explain in peace and quiet and greater detail what exactly we're dealing with here? Or words to that effect. Or not to that effect at all, because unlike the dust-busting brigade in my homeland whose daily work involves getting cats out of trees, the Italian *carabinieri* are an army that have been fighting organized crime for decades. Blind eyes are sometimes turned in their prison cells. They know how to get a person to confess. They have plenty of experience.

I had to go to the sea. Nervi. High cliffs. No beach. I should weigh down the bag with stones, but I didn't want to open it another time and smell what I never wanted to smell again. I should have put another bag around it and put the stones in there. But there was no way I was going home again. I had to get rid of it as quickly as possible. Maybe I could try to throw stones onto it. Or something like that.

I took the train from Brignole Station. It stopped at Sturla, Quarto, and Quinto before it reached Nervi. It seemed to take forever. Commuters wrinkled their noses. Yes, I'm sorry, I'm aware of it. I'm sitting here with a rotting leg in my bag. And as a matter of fact, everything you have in your briefcase is probably much worse. I don't even want to know. No, I really don't.

Nervi's station is on the seafront. By now, I'd really had it up to here with the whole business, so much so that I couldn't summon up the energy to look for a special, secret, well-chosen place and just dumped the bag into the sea from the platform. The waves were on my side. Pure luck. The bag floated away. There were black clouds above the mountains on the other side of the city. Forest fires. A yellow fire-fighting plane maneuvered above the bay. Tomorrow was going to be hot again. I used the same ticket to take the train home.

18.

Sunday had descended upon Genoa. The city lay like a woman with a bad cold who'd decided to spend the day in bed. The pillows were damp, the bottom sheet damp, the duvet twisted in its cover, but she didn't have the strength to change the sheets or make the bed. Bright sun shone through the window onto her snotty face. She turned over and closed her eyes. Yesterday's dirty dishes were still piled up on the counter. Her risky evening dress lay in a corner of the room. She wouldn't be swishing and swirling before the hungry eyes of the night this evening. She reached with a sigh for the half-empty packet of cigarettes on the bedside table and the lighter. After two drags, she extinguished the cigarette on the saucer under the cup of her now-lukewarm tea. Everything tasted funny today. It was hot, unbearably hot. She kicked the duvet half onto the floor and fell asleep. She didn't dream about anything in particular. She dreamed gray, lingering dreams like a boring, tacky film, and would remember nothing of them. When she awoke it was the evening. But she didn't feel better.

I shuffled through the empty streets of my new city. The shutters had been lowered in all the alleyways. The hawkers' raucous arias were nowhere to be heard, and nowhere to be heard was the fierce barking or scornful throat-clearing of life. Even the beggars had taken the day off. Scattered about were a few bars that were reluctantly a little bit open, yawning behind their façades. The Bar of Mirrors was closed. I felt like a man who had done his best with roses and champagne, had ironed his best suit to the nines and lightly sprinkled his cheeks with his most expensive aftershave, ready for the evening and the rest of his life, and the woman he has a date with fails to show up. She doesn't send a text until late that night. "In bed with a bad cold. Sorry." And he replies, "No worries. Better for me too anyway. Get well soon. Hope to see you." And he throws a wine glass in anger. Then sighs deeply.

He gets to his feet to tidy away the broken glass, cutting his finger in the process. A drop of blood stains his suit.

I was alone. Of course I was alone. I'd had that feeling for the past couple of days, but on this Sunday, it broke through like a heavy cold, dampening my desire to do anything at all. I tried to reflect on this, but didn't feel like it. Loneliness had nestled in my cavities like a gray lump of snot. It made my face hurt. The heat was unbearable, even in the darkness of the narrow alleyways I knew like the inside of my pocket. I didn't feel like sweating, either, but I was. Maybe I should have stayed in bed. But I didn't feel like that, either.

What have I achieved up to this point? Back home everyone recognizes me and I'm pestered every day for an autograph or an opinion about something. Not here. I have taken up residence. I carry a key to a real Genoese house. It is a large, real key with a fat bow on a long steel shaft, which has to be forced with conviction into a heavy old door, and you need to use force to turn the key. I didn't intend this as a metaphor, but in retrospect it could be interpreted as such. Go ahead then, my friend. Invent something beautiful about heavy doors and the large, indigenous keys needed, along with conviction and force. I'm sure you can do it. Think about Rashid too. I don't feel like pre-digesting it for you. It's Sunday. I'm alone.

Out of boredom, I try to remember the Sundays of my child-hood. They had to do with paving stones and ants that had taken up residence in the strips of sand between the paving stones without a permit. I considered that illegal occupancy and tried to chase them away with spit and sticks and, when that didn't help, warm yellow piss. In the olden days, it was always hot on Sundays.

In Genoa, the pavements were as gray and solid as the walls of her palazzi. Big blocks of sagging stone. You'd need three men to lift one of those boulders and set it straight. The cracks between them were the city's ashtrays. There wasn't a single ant that would dare start a family here. In many places, there was barely enough space between the stones for a rat's nest. In Genoa's glory years, from above, it must have looked like a stone floor of gray palaces with cracks and crannies between them where rats could come and go as they pleased. In their glory years, God tried to fight them with spit and sticks and, when that didn't help, warm yellow piss. The city still looks like shit. But God is no longer who he used to be and he's given up. La Superba beat God by blocking his view of the alleyways. Every kind of dirt and decadence can run rampant in the cracks and cavities of this city. There are even transvestites here, it seems. I haven't found them yet. I mean, I haven't run into any yet.

I'd invented a game, and also come up with an official name for it. You're either a celebrated writer or you aren't. It's called "girl surfing." The rules are simple. You pick out a random girl as she walks by and start to follow her. If you tend to go on aimless walks anyway, you might as well walk after a random girl. As you follow her, you fantasize about her. About what she's like up close and under all those clothes, about how she'd sigh and reach for a half-empty packet of cigarettes on your bedside table. You keep on doing this until you see a prettier girl. Then you swap and carry on following her until you see an even prettier girl. The game becomes more and more satisfying the longer you play it.

And in the meantime you get to know the city. To add a didactic element to the game, I invented the extra rule that I had to fantasize in Italian. I would learn the most by doing so out loud, but I realized I'd better be careful with that. I caught a fantastic wave during the week, one of the best since I arrived in Genoa. She was small and olive-colored with a nonchalant miniskirt and racy boots. I got to follow her all the way from Maddalena, past Molo, to Portoria. My fantasies became ever more colorful and explicit. I was able to express them beautifully in Italian. But at a certain point, I was standing close to her in a herd of commuters waiting for a traffic light to turn green, and I'd forgotten that, for autodidactic reasons, I was speaking out loud. I decided to switch then, even though my fantasies at that very moment were about what I would do when she reached the heavy door to her house and rammed the big key with conviction and force into her lock.

Not much surfing to be done today. Even for the waves it was Sunday. Here and there, a tired tourist in Bermuda shorts was encouragingly patted on her fat rolls by the skinny man of the moment carrying the map and the rucksack containing important things firmly strapped to his back. "Where are our international travel insurance papers? Have you seen our international travel insurance papers?" And she didn't even recognize me. I was alone.

What had I achieved up to now?

19.

"You've made a big impression in Centro Storico. Everyone knows you."

Her name was Cinzia. She was a young, pretty girl with a long face. I recognized her as the waitress from Caffè Letterario on Piazza delle Erbe. The one with the red tables. I often went there since I knew what it was called. But there was something odd about her. I saw her too often during the day, and too often on her own for an Italian girl of her age, especially for an Italian girl that went about dressed in a suggestive top, deeply cut, with an open back, no sleeves, and shorts. She had lovely legs and wore high heels. She wore makeup, but it was subtle and tasteful. Almost every afternoon she sat on her own at a table in the Bar of Mirrors, studying. She came from Sardinia and was studying education in Genoa. She'd been here two years. Sometimes I saw her with Don, an emeritus professor of English language and literature in his seventies who had been living in a hotel room for twenty years with a view of the seven bars on the Piazza delle Erbe. He had a Union Jack hanging out of his window, didn't speak any Italian, and survived on a sole diet of gin and tonic. "*Capuccino senza schiuma,*" as he called it. But I hadn't seen him for a few days now, and she was sitting on her own in the Bar of Mirrors, and she came outside to smoke, and because there weren't any free tables on the terrace, I invited her to join me at mine.

"That's what you say."

"It's true. I was sitting at this table yesterday, too, and there were other people sitting here, people I didn't know, and they were talking about you. About you. They were wondering who you were and what you were doing here."

She was attracted to older intellectuals. That must be her problem. You saw it every evening on Italian TV. It didn't matter which program you watched. Whether it was infomercials, which it mostly was, or a talk show, or a quiz, or a sports program, there was always a light blue background with a handful of young, pretty, stupid girls in bikinis and a single older intellectual, sweating in his suit, making jokes about the girls—only they were too thick to understand them: a golden formula, I give you that. The man uses a few subjunctives, one of the girls doesn't get it and says something ungrammatical, the audience screams, and the girl has to take off her bikini top as punishment, causing the intellectual of the moment to make another cutting remark, causing the audience to scream again.

All of Italy is made like that. It's the man's job to make cutting remarks and the woman's job to take her top off afterward. In any case, the gender roles are clear. You know who's who. That's the way the Church likes it. A man shouldn't suddenly turn out to be a woman or vice versa. I wondered what it would be like to take off Cinzia's top.

"That's what I like about you. I really appreciate that. You are the first—no, second—man I've met who hadn't immediately wanted to take off my top after we've exchanged just a couple of words."

"Maybe that's because I'm not Italian." I smiled in a very mysterious, intellectual manner.

"Maybe." She fiddled with her top a little.

"I always find Italian men quite—how do you say it in Italian—quite expressive."

"Women too," she said.

20.

Before she left, Cinzia gave me a mission: I had to find the Mandragola. I was charmed by the medieval allure of the quest, and I wanted to ask her whether I could wear the silken handkerchief embroidered with her initials beneath my shining breastplate during my long, long journey to traverse sevenfold mountains of sevenfold rivers, and sevenfold woods. I would count upon her snow-white handkerchief to protect me from griffins and seas of fire, witches and dragons that drenched themselves in the dripping blood of druids.

The Mandragola is a legendary flower which grows in just one place and blooms only once in a hundred years. The magic scent of her blossom could save mankind. "It's a bar. More like a kind of nightclub." "And where is it then?" "I'm not telling you. I'll be working at the Caffè Letterario tomorrow. Come and let me know if you've found it."

Her handkerchief certainly came in handy. My first hunch was that it would be in the area around Maddalena, which has those kinds of little squares like Piazza della Lepre, Piazza delle Oche, and Piazza della Posta Vecchia—squares as big as a parking spot, which translocate mysteriously each night. There are tiny bars on them but they translocate, too. The art is to catch the streets during their nighttime displacements. But it happens inaudibly and very fast. Or very slowly. I'm still not sure about that. I walked in circles and squares around Palazzo Spinola, Vico della Rosa, Vico dietro il Coro della Chiesa die Santa Maddalena. These are places where the sun never shines. It was nighttime. The shadows had eaten up the sun. The prostitutes and tourists had gone. The alleys were the domain of rats, pigeons, and pickpockets, as they almost always were. Witches hissed at me. A person I didn't trust asked me for a light. A rogue roared with laughter in an alleyway.

I went off to search the other side of the Via Luccoli, in Sestiere del Molo. I knew this neighborhood better but I realized that there could be streets between Via San Bernardo and the towers of the Embriaci that I didn't know. It all goes uphill there toward Castello, to the architectural faculty and the Sant'Agostino cloisters, and I don't like going uphill. So the Mandragola might very well be located there. These paths had not been trodden recently. Or if that wasn't the case, they'd been shat upon by vermin even more recently. There was a tinkle of glass in the distance. Closer by there was screaming. I strayed until I happened upon the Piazza Sarzano, near the Metro. I hadn't found the Mandragola. But in any case, I knew where I was again. And that wasn't good. I don't feel at home in this neighborhood. During the day Piazza Sarzono is too hot, and at night it's deserted, while the alleys like Via Ravecca are populated by distrustful elderly Genoese who don't want to have anything to do with foreigners, not even white ones.

"How's business, maestro?" It was Salvatore. I felt a two-euro coin in my pocket. But of course I didn't give it to him. "Sorry, Salvatore." He came up to me and whispered in my ear, "The man you were sitting on the terrace with yesterday is a Moroccan. Did you know that?" "So what?" He held his finger to his lips meaningfully and hobbled off on his good but purportedly bad legs.

I knew how to get to the Cantine della Torre dei Embriaci. That's a bar I'll have to take you to sometime, my friend.

It's in the cellars of one of the medieval watchtowers. The space is amazingly big when you go in and renovated in the best possible taste, preserving all its authentic features. The owner is called Antonio. He's in love with his own bar. If you're there, it doesn't matter whether it's in the morning, afternoon, or evening, he'll be busy improving his café by moving a halogen bulb or two just less than two millimeters to the left. Or to the right. When you go in it's always empty. And if you cautiously ask Antonio whether he's open as he stands on a bar stool tinkering with his light bulbs, he'll say, "It was a madhouse." Or he'll say, "It was a madhouse yesterday." Or, "It's quiet now but tomorrow, pff…It'll be a madhouse." Then he'll get down off his bar stool and ask what you want to drink. No, I'm saying it wrong. First he starts complaining about Italian laws, then he goes outside to smoke, then he comes back, and only then does he ask you what you want to drink. "A beer." Wrong answer. He has sixty different kinds of beer and likes to serve them with a shot of whisky and a little cocoa powder on the foam. Which whisky would you like? And which beer? If you like, you could also have it with honey, but then it would be quite a different kind of drink. Then I'll have to add Limoncello, too. Or, on the contrary, something salty. But perhaps he might make another suggestion. A surprise. No, don't ask. I'll make you a beer. You can tell me what you think of it later.

Then he brings a few snacks. My God, does he ever bring the snacks. Cured anchovies with a salt crust. "Made them myself. This afternoon." A bowl of *penne all'arrabiata* with extra chili. "I always make a bit of this on Thursdays. For my friends." Meanwhile you drink English strong ale, pimped up with two measures of grappa and a shot of Benedictine, with cinnamon on top. "I always give my friends a glass of vermouth to go with it. Maybe you'd like one? With or without basil and brown sugar? You know, my friends are the reason I own this bar. I like to give something back from time to time. Shot of Grand Marnier in the vermouth?"

His bar is devoted to the memory of Fabrizio De André, the brilliant poet and singer whom almost no one outside of Genoa knows. I know who he was. He was really brilliant. Antonio has constructed a wall of memorabilia: photos and paintings and a real guitar. Only his music is played in this bar, preferably on vinyl on a crackly record player in the corner. "I knew his mother. Her aunt was friends with my gym teacher and she was his cook. That's how."

It was pretty much empty when I went in. "Pfff. It was a mad-house this evening. Look at all these dirty glasses. All friends of mine. But I'm happy to oblige." There were still a couple of tufts of windswept people. A valiant small girl took the guitar down from the wall and began to play. It was the official sacred guitar but it was allowed. She sang. She sang Fabrizio De André songs. I've never heard anything like it. She sang for an almost empty bar and she sang with a voice that gave me goose bumps. She sang very differently from Fabrizio De André, but with deadly accuracy, taking no prisoners. It was also the fact that this was Genoa and that this was all living culture and that a valiant girl was singing all those songs I really love just like that in a bar in the night, so unexpectedly and on the holy guitar and almost solely for me— I sat in the corner and wept. Tears poured down my cheeks. They really did, my friend, I know you don't believe me. And for one reason or another, I had to think of her, the waitress at the Bar of Mirrors, the most beautiful girl in Genoa, and I thought how wonderful it would be to share this moment with her, which made me cry all the more.

And there I sat in Genoa without a handkerchief. "That girl," I said to Antonio. "That girl who sang, I'd like to thank her if you see her again. She's really special."

"Oh sure, with pleasure." Then he bent his head over my tear-streaked cheeks and admitted, "She has a lovely cunt that one, it's true."

21.

These days I'm visiting the Bar of Mirrors every day for the aperitif, from around five until they close at nine and after closing time I hang around the neighborhood for a bit, and naturally you understand why, my friend. She works there every day during exactly those hours. And when she comes out around ten, after cleaning up, in her normal clothes, carrying a scooter helmet under her arm, sometimes I manage to walk past by complete coincidence and say "Ciao" to her before she goes home. Or to her boyfriend's flat with his ugly gelled head, the bastard. Or maybe they live together. No, that's not possible. It's simply not allowed.

Usually I sit on the terrace on my own. Sometimes the signora drops by, but when Bernardo Massi, the old man with the wild white hair and the wild Hawaiian shirts, rumored to be powerfully rich, is there, she prefers his company to mine. And he's almost always there. He's the owner of the entire palazzo which the Bar of Mirrors is part of, it seems. But I like sitting on my own.

That way I can watch people undisturbed. I'm afraid she is starting to become a real obsession. I get goose bumps when I see her. She glides before my eyes like a poem written in calligraphy. She's like an elegant swirl in an art nouveau ornament. I can't keep my eyes off her. And I time it so that I take the last sip of my Negroni when she comes out of the porcelain grotto onto the terrace so that I can order my next drink from her rather than from one of her nondescript colleagues. I'm as polite and respectful toward her as possible. I never try to speak to her, except to order something. That's also because I just don't dare. I know it sounds crazy but I really don't dare. I'm afraid to ruin the fragile fairy tale by saying something trite. Meanwhile, I'm waiting for the moment when she'll say something to me.

With this in mind, I always sit writing on the terrace. Almost everything I'm giving you to read has been written there, in that outside space with the dark green tables on Salita Pollaiuoli with a view of her. Maybe that's the reason I write about her so much. Maybe that's the reason I write so much, my friend. Just be thankful to her.

Because sooner or later her curiosity will have to be piqued. If you have a customer who comes back every day, polite and irreproachable in his newly-purchased Italian wardrobe, which obviously must have cost a fortune, with a real panama hat, everyone knows how much they cost, a foreigner who has clearly settled here and who sits at a table on his own every evening writing in small, meticulous handwriting in a Moleskine notebook—an artist but also a professional with an income who is probably a celebrity in his home country—then sooner or later your curiosity would be piqued, wouldn't it? "May I ask what you are writing, sir?" "Oh, just some notes for myself. Actually I'm a poet." "Really? A poet? I've always wanted to meet a poet. Are you famous?" "Ach, what can I say...?" "How exciting! Will you write a poem about me sometime?" "With pleasure. But I'd have to get to know you better first." Name. Phone number. Date, kiss, and into the sack. And the bastard with the gelled head goes to the back of the line.

But she never speaks to me. And meanwhile I'm falling more and more in love.

22.

The old stones are steeped in the smell of rotting waste, piss, and something else, something acidic, something you taste on the roof of your mouth more than you smell it. Rats dart away and climb into the crevices. Their gnawing sounds like an evil thought. The sea wind brings a heavy salt spray, causing people to pant and groan. They'd love to throw off that last suffocating item of clothing. It is as damp as the forbidden cellars of the secret hunting lodge of a perverse prince. The mold and shadows that rub themselves up against the clammy walls day and night leave behind scent trails. No one need be afraid of anything chivalrous here.

They act like this is their city. They pretend to be walking along the street. But their expressions are too dark for that, their legs too long, their steps too small. No one is going anywhere. No one walks past only once. No one walks past without shining like a gold tooth in a pimp's rotten grin.

I walk over the curves and between the crannies and gashes of this city I know my way around like no other, where I pretend to be out walking, where I repeatedly and deliberately get lost like a john on his rounds. The pavement yields willingly under my feet. Underneath flows the morass of pus we'll all plunge into once we find the opening.

They act like this is a city. They act like they're walking and wearing clothes. But underneath those clothes they are continuously naked. They touch themselves with their hands while pretending to be looking for their keys, a mobile phone, or loose change. Their thighs rub gently against each other as they walk. From time to time someone will just pause for a moment, happy, self-absorbed, as though standing under a hot shower.

I wander in circles around the labyrinth like a corkscrew being screwed into a cork. When it's freed, a bouquet of tarry, sweet wine with legs like dripping oil, matured on groaning rotten oak, with full notes of earth, decay, pleasure, and piss will rise up. We're all drunk before we even start, as we screw ourselves deeper and deeper into the cork, into the smell of the cork, into the promise of smell. What do you mean, prejudice? This is no city for a lone male. I have to come up with something. I have to do something about it before I do something, God forbid.

It was a tiny item in the local paper, *Il Secolo XIX*. I chanced upon it. In the burned forests above Arenzano, a charred woman's leg had been found. Using DNA testing, the authorities had managed to link the leg to a crime committed some time ago. The victim's name was Ornella. It was the name she'd used when admitted to hospital. She had never formally reported the crime. Her real name was unknown. She had disappeared without trace.

It slowly sunk in that this was my leg. How many severed limbs could there be knocking around Genoa and its surroundings? But how could it have gotten there? And then I remembered the yellow fire-fighting plane maneuvering above the bay of Nervi. I closed the paper in shock. But then I realized I should be happy. In any case all the traces had been wiped out. I was relieved. For a moment, I toyed with the idea of trying to track down the mysterious Ornella the leg had been attached to. If she was as I'd imagined her, a missing leg didn't have to be a problem. In fact, if I'd managed to fantasize her onto one of her legs, I'd surely be able to compensate for the lack of a single leg with my imagination. But I knew that wasn't right. The less reality there is to disturb the imagination, the more effective, attractive, and exciting the fantasy. And what's more, she'd see right through me. "Hey babe, you won't remember, but we've already met." I should count my blessings that it had all gone so smoothly. I needed to forget that entire leg, including the Ornella I'd imagined onto it, as quickly as possible.

23.

I went for a so-called spontaneous stroll with my hand in the pocket of my trousers. It was beautiful weather, but we all know only too well where I was off to. It was the white hour after lunch, the blank page upon which some secret language could be scribbled in pencil, something that should be rubbed out again instantly as soon as the shutters were raised and life started again in black and white with profits, proceeds, and protests. For the time being, the city lay dozing, her belly bulging into the dreaming alleys, which nonchalantly changed their position with a soft sigh, the way a woman would languidly roll over on the couch she'd settled upon after the digestif. Suddenly, all the alleys led to Maddalena. She lived nearby in Palazzo Spinola four centuries ago, among the glory and splendor of the family she managed to marry into. Portraits of doges and admirals stared down at her body with the dusky glances of age-old lecherousness. Sometimes, at this hour when the palace sleeps and the men are at sea or wherever they are, she undresses in front of the cardinal's life-sized official portrait. Soon she'll have to sit and keep quiet again. She doesn't have anything else to do. She has a lot of servants. She lies on her day bed and stares at the ceiling upon which a scene of half-naked Romans kidnapping naked Sabine virgins has been painted. If only she were a Sabine virgin. Her husband, the Doge, says that they'll lose everything if they lose the war and that this is why he is often away. "Even my clothes?" she'd asked. "Yes, even your clothes," he had replied, after which, with a serious expression on his face, he'd gone out to continue his war. Who were they fighting again? She has no idea and she doesn't care, either, as long as they rip the clothes from her body. Pisa probably, otherwise Venice. They are always having wars against Pisa or Venice. Or perhaps it's the French. Might the French soldiers also be half-naked when they come to kidnap the Genoese women? It wouldn't surprise her, she's heard all kinds of things about the French. Brutish beasts they are, without a jot of respect for a lady's honor. Her husband has often told her that, adding that she doesn't understand a thing about state affairs. She understands enough to hope that Genoa will lose a war for once, by preference to the French. Through the open window of her bedroom, she hears a woman screaming like a stuck pig far below her in the alleyway. Brutish beasts they are, oh, brutish beasts.

Suddenly all roads led to Maddalena. I tried to walk from Piazza Soziglia to Piazza Fontane Marose, but in the place where the Via Luccoli was located at other times of the day, there was a dark alleyway which turned back on itself, coming out on the other side of Piazza Lavagna, where grubby men with their hands in their pockets walked along alleys with poetic names that were all called Maddalena, and where darkly-scented women, who were all called Maddalena, said I had pretty hair and that was why I had to go with them. They asked whether I was French. They asked whether I knew the secrets of the jungle where it could be night all afternoon in their hands. They grabbed me by the forearm to go explain it better somewhere else. They twirled my hair around their fingers and said that there was something feminine about me. They stroked the hand in the trouser pocket. Brutish beasts, they were.

She rolls over once again on her daybed. The ebony paneling nauseates her. She gets up to open a window. There's not enough light in this room in this house, in this much too grand house. There isn't enough light in Genoa. The biggest problem with women is that they are inclined to expect something from men. The biggest problem with men is that they realize that something is expected of them. This realization scares them. That's why they prefer the company of other men, men with whom they go rushing around in great seriousness, in the delusion that the city's future is at stake. And that's why nothing ever happens. A man wants to possess his wife, but if she wants to be possessed, he flees.

It's so tiring, waiting for the French. She stands at the open window. Far below in the alleyway there is loud laughing and joking in languages her husband won't let her learn. She hears someone running away. She imagines he has one hand in the pocket of his trousers. She falls back onto her day bed with a sigh. She looks up at the ceiling painting.

We all know damned well where I was going. San Luca is at the end of Maddalena. I turned right there. I walked to Via del Campo. Just before the end, ten meters before the Porta dei Vacca, was Vico della Croce Bianca.

24.

This neighborhood is known as the Ghetto. The name is meant ironically, but even during the daytime, it takes courage to go there. It's dusky all day in other alleys. Here it's always night. It gives the appearance of being renovated. And it's in dire need of that, which you realize the moment you set foot in the area. There's no pavement and almost everything is crumbling or half-collapsed. But it's not being renovated. For years, the narrow, tall, impassable streets have been covered in rusty scaffolding that has no other purpose than to deny all pedestrians even that tiny strip of blue sky.

If you look on the map, it's a question of five or six small alleys: Vico della Croce Bianca, Vico del Campo, Vico di Untoria, Vico dei Fregoso, Vico degli Andorno, and perhaps Vico San Filipa. But the map isn't quite right. There are also gaps between the walls, and toppled palazzi form new squares without a name. The rats are as big as lapdogs. They know their way around and take to their heels, just like the Moroccans who rub along the mildewed walls as skittish as ghosts. And everywhere I saw the same sticker that was stuck to the pipes on my house:

derattizzazione in corso
non toccare le esche

I still have to look up what that means.

The transvestites live here. The famous transvestites of Genoa that Fabrizio De André sung about as *le graziose di Via del Campo*. They are men in their fifties wearing high heels and fishnet stockings over their hairy legs, a sexy dress straining over their beer bellies, and a wig. They beckon you into their caverns with their stubble and their irresistible baritone voices, where, for a pittance, you can grapple with their self-made femininity. Muslims who may not deflower a woman before they've committed a terrorist attack eagerly do the rounds of the hairy asses on offer. A condom spurted full is worth four dead rats, and four dead rats are a meal. She doesn't have any tits, her bra's full of cotton wool, but if you pay extra, you can suck on them. And if you don't pay, she'll stab your eye out with one of her stilettos.

I heard a story: in the nineteen-sixties a real war waged in these alleyways. For three days. The harbor was full of American warships. An American marine had broken the explicitly worded rules and ventured into these streets one night. Into the Ghetto. He had fallen in love. To him, she was the most beautiful girl in Genoa. He had the blushing privilege of being able to shower her in cigarettes, chocolate, and fishnet stockings. He secretly wrote poems for her in his diary. It was the most wonderful night of his life. But exploring between her sticky thighs afterward, he discovered the truth.

He felt betrayed, swore he would take revenge, and fetched his friends. Forty heavily armed marines invaded the Ghetto. And the transvestites fought back. Stilettos vs. night-vision binoculars. Boiling oil poured from the top floor. Fences falling as soon as the troops reformed. In the meantime, running across the roof-tops and the rusty scaffolding. Diversionary tactics with fishnet stockings. And the street you came through, the one guaranteeing your retreat, suddenly doesn't exist anymore because it seems to have been barricaded with a portcullis. They won. The trans-vestites won. The neighborhood was declared a no-go zone for American marines.

It's a place that has an unusual pull on me. Probably partly due to that story. Or because it's the place that is the furthest away from my fatherland. Or for other reasons. I don't know. We'll come back to the subject.

25.

Rashid was limping when I saw him again. He had a black eye as well.

"Come and sit down. I'll order you a beer. Sorry about last time. And thank you. But what happened?"

"A disagreement," he said.

"Did you go to the police?"

He tried to giggle but it made him cough, which clearly hurt his ribs.

"Are you here illegally?"

He stared into his beer.

"Sorry, Rashid. Perhaps you don't feel like talking at all."

"Could you order a few of those free appetizers for me maybe? What are they called again? *Stuzzichini.*"

"Of course."

"Sorry to ask but there are some things here that a foreigner like you gets more easily than a foreigner like me."

He ate like a dog. He ate like someone who hadn't eaten for a week.

"I haven't eaten for a week, Ilja."

I ordered more free snacks for him under the pretext of ordering them for myself.

"And I'm privileged," he said with his mouth full. "Can you imagine? Where I live, we live with eleven or nine or thirteen, it's different every day. Two rooms. Nine hundred and eighty euros a month. Most of them are Moroccans like me. But there are also a few Senegalese. It's even harder for them than it is for us. But they make it difficult for themselves, I have to say. I'm not a racist but those black people ruin it for all of us. I mean, I came here to work, Ilja. I'm an honest man. Tell me it's true. I'm a good Muslim, even if I do have the occasional beer. But those blacks have a completely different mentality, you can't do anything about it, it's just like that. They steal. They even steal from their own housemates. And if you say anything about it, they kick the shit out of you and give you a black eye. They're used to taking advantage of others. It's not even their fault, really. It's their culture. You have to respect that. You'll agree with me about that, Ilja, that you have to respect their culture."

I began to feel more and more uncomfortable about this conversation.

"But to return to your question," Rashid said. "No."

"Sorry, I lost the thread."

"I'm not here illegally. I have a temporary residence permit. Not like those blacks. I have the right to be here. They arrive on rubber boats via Lampedusa, Malta, or the Canary Islands. I came here with a passport. I'm a skilled worker. I installed air-conditioning for work in Casablanca. I'm a good person, Ilja, do you understand?"

"And why did you come here?"

"Do you want an honest answer?"

"No."

Rashid had to laugh and then cough and then his ribs hurt again. He slapped me on the back.

"Really, you're my only friend here," he said. "It's quite an honor for a white man, me saying that, you should know that. Since you asked, I'll give you a dishonest answer."

He took a sip of his beer.

"I came here to write a book and not to earn money. I came here to gather inspiration and to enrich my life with new experiences, like being robbed and beaten by my own housemates, and I didn't come here to survive. I got bored with my work in Casablanca. It was the same old. I came here to look for a new challenge. Like not even being able to get the most basic job with a name like mine. Here I'm a pariah. But it's fascinating sharing a two-room apartment with nine or eleven or thirteen others, plus the rats. It makes me resourceful. It makes me creative. It keeps me on my toes."

"I'm sorry, Rashid. I understand what you want to say. But why don't you go back?"

"You don't understand a thing, Ilja. I've already explained it to you. The first time we met. Don't you remember?"

"Yes."

"You're lying. But I'll explain it to you one more time. If you'll order me another beer."

I ordered him another beer with *stuzzichini*.

"Let's take one of my housemates as an example. So that it's not about me but someone else. That makes it easier. He comes from Senegal. He's black. His name is Djiby. Yes, write that in your notebook: Djiby. Got that, concerned white citizen of the world? Great. He's a man with a spectacular refugee story. Go and interview him. I'd be happy to introduce you to him."

"Thank you."

"But the principle is the same."

"What principle?"

"My family saved up, too. I have five brothers. And a couple of sisters, but they don't count. Apart from that, I have about forty cousins. The family picked me out. The crossing and the documents cost a couple thousand euros. The illegals, like Djiby, paid even more. But in Africa, it's considered a wise investment. Everyone knows how difficult it is to get into Europe. That's why they choose their best sons or cousins. The people with the best chance of success in Europe. They picked me because of my professional training and because I speak English. And everyone knows the investment is returned. Because if he manages to reach Europe, he'll automatically get rich and send back money, fridges, and cars to the family members who took out loans to get him there."

"What if it doesn't work?"

"That's not an option."

"But it happens."

"In almost one hundred percent of the cases. But it's not an option. Because they've invested too much in you. And apart from that, you'd be the first."

"The first?"

"Not to make it in Europe."

"And all those others then? All those Moroccans and Senegalese like the ones you're sharing the house with?"

"The legals get themselves knee-deep in debt so they can return to the homeland in August in a hired Mercedes with a trunk full of Rolexes."

"And that keeps the fairy tale alive."

"Fairy tales aren't fairy tales if no one doubts their being true."

"And the illegals?"

"It's a fairy tale paid for with the family's entire assets. Do you know how much money that is in Africa, a couple thousand euros? In Casablanca, they assume that I'll immediately start earning that on a monthly basis. Because I'm in Europe. Because I managed to get to Europe."

"What would happen if you went back and admitted that the project failed?"

"The illegals do the same as us. Except they can't go home. They spend the whole day sweating in call shops, explaining in their language why the money transfer hasn't arrived yet. It seems like all of Senegal hangs out on the pavement in front of the Western Union. And they use that money not to buy food or to open a shop or start a business—they buy Rolexes to show their friends they've made it because they have a second cousin in Europe."

"And how much do you earn now, if I may ask?"

"If I returned empty-handed, without fridges and Mercedes for the whole family, it would mean that I, the chosen one, was the first to violate the sacrifices and trust of my kinsfolk. I would be disowned by my family and friends and I wouldn't have any family or friends anymore. I'd be the ultimate loser, a pariah no one would ever want to have anything to do with. I'd be as good as dead.

"These roses are imported and stripped in the Ghetto. They are sold illegally in the early morning on Via della Maddalena for fifty cents apiece. I take forty on weekdays and a hundred and twenty on Fridays and Saturdays. I sell them for a euro. And I rarely manage to sell them all. I have to pay my rent and in the meantime my family keeps asking where the Rolexes have got to."

"And so?"

"And so and so and so. And so everyone does what I do. From time to time, I send them fifty, a hundred, two hundred euros."

"And you borrow that?"

"I borrow it."

"And how are you going to pay it back?"

"I live in a fantasy, Ilja. And not even one I made up myself."

26.

An interviewer in my home country once asked me, "Why do you keep falling in love with waitresses?" I have no idea where he got his information from. I didn't have much time to think about it; I had to come up with a witty response: "Because they can't escape my gaze."

I'm writing to you, my friend, because I'm afraid things are about to get out of hand with the waitress from the Bar of Mirrors. I say afraid, and I mean for you, because she is, as I've repeated to the point of boring you with it, the most beautiful girl in Genoa. You'll never see me again anyway, but given the most recent developments, I'm afraid I have to admit the fact with an ever-broadening grin on my face.

To maintain the suspense, I'll tell you something else first. I found the Mandragola. You'll remember I told you about my new friend Cinzia and she gave me the romantic or more accurately medieval task of going off in search of it. I used that as a reason to penetrate even more deeply into the alleyways than I usually do when I got lost. This was right at the start of my time in Genoa, when getting lost was one of my main pastimes. Cinzia is an intelligent girl. She understands stuff. I didn't entertain for a moment the illusion that the Mandragola actually might exist. But still, I went in search of it. Anyone wanting to make their home in a new country can't ignore orders given by clever, well-meaning local residents. You can't ignore an order given by any woman, until you're married to her and can secretly ignore her orders. But I'm getting ahead of myself.

The Mandragola exists. It's a restaurant. I went there yesterday. There were tables outside on a square the size of a service court when you're playing tennis. In front of a blackened Roman church that through the centuries has been grilled, roasted, and burned down so often it has carbonized to its essence and can decay no more. The minuscule, crammed terrace is shared with a café located in the crypts of an adjacent building in medieval cellars that would be an excellent torture spot if only for the reason that the walls are so thick cries for help would never reach the outside world. And you can descend even lower, to the underground river, where there are cushions on the floor and burning torches. I don't think I'll ever be able to find this café, this square, or the Mandragola ever again, assuming it would all still exist the next time, if it did exist yesterday and wasn't just a figment of my imagination. Because the way it exists, it exists in the shadowy net of dark alleyways at the foot of Santa Maria in Castello where even the rats get lost.

I was there with her. No, not with Cinzia, but with her. Really. When I finally found the Mandragola, it was thanks to the most beautiful girl in Genoa.

27.

I broached it in a really smart way, if I may say so myself. I did the unimaginable. I spoke to her.

"But…" I said.

I'm picturing a traditional Italian wedding. With a white dress and a church. Friends who fly in for it and a long table on a piazza. We've talked about nothing but the menu for months. *Antipasta misti*, we agree about that. Sardinian salami and Spanish pata negra was my suggestion. A few *ripieni*. Courgettes filled with minced meat. And something for the vegetarians, of course. Carpaccio of swordfish, tuna, and salmon with wasabi sauce. And fried *melanzana*. *Acciughe impanate* too, breaded anchovies, fileted and opened out so you can eat them with your fingers. But you said that wasn't an antipasto but a secondo. And those Calabrese meatballs of yours then?

You do have a white dress. So in any case we should serve food that doesn't stain, because I know you. *Crudité di gamberoni crudi.* And *vongole* with *cozze. Penne al gorgonzola.* As a primo. For a wedding? Pears with Parmesan cheese, is that a primo or a secondo? I think it's a dessert. Or let's do trout with almonds. But that's definitely a secondo. *Tagliatelli al salmone.* But are you sure with your white dress? Duck à l'orange. Not Italian enough. Then we might as well go to the Chinese restaurant. But my father would shoot himself. What, Chinese? No, ducks, you imbecile. The Chinese shoot imbeciles. And then we kiss. But still no menu. Kiss again. We'll see. No, we have to arrange it. Cheese fondue, then? Good idea! It was just a joke. But it really is a good idea. But it really was a joke. We'll start at the beginning. We'll have *fave.* Broad beans with Sardinian goat cheese. It won't be the right season. It's always the right season for goat cheese, what do you mean? But not for broad beans. Not in the greenhouses? Sure, in the greenhouses in your country, maybe. Alright then, no broad beans. Risotto. Risotto? At a wedding? Yes, risotto. How? With asparagus. Brilliant idea. It doesn't stain. With butter and ham. Are you mad? It's summer. Then we'll serve a tomato and mozzarella salad on the side. On the side of what? With the lamb shanks. We haven't even discussed the secondo, let alone lamb shanks. Kiss. You see? Do I see what? That you like lamb shanks. No, I like kissing.

Go and rent yourself a suit, my friend. We still need to talk about the menu, but the white dress has already been fitted, in a manner of speaking.

28.

"But," I said, "do you work every single evening?"

"Yes."

"But then if you, you know…"

"I'll be finished early tomorrow."

"For me, tomorrow's…I mean…"

"Pick me up here. We'll go for an aperitif. You can pick a nice place for us. You know Genoa better than I do."

That night I couldn't sleep. I'd picked a special place long ago. Walking distance from the sea. A kind of pier in the harbor with a view of La Lanterna and the big ships sailing far away to fairy-tale destinations like the coast of North Africa, where a purple sunset will be sent back in return. Sorry, I was lying there quite romantically awake. And I could actually see her standing before me in her white dress. While I fully understood that everything was just on the point of beginning…Let's not get ahead of ourselves, for heaven's sake. I still didn't know her name. But we had a date and that was the most important thing.

When I went to pick her up at the Bar of Mirrors the next day, she'd already gotten changed. This was quite an understatement in her case. She'd swapped her waitressing uniform for…for practically nothing. Two boots and then a long stretch of nothing. A kind of short frayed denim skirt. And I can't even remember what she was wearing on top, perhaps because I didn't dare look. She was playing the game. She was playing the game with verve.

You have to change your life, is what I thought when I saw her like that. And I realized that that was exactly what I was doing.

We watched the sun set that evening. It cost me an arm and a leg because in the special place I'd chosen they know better than anyone that they're a special place that is chosen, at great cost, to make an impression with their free sunset. We should talk sometime, too—about money. But not now.

And when the moment came that she had to go home, I asked whether perhaps she'd like to go for a bite somewhere. To my astonishment, she said, "We'll go to the Mandragola. Have you ever been there?"

And when, many hours later, I walked her to her scooter, she said we'd see each other again very soon and kissed my cheek. I finally dared ask.

"What's your name?"

And she told me her name.

29.

That night I lay awake, even awaker than before, if you can say that. My dreams were keeping me awake. The footage of the evening played a hundred times over in my mind, and it seemed like a film. Everything had happened exactly as it happens in films. I couldn't find a single fault. We had talked. We'd had long, pleasant conversations about wonderful things. We'd looked into each other's eyes. Not a cliché had been eschewed. We'd even had recourse to a sunset. And I seemed to remember a soundtrack of sloppy film music with softly swelling violins timed to her slow gestures and her subtle, precise curves. I ran my fingers along her leggy youthfulness in lengthy fantasies and felt the afterglow of her kiss on my cheek like the crimson tinge of a sacred seal.

And we had looked into each other's eyes. Or did I already say that? I could repeat it a hundred times, as that night, dreaming with my eyes open, I gazed a hundred times into her eyes. And there, through the magnifying glass of her dusky, self-assured gaze, I found myself in a different world, where nothing was sure anymore and everything tottered. Under the gentle force of those eyes, I would deny myself three times before the cock crowed without a second thought. In those eyes, I'd get so drunk without drinking that I'd feel the billowing morass under the crust of civilization that was the gray granite pavement. If I stood up, I'd be weak at the knees. But I didn't stand up—I swam like any person not able or willing to sleep, and finding it ever harder to separate dreams from reality.

Take me to the underground river with the flaming torches in the medieval cellars of that next-door café and torture me, please, torture me, because nothing can cause greater and sweeter pain than your towering legs of sorrow in your prettiest torture skirt as you look at me with an expression that singes me, gives me hope, and spurns me all at once, and which burns all my hopes and dreams down to a single plea for this to go on. As I re-dreamed the evening in my rickety IKEA bed in my apartment on Vico Alabardieri, I had more and more difficulty believing that this evening had really taken place. The only thing that could convince me that it really had was the fact that the fantasy had been more wonderful than anything I could have imagined. I'd been on a date with the most beautiful girl in Genoa. Just those words: a date. I'd written them down before I'd thought about it. I don't think I'd ever written those words down before with all their connotations of a neatly orchestrated evening from an aperitif by a sparkling crystal sea to a kiss on the cheek after midnight. I don't think I've ever been on a date with anyone before. Sure, I've sat in a pub with a woman on occasion. But that wasn't a date. That was just boozing and then tumbling into bed together afterward. Or not. But seeking out a romantic place for a girl, somewhere you'd never go to on your own, and making a particular effort to make it a special evening for her—that wouldn't even occur to me in my home country. But I know how Italian girls think. In my new home, I was changing from a blunt Dutchman into a suave Casanova who could even organize sunsets. One who is attentive enough to even think of doing it. And this transformation was due to her. The most beautiful girl in Genoa had bestowed upon me a full evening—long with her full and uncensored presence. Not bad for an immigrant. And when we'd said goodbye at her scooter, she'd even said we'd see each other again soon. And she'd told me her name.

To cut a long story short, what I wanted to say was that I think your friend is in love. I think I know it for sure. And if earlier I might have jokingly written or suggested that I was in love, I was only joking. Now it's real. Now it's finally real. And that's what was missing. That's what I'd been searching for all that time. Instead of losing myself passionately in my new life, the first contours of a legitimate reason for me to settle here with passion were finally beginning to take shape. Anyone opting for a new life might find the new life not new enough. This is exactly the adventure I needed because it affected me in a new way.

I know, my friend, the way I'm expressing myself is a little muddled. Or maybe "tentative" is a better word. But in any case, this is precisely the main reason I left my fatherland. Not because anything there drove me away, but because to me the story was old and stale. I needed this so that I could invent myself in a new life. Emigrating is like writing a new novel whose plot you don't yet know—not its ending, nor the characters who will prove crucial to how the story continues. That's why everything I write has something tentative about it.

But now that I've gotten to know the decor and feel at home, the curtains can go up on the opera. Everything is just beginning. Everything is just on the brink of beginning.

30.

There are two shops on the ground floor of Palazzo Agostino e Benedetto Viale opposite the Bar of Mirrors on Salita Pollaiuoli. On the right at 74 rosso, Laura Sciunnach's jewelry shop, and on the left, at 72 and 70 rosso, in a property twice the size, a lady's fashion shop called Chris & Paule. Both are specialist shops in the sense that almost no one ever goes in them. Both look nice with well tended window displays and tasteful window boxes on the wall. These are the things that attract the customers who do flutter into them, without the intent to actually purchase anything. Set against this is the fact that the products in both shops are exclusive and that one or two customers a day are sufficient to keep the business going. The staffing costs are low. Both shops can be easily kept open from early morning 'til late at night by a single store manager; to the right, Bibi; to the left, a beautiful and sad lady of a certain age. They are what I wanted to talk about.

There are some rifts in Genoa that can never be bridged. In the labyrinth alone, there's an invisible, electrically charged curtain at the level of Via Luccoli separating the Molo quarter from the Maddalena quarter. Tourists aren't aware of it and I wasn't, either, at first, but the force field gains intensity the longer I'm here. It exists in that special gaze of the signora as I tell her that I had coffee on the other side, in Via del Campo or on Piazza Lavagna. I know every rose seller and every busker in Molo—they don't venture into Maddalena, just as its beggars don't dare venture into Molo. The girls there are different, the dogs bigger. Thugs and whores and the old, flaking transvestites from the Vico della Croce Binaci, the middle-aged men with beer bellies and fishnets with two packets of cotton wool in their bras—they all live in Maddalena.

In the same way, there are two football clubs: Genoa and Sampdoria. One is the best club, the other always wins. As the oldest football club in Italy, one of them fosters tradition, the other has the money. They share a stadium in Marassi and when one is playing home, the other plays away. Their supporters never meet, except at the derby. And everyone in Genoa supports one of the two teams, including the women and children. They don't have to wear the club's colors. You can tell from a person's nose whether they are familiar with the depths of suffering or whether they've plumped for success.

Nor will you ever be able to close the gap between the inhabitants of the labyrinth and the hundreds of thousands of others happy enough to call themselves Genoese—those who occasionally travel in cars or on Vespas to the historic center from their luxurious lives in outlying apartments with sea views ten or twelve kilometers away in Quinto or Nervi so they can poke around in cute little shops like Laura Sciunnach's or Chris & Paule and carry on like it's their city—while just twenty meters beyond their shops they'd be hopelessly lost. The store managers come from outside, too. They arrive every morning with a scooter helmet dangling from their wrists and every night, carrying the same helmet, they go back to their sad, ordered lives in the flats of San Fruttuoso, Marassi, or Castelletto without knowing about the rats, the whores, the old transvestites with their beer bellies, and the foul-mouthed fishmongers around the corner.

Bibi and the beautiful, sad lady traveled in like this in the morning, arriving around nine thirty. Bibi was usually the first. He'd raise the security shutters. He'd put two of the three flowerpots on the pavement outside and then rummage around in his shop. The third flowerpot is kept inside the clothes shop at night and is put out by the beautiful, sad lady. She waters all three of the plants, cuts off the dead leaves, and carefully puts the three pots in the window box. Then she goes back inside.

At that moment, Bibi comes outside to hang up the tin bucket on the nail in the wall between the two door openings. The bucket functions as a communal ashtray. He inaugurates it by leaning indifferently, not to say expressionlessly, against the doorpost smoking a cigarette. When he's done, the beautiful, sad lady smokes a cigarette in her door opening. Usually she wears boots, although I don't know why it's of interest to tell you that. She throws her stub in the bucket.

As I said, there aren't many customers. The entire day—until long after the candles have been put out on the tables in the Bar of Mirrors and the Prosecco twinkles between conversations in the trapeze of art, poetry, and politics—they will smoke lots and lots of cigarettes in their respective door openings—Bibi on the right at 74 rosso, her on the left at 72 and 70 rosso. They'll carefully aim all of their stubs into the bucket. The yellow flowers in the three flowerpots will look lovely. They won't talk to each other, not because they don't like each other, on the contrary, but because there isn't much to say without candlelit Prosecco. Various girls will call on Bibi; they won't want to buy bracelets or rings, but each of them believes she is special to him. He will look down on them with scorn. He will hardly speak to them, either. They'll slink off and you can count on them returning in boots with even higher heels.

Very rarely, they'll almost touch, but they don't realize it—I'm the only person who can see it. From the terrace. Sometimes Bibi will reach for a catalogue on the right of his counter at precisely the same moment she is rearranging the skirt suits on the racks to the left of the register. There's nothing more than an old medieval wall, twenty centimeters thick, between their two hands.

They close at seven thirty. The yellow flowers go back inside, two pots in his shop, one in hers. The last thing Bibi does is to get down the tin bucket from the hook. She rolls down the shutters and padlocks them to the marble shop front. She closes the cast iron fence and secures it with a chain lock. Then they exchange a few words. He says "Ciao." She asks whether he might like to drink a Prosecco on the terrace. He says he's tired. Then they both return to their own flats with a scooter helmet dangling from their wrists—his with a Sampdoria sticker, hers sprayed in the tragic red and blue of Genoa.

31.

I could barely repress the urge to tell all my new Genoese friends about my fairy-tale evening. But it turned out to be entirely unnecessary. Everyone knew about it already. I flattered myself with the thought that she'd gone around telling everyone but realized at the same time I shouldn't entertain any illusions, because everyone always knows everything already in Centro Storico. "Entertain no illusions," she said. "You know I had my bathroom redone recently? The work was done by two *carabinieri* wanting to earn a bit of cash on the side. The day before yesterday I met them in a bar around the corner from my house to pay them. 'You've been hanging out with that foreign poet a lot recently,' one of them said. And I don't even live anywhere around here."

"Why are you looking at me like that?"

"Like what?"

"Like that."

She was silent.

"Aren't you happy I completed your quest and found the Mandragola?"

She still didn't say anything and didn't look very happy, either.

"Are you jealous?"

I shouldn't have said that.

"Who do you think you are?" she said. "Who do you think

you are? You parachute yourself and your colossal body into our streets and then you think you understand everything. You're still messing up the subjunctive and you don't understand anything, Ilja. Ilja Leonard. Leonardo. You don't even deserve that honorable title you invented for yourself. You still have to earn it. Go and write it all down in your little notebook. All those things you think you've understood. Have you already explained why the English flag is identical to the Genoese flag? That because for a long time our fleet was the mightiest and that we rented out our flag to the English for a lot of money so that no one would dare attack their ships anymore? It's a famous story, you know. Your readers in the Far North are really fascinated by that kind of thing, I'm sure of it. And no, I'm not going to dictate it to you. Go and google it yourself, Leonardo. You're the writer. And have you already written down that the city's old nickname is La Superba? I guess so. And I'm sure you've given it a literary twist? Since you understand everything, don't you, Leonardo? Let me guess. It means superb and reckless, beautiful and proud, alluring and unapproachable; you must have learned Latin and I don't doubt you've given it a deep, etymologically justified slant. And what have you called me in your notebook? Cinzia? My real name? If that so-called novel of yours is ever published, I'll set my family's lawyers on you. They'll tear you to shreds. You won't stand a chance. You don't understand anything, Ilja. And what have you called her? Or don't you dare? Do you know where she comes from? Do you know her family? Do you know which of her brothers, lovers, or lawyers will come banging on your door tonight, if they haven't already soldiered their way into your miserable apartment? Everyone knows you. Everyone knows where you live, Ilja. I'm trying to make that clear to you. You think this is Europe because you can get here on EasyJet within an hour and a half from your efficient fatherland. You're mistaken. You're in Genoa. This is Africa. This world is totally foreign to you.

"And another thing. Imagine it all goes well. Imagine it all goes as you've gotten it into your head that it should go. Imagine she does become your girlfriend. Imagine. How on earth can you imagine that? How on earth are you going to keep a girl like that happy? You can't afford an Italian girlfriend, Ilja. You've no idea how demanding she is. And not just in a material sense. You think she'll find you interesting because somewhere far off in a foreign country you're a famous writer who writes books in a language we can't even read, but don't fool yourself that will be enough. You'll have to be constantly on your toes, like you're in a porcelain grotto, and think up more and more new romantic places where you can spend a fortune on her aperitifs. And I also hope for you that you have an indestructible prick. And you'll have to change your life, be home at half past twelve for *pranzo* and eight o'clock for *cena*. After that, you'll have to watch television because she wants to, then she'll complain you never do anything fun together and only watch television, or, you'll take her out somewhere and she'll complain that she's tired and would have preferred to stay home and watch television. You won't be able to drink anymore, even if it's just for the simple fact you no longer have time to. And yet she'll keep on complaining that you drink too much. And if you do everything right and manage to pull off the improbable and keep her more or less happy, your reward will be that she'll want to marry you and have children. Then you'll get a whole Italian family on top. With Christmas dinners and seaside holidays in August. Just think about it, Ilja."

So she was jealous. I had to think of a way of staying friends with her.

"Give me a new quest, please."

She said nothing. She stared into the distance. I had plenty of time to tug at her top in my thoughts, if I'd wanted to, but I didn't want to because I was officially in love, everyone knew that. The sanitation department's van came to empty the containers. Somewhere in the distance a dog started up. And then she said, "Ask her about her wounds."

The fat lesbian grinned at me from behind her sunglasses.

32.

Like an old hand, I waited a few days. I avoided the Bar of Mirrors, even though it physically hurt to have to do without the intoxicating sight of her. It almost felt like cold turkey. I'd become addicted to my daily dose of staring at her. But now I'd been promoted to the next level. The time of just gawking was over. I had penetrated into her life. I knew her name. She had kissed my cheek. She'd said we'd see each other again soon. So I couldn't just go and sit at my table and let her serve me as though nothing had happened. That would be tantamount to a denial of the most beautiful evening in Genoa, the evening that we found the Mandragola together and gazed into each other's eyes. From now on, I'd have to play the game according to different rules.

For a few days in a row, I had my aperitif on Piazza delle Erbe.

Three days was what I'd thought of. Just long enough not to come across as too eager and pushy, and not too long to seem indifferent. In the best-case scenario, she'd miss me. She'd certainly miss me—at least as a customer. Missing is good. But it shouldn't last too long. So on the fourth day, just before nine, just before closing time, I went to the Bar of Mirrors. I didn't sit down but waited at the door until she came out. I asked her whether she might be thirsty the next evening.

She smiled. "Sure."

I took her to a chic bar I'd discovered on the square on Via di San Sebastiano opposite the Best Western City Hotel, between Via Roma and Via XXV Aprile. It was an un-Italian hip designer bar with expensive cocktails in designer glasses with a buffet of seafood and oysters. The venue didn't fail to have an effect. I could see that she felt celebrated. She imagined she was in London or New York, or in another city far from Italy where real, fast, frantic life was lived. At least, that's what she said.

After that I took her to dinner at Pintori. On Via San Bernardo. My favorite restaurant run by a Sardinian family, with mamma in the kitchen. Normally I only go there when someone else is taking me out. It's one of the most expensive restaurants in Genoa. I said she should order the *spaghetti neri alla bottarga* and then lamb shank. She did what I said and was impressed afterward that I'd given her such good advice.

And when, after a full, sparkling evening, I'd walked her back to her scooter and was saying goodbye, she asked me, "Why did you come to Genoa, Leonardo?"

"For you," I said.

She slapped my face as punishment. I went to kiss her cheek but she'd already put on her helmet, though I only realized that once my face was right by hers, so I clumsily jerked my head back. She smiled. She took my face between both hands and kissed me on the lips. Then she drove off, without saying a thing.

33.

"I have to tell you something, Leonardo."

"If I could invite you to my table, signora, that would make my day."

"You're still making mistakes in the conditional tense."

"What are you drinking, Signora Mancinelli?"

"Stop trying so hard. I'll order myself."

"What was it you wanted to say?"

Her drink was served. It was a kind of indefinable alcohol-free cocktail with pear juice, coconut, and strawberry. She drained the glass in one slug, got a bottle of rum out of her handbag, filled her glass to the rim, and held it up for a toast.

"I've heard that you talk to that Moroccan regularly," she said.

"You mean Rashid?"

She laid her finger to her lips to show me I was to keep my mouth shut. She looked around to check no one had heard.

"But he's a good, intelligent young man," I said.

She shook her head.

"Do you have something against Moroccans, signora?"

She gave me an angry look. "I've been going to India for years, Leonardo. I used my alimony payments to set up a school there."

"What's India got to do with Morocco?"

"The basic principle. That's the difference."

"What do you mean?"

"I go to India to help. But the Moroccans come to us."

"So?"

"It's the same difference as inviting someone to join you at your table for a drink and someone who sits down uninvited."

"Like you."

"Don't try to be clever, Leonardo. And whatever you do, don't try those politically correct arguments on me. I'm wise to that kind of talk. You just cannot trust those Moroccans for the simple reason that it is impossible for them to survive on selling roses and even more impossible for them to find a decent job. Because no one trusts them. And so sooner or later they'll start stealing or selling drugs. Because it's the only option. In no time, your so-called intelligent friend will be in Marassi prison, mark my words!

"What's more, we're in Genoa and it's a porcelain grotto. You have to associate with the old aristocracy here, or at least pretend to. Investing family money in a school in India is noble. Drinking beer with the first Moroccan rose seller you run into isn't. What do you think my friends will think of me if I'm friends with a foreigner who associates with foreigners? You need to take my status in my network into account. You owe that to me as a friend. Can I make it any clearer? You want to be part of this world, don't you? Then make sure for starters that you don't have the wrong kinds of friends. Otherwise I won't be able to invite you to my wedding."

"Are you getting married, signora? At your age?"

"Viola needs a grandfather, let's put it like that. And I've found a suitable party. He's a widower and quite a bit older than me. Bernardo Massi. You know him. I've discovered that he's even richer than I thought. Now all he has to do is ask me. But I'll take care of that."

"I'm getting married, too."

She looked at me in astonishment. Then she began to laugh. "With that girl from the Bar of Mirrors you've been out with twice?" She roared with laughter. "You only see the exterior. I've already told you that, haven't I? You live in your dreams."

34.

A few days later she took the initiative. Just before closing time, she brought me my last Negroni, and with a conspicuous gesture laid a folded-up napkin under it as a coaster, and winked. I unfolded the napkin. "Tomorrow evening, 9.30pm at Gloglo on Piazza Lavagna. X." She looked at me via the mirrors. I blew her a kiss to show that I was confirming the date.

We dined on the terrace and talked. She wanted to know everything about my country. I didn't feel like talking about it but enjoyed the fact that she was hanging on my every word. And before we knew it, it was half past one. The waiter brought the bill. They were closing.

"Should we maybe go somewhere else?" I asked.

"It's late," she said.

"You can sleep at mine, if you like. I live just near here."

I almost jumped out of my skin. Had I really said that? Yes, I'd really said that. The echo of my words hung like an accusation in her painful silence. Or something like that. Even my style gave away my despair. In a panic, I tried to come up with something that would undo my words, but my thoughts raced too fast for me to be able to think.

"Alright," she said. "But let's go now, then."

I felt like I'd landed in my own fantasies. I was walking with the most beautiful girl in Genoa on my arm through the deserted night-time streets to my apartment on Vico Alabardieri. This was Italy, my new country. I was wearing an Italian suit and Italian shoes and I was walking with an Italian girl through Italian streets to my Italian house. We'd spoken Italian all evening. I had seduced her in Italian. I regretted the fact that it was so late there was no one around to see us together. I would have preferred jubilant masses. On either side of the red carpet. Applauding us and clapping loudly. She smiles haughtily in her white dress as rose petals rain down on us.

I lit a candle and opened a bottle of wine. "So you live here," she said. "Nice." She almost seemed shy in what were for her unfamiliar surroundings. She was more beautiful than ever by candlelight. We drank a single glass and then she blew out the candle. "Come. Let's go to bed."

She undressed. It was a sacred moment that I can hardly describe. In the silvery-white moonlight that fell through the windows, I saw the breathtaking curves that I had so often imagined. She was like a nymph, like the goddess Diana herself, bathing in her own silvery light. I couldn't believe that the most beautiful girl in Genoa was standing naked before me in my own home. Every thought of sex evaporated. She was too sacrosanct for that. My only desire was to worship her. She lay down next to me and I worshipped her with my hands. I stroked her even more gently than the moonlight. And then I felt her wounds. They were on her elbow, her wrist and her ankle. They had almost healed and were virtually invisible. But I could feel them. I remembered the quest Cinzia had given me. Her first commission had brought me luck. The reason I was lying there was thanks to having found the Mandragola. I asked her what had happened.

"What do you mean?"

"Your injuries. I still remember you waiting on me with a bandage and red antiseptic streaks. You can't see anything anymore, but I can feel them. What happened?"

She went rigid.

"Did I say something wrong? I'm sorry. It was only a question. I was curious. But it's not important. Leave it."

"I was bitten by rats," she said

I laughed. "I don't believe you."

She stood up. I tried to stop her.

"What are you doing?"

"Let go of me."

She began to get dressed again.

"I changed my mind, I'm going home."

She slammed the door behind her with a loud crash.

35.

But she cannot escape me. She's a waitress, after all. She works in a public place. The next day I went to the Bar of Mirrors for my aperitif. Even before I could sit down, she came over to me. She gestured for me to follow her. We went into the porcelain grotto, the small space where she prepared the *stuzzichini*. She closed the curtain behind us.

"Listen, Leonardo," she whispered. "Promise you'll listen to me properly and won't interrupt. I'd rather you didn't come here for a while. Don't worry. It's not your fault. But I need some privacy. You have to give me some space. I need to think. So let's agree not to see each other for a while. Two or three weeks or so. There are enough other bars. Go to the Piazza delle Erbe. OK?"

I nodded.

"And you were right. Naturally you were right. Of course I wasn't bitten by rats. I will tell you the truth. I fell. Down the stairs. And it wasn't really an accident. He pushed me. Francesco. My boyfriend. I'm sure you've seen him around. I told him about you, about the interesting new customer I'd met who was always so well-mannered and polite and who always sat writing in his notebook. I told him I thought you were a poet. And then he got so jealous he pushed me down the stairs. It was a bit unfortunate that you reminded me of that last night. But you couldn't know. So I'm not blaming you at all."

"And that's why you broke up with Francesco?"

She gave me a confused look. "What do you mean?" she said. "No, I didn't break up with him. He's still my boyfriend. It actually means that he really, really loves me. Getting so angry when I'm talking about another man that he can no longer control himself. He's a passionate man. Really different from you."

"So why did you come home with me last night?"

"That's exactly what I want to think about. Go now."

I understood. Oh my God, how I'd understood. How could

I have been so stupid? Of course she had a boyfriend. And now that boyfriend had a name, too. Francesco, the bastard. Of course she'd never leave him. If she managed to interpret domestic violence as proof of his love, what would it take to get her to leave him? I'd been living in my dreams. The dream that she could be mine. But Cinzia and the signora had been right. She was an Italian girl with a passionate Italian boyfriend, and she'd never be capable of taking the step toward a new life. She would always take the certainty of his heavy-handedness over the uncertain adventure of my hands that had stroked her more gently than the moonlight. Fine. This was it, then. I decided to cherish the night before as a precious memory and for the rest, forget about her.

36.

I'm sorry, my friend, that you haven't heard from me for a while. I'd taken a break from my pleasurable obligation of keeping you up to date, via these notes, on the vicissitudes of my life in the labyrinth of my new city in my new homeland, and my striving to force myself—by fulfilling this pleasurable obligation—to mine the crude ore from which I'd win the liquid, red-hot, precious metal that would stream, shine, and scorch as my next novel, in order to dedicate myself to an even more enjoyable task if possible, which for obvious reasons will have no impact on my book, if only because real people are involved, with real feelings, and a family with three small children and a jealous husband whom readers in my home country might know. Thematically, too, this short, piquant episode has no relevance to my novel, which, as you will have understood, will have to focus on the big topical issue of immigration, whereby I will contrast my own successful expat lifestyle with the deplorable fate of all those poor fellows from Morocco and Senegal who got lost in these very same streets in their dreams of a better life and guaranteed wealth in Europe, and whom the authorities, who have declared a state of emergency, are exterminating like rats. The novel will also have to be about my own fantasy of making my long-cherished dream of a jealousy-inducing rich and carefree Mediterranean existence among true, authentic people who haven't yet unlearned the art of attributing importance only to the things that really matter: perfume, taste, elegance, and a natural, noble way of life. Italy, oh Italy. The balmy, humming summer's evening skies, pregnant with scooter girls, and the light-footed *opera buffa* of daily existence are perfectly isotonic with my soul. Being in this country has always felt like a process of osmosis, of my fusion with my natural habitat. The labyrinth of Centro Storico is just as much a metaphor for my dreams as it is the desperate fairy tale in which Rashid, Djiby, and others have lost themselves.

Genoa's old nickname is La Superba. You can interpret the name in two different ways and you understand this best when you approach the city from the south, across the sea. All of a sudden there she is: a beautiful piece of scenery with towering palazzi in a mountain basin. But while you are enjoying it, you realize that the pomp and glory form an impenetrable wall. She is beautiful and heartless. She's a whore who beckons but whom you can never make your own. She is alluring and reckless. She seduces and destroys. Like the rats lured into traps with poison

that tastes like honey. In that sense, Genoa, La Superba symbol-
izes Europe as a whole. Behind her impenetrable walls of border
checks, asylum procedures, investigators, and forced expulsions, she
lies there showing off her promise of new Mercedes and BMWs.
Anyone managing to force their way in takes this as reason enough
to believe they've achieved their dream. They're in paradise. The
rest will follow as a matter of course. And then they'll wither away
in a leaky two-room apartment with eleven of their countrymen
and be exterminated like a rat.

That's what it should be about. And about the past. Seven score
and ten years ago, millions of destitute, desperate Italians boarded
ships in the ports of this very city, dreaming of a better life and
guaranteed wealth in La Merica, as they called their wonder-
land on the other side of the Atlantic Ocean. In the place from
which millions once set sail, now millions are chased away like
rats because they are doing exactly what their hosts did fifty and
one hundred years previously: hope. That's what it should be
about, for fuck's sake, and not about the trivialities I contemplated
telling you.

Alright. Of course it also has to be about her, too. You're much
too good a reader not to have picked that up from the first line
I wrote to you. Of course it has to be about the most beautiful girl
in Genoa, who, as befitting the most beautiful girl, works among
mirrors. She is a fairy tale. I'm not sure which role I'm going to
invent for her in my final work of art. It depends of course on
future developments. If there are any future developments, which,
to be honest, I seriously doubt. She was La Superba. And she was
the fantasy in which I have gotten more and more lost. This was

another good reason for taking a break for a few days and devoting myself to a juicy reality. I'll tell you about it, my friend. But I'm presuming that you understand that I'm trusting you to keep to yourself what I'm about to tell you.

37.

The story actually began a few years ago. I was at one of those many compulsory literary parties in my homeland, which I always frequented with great displays of bravado and bluster and which I miss like a hole in the head. As I was standing there holding forth on an interesting topic among a group of jealous admirers and jealous rivals, a woman came up to me and introduced herself as my German translator. She was blonde and statuesque, slightly plump, but all in all pretty impressive. She'd just been asked to translate a selection of my poetry. I'd heard about it. Her name was Inge. Maybe I've mentioned her to you before.

After that first meeting we saw each other with some regularity to discuss her progress. Generally, I like to have as little contact with my translators as possible, but in her case it was a pleasure. I noticed—or perhaps just fantasized it—that she got dressed up especially for our meetings. Or in any case, she could have chosen to show off a less deeply-cut top at a work meeting with one of her authors. You could put it another way. In complete concordance with my poetics, she accentuated her excesses. On my part, I didn't have to make any effort at all. I'd already written all my poems. I didn't even have to spray my armpits to give her the idea that she had the right to flirt with me.

Last week she sent me an e-mail saying she'd like to talk to me because her translation was as good as finished. I replied by e-mail that it would be a great pleasure and that I was keen to see it, but that I was living in Genoa at present. She wrote back saying that, in that case, she'd come to Genoa. I said: OK. And then she came. She'd booked a flight to Milan–Malpensa and reserved a place on an intercity. She texted me a specific time of arrival.

She was married…is still married to an American agent who has been frequenting parties in my homeland with great displays of bravado and bluster since time immemorial and still hasn't been able to muster the decency to lose his all-American barbecue accent. He's a bastard. They have three small children. For form's sake, I'd taken an option in her name on a grimy hotel room in the Doria on Vico dei Garibaldi, the worst hotel in the neighborhood, which she'd certainly want to swap for another after the first night and then it would be a Saturday and all the hotels in the city would be fully booked. But the ruse was completely unnecessary. I waited for her at Palazzo Principe station at her specific time of arrival and she came running up to me in all her flamboyant, un-Italian blondeness. She embraced me like she never would have done in the fatherland, kissed me on the lips, and asked, "Is it a long way to your place?"

And I didn't have to make up the guest bed that night. She joined me in bed like a sumptuously shaped cloud. She smelled of the north, not of Genoa. I wanted her to undress, but she said I had to dance for her. She watched me as I stroked my own body tauntingly slowly. I looked in the mirror to see the way she was watching me as I watched myself like a pole dancer.

Then she said she wanted to see the most beautiful girl in Genoa. Then she said we should undress her together. She began to kiss her. I kissed her while she enjoyed my fantasy. We played with the girl in the mirrors for hours on end, the two of us, and we were given ourselves in return, as shining and clear as our own reflections.

It's just struck me that it sounds a bit odd when I tell it to you like that. And yet it was exactly as I said. I had soft, sweet lesbian sex with Inge, about whom I'd long fantasized, and with my own fantasy. And then it got even crazier.

38.

The next day it was raining. We went to have coffee in the Bar of Mirrors. The girl was there, but she didn't seem to want to have anything to do with us. She didn't greet us, let the other waitresses serve us, and didn't look at us. When the rain had stopped, I paid her, leaving a big tip. She didn't even thank me. When we walked out, I saw her watching us in the mirrors. She quickly turned her face away when she saw in the mirrors that I was watching her in the mirrors. But I'd seen it in the mirrors. She was crying.

I took Inge on a long walk through the labyrinth. We walked to Porto Antico and back up via the dirty streets near San Cosimo and Santa Maria in Castello, over the cobblestones I love so much, through the gates and arches so fond to me, past the names which sing so in my ears, downwards along Vico Amandorla to Campo Pisano. The sun broke through. But I had a strange, dark feeling in my stomach. She was crying. I was sure of it. I'd seen it.

Every time I thought about it, I felt a nest of baby rats gnawing at my innards, at my masculinity, and my convictions. But Inge was walking along very obviously enjoying herself. Her blonde hair shone like Saint Elmo's fire in the night. It was all strolling hand in hand for her. It was all getting lost in a fairy tale to her. It was, for her, like it was for me the first time I got lost. And when we passed the high bridge under Ravasco, which is the bridge to Carignano, and caught sight of the colossal spaceships stranded in the no-man's-land of the Giardini di Plastica, she said, "It looks like some kind of virtual world, like Second Life. It's amazing." She took a picture of me with her mobile phone.

Later in the afternoon, we walked the long route parallel to the sea, from Via Canneto Il Curto, Via San Luca, Piazza Fossatello, and Via del Campo toward the Pré. I wanted to show her Africa. I wanted to see how exotically she, in all her colossal blondeness, would stand out against the dark background of alleyways filled with danger and grinning white teeth. She was surprised by how many wig shops there were. "Which would you choose?" she asked. "For you?" "No, I'm already a dumb blonde. For yourself." I pointed out a blonde wig that looked a bit like her own hair-style. "No, no need to be sweet. I know you want that one." She pointed out a wig of beautiful, long, dark Italian hair you'd be able to wear up, just like the girl in the mirrors. "Then you'd be the most beautiful girl in Genoa," she said. She kissed me on the lips. Then she burst into a fit of giggles.

After that I had to show her the transvestites in the Ghetto around Vico della Croce Bianca, you'll understand that. She was frightened in the dark streets filled with the shadows of scummy men searching for hairy-assed fifty-year-olds in fishnets.

I had to hold her. She pressed herself to me as though I were a local guide who could protect her from the savages. But she found the transvestites themselves endlessly fascinating. Although she was frightened, we had to take the same route three times. "That was the most impressive bit of Genoa," she'd say the next day when we said goodbye at the station. "After you, of course." And again she'd burst into a fit of giggles.

39.

In the evening, I wanted us to go to Capitan Baliano to watch the match. She had no interest in football, but it was the derby that evening and I told her the experience would crucial to her understanding of the city. I had to see the match, I'd been looking forward to it for weeks. For days, I'd read about nothing else on the pink pages of the *Gazzetta dello Sport*. The bar was packed. She was one of the few women there and was therefore offered a seat. She sat there sending text messages to her American husband or her three children. I stood behind her chair and laid my hand on her shoulder.

All of a sudden, I saw her in the big mirror behind the bar. She was looking at us, still crying. I searched for her in the crowd but couldn't find her. Is she a girl I can only observe through mirrors? When I looked in the mirror again she had disappeared.

I couldn't concentrate on the match. In the second half, Milito, the Prince, scored the only goal. An inferno of joy burst out. People jumped in the air, their fists clenched. Beer and coffee poured over the tables. Fabio the barman danced for joy in front of his flat screen. I hugged Inge so I could celebrate on a busty note and then I saw her again. She was standing motionlessly in a corner, crying. I went over to her but she wasn't there.

Genoa won the derby against Sampdoria 1-0. The city's statues were covered in red and blue flags. Cars drove along the Sopraelevata tooting their horns. The fountain on Piazza de Ferrari was danced empty. Fireworks were set off on Piazza delle Erbe. We watched it through the windows of Caffè Letterario, where we had good, long conversations about beautiful things. We kissed. "Isn't that that girl?" Inge asked. I couldn't see properly through the smoke from the firecrackers and rockets. I went outside and saw her running away along Vico delle Erbe toward Piazza Matteotti and Palazzo Ducale. I tried to catch up with her but she was too far away and the square was too full of frenzied joy. I tried to find her in the alleys behind Palazzo Ducale and even ran all the way to Piazza Campetto, but she had disappeared in the labyrinth that was pretty much impenetrable thanks to the hordes of boisterous football fans.

When, deep in the night, we walked back to my apartment along Via San Bernardo and Vico Vegetti past the smoldering embers of a memorable day, I was certain she was following us and thought we'd be too intent on each other to look back. I didn't look back because I knew she'd have run screaming back into the underworld of the labyrinth.

That night, Inge played gently with me like we had played with her together the night before. She squeezed my tits and kissed my nipples. She slowly stroked my fat belly full of gnawing rats. She burst out laughing. "What is it?" "I just remembered that you're a very famous poet." She moved her hand downwards and began to work my cock a little. "You're a very strange girl," she said.

"You're a pregnant transvestite." She kissed me and fell asleep.

40.

I dreamed that I woke up next to the most beautiful girl in Genoa. She wasn't in the Bar of Mirrors where she belonged, but on a double IKEA mattress on the flagstones of the sitting room in my apartment on Vico Alabardieri. She was lying there asleep with a lot of cuddly toys. I was lying on a rickety one-man IKEA sofa bed with my head facing the other way. I started, because instead of her shining, chestnut Italian hair she had short white hair with various bald spots. I stroked her head and she smiled. She stirred slightly, slipped into my bed, squeezed my nipple, and began to carefully and gently fuck me. No, that wasn't how it went, because I climbed out of my creaky bed to go feel her pink hair. I lay down next to her on the big mattress. She was small, almost as small as a cuddly toy. She stirred slightly and said, "Don't I have any goddamn right to privacy?" I said she shouldn't worry. I actually wanted to say that the crux of what they call love is trying to get closer to someone during difficult periods, not shutting the other out. Or something like that. I couldn't quite articulate it. She had already gotten up and dressed in a lot of very thick, gray clothes. "Where are you going?" But she'd already closed the door behind her. She'd already turned the big long key twice in the lock.

Then I dreamed I'd fallen asleep again and that I was dreaming I was in an English pub in the middle of Genoa. I was allowed to smoke there and everyone spoke Italian. It was dark and there were nice seats to sit on, like in a bus. There were names and hearts scratched into the tables. On the seat I was sitting on, someone had written in Italian in felt pen, "I have no money or things I can give to you, only all of myself and the nights we spend together." From the grammatical form of "all of myself" I could tell that this outpouring had been written by a woman. Swedish music by ABBA was playing; they were singing in English that breaking up was never easy, but knowing each other the way they did, it was the best thing to do.

I woke up and thought it might be better to go and lie back down on my sofa bed, because if she returned, she'd certainly think she had a right to her privacy on her enormous mattress covered in cuddly toys. She was certain to come back. Though it wasn't certain that everything would be fine and I would be happy.

I dreamed that she came back. She opened the heavy lock and closed it behind her with the long key. She said nothing. In my dream, I secretly opened one eye to look at her. She wasn't wearing thick, gray clothes any more. She was naked like a sick rat. I saw her wounds. On her feet, her leg, her lower arm, all over. She'd turned them pink with iodine, perhaps hoping they might stand out less that way. She was bald, small, wounded, and helpless. I was the only one who could save her. If she allowed me to. If she wanted me to. She didn't look at me. She was too proud to even cry.

I dreamed that the next day she'd be beautiful again and that she'd bring me *stuzzichini* as though nothing had happened. As though everything that had happened was of no importance. As though we all had a different life than the one we had. As though we'd never meet because of this.

41.

Someone who looks like a banker walks into the BNL bank on Piazza Matteoti. Someone who looks like a crook—with a broken nose, low forehead, and big, protruding ears—comes out of the police station next door, while eight *carabinieri* stand smoking on the pavement and laughing and acting out on a friend how they'd arrest him. Someone who looks like an elderly Italian gentleman saunters past as an elderly Italian gentleman would saunter on his afternoon stroll along the Via San Lorenzo to Porto Antico where he'll sit on a bench to look at the ships.

Everyone is the embodiment of their own fantasy. Everyone looks the way they imagine and lives the life that goes with that. The butcher on Via Canetto Il Lungo looks like a butcher— a colossal hunk of meat with a bloody apron and magisterial claws made to plow through carcasses. He looks like that because he immerses himself so well in his fantasy of being a butcher. And the elderly Italian gentleman sits on a bench on Piazza Caricamento near Porto Antico, looks at the ships and fantasizes about far-off destinations: Barcelona, Tunis, Panama, La Merica. And when he returns home obediently in time for dinner, he feels satisfied, enriched, and somewhat tired, like a man returning home after a long, adventurous sea voyage. His grandchildren wanted to offer him a cruise to Barcelona but he refused the gift because he'd been going there every afternoon all those years and every afternoon it was beautiful weather and the most beautiful people strolled along the unnaturally beautiful boulevards toward the seafront to sit on a bench every afternoon and fantasize about Genoa,

La Superba, that robbers' den on the Mediterranean, where the whores are as black as the endless night in the alleys, where the only light flashed off flicked-open knives, and where you might be kidnapped on every street corner and sold as a white slave in the slums of Tangier or Casablanca. Every afternoon, the elderly gentleman had to smile about their fantasies of his city. But he's grateful for them because the myth they invent makes Genoa deeper, richer, and more beautiful. And there are days when he's in the mood to believe their myth. Those are the days he returns home a little later than usual, almost too late for dinner. And like every evening, he says nothing about his adventures.

Everyone's had the nightmare that the world around him has been created by an invisible director—that he's living in a stage set populated by extras and that everyone knows about it apart from him. Like in that film. What's it called again? I've written about it before, in another book. Look that up for me, my friend, would you? Entire religions have been built on that nightmare. Almost every religion. At least, every monotheistic denomination. The world we think we see is in fact the perverse fantasy of an omnipotent director who wants to test us in a complicated game. It's up to us to guess the rules of the game. A fantastic game show of life and death. If you guess right, you get seventy times seven vestal virgins under streams of ambrosia and harp music in the blinding artificial light of the Almighty One. If you guess wrong, you burn in Hell for all eternity. A golden formula that scores high viewer ratings among the ever-critical, ever-bored audience of immortals.

Everyone is familiar with the opposite fantasy too. Everyone has played God at some point in their thoughts. The world around us exists only because we observe it, give it meaning, and invent it. Without our eyes and thoughts, the world wouldn't exist or would just hang around pointlessly on its own somewhere like a far-off galaxy still waiting for us to discover it, see it, and give it a name. Everything that exists exists only in our minds, otherwise it doesn't exist. And who says that there are many of us? Who says I'm not the only one? Who says that you exist, my friend? It's much more likely that I've made you up. In the same way, I've made up the street names, the pavement, and the people strolling by. And not just because I'm a writer. I only see what I want to see, as all people only see what they think they know or expect. If I invented a butcher, I would invent him exactly like that: a colossal man with a bloody apron. Maybe he's a banker and the redheaded girl on a scooter is the butcher. But it isn't like that because it's not like that in my mind. And as soon as I see an elderly Italian gentleman sitting on a bench watching ships, I'll imagine what he's thinking. It's my job. But that's not the point. We're all like that. You too, my friend. We all live in each other's invented worlds without any real contact. We are extras in each other's fictional autobiographies. We are the decor of each other's illusions.

Of course I invented Genoa. In some ways, the city also exists without me, at least I'd be happy to assume that. You can go there yourself. It has an airport named after Columbus, who supposedly came from Genoa. He's the man who invented America. His dream was to reach India by going west and get rich. He reached Haiti and saw people in funny clothes. "Oh, you must be Columbus," they cried elatedly. "Hooray! We've been discovered!" His fantasy was that he'd reached India and that's why he called them Indians. And that's where the fairy tale that cowboys have to shoot Indians comes from. In the meantime, Genoa had become rich off the silver from the wilderness now called Argentina. But when the cowboys had well and truly won and built skyscrapers, tens of thousands of destitute Italians left from the Port of Genoa, following in Columbus's footsteps, chasing the dreams of wealth and a new life. But flights to Christopher Columbus Genoa International Airport are rather expensive at the moment. I'd advise you to fly to Pisa or to Milan–Malpensa. Then you'd arrive late at night to Brignole station or Palazzo Principe. From that second station, you can easily walk along Via Balbi past the budget hotels to Largo di Zecca, Via Garibaldi, and Piazza de Ferrari. But you can also go straight from the station to Africa, to sailors, whores, and danger. The best way to arrive is by boat from the south. Then the city looms up like an impenetrable wall of overconfidence. Genoa, La Superba. Of course you can come here. But of course I invented it. You'll never see it the way I see it, until I tell you how to.

I've also made up the fact that this is my city, the natural home of my true soul, where I will be truly happy for the first time, as I'd previously made it up that Leiden was that place and, before that, Rijswijk in Zuid Holland, and as Casablanca, Tunis, Zanzibar, or Gotham City could very well be in the future. Not that I'll ever leave this place, but it's about the principle. I watch the ships every day. And if, on a windy morning, a large ferry from foreign climes docks in the distance behind Darsena, and the labyrinth fills with fresh strays, then, on a morning like that, in my city, at walking distance from Capitan Baliano, Piazza delle Erbe, and the Bar of Mirrors, as the fishermen curse and the whores want to love me, as dark clouds gather about the fortresses on the hills, then I feel…strange to say it…then I feel…strange to believe in your own fantasies…but then I feel truly happy at the same time.

As I write this, a tramp who looks like a tramp shuffles by. He is wearing a kind of alien costume made of *objets trouvés* and junk. Bedraggled teddy bears dangle from his suit of armor. He has a magic mask made of compact discs. He uses a found stick to rhythmically beat an empty Coca-Cola can as he walks by. He is a shaman. He is God in the depths of thoughts. He sees nothing and nobody. He makes us up when he needs us. He lives entirely in his own fantasy. He looks completely happy. I feel very much akin to him.

42.

"What do you think my biggest problem is?"

She didn't answer. She didn't look at me, either. She took a sip of her cappuccino, slowly lit a cigarette, and stared across the square. Her gaze was cold. She didn't look like a person pondering a difficult question but like someone demonstratively ignoring the questioner in annoyance at the fundamental lack of understanding the question testified to. She exhaled her smoke, but it was as though she was sighing. She didn't move, but it was as though she was shrugging. She was beautiful. She was even more beautiful than normal. She had changed from an Italian girl into a sculpture of an Italian girl. She was a Madonna in the Doge's private chapel, sculpted from the finest Carrara marble. He delighted in the fine features of her immobile, silent face each morning during prayers and once again at vespers. He kneeled, hands clasped, and was amazed at the way her nose, her chin, her jawline could be both angular and soft at the same time. She was noble. During his prayers, he imagined what it would be like to kiss her. And her wrists and ankles looked so breakable. It was incomprehensible that she could exist in marble like a featherweight fantasy of spun sugar. And in real life, in real life—he imagined how her hands, her arms, her whole body would succumb like a snow-white butterfly to his embraces and caresses. The statue had become more precious to him than his own wife. It was to her he prayed. He had ripped off the artist with a budget price for which the Doge couldn't even organize a banquet.

What he didn't know was that the destitute sculptor had modeled the Madonna on his great love, the daughter of the baker on Piazza Fossatello. He dreamed of her every night. Every morning, he went to the bakery to catch a glimpse of her. She never showed the slightest bit of interest in him. She never even gave him a second glance. For her, he was just another bum from the alleys. But for him, just seeing her was enough. A day that began with the sight of her was a beautiful day with golden yellow sunshine on the palaces of Genoa. A day that began without her, because she was ill or had been sent on an errand that morning, was as black as the night with bitter rain in the dark alleys. He worshipped her. Oh, if only she knew who he was. If only she could come with him to the Doge's Palace and see how he had caressed her into existence with his hammer and chisel. But how could a baker's daughter ever gain access to a Doge's private chapel? His own access to the palace had been blocked the day he'd completed his masterpiece and received what he saw as a very generous payment.

But one day the baker's daughter did enter the Doge's Palace. She'd been sent on an errand that morning. She had to deliver baskets full of focaccia for the banquet being held that evening. She happened to come out of the kitchen just as the Doge was coming down the stairs. She'd taken the wrong door, and to her horror, found herself in the large stairwell used by the noblemen and women. He saw her. She was the spitting image of the love of his life. She had the same angular and soft lines in her face. There was the same flimsiness to her ankles and wrists. Her hands looked like fragile confectionary concoctions.

"You live in your fantasies too much."

She still wasn't looking at me. But she'd replied. She had actually deigned to give me an answer. Although it was intended as a reproach, it was still an interesting answer. I heard three deep blasts of a ship's horn. In the harbor, a large ship was about to set sail for Barcelona, Tunis, Jerusalem, or La Merica. Of course I live in my fantasies too much. It's my job. Every day I have to reinvent Genoa and populate it with the people I see and bring to life the thoughts they have. I have to caress Genoa into existence each day out of the meaningless, rough blocks of marble from the palazzi with my hammer and chisel, and model them to fit the image of my imaginary beloved. I have to fantasize myself in her arms and invent that I am at home in her embrace, and happy. I have to fantasize myself into a Genoese. I have to blow the salty sea wind from my lungs into the alleyways. I have to make the shutters rattle and every baker's daughter or fishmonger curse. I put the *stoccafisso*, the *cima*, the *trippe,* and the pesto on the shelves of all the stinking shops in Via Canneto Il Lungo, in Macelli di Soziglia and in the Sottoripa arcades. I have to paint the whores black and make the knife shop on the corner glitter. I have to construct the terraces and the roofs, the corners and the cracks, the squares as big as a Fiat Cinquecento and the alleys as wide as a handcart. I have to spit out the dirt, the stench, and the rats into the labyrinth. I have to make the Moroccans and the Senegalese suffer, eleven to a room.

"But is that bad?"

She didn't answer. With a snow-white cappuccino in a snow-white cup on a snow-white saucer, she stared across the snow-white marble square in front of the Doge's marble palace.

"You think you're a good man," she said. She took a drag of her cigarette and stared into the distance. The tourist train from Porto Antico to Porta Soprana jingled past. "But that's just your imagination."

And how things turned out with the baker's daughter and the Doge is something you can come up with yourself, my friend. Did they get married? What do you think? And when nine months later her disgrace saw the light of day and she said he was the Doge's son, do you think they believed her? And what if they didn't? Just fantasize, my friend. Unfortunately, as is generally the case, your darkest fantasies will turn out to be the truth.

43.

I hadn't seen Rashid for quite a while. Other rose sellers had taken over his neighborhood. They were even less successful than he had been. I would be lying if I said I'd thought of him often.

From time to time I thought of him, but I didn't go to any trouble at all to try and track him down.

And then all of a sudden I saw him at the end of the Via del Campo, close to the Porta dei Vacca. He had visibly gained weight and was wearing a nice suit with an Italian cut and a pair of sophisticated shoes. I greeted him. He didn't see me. I greeted him again.

"I'm busy, Ilja."

I apologized. "You look well, Rashid. Did you find a job?"

He nodded.

"As an air-conditioning installer? The same work you always did back in Morocco?"

"Sorry, Ilja. I have an appointment."

After that I saw him a couple more times, mainly on Piazza delle Erbe, toward the end of the evening. He had stopped greeting me. He avoided my eyes. He usually installed himself at the yellow tables of Bar Gradisca. He waited for others and when they appeared, he went into the labyrinth with them. Sometimes he came back later to wait for other clients, sometimes he didn't. He had become a businessman and didn't deem his old friends worthy of a second glance.

And after that, he disappeared completely. I asked Oscar, the owner of Gradisca's, whether he knew anything. He shrugged. When I continued to ask, he walked away. I asked Mustafa, a fellow Moroccan who put the tables out in the morning for Oscar, whether he'd heard anything. He said that all his friends were Italians, that he didn't know a single Moroccan, and certainly no one called Rashid.

A few days later, Oscar took me aside. He didn't say anything. So that I could never say he'd said anything. He put his index finger to his lip to emphasize the point. After that he closed one nostril with the same finger and made a snorting noise with the other. Then he put both of his wrists together in a gesture that suggested handcuffs. "Marassi," he whispered. And I'd been in Genoa long enough to realize he didn't mean the stadium but the prison in the same neighborhood.

44.

And one evening, when I came home, I found a letter. It wasn't in an envelope. It was nothing more than a single, folded sheet that had been shoved under my front door.

"Dear Leonardo, I'm so sorry things turned out the way they did. Like I said the last time we saw each other—your problem is that you live too much in your fantasy. You think you understand things, but everything you understand you only understand in your own thoughts. If you paid more attention to reality, none of this would have had to happen.

"I was in love with you, Leonardo. I loved you. But those feelings were so strong and so new, they confused me. That's why I needed time. That's why I asked you to leave me alone for a couple of weeks. And do you know what? I had a really good think. I began to understand that the things you said about Francesco were right. Or didn't say but thought. I began to understand that I wasn't obliged to stay with someone who pushed me down the stairs. I began to understand that I had the right to make my own choices and that I could also choose adventure. Nobody could stop me.

"And you know what, that very day, two days before the derby, I had made up my mind. I had decided to choose you. And I broke up with Francesco, however difficult that was. I dreamed of being with you and maybe even going to your country one day. I dreamed of learning your language, being able to read your poems and beginning a new life in the north with you one day. I couldn't wait to tell you.

"And the next morning you turned up with her. With that blonde girl who was the opposite of me in every sense. And I saw the two of you talking in your own language and looking at each other. You paid absolutely no attention to me. You seemed to have completely forgotten me. Or you were deliberately ignoring me. And during the derby I saw the way you laid your hand on her shoulder. And after that on the Piazza delle Erbe, I saw how you were talking like two people in love. I saw you kiss. And after that I followed you. I watched you walk back to your house, hand in hand, that same house where I lay in the moonlight in your hands and where in my dreams I had wanted to live with you until we went to your country. How could you be so heartless, Leonardo? How could you forget me so quickly?

"Well, that's what I wanted to say. Now you know.

"And, oh yes, one more thing. Feel free to go to the Bar of Mirrors. I don't work there anymore. I handed in my notice this morning."

FIRST INTERMEZZO

We All Live in a Yellow Submarine

I.

It was Don's birthday and there was no way we could forget it. He was turning seventy-three. That morning I saw him sitting with Boar—that's Elio's nickname, the manager of the Schooner, a restaurant on Salita Pollaiuoli, you go past the Bar of Mirrors and it's a bit further along, toward Via San Bernardo and San Donato. Boar has a simple strategy. No one can smoke in his restaurant unless it happens to be empty. That's why the restaurant is closed pretty much all day. Boar stands there in his dirty wife-beater, puffing away behind the counter under the NO SMOKING sign. Sometimes the door is open to let in some fresh air. Unsuspecting, high-spirited tourists, wandering in for a bite to eat in the world famous Schooner restaurant, are bundled off by the Boar. *Chiuso*. Closed. Shut. No, no restaurant today. Because otherwise he'd have to get changed, clear the ashtrays from the tables, look for the menus, work. He'd rather close the door again and turn up the music. Ella Fitzgerald. Listen to this. Sarah Vaughan. And then something with a sousaphone solo. His vest turns as yellow as his fingers, steeped in nicotine. Wine. Beer. Gin and tonic. Don. And anyone else in there has to be a friend of either Boar's or Don's.

Even at eleven in the morning.

Italian humor mainly consists of laughing very loudly after you've told a joke and then raising your voice and re-telling the same joke three times over. Sarah Vaughan sang a song called "You Are My Honeybee." Boar, who, unlike the rest of them, understands a bit of English, translated the line into Italian. "She sings, 'You are my honeybee.' That means he comes along and pricks her, know what I mean?" He accompanied this with a vulgar gesture. While there was laughter around the bar, he raised his voice, clearly as pleased as punch with his minor success, and continued, "You are my honeybee. Get it? He has a sting…He pricks her with his…you know. And then she sings that he's her honeybee. Get it? Get it?! You are my honeybee. Unbelievable. That's what she's singing. And he's pricking her…" Again and again he made the same obscene gesture. And if anyone else tried to chime in, he defended his personal success by repeating the same thing even more loudly. An Italian party consists of telling as many jokes as possible, as often as possible, and drowning out any others trying to do the same.

And among it all, Don floated, flourished, triumphed, and warbled like a jamming device. He danced along on a giant woolly cloud of gin and tonic. It was his birthday for sure. He had been in Genoa for more than twenty years by now, and he still hardly spoke any Italian, but he knew the obscene gestures as well as the next person. And as soon as the next girl came tripping in to wish him a happy birthday, he spread his arms and sang, "You are my honeybee," to Boar's great amusement and that of all the other Italians at the bar. Don knew how to make friends in Genoa, or anywhere else in the world—he didn't care, as long as they served gin and tonic with as little tonic as possible, and as long as he was given special dispensation to smoke with the barman in a bar where you couldn't smoke. He slapped women's bottoms, squeezed their breasts, and laid his head on their laps. Clearly, a seventy-three-year-old alcoholic with an English accent could get away with a lot.

"We're just as scoundrelous as all those Italians," he said to me in English.

"We're anthropologists," I proposed.

"Here's to anthropologists! Let's drink to that! Cheers, big ears!" And then he began to dish up a long, priceless anecdote about an anthropologist he'd met in Burma or Malaysia. I'd heard this anecdote ten times already, but each time I'd been denied the punch line because of the arrival of yet another woman needing to be serenaded, hugged, or felt up.

At the time, Don was my dearest friend in the labyrinth. He was the only one who, by getting profusely lost every day, never got lost. His world had shrunk to a handful of bars near his hotel on Salita Pollaiuoli and although he regularly couldn't find his way back to his hotel from the Piazza delle Erbe, which his room looked out on, in his unbroken delirium, he was the most constant, stable, reliable, and most realistic of all the people I knew. And I don't mean that as a funny way of saying that he was predictable and easily locatable at any given moment of the day. He was the only one who understood. He didn't live in a fantasy world; because in all its modesty, he had made a beautiful fantasy come true: drinking himself to death, laughing and dancing among cheerful sweet nothings, smiling Italians, and a few bottoms to slap and tits to squeeze. He no longer had any illusions. Instead, he had decided that every day was a party. Every day was Don's birthday for Don. *Grande Don.*

2.

His real name was Donald Perrygrove Sinclair, but because he was the godfather of the square and, on a busy night, hundreds came by to kiss his hand, he was called Don. He was the English Professor. The little Italian he spoke he pronounced with such a heavy Oxbridge accent that he turned himself into more than one English Professor: the way he said it, it sounded like *Il Professori Inglesi.* And everyone copied him, because it seemed to fit. He was too magnificent to make do with the banal singular.

And he *was* several people, too. He was the rumpled, soiled old age pensioner in the morning with a gin and tonic in his shaking hand. He was Oscar Wilde in the afternoon, a ravishing conversationalist who, while enjoying a gin and tonic, sailed along on the currents of art and literature, sublimely acting out what pleased and rankled him, quoting Shakespeare and his own verse, dishing up priceless anecdotes. He was the Don the Italians loved after sunset, the pissed clown who sang and danced with a glass of gin and tonic in his hand, without a care for decorum or even any recollection of what the word meant. There was no way he could remember the names or faces of the dozens of friends, male and female, who filed past his table after sunset whom he'd undoubtedly met before at some point, but also after sunset.

This was why he hugged and kissed everybody. He resolved painful misunderstandings, which were inevitable, by bursting into song. He had a large repertoire, but his favorite was "We all live in a yellow submarine." He was the Don who tripped and injured himself after closing time. This was because he suffered from dizzy spells, according to his own diagnosis. He actually went to the doctor once to ask what was causing the dizziness. "And what did the doctor say?" I asked when he returned. "He's an old friend of mine. I can't lie to him. He asked me how much I drink and when was the last time I'd eaten. I'm a very intelligent man but not that clever."

He was seventy-two when I met him for the first time. He told me he'd come to Genoa more than twenty years earlier to teach English. He had a one-year contract. He never left, not even once he retired. He had lived in the hotel on Salita Pollaiuoli for more than twenty years, close to the Bar of Mirrors. He had four girlfriends who were venomously jealous of each other. He had more than four girlfriends. He kissed, felt up, embraced, and pawed everything with a pair of tits, and then he'd say, "I love you." And all that about a hundred times a night. "Shot by a jealous husband at the age of ninety-five. That's my ambition. What a way to go."

His greatest mistress was undoubtedly his glass of gin and tonic. He often said it himself, "I've abandoned nine women, but never a glass of gin and tonic." *Cappuccino senza schiuma*, he called it lovingly. He never emptied his glass, but cherished, adored, and nurtured it the whole day long. Each time he was halfway, he'd ask for extra ice and a *lacrima*—a tear, a shot of extra gin. "Drunk on tears. That would be a wonderful name for a pop group." Early in the afternoon, it was already pure gin with a dash of the memory of tonic. "Enough gin to keep the Titanic afloat and enough ice to sink her." He was a professional alcoholic who didn't spend a single second of the day with an empty glass. And at night, at closing time, there wasn't a barman who knew how much gin and tonic to put on the bill. All things considered, he'd only drunk the one.

"I had my first gin and tonic when I was eleven, with my Uncle George. It was all his fault. He was a great character. The man never uttered a word of sense in his life, until he suddenly came out with: 'They say you live longer if you don't smoke or drink. But that's not true. It just *seems* longer.'"

He didn't like moving around, that much was clear. He liked Genoa. "My hotel room looks out onto seven bars. Eight if you count the Internet café. Please stay. Please stay in Genoa, Ilja. It's heaven. Everything you need is here."

3.

Apart from gin and tonic, Don only needed one other thing to survive and that was attention. He was the king of the Piazza delle Erbe, where all the tables were crooked. He would install himself, by preference, on the high side of one of the higher tables, because sooner or later a bottle of tonic would topple over and in accordance with the rules of gravity, would land not in his lap, but in the lap of whoever was sitting opposite him on the lower side of the table. He was a professional. He thought of everything. When it came to drink, he didn't leave anything to chance.

Usually he sat on his own on the high side of his high table and held court. The crowds greeted him and moved on. The two most common words in Genoa were "Ciao, Don." He sat there like a retired cabaret artist waiting for an audience. Like a sleeping monkey in an old-fashioned machine, the kind you had to put a coin into to wake it up and then it would do a little song and dance. Don was like that, prepared at any moment of the evening to do his act as soon as a grateful audience presented itself. In the meantime, he'd doze off behind his sunglasses with a half-liter of gin and tonic in front of him on his high table.

And like every cabaret artist, he was in constant need of new spectators. His repertoire was large, but sooner or later he'd lapse into repetition. The gin and tonic didn't help, either. He was capable of dishing up the same priceless anecdote three nights in a row because for two evenings in a row he'd forgotten he'd told it the night before. Though this wasn't a real problem, because the combination of his antiquarian Oxbridge accent and the gin and tonic made him as good as incomprehensible, so you had to hear the same anecdote at least three times to understand it.

His favorite audience members were the *boaties*. Ah, the boaties. How should I describe them? Genoa is a port city, right? The cruise ships moor to the west of the Centro Storico; further to the west are the ferries for Sicilia, Sardinia, and Africa, and even further to the west from there, kilometers and kilometers of container ship facilities. But all the same, we're talking about the Mediterranean. So there's also a large harbor for yachts. And that's in Porto Antico, right beneath the Centro Storico, at walking distance from the Piazza delle Erbe. That's where you find the luxury motor yachts, the over-forty-meter crew. If the owner isn't there. If he is, they go to Sardinia, Portofino, Saint Tropez, Saint Tropez, and Saint Tropez. But the owner is only there two or three weeks a year. Aside from that, they also have a few charters, but for the rest of the year the boat stays here. And to maintain a luxury motor yacht of more than forty meters moored in the haven, you need a crew of ten or eleven. There's a German or a Russian captain everyone hates; half are Filipinos, who do the hard work and cook for each other; and the other half come from the Commonwealth. They're the boaties. Australians, Kiwis, and Canadians with much too much money and far too many gadgets, off on an adventure in the Mediterranean, only it's not a real adventure because they hang out together all the time in overpaid luxury. They come along to the piazza from time to time with their iPhones to noisily throw away hundreds of euros on cocktails and leave a stupidly large tip for all the glasses they've broken and all the nuisance they've caused.

They were Don's most appreciative audience. It also meant he didn't have to speak Italian, which he couldn't anyway. Spoiled young men from the colonies found his archaic Oxbridge accent hilarious. Sometimes it seemed as though they expressly sought him out. As though he had been explicitly marked out as a tourist attraction in their travel guides. With three stars. And up he'd pop. As though someone had put a coin in the machine. He'd do all his anecdotes and all his jokes. He satisfied every expectation. And they would buy his next gin and tonic just like you'd throw a new coin into the monkey automat. And at the end of the evening, when he could no longer talk, he'd begin to sing. They already knew the song. "We all live in a yellow submarine…"

4.

He considered me a new member of the audience, too. He told me stories about his own life. He was a brilliant storyteller. At least, after his third gin and tonic and before his thirteenth, which on average left a window of opportunity of between three and six hours. He told me how he had been expelled from school almost a century ago. Of course with a surname like Perrygrove Sinclair and a father who'd ascended to great heights in Her Majesty's Royal Army, he'd been sent to one of the most prestigious public schools in the United Kingdom.

"In my second to last year, we got this math teacher from India. A brilliant man, I've no doubt about that. But he had a terrible stutter. And I wrote a limerick about it in my exercise book. But he saw it and confiscated my book. He read the limerick. And then there was trouble.

"The next morning I had to go to the headmaster's office. Along with my father. The headmaster had my exercise book lying on his desk. He put on a stern face, opened the book, and read out the limerick. I sniggered. 'There's nothing funny about it, Perrygrove Sinclair. Did you write this?' My father sat motionlessly in his chair, resting his weight on his walking stick. He'd adopted a stern expression, too. 'Although it might not be perfect in terms of meter,' I said, 'I'm not ashamed to admit that I'm the proud author of this poem.' The headmaster slammed his hand on the desk. 'There's isn't a single reason to be proud of this filth.' Then my father stood up. 'I agree with you completely, headmaster. My son has sullied the good name of the many generations of

Perrygrove Sinclairs who have been educated here.' He decided
to take me out of school and sent me into the army."

Don took a sip of his gin and tonic and asked the passing waitress for some extra ice and a *lacrima*.

"And now, of course, you'll ask whether I can still remember
the limerick.

A math teacher from Calcutta,
was stuck with an incredible stutter.
But his girl smiled with glee,
for she found out that he
took more time than others to fu…fu…fu…

"Only the last line still rhymed, you know. But you got that already.
When I read it out to my mother that evening, she laughed. She
kissed my forehead. The next morning I took the bus to the barracks.

"A year later I was in Malaysia. For the so-called Emergency.
You weren't allowed to call it a war, but it was one. It began in
1948 and didn't end until 1960 or 1961. I was in the parachute
regiment. One day a grenade exploded a little too close by. All
my guts were blown open. I'll show you the scars. Look. See that?
I almost died. Because of a limerick. I almost died because of a
fucking poem."

5.

Quite frequently he'd emerge from his hotel in the afternoon
with visible wounds from the night before. Scabs on his head
or elbows or bloodstains on his shirt. When I asked him once
what had happened, he spread his arms and replied triumphantly,

"I can't remember anymore." And when I carried on asking, he said, "Normal people fall down the stairs, I fall up the stairs." And when I carried on asking some more, he said, "There's a security camera next to the entrance to my hotel. I'd love to see a compilation of all my spectacular homecomings."

Slowly something else began to dawn on me, something he kept carefully hidden behind his suits and ties, his impeccable appearance—a few bloodstains notwithstanding—his Oxbridge accent, his *lacrima* gin, and his residency in a hotel room from whose window he'd hung a Union Jack. He was totally broke.

It became clear to me one evening when he asked me to come up to his hotel room to fix his television. Repairing it wasn't the problem. That was a simple matter of putting the plug in the socket. But the socket! A kind of pre-war construction made of several cracked Bakelite components. There were bare wires. "Is this yours?" I asked. "No, it's the hotel's." And then I took a closer look. There were patches of damp everywhere. The wallpaper was peeling from the walls. His bed was a yellowed mattress on top of an old door. I went to the bathroom, but I'd have been better off not going. There were empty gin bottles and the remains of kebabs all over the place.

"How much do you pay for this room, Don?"

"I've been here so long. The owner's an old friend of mine. I've known him since—"

"How much do you pay for this room, Don?"

"Two hundred."

"And how often do they clean it?"

"Sometimes."

"How often?"

"The problem is I have to clean it myself before the cleaner dares come in."

We carried on our conversation out on the square. He took a sip of gin and tonic.

"Just before my father died," he said, "he summoned me to his study. It was the first time we'd spoken to each other since he took me out of school. Well, to say 'we spoke to each other' is an exaggeration. He gave me a file. It contained all the paperwork for his pension, his life insurance, my mother's, and my pension, all perfectly documented and ordered and all of them with one of the most traditional and reliable banks in England."

A waitress went past so he ordered ice and a *lacrima*.

"Barings Bank."

He paused for a moment.

"I don't know if it made the news in your country at the time. In England it was a drama. Ten thousand respectable, honest, hard-working people lost all their savings in one fell blow."

His eyes filled with tears.

"Nick Leeson. I'll never forget his name. It was 1995. He was a trader for Barings Bank in Hong Kong. He had gambled away millions of their capital on the stock market and then billions more in an attempt to make good on his loss, then he fled to Thailand in his Ferrari. They got him in the end, tried him, and sent him to prison. He did his time. Then he wrote a book that became a bestseller and made him a multi-millionaire again. But Barings Bank was bankrupt. And do you know what it means when a bank goes bankrupt? I know you know what it means.

"If I add it all up, what with my time in the army, my work as a Cambridge professor, everything I did in Italy after that—not to mention the work I carried on doing for certain British contacts, but I can't tell you anything about that unfortunately—and then my father's money and a little from my mother on top—if you'd added it all up, I'd have received a pension of more than eight thousand pounds a month. How much is that in euros? But I lost the lot. I'm one of the Barings bankruptcy victims. I'm one of Nick Leeson's victims. And now I live on a small state pension of a few hundred euros. Just enough to pay for that shithole I live in. And the rest goes on drink and cigarettes. And every month I have to choose whether to take my shirts to the drycleaners or get my shoes resoled. That's how tight things are."

He took a large sip of gin and tonic.

"That's how tight things are. But you can also look at it another way—imagine if I'd had eight thousand euros a month to drink, I'd have been long dead. Cheers, big ears. Here's to Nick Leeson."

6.

We began to worry about Don. The crowds that filed past his table every evening to embrace him and kiss his ring couldn't see it. They saw the clown they hoped to see, and he delivered on cue. We were a handful of foreigners—a Scot, a Paddy, a couple of Brits, a Pole who'd married in, a Czech—who saw him most days on the square. It was a group of good friends, from whom I often distanced myself because the language of communication was English. And that wasn't even the real problem. It was the kind of small, expat community that talked about the test match results, the Queen Mum, and the best place in Genoa to buy Marmite. The aftershocks of British colonialism. Speaking their language allowed you into the club—but let's see if you really are civilized and know the cricket scores. And in the meantime, have a laugh about the Italians who happen to have the privilege of temporarily welcoming you, with your superior culture and your superior irony, to their corrupt and endlessly inefficient country, at which you shake your head pityingly, because there is still scaffolding up that was there six months ago and your doorstep hasn't been repaired yet. I didn't come south to listen to superior shorts-wearing northerners cracking jokes about the south in their superior language, with all kinds of puns on the names of English cricketers and little else that was of importance that day in the Commonwealth. But they were friends of Don's. And they were nice people. So I couldn't and didn't want to keep ignoring them.

We had a crisis meeting in a place Don would never find us: the Mandragola. Rebecca, the owner of Caffè Letterario was there, too, because as manageress of his favorite haunt, she was best placed to pass judgment on Don's situation. The meeting was opened by our Scottish friend, who thanked us all for attending and emphasized that this meeting should never come to Don's attention. We all nodded obediently. Then he explained in a nutshell what our problems came down to by describing Don's skin color. He said it was "olive green." At this, a lively discussion sprung up. The lobby for "moss green" seemed to gain the majority stake at first, but after a veto from the Eastern Bloc countries, a compromise was reached: "puke green." The next item on the agenda was his physical health.

A small minority described him as "skinny." But they were over-ruled by a majority who considered him "emaciated." The debate finally moved on to his many injuries and their failure to heal properly and the cause of his strangely swollen stomach. Our Scottish chairman suggested a compromise: that Don, despite the differing interpretations the various parties might have, was looking unhealthier by the day. This motion was unanimously approved.

At that moment, Rebecca took the floor. "I love Don," she said. "He's a living legend. I don't mind if he drinks himself to death on my terrace. He's an adult. It's his choice. And in some ways, I feel honored, although perhaps that's the wrong choice of words. I mean—"

We nodded understandingly. We knew exactly what she meant.

"What I mean is this. On an average evening, he easily drinks a whole bottle. Gin. A liter. That's forty euros, retail price. And he can't even pay the cost price. Sorry to be so prosaic. Don is a poem. But I still have to cash up at the end of the night."

There was a silence. And suddenly all of Don's friends had places they needed to be. I stayed behind with Rebecca. "The most important thing," I said, "is that Don never finds out that we met up to try and help him. He has his pride. It's the only thing he has left. He would never forgive us."

Rebecca didn't say anything.

7.

"After Malaysia, I was posted to Japan and Korea. Japan was a doddle. It meant drinking G&Ts with the Japanese. I'll give you two guesses who won. And in Korea I had a kind of admin job. For a month. And after that I was at a secret British naval base in Saudi Arabia for a while. It was so secret, even in the upper echelons of the British Army there weren't many people who knew of its existence. But the Israelis knew about it. And they demonstrated that by flying over on a weekly basis and bombarding the runways. Symbolically. With flowers. As a warning. To make it clear that they were keeping an eye on us and that nothing would stop them if they did decide to bomb us because we weren't keeping our heads down. Sometimes they'd come a day earlier or later. And once the Saudi pilots had just gone out to train when they came along. All the pilots were princes. Terribly spoiled. And terrified of the Israelis. And two of them were so terrified they used their ejector seats and let their expensive fighter planes crash in the desert. We laughed a lot about that.

"But Malaysia was tough. That was real. We were given a jungle survival training course in Kuala Lumpur. What was edible and not. How to make drinking water from your own piss. There were these plants with huge leaves. Really. This big. We called them elephant's ears. They're poisonous. If you eat them raw, you die. But if you soak them for a night in your own excrement, they become extremely nutritious. And in case of emergency, I always carried a bottle of gin in my rucksack.

"We were hunting CTs. Communist terrorists. These days I'd call them freedom fighters. Pitched our tents behind their lines. The stress. The stress was the worst thing. Four men keeping guard and after four hours being relieved by the other four. Taking turns to sleep in four-hour shifts. And never shooting. If only that was true. That would have made it a little more bearable. I have my doubts those CTs existed. I never saw one.

"There were Frenchmen, though. On our rugby pitch. They came from Vietnam. Their base was surrounded and they were evacuated by helicopter. To our rugby pitch in Malaysia. They'd had a lot thrown at them, you could see that. Wounded. Torn uniforms. Lice, leeches, gunshot wounds, and no gin and tonic for weeks. So, us Brits, we started by giving those Frenchmen a good wash. A great heap of tattered uniforms on the rugby field, gasoline, and a lighter. And there they were, stark naked in a row in front of the showers. The officers, too. Their beer bellies gave them away."

He ordered ice and a *lacrima*.

"We called them the FBBs. Fat beer bellies."

8.

"In total, I spent eight years in the army. Eight fucking years of my life. It was a complete waste of time, all things considered. I learned nothing but skills I hoped I would never ever need—like shooting freedom fighters, cooking elephant's ears in my own excrement, and catching shrapnel in my stomach. It was finally time to do something useful with my life. Useful mainly in the sense of easier to combine with my thirst. I wanted to sit in bars like a civilized human being, not in submerged manholes in the jungle. I could put my talents to better use. And my illustrious career proved me right.

"I decided to study. English literature at Cambridge. But there was one problem. I'd never finished school. I didn't have any

A-levels. And you need A-levels to get in, don't you? I mean, that wasn't enough, you had to submit essays, too, take entrance exams, that kind of thing; but without A-levels, you didn't even get the chance to try. So I had to come up with a plan.

"I had a mate in the army, a simple lad from Birmingham. He couldn't write his own name, but he was brilliant at drawing. He made clever cartoons of our officers on the backs of bread packets or whatever he could lay his hands on. It was a wonder it never got him into trouble. They were so cruel, so accurate, so good. I thought: that's the man I need.

"I can't remember his name. Peter. Something like that. Or Brian. But that doesn't matter. He was brilliant at drawing. Or did I already say that? And he owed me a favor. Ha-ha! It still makes me laugh to think of it. That was in Japan. No! Korea! It was in Korea. I remember it well. He had a lady visitor—that was our euphemism at the time. A scarlet lady. They popped up fairly often on Her Majesty's Royal Army base. But of course it was strictly prohibited, you'll understand. To pluck the fruits. To consume, for a modest fee, the ripe fruits that had fallen on the ground in front of your very feet. We were British, weren't we? Ha-ha! And this Richard or Mark or whatever his name was had found one who screamed like a stuck pig. I still remember it well. I was standing in the corridor keeping a look out. And then one of those five star generals came along 'to inspect the troops,' as it were. Can you imagine? No, listen. That Korean floozy lying there screaming like all the karaoke bars in Taipei put together and the general coming down the corridor. Do you know what I did? I faked a coughing fit. I coughed her out. I coughed a hysterical little Korean whore all the way home. The general was worried. 'Asthma, General. I suffer from terrible asthma. And being in the tropics doesn't make it any better. The medical examiner didn't want to pass me when I signed up. I got down on my knees and begged him to show some mercy. My greatest desire was to fight for England, the queen, and the free western democracy.' The general gave me a pat on the shoulder and walked on.

"So that John or Edwin or whatever he was called owed me a favor. He was a simple lad. But what you need to know is that he was really damn good at drawing. Or did I say that already? So I gave him a copy of my brother's exam certificate. Don't ask me how I managed that. It's a long story. And Michael or Steve or whatever he was called copied it. He faked my exam certificate. I could apply for university. My essays on James Joyce and the English metaphysical poets went down brilliantly. That's how I ended up at Cambridge."

Don took a big sip of his gin and tonic. "Cheers, big ears." He fell into a coughing fit. When he'd finished coughing, he said, "I can still do it. I'm one of the great coughers of my generation. Didn't Oscar Wilde have a clever quip about that? Anyway, it was a close call."

A group of teenagers walked by. They found it important to greet Don, one by one. To ask his opinion about Sampdoria, which had been on a losing streak for weeks. He stood up and hugged them all, while getting all their names wrong, which he made up for by singing the Sampdoria club song. That was the way it always went.

"What was a close call?"

"Almost getting kicked out in my first year."

"Tell me."

"No, Ilja. I'll tell you tomorrow. Otherwise you'll put it all in the same chapter."

"Since when have you worried about my novel's structure? You're a character, try to remember that!"

"And what a character! Ha-ha! Let's drink to that. But I do want a bit of space for my story. I can't write it all down myself anymore. So I'm using you for that. And make sure you don't make stuff up. I'm much better at that than you. Ha-ha! We all live in a yellow submarine."

9.

When I bumped into Don the next day on the Piazza delle Erbe he looked radiant. He was glowing. I was almost worried. "Don, what happened?" He removed a newspaper from his inside pocket with a triumphant gesture. It was the Sampdoria club paper. "Page eight," he said. There he was. A full-page photograph. With the caption: *Don, one of Sampdoria's biggest supporters.* I congratulated him on this corroboration of his fame. He dismissed the compliment, beaming. "Oh, well, Ilja. I've been in this city for so long. I know them all. Vialli and the rest. I've given them all English lessons. Gullit, too. But to be honest I thought he was an arrogant bastard. I don't go to the stadium these days. I'm too old. And I suffer from dizzy spells. But I used to go to every home match. The last time was on my birthday. Four or five years ago, or maybe even six. And they knew. At a certain point the entire stadium was singing, 'Happy Birthday to Don.' It was moving. The referee held a two-minute silence. All the players came to the *gradinata sud* where I always sat and applauded me. It was the nicest birthday present I ever had.

"All my friends are *Doriani*. You know, there are three sounds I cannot bear: breaking glass, the sound of shutters going down in the bars at closing time, and '*Forza Genoa.*' You are a Genoano, I know. Even though you seem like an intelligent man. But there are other things about you I don't understand, either. For example, why you carry on drinking those disgusting cocktails instead of becoming a member of the Gordon's Club, whose chairman, secretary, and treasurer you have before you.

"I was there at Wembley, too, when Sampdoria played in the Champions League final against Barcelona. Simon arranged it, a friend of mine who was working at the aquarium as a dolphin trainer at the time. He called me a few days before the match. 'I have good news and bad news. The good news is that I've found cheap flights. The bad news is that we're flying via Amsterdam with a four-hour transfer.' Yippee! We went to a coffee shop and got as high as a kite. After the match, they gently broke the news to me that Sampdoria had lost. The entire match had passed me by.

"And on the return journey, too—the same coffee shop. Or another, I wouldn't be able to say. They all look terribly similar, don't you think? When it was time to go to Schiphol to catch our flight back to Genoa, we still had a big chunk of hashish left. 'Don't take it with you, Simon. Think about it. Give it to those two boys at that table.' 'You're right, Don, that would be a better idea. But I've just flushed it down the loo.'

"At Genoa airport, the sniffer dogs lunged at us. They jumped all over Simon. 'Fuck, Simon,' I said, 'you didn't…?' But they couldn't find anything. 'It's on our clothes,' we said. 'We've spent the entire afternoon in a coffee shop in Amsterdam. The smoke's on our clothes. That's what the dogs can smell.' And they let us go because they couldn't find anything.

"In the taxi from the airport to Piazza delle Erbe, Simon said, 'Do you fancy a joint, Don?' He had shoved the hash up his arse. In a condom. He'd gone to the loo in the coffee shop in Amsterdam to get a condom out of the machine and put the hash up his arse. Can you imagine? And that's without even mentioning whether I still felt like smoking it once I knew where it had been for the entire flight.

"And this brings me to something completely different. Do you remember accusing me of meddling with the structure of your novel last night? You might have forgotten it, you drunkard, but I haven't. Because what do I still have to tell you? Well? Exactly. Why I almost got sent down from Cambridge in my first year. And that didn't have anything to do with hashish. But everything to do with a condom.

"Back in those days we still had servants in college. Kind of butlers for the students who made their beds in the mornings. We called them 'bedders.' One of the bedders found a used condom in my bed, something which didn't surprise me at all, by the way. I was summoned by the dean. He pulled a face and got it out of an envelope with the tip of a pencil. He dangled it in front of my nose. 'Is this yours, Perrygrove Sinclair?' I put on my glasses to get a better look. I studied the condom carefully. And do you know what I said? The dean laughed so much he had to let me off. You should be able to guess. I just said it. If I'm interfering with the structure of your novel, I'm doing a good job."

He took a formidable sip of gin and tonic and gave me a triumphant look.

"They all look terribly similar, don't you think?"

10.

Don could be irresistible at times. He had a talent for making himself lovable and used this to gain personal favors, which he then considered his right and a legal basis for further favors. Catering staff were his main victims. He used his charm to take advantage of them. What began as an extra ice cube would imperceptibly morph over the space of a few weeks into his own glass of maximum volume, a personal chair, permission to stay on after closing time, and liters of free gin. And whenever a bar owner was brave enough to move Don's process of appropriating the bar back a step, he'd explode. When a self-created privilege was taken away from him, he could be unusually unpleasant. Like a spoiled child not getting its own way.

And he lost control completely when his drink supply was stopped; for example, when the barman concluded, after he'd fallen over three times, that he'd had enough. Even if he didn't have any money left to pay for his next gin and tonic, he'd consider it a universal human right to be allowed to drink one more, and anyone disagreeing was a fascist or much worse.

A lack of attention was also catastrophic. He could have an angry outburst when a group had collected at his table and didn't consider him the cornerstone of the company—for example when no English was spoken or when English was being spoken, but he was being ignored because he was too drunk to say anything sensible. During an angry moment, he'd wake up out of his stupor and call them every name under the sun.

But worst of all was when he felt his pride had been injured. He disgraced himself on a daily basis, but when he got the impression that someone else was trying to do that, the piazza was too small for the both of them. *He* cracked the jokes, including the jokes about himself, and anyone getting it into his head to make him the butt of one became an arch enemy, at least for as long as he remembered, and that was never very long, and in any case never longer than until the next morning.

But outbursts like this were relatively uncommon. I began to worry about something else. There was also a quiet, dejected, melancholic Don, and I began to see him more and more often. The expat friends we had in common noticed it, too. When we asked after the cause, he'd just say he was thinking. And if we carried on asking, he'd say even less. But we could guess what he was thinking about. A lack of money put a recurring damper on the party mood. His depressions almost always overcame him during the last week of the month. As soon as he'd been to the bank to collect his pension he'd drown himself in happiness again. But it went deeper than that. Sometimes he'd get a card or a letter from his sister in Birmingham. He would carry it with him in his inside pocket for days and tell us night after night that he'd gotten a card or a letter from his sister in Birmingham. He seemed just as surprised as we were that he had a sister and it made him melancholic, like someone taken unawares by a realization of lost time.

Don's family was a concept no one could get their head round. He was one of those rare characters who, like Athena, must have sprouted fully armed out of someone's head. Don was born with a gin and tonic in his hand; it was the only possibility, because without a gin and tonic in his hand, Don wouldn't be Don. It was inconceivable that he'd ever been a normal toddler with anything as banal as a sister. Even more unimaginable, if that was possible, was the thought that he'd had ever had children himself. He was much too happy with his own cocky independence and his role as a maverick singleton at the heart of the crowd and much too faithful to his glass, his only mistress. And yet he had them. He had a daughter, who lived in Greece, and a son whose stage name was "Dicko" and had made a fortune in Australia playing a malevolent judge in TV talent contests. We found this out by chance. Don never talked about them. All contact had been cut off. And there must have been a wife involved, or in any case a mother to his children, but we never found anything out about her, not even by chance. He was in denial about his hidden past and trying to forget it, but its ghosts haunted his mind more and more often when he didn't have enough money for the gin he needed to deny or forget.

He was getting old, that was it. He began to grow older than he'd ever imagined possible. He no longer had the strength for his forward flight every evening. He was being sucked back into his own past, which he wouldn't share with anyone whatever bottle you plied him with. He resembled a wounded animal, hiding away under the roots of a tree to die out of sight of the cameras that continued to play for as long as he could see them.

11.

"I really can't talk about it, but I know I can trust you. I'll tell you on the condition that you don't write it down. It was just before I graduated from Cambridge. My thesis on the metaphysical poets had been approved. Better still, I'd been given the highest possible grade. I'd been celebrating that in my own way for a few days. And one evening I came home and found an official letter from the dean on my desk. One of the bedders must have put it there. This was highly irregular. The college post was always delivered to the pigeon holes in the main hall, just next to the entrance. The next morning, when I'd sobered up, I opened the letter. The dean had invited me for tea at his home. This was highly, highly irregular.

"I was received in the drawing room. The dean's wife served tea with a wide assortment of sandwiches, cakes, and petits fours. The dean joined us in the drawing room and began a very amicable conversation about a series of amusing trivialities. He told me stories about his time as a student and the short period during which he had been politically active. He seemed exaggeratedly interested in my thesis's conclusions and my other views on English literature. He nodded and smiled friendlily at everything I said. His wife kept on topping up the teacups and proffering new delicacies. Meanwhile I felt more uncomfortable by the minute. Something was fishy about this. It was highly, highly, highly irregular. What was going on? What did he want from me?

"'I know you have a great fondness for orchids,' he said, 'Come. I want to show you something.' Where on earth had he gotten that from? I didn't like orchids at all. But I went with him. We went outside through the back door, and right at the back of his large garden there was a greenhouse in which he cultivated orchids. He gave me a tour and at a certain point, while he was clipping away a couple of superfluous leaves with a small pair of shears, he casually asked, 'By the way, have you ever considered joining the Service?'

"I didn't have the foggiest what he meant. He carried on coolly trimming his orchids. It was a very finicky task. He leaned in close to scrutinize his work and said, 'We have selected you as a potential candidate. You aspire to an academic career, don't you?' I nodded. 'That can be arranged. It won't get in the way of your work for the Service in any way. On the contrary, it would be an advantage because an academic career is a most suitable cover. You'd have to attend a lot of conferences abroad, but you wouldn't have to worry yourself about that. We'd organize that for you.' I still didn't understand where this was heading. He said, 'What I mean is this: if you cooperate, the Service would guarantee the preconditions, like a lectureship and, in time, a chair. That goes without saying.'

"I couldn't believe my ears. 'Why me?' I asked. 'Because you are one of the few here with a military background. Besides, there are certain facets of your personality that make you a very suitable candidate—you seem to value a varied social life and you are very credible in places where a lot of alcohol is drunk and people tend to be rather more loose-lipped than usual. That's a characteristic that might come in useful. What's more, you don't clam up under pressure. I noticed that when I put you to the test with that condom that ostensibly had been found in your bed. And if you are still not convinced, I'll give you one final argument.'

"He walked to the back wall of the greenhouse, where there was a tool cabinet. He took out a rolled-up piece of paper. 'Do you recognize this document?' It was my A-level certificate. 'It's a forgery,' he said. 'Not a bad forgery, I'll admit, but we're no fools. Listen, let me put it this way, as an employee of the Service such a demonstration of improvisational ability works in your favor, whereas under different circumstances it might be considered a punishable offence. Do you get my meaning?' I nodded. 'To prevent any misunderstanding, I'll make myself more explicit. If you accept, we'll put this document back in our archives and you'll get your first class honors next week and we'll underwrite your future academic career. If you refuse, I'll unfortunately find myself compelled to take steps. To start with I'd have to cancel your graduation and following that, legal proceedings would be put into motion.' I swallowed. 'So I don't have a choice?' Smiling, he laid an arm around my shoulders. 'No.'

"That's how it happened. That's how I got recruited into the Service. But once again: you have to swear that you won't mention this to anyone else." He took a generous sip of his gin and tonic.

"But what kind of service was it?"

"Ilja! Don't you understand anything?" He looked around to make sure no one was listening. He leaned toward me and whispered in my ear, "MI6. Her Majesty's Secret Service."

12.

"In the early years, I was a kind of delivery boy. As a PhD student and later a professor, I was regularly invited to international conferences on the English metaphysical poets. It amazed me that there was so much interest in them worldwide. And the curious thing was that they were mainly held in places in countries which, to put it subtly, were 'at odds' with the United Kingdom. Peking. Bucharest. Havana. I gave lectures in all those places. And there was a lot of interest in metaphysical poets in Moscow. I went there at least ten times for conferences. And while my international colleagues debated my hasty conclusions, I was supposed to deliver a parcel. A parcel is a bit of an exaggeration. It was usually a newspaper. Or a magazine. It probably had a microfilm hidden in it. They never told me what I was carrying. It wasn't my business. And I wasn't supposed to ask questions, I was the delivery boy.

"I remember one time in Greece. That was during the military junta of '67-'74. I was in the train. All of a sudden five Greek policemen entered my carriage. I was shitting myself, in a manner of speaking. I didn't know what I was carrying but I knew I was carrying something. But the other five passengers in my carriage turned out to be Turks. They stripped them from head to toe and left me alone. It didn't sink in until later that we'd planted those Turks there. But Ilja, you can't imagine how petrified I was."

He asked for some ice and a *lacrima*. "My darling," he said. "My darling," the waitress said back.

"I love young people, Ilja. I love young people. They say they keep you young. I believe in that with all my heart. That's why I was always so popular when I was teaching at the university. I always behaved like one of them instead of their professor, but that's how I felt, too. I remember it well. It was in 1968 or '69. One day, my students came up to me after a lecture and asked,

'Professor, do you fancy coming to a concert with us tomorrow? It's a bit of a drive. But if you want, we'll come and pick you up tomorrow morning in the car.'

"The next morning I stood there waiting in a dinner jacket and bowtie. Ready to go to a concert. They said, 'Professor, you might be a little overdressed. We're not going to the opera. It's a different kind of concert.' 'That doesn't matter,' I said. 'I like to dress up for the performers. Out of respect.'

"It was indeed quite a drive. We were hours away from the city. We drove along country lanes. They said we were close. It seemed an improbable place for a concert. 'I think we're lost,' I said. I could see a farmer on his tractor in the distance. 'I'll ask him the way. What's the name of the place we're looking for? Stockwood?'"

He still found it hilarious.

"Had you stopped working for the Service by then?"

"No, I'd only just begun. As a delivery boy. Later I was deployed for more serious missions. Well, I don't know whether they were more serious. You never know with MI6. But I had to gather information. I was brought into contact with rulers and dissidents. I had to drink G&Ts with them. That's what it came down to. And I'd be debriefed in London. Of course I wasn't allowed to write anything down—that would have been much too risky. I had to remember everything. That's where I got my excellent memory. I was never allowed to tell the same story or joke to the same person twice. And in London I was expected to relate everything they'd said. I wasn't to judge what was important and what wasn't, that was their business. My job was to relate everything exactly as they'd said it.

"And to be honest, that's how I... But wait. You really have to promise me that you won't mention this to anybody."

I promised.

"But I'm serious." He disappeared into his thoughts.

"Cheers, big ears." He remained silent. "And to be honest, that's how I witnessed a few important developments. Not to say caused them."

I ordered him another gin and tonic.

"You understand."

"Well?"

He stirred the gin and lime in his family-size glass. "In 1989, I was in the GDR."

"For a conference on metaphysical poets?"

"Yes. And what's his name again? Kraut. Egon Kraut. I have an excellent memory. No! Krenz. Egon Krenz. I said to him—"

Some Italians came to kiss his ring. "We all live in a yellow submarine," I said.

Don gave me a withering look. "That's my line," he said.

"Sorry. But tell me more about Egon Krenz."

"No."

13.

I hadn't seen Don for a couple of days. People on the piazza began to worry. It was almost the end of the month. Maybe his money had run out. On the other hand, this had never prevented him from clamoring for his right to an advance on next month's tab before, given his special status. The shutters on his hotel window remained closed. He didn't answer his phone, but that happened quite a lot because he didn't know how it worked. And just when we really began to worry and seriously consider calling someone, like the police or the hotel owner, he came coolly sauntering onto the square in characteristic fashion, like a gentleman who has assumed a slow and dignified gait to camouflage the fact that he is struggling to keep his balance.

"Where were you, Don?"

He didn't say anything. He stuck out his arms and crossed his wrists. The gesture meant that he'd been handcuffed. I had to laugh. He didn't.

"What happened, Don?"

He sat down, ordered a *cappuccino senza schiuma*, and didn't say anything. He didn't begin to talk until after his third *lacrima*. What he said was: "Cheers. To Nick Leeson."

A man came by selling roses and Don tried to wrangle a free rose for his buttonhole. After a while, the rose seller became rather receptive to the idea that Don shouldn't pay for the rose because he was a pensioner, but the deal fell through in the end because Don didn't like the color. He was wearing a pale blue shirt with a white tie that day and couldn't compromise on a yellow, pink, or red rose. The rose seller apologized profusely and promised to return the next day with white roses.

"But hey! White means white! Understood?"

"Sure, Don. Sorry, Don."

The rose seller moved on. Don drank. I waited. Don sighed. "I've told you how tight things are sometimes," he said. "Everything goes on rent, drink, and cigarettes. And it gets less every month because the pound keeps going down against the euro.

Last month, the hotel owner raised the rent for that shithole. Not much, but every tenner counts. I protested but he said that I was the only person in the hotel who'd been paying the same rent for years. What can I say? He's an old friend of mine. And I'd pay at least double that everywhere else. At least.

"I don't usually make it to the end of the month anymore. That's not a real problem for the alcohol—I have tabs all over the city. But my shoes need to be re-soled. And I have to go to the dry cleaner's. I've run out of clean shirts. And you know how important I find it to look tip-top. My dignity is the only thing I have left. If I lose that, I've lost everything. Do you understand?"

I understood. And because I understood about his dignity, I decided to change my mind and not offer to lend him any cash.

"So." He stirred his glass pensively with his straw. "Do you know Bruno? From Le Cinque Vele in Porto Antico. It used to have a different name: La Sirena. He has three or four bars around there. I'm sure you know him. He was one of the biggest drugs dealers in Genoa. Years ago. Everyone knew. In the end he got arrested, but he did a deal with the police. He gave up his supplier in exchange for being acquitted or at least avoiding a long prison sentence and then stopped. But what not many people know—"

"Is that he didn't stop?"

Don nodded. "He mainly delivers to the luxury yachts. To the boaties. I know them all, and I know nearly all the captains. They trust me, and Bruno needs a delivery boy from time to time. Which happens to be my former occupation, shall we say. He doesn't pay much—a few tenners. But I can use the money."

I give him a shocked look. "But, Don, what the fuck are you

saying? I mean—drug-runner? At your age?"

"I know, Ilja. I'm a very intelligent man, but not that clever. And I was incredibly lucky, too. When they picked me up, I didn't have much left on me. A few grams perhaps. Less. I'd already delivered the rest. But still. I had to go to the station. They kept me for a couple of days. They wanted to know who I worked for and who I delivered to. They knew damn well that I was a runner, they're not stupid. But I didn't give Bruno away, or the boaties, either. I maintained it was for personal use and that I'd bought it from some Moroccan guy on a street corner in the Maddalena quarter. And of course I wouldn't be able to recognize that Moroccan again. 'They all look terribly similar, don't you think?' They didn't find that very funny. And they didn't believe me. But they didn't have any proof.

"But the biggest piece of luck was that the police chief is an old friend of mine. He only showed up after a couple of days. To be honest, I think he works for a different department as a rule. I'm not sure exactly how it works. But as soon as he saw me, he was all, 'Ciao Don. *Cappuccino senza schiuma*. We all live in a yellow submarine.' He asked me what had happened. I told him that it was all a misunderstanding and that he should ring the British Consulate at once. I had already said that to the other *carabinieri* who had questioned me, but they had refused. He knew I still had special protection because of my work for the Service and he was happy to help me. It was all sorted out with a single phone call. I could go.

"That was an hour ago. So you'll understand, Ilja—I could use a G&T."

14.

A few days later I was drinking coffee and reading the papers in the little Sicilian bar on Piazza Matteotti early in the morning, when Don popped up from the wrong direction. His hotel was on the Salita Pollaiuoli but he came from the Piazza de Ferrari. It was highly irregular to come across him at such an early hour, but he'd clearly been somewhere else even earlier. He sat down next to me. His face was troubled. He ordered a coffee. That was even more irregular, if possible.

"How are you doing, Don? Where've you just been?"

He pointed his thumb back over his shoulder in the direction he'd just come from. "From the British Consulate."

"Because of that little incident? When you got arrested?"

Don shook his head. "Well, indirectly. They called me two days ago to make an appointment. Which was this morning. They were very friendly. They asked about my health and in particular my financial situation. I told them the truth. I told them how difficult it is sometimes. They knew everything already and told me they might be able to help. 'There are two gentlemen here you probably know. They'd like to have a little chat with you.' The door opened and they came in. And indeed, I did know them well. I knew them only too well."

He stared dejectedly into his coffee. "Maybe I need something stronger."

"And who were they then?"

"Unfortunately I can't tell you, Ilja." He downed his gin and tonic in one gulp. He looked a lot better for it. And when he'd finished his second, he said, "They wanted me back. They wanted me to work for them again. For the Service. But I'm too old, Ilja. I'm too old.

"The two men were my former boss and his right hand. They'd come to Genoa especially to talk to me. Undoubtedly the Consulate had informed them about my lack of money and my recent act of desperation. We went for a coffee in the bar on the corner. I already knew what they were going to ask me, but I pretended not to. We talked about this and that and the good old times for half an hour and then the truth came out."

"What did they want you to do?"

"They never tell you beforehand, they only explain when they're one hundred percent sure you're going to do the job. And just the bare minimum. You only get told the things that are absolutely essential to completing the mission. And then a lot of the time it's probably about something other than what they've told you.

"But they let it drop that they were thinking of several missions. Abroad. The word Cairo was mentioned a couple of times. They told me about a good friend of mine from Cambridge. Another literary type. Turns out he's a professor there, at the University of Cairo. They told me he was planning to organize a big international conference shortly."

"On the metaphysical poets?"

"I didn't know he worked for the Service, too. I should have suspected, of course. And they did offer me a generous fee. About twice as much as I used to earn from them. And they knew all too well that I'd be receptive to their offer."

"So you agreed?"

"I can't do it anymore. All that traveling. I'm too old for it. I'm too old, Ilja."

15.

A week later he was dead.

It was a lovely summer's evening. The terraces were buzzing. It was the high-pitched note of a warm day that hadn't yet tired itself out but was satiated enough not to demand anything more of itself than this gentle and effortless slipping by in warm, slow gestures. Here and there, the metallic tinkle of a toast. Street musicians went past. They played slightly slower and their sound was slightly purer than usual. Beggars smiled. The swallows flew high above the pastel-colored palazzi. Pigeons pecked around the square without having to worry about the seagulls who'd flown far offshore over a calm sea. The fire brigade's red helicopter flew high overhead to put out forest fires in the mountains. Tomorrow was going to be another wonderful day.

I didn't speak to Don that evening. I sat a few tables away from him with three Italian girls. He'd been attended to at his high table by a group of boaties. Don had been at his most Donnish. I had seen him gesturing enthusiastically and heard his loud laughter. Shoulders were slapped heartily again and again. He had been able to run through a large part of his repertoire. His stories had met with warm approval. They had sung along to his songs, and he'd been generously rewarded with many brimming glasses. He had been the focal point of the evening. He had gloried.

When they left, he'd drifted off behind his sunglasses. There was a full glass of gin and tonic in front of him. He had a smile on his face. The crowds filed past his table. "Ciao, Don." He didn't reply. Just smiled. "*Forza Sampdoria.*" They slapped him amicably on the shoulder and carried on. "*Grande Don.*"

Closing time drew near. Various waitresses had told Don in passing to finish his drink because they were about to shut. He'd listened with an affable smile.

When the bar's shutters had been rolled down halfway, Rebecca, the owner, came out to shake him awake. His glass was just as full as before. "Don, we have to close." His sunglasses fell from his head. And still he didn't move. He was cold to the touch.

The ambulance arrived immediately. But there was nothing they could do. He was dead.

"How long's he been dead?"

"It's hard to say. But at least four hours or so. Didn't you notice anything?"

"We thought he was happy."

16.

The news spread through the city like wildfire. The next day, people from the suburbs were already arriving in Piazza delle Erbe to ask whether it was true. It was true. In the absence of anyone to offer their condolences to, they offered them to themselves. Rebecca had placed an improvised book of condolences on the bar in her café: an empty scrapbook with kittens on the cover, which she'd had lying about somewhere; a photo of Don, which Nello from the Internet café had printed out and framed;

and Don's last gin and tonic, which they hadn't had the heart to empty down the sink the previous evening. The rose seller had laid a white rose next to it. Rebecca had tried to pay him for it but he'd refused. Halfway through the evening the scrapbook was already full. Nello dug up a large exercise book in the Sampdoria club colors from somewhere. That, too, was soon full. And everyone asked when the funeral would be.

That was a good question. Not least because it wasn't exactly clear who would arrange it. Or, rather, it was all too clear. Don knew hundreds of people in this city who called themselves his friends, but he had no friends, apart from our small group of expats who had always worried about him instead of cheerfully slapping his fragile shoulders in passing, which by the way, he had always preferred to anyone worrying about him. If we didn't organize it, no one would.

We had to notify his family, but that was easier said than done. We knew of the existence of a son in Australia, a daughter in Greece, and a sister in Birmingham. We tracked down the son quite quickly. He really had become famous as "Dicko," the bad guy on TV talent show juries. We tried to contact him through his management. There was no response. There wasn't a single trace of the daughter. No doubt she had a different surname by now. The same went for his sister, but we did finally manage to trace her with a lot of effort and a bit of luck, thanks to friends of friends of our friend from Liverpool. She reacted calmly to the news of her brother's death. "I'm glad it happened like that," she said over the phone. "That's the best death he could have wished for, the drunken bastard."

We had a lot of contact with her over the days that followed. No, the body didn't need to be shipped back to England. It was better to bury him in Genoa. "Let him take his nuisance where he spent his money. All those so-called friends of his are there. No one knows him here anymore." And no, she wouldn't come for the funeral. Her brother had always considered himself better off without her. He'd never wanted to listen to her when he was alive and she thought the chance very small that things would be any different now.

And his children? "Don't bother." Why not? "Let it lie. I don't want to say anything bad about him." But we need to keep them informed at least? "He never found that important when he was alive. He's been dead to them for more than thirty years. From the moment he started drinking again. If he ever stopped. But for a while he acted as though he had, when the children were still young. And when he couldn't keep it up anymore he just disappeared, from one day to the next. He didn't even leave a letter on the kitchen table and he never got back in touch. We only heard by chance through the grapevine years later that he was in Italy."

We asked about his professorship post. Perhaps the University of Cambridge would be interested in publishing an obituary or might be inclined to donate something as a sign of their gratefulness and respect? She burst out laughing. "Is that what he told you? Typical Don." Wasn't it true, then? "But when, then? Think about it. He went to university when he got out of the army. He was a mature student, as we call it. When he started his studies he was about twenty-six. He was over thirty when he graduated.

His children had already been born. He started a Master's thesis but never finished it, he ran off to Italy before that."

But nevertheless, over the years he was a welcome guest at international academic conferences, wasn't he? In particular, ones on the metaphysical poets? "Don't make me laugh. He never left Italy. It wouldn't have been possible. His passport ran out more than twenty years ago. I still remember the letter. His ex-wife gave it to me. I think I've still got it somewhere."

And that astronomic pension, then? "Which pension?" The one he had at Barings Bank and lost because of Nick Leeson's activities? "All the private investors were reimbursed before the bankruptcy. The truth is that Don never worked in his life, apart from perhaps a few private English lessons and a little translation job now and again. He didn't have time to. He was a full-time alcoholic. His whole life long. He was already an old drunkard long before you knew him as an old drunkard. It's a miracle he kept it up for so long. I'm happy he had such a pleasant death, because I do love him. Bury him there among his so-called friends and keep us out of it. And cherish the stories he had you believe. Let things be as he wanted them. I don't want to hear anything else about it. I'll transfer a contribution to the costs. That's all. Thank you."

17.

In Via Canneto Il Curto, in the stretch between Via San Lorenzo and Piazza Banchi, there's a dusty little shop where you can buy old coins and medals. I'd never seen a customer go in, and although

I'd never noticed a shopkeeper, either, he did exist. He heard the shop bell ring and came shuffling out of a back room in his dressing gown. He was even dustier than his shop. He asked me how he could be of assistance. I told him I needed one or two old decorations. He stared into space, deep in thought. Medals, I clarified, pointing at the shop window where medals of all shapes and sizes were displayed. Something gradually began to dawn on him. He nodded circumspectly and asked me what kind of medals I was thinking of. "English medals," I said. "Decorations for bravery in battle or other exceptional services to the fatherland." "English?" "Yes, English." He shook his head and began to shuffle to his back room. I stopped him and said I'd take any other medals that were good. I chose four: the biggest with the most stars, crowns, and aureoles, with the most fake gold and the most colorful ribbons.

The funeral took place in the historic Staglieno cemetery. Our Scottish friend had been able to arrange a modest but pleasant spot through his contacts there for a friendly price. He didn't want to say much about it, but I suspect he'd gotten a bulk discount by signing a contract for us all to take options on plots there at the prevailing rate at the moment of first use. To keep the costs even lower, a slot was chosen on a Tuesday morning at eight o'clock. We announced the time and place in an advertisement in *Il Secolo XIX* and a letter on the door of the Caffè Letterario on Piazza delle Erbe.

Despite the early hour, it was unbelievably busy. When the ceremony started with an a cappella performance of Don's favorite aria "*O mio babbino caro*," by his good friend Irene Cenboncini, the soprano from the Carlo Felice, there were hundreds of people around the grave, including pretty much every barman from in and around Genoa. Our Scottish friend gave an impassioned speech in Italian, in which he dwelt at length on a number of Don's merits— ones he'd always been too modest to share with his Italian friends, such as his heroic role in various battles in Korea and Malaysia and the crucial role he played in a number of key moments in the history of the twentieth century as an agent for the British Secret Service. The medals shone on his coffin.

And then the coffin began to drop and, in a silence that resounded with respect, the grave stone was slowly revealed. It was a simple block of granite in the classical form with a curve at the top. And the only thing carved into it were the two words which had been the two most spoken words in Genoa all those years and which now rang out in silence for the very last time:

ciao don

18.

There was a long procession from Staglieno, along the banks of the River Bisagno back to the center. We passed Luigi Ferraris Stadium in Marassi. There was a large banner hanging above the main entrance, changing the name of the stadium to "Stadio di Don."

On Piazza delle Erbe, all seven cafés were running at full fighting strength. The terraces had been set up outside at their maximum capacities and all the temporary staff had been called in. This turned out to be necessary. On that Tuesday morning, when all of Don's friends flooded the square to raise a final toast to him, it was busier than a busy Friday or Saturday night. And even though nothing had been agreed beforehand, everyone drank gin and tonic, which everyone ordered as *cappuccino senza schiuma*. This led to some debauched scenes quite early in the day.

The game soon became who could remember the most jokes from Don's immense but worn repertoire. Anyone telling a joke laughed louder than everyone else and then told it again a few more times in a loud voice to prevent others from cutting short their victory by telling a joke of their own. This Italian habit, which usually annoyed me, had something almost likeable at the time, because ultimately these were Don's victories that were being celebrated with so much determination and noisy envy.

The next game was to do an impression of Don. Elio, Boar, imitated how Don sang Sarah Vaughan's "You are My Honeybee" to every girl who came in. 'You are my honeybee, he sang, and he pricked her...' He made the accompanying obscene gesture. "Get it? Pricked her...And then squeeze some tits. I'll demonstrate. Look. Like this." Boar squeezed a random friend of Don's in the tits. But there was a degree of self-interest in it, I thought; it wasn't just part of the imitation. From time to time, someone would fall off his chair, blind drunk. But in those cases, too, it wasn't clear whether this was part of the game or whether it was due to the gin and tonic. But at the end of the day it came down to the same thing.

Don's funeral gradually turned into Don's birthday. And because at his own birthdays Don generally featured more as a shadowy presence than he was actually present as a concrete person, he was barely missed. He was there that day on the Piazza delle Erbe, there was hardly anyone who doubted that. And no one doubted it at all when, suddenly, spontaneously, without agreement or sign, across the square hundreds of voices joined together in his favorite song:

We all live in a yellow submarine.

In the evening there was a passionate debate about how we could get the council, the province, or the region to replace a small, battered statue of a *putto* on the Piazza delle Erbe with a statue of Don holding a glass of gin and tonic. And when, hours later, after the legal closing time, the shutters rattled downwards and everyone stumbled home blind drunk, we heard Don's piercing peals of laughter echoing through the city's silent alleyways.

He was a living legend and it will be difficult for the city to get used to the fact that he is now a dead one. Smiling behind his sunglasses, he drank himself to death and laughingly invented a life story to go with it. The bum. The drunken bastard. He enticed all of us into the labyrinth of his fantasies. And he succeeded—he was the most popular immigrant, the most successful foreigner in the whole of Genoa because he never assimilated, never fit in, and always stayed himself. In fact he had refined himself into a caricature of himself. And on the day of his funeral, hundreds and hundreds of friends had drunk *cappuccino senza schiuma* while having serious conversations about a statue. Hundreds and hundreds of drunken voices had joined together to sing his favorite song. We all live in a yellow submarine. He had always known that it would end like this. *Grande Don.*

PART TWO

The Theater Elsewhere

I.

It's like a bath. The plug's in and the tap's on. There's nobody home.
The person who turned on the tap has forgotten it. She's gone
out. Slowly but surely, the bath gets fuller and fuller. And it's a cast
iron certainty that at a certain point that can be calculated math-
ematically it will overflow, immediately causing a new situation
because the apartment will be flooded and so will the downstairs
neighbors'. That's August.

The plug is plugged in the early springtime and the warm tap
is turned on. Gradually, day after day, week after week, month after
month, the city becomes filled with summer until, on a mathe-
maticallycalculable day in August, when almost no one is home,
it floods. It's not that it's only a bit warmer than the day before,
the same as when a bath overflows, you can't say that it's only
a bit fuller than before. The city suddenly becomes white with
heat in August. And when the inhabitants return from holiday in
September and rush to turn off the tap and pull out the plug, it
takes another couple of months to mop up all that summer.

The August heat is aqueous. And I'm not referring to the sweat
that pours from your forehead when you feel the urge to raise

a slow hand to mop your forehead. Although it's related to that. The water from the sea evaporates and has nowhere to go. Right behind the city, there are mountains. In other places in the world, you're grilled or roasted at such high temperatures. Here you're steam cooked in the hot vapors. From the mountains it looks like there's mist hanging over the city. But in the city itself the sun shimmers. The mist is the air we breathe. In the city, this goes by the fairy-tale name of *macaia*, a word that can only be whispered, otherwise they'll reach in through your open windows while you sleep and choke you with their soft hands. If the Genoese, who always complain about everything, complain about one thing more than anything else, it's these clammy days and nights of suffocation that paralyze even your thoughts. *Macaia* is made up of the sighs of the Genoese.

The August heat is liquid. You stretch out in it like in a steam bath and immerse yourself in it. You swim through the city's alleys. The heat is tangible. It streams between your fingers and over your skin as you drift on her slow waves. It takes three times as long to reach nearby destinations in the deserted city flooded with summer, such as the *latteria* on the corner, if it's even open. Perhaps it's better not to even try to find out.

I feel like a fish in water in the deserted, liquid city of August. While everyone who can afford it has fled to the coast or to the mountains, I try to survive in this shimmering post-apocalyptic playground, along with the rats and a few similarly minded. Nearly all the attractions are closed. We, the group of survivors, show solidarity and exchange information that could save each other's lives, like the addresses of tobacconists that are still open. There's nothing to do, but doing something has never been my strong point—it has never been my burning ambition. To be honest, I consider it a rather overrated concept, that whole palaver. And the paralyzing heat is the ideal excuse to dismiss every kind of plan in advance without anyone thinking to criticize you for it. And so I swim small laps in the alleyways, smiling, using minimal physical effort. I don't need to go to the sea to swim.

2.

I'd already sent the previous letter when I realized I'd forgotten to tell you something important. Something that will interest you. Let's not be coy.

Let me put it this way. When everyone's at the beach, parading around in only their bikinis in front of overheated, thirsty eyes that try to melt away the little fabric in the way (even my style is becoming lewder and exhibitionistickier, if that's a word, perhaps you noticed; I'll have to smooth it all into the correct, Calvinistic form when I rework these notes into a novel, but in the meantime I'm enjoying the freedom to speak the truth, to you at least, in overheated terms, the naked truth, we might say, if you'll permit me this lame pun, but all of this between parentheses), then the people left in the city try even harder. So as not to look left out. To make it look like a conscious decision to be in the city in this weather. I guess you don't understand that. But what I mean is this:

I'm sitting there innocently eating my lunch on the terrace of Capitan Baliano. On my own, newspaper in hand, a picture of innocence. It's August. Boiling hot. Somehow this young man is sitting in the middle of the catwalk. The fashion this summer? As little as possible. There's a financial crisis, right? Economize on fabric. But between us men, they take it to extremes. Just because they're not on the beach doesn't mean they have to wear clothes. In fact, they're wearing even fewer clothes than on the beach because they want to make it clear we don't have to pity them for not being on the beach.

Today. Four long, brown, bare legs in some kind of shorts too small to cover pubic hair that would be freshly budding if it weren't epilated. On top: the suspicion of a vest in which juvenile breasts watchfully wait their chance. Copper thighs as thin as my wrists clasping a roaring scooter. Girls wearing just four things: a drop of Chanel, two high heels, and a fluttering summer dress. A small earthquake would be enough to make them come on the spot. I only have to stick out a finger to find myself in something wet that groans, while at the adjacent table the last transparent nothings are taken off with a sigh because it's so fucking hot.

I'm exaggerating a little. I'm acting out my fantasies. Let's call it an exercise in style. But the fact I'm exaggerating doesn't mean that what I'm saying is untrue.

And don't blame me for only being able to talk about one thing since I moved to Italy. That's just like the joke about the student who is so sexually frustrated they send him to a shrink. He does a test. He draws a square and asks the student what he sees in it. "A square room full of naked women." Then he draws a triangle. "A triangular room full of naked women." Then a circle. "A round room full of naked women." "I'm terribly sorry," the shrink says, "but you really are horribly sexually frustrated." "Talk about the

pot calling the kettle black with all those filthy drawings of yours!"
And that's what it's like. That's exactly what it's like. I'm doomed
to live in a city where half-naked nymphs parade past me like doe
in a wildlife park, and you blame me for being frustrated? That
comparison with the joke isn't entirely accurate, but it is like that.

But in a different way, you do have a point. When I rework
these notes into a novel, I'll need to pay attention to the balance—
you're much more aware of that than I am. On the one hand,
I need a large dose of southern sensuality, partly to do justice to
my fantasies, and partly to do justice to the clichéd image that
readers in my home country have of Italy. Clichéd expectations
deserve to be frustrated, but it would be a pity to go that way
on this subject. On the other hand, I shouldn't let this reach an
orgiastic mess, though many of my readers would have no objec-
tions to that. It has to have a minimum of thematic relevancy,
let me put it that way. But I've already thought of something for
that. One of the main themes will have to be that the various
characters, including the first-person narrator, disappear into the
fantasy of a new, better life in various ways, like tourists getting
lost in the labyrinth of the alleyways. By giving my own fantasies
free rein, or if necessary exaggerating them, I'm underpinning
this theme. It would be nice if something else could be added. If
the self-conscious machismo of the first-person narrator in such
passages could stand in contrast to something else, for example,
the increasing effeminacy of another character, leading to his ruin-
ation. I haven't met a character like that yet. Perhaps I'll have to
make him up.

3.

There was a TV crew on the piazza this evening.

Back home, I've had plenty to do with them, I don't need to tell you that. There's always the interviewer who has left everything to the last minute and thinks his lack of preparation gives him the right to insult you. He brings a cameraman with an enormous camera. His status comes from the size and weight of the camera. He sighs before he's even over your doorstep. This is related to having had to lug his enormous camera up all those stairs. And he blames me personally for that. His gaze accuses me of having got it into my head to live so far up and having made my home only accessible by way of a medieval torture device called a stairwell, while, given my status, I should have known that camera teams would be constantly coming to visit. Cameramen are always fat too. It doesn't help. And while they are still sighing on the stairs, they start to complain in advance because what they finally encounter on the top floor after their long journey up the stairs doesn't meet their high artistic and professional standards in any way. The light is wrong. They'd seen that when they parked in front of this goddamn building you took it into your head to live in. And given the shitty light, the arrangement of your furniture is downright catastrophic. They start to drag around your sofa, your dining table, and your bookcases, still panting from the stairs, without even taking off their jackets. "Would you like some coffee perhaps?" you try. The interviewer does fancy a coffee but doesn't dare say so because the cameraman has made it quite clear in both word and deed that he wants to get this over with as soon as possible because such horrific amateurism hinders his work, and, anyway, he should have picked a different career. The final interview is usually conducted in shy whispers under the evil eye of a person who had this pegged as hopeless in advance and whose every unfortunate hunch is confirmed on a daily basis. Why does no one ever listen to him? His bosses at the station, oh, the station. If only he were a freelancer, he'd be better off. There'd be none of this bullshit for a start.

An Italian camera crew has a different makeup. The cameraman is a shy working student who gets down on his hands and knees and thanks God for every small job he gets; he's had to buy his own equipment, which he has scraped together over the years with the help of a friend who gave him discounts on outdated models and a competitor who wanted rid of all of his stuff for too much money because he could afford better now. The Italian cameraman is an invisible slave who would descend, panting, into the deepest underground vaults to do his utter best to film something in the impenetrable darkness, all while muttering his humble apologies.

The team is completed by at least three female editors. They walk around with factsheets and storyboards. It's what gives them their importance and the fact that no one sticks to them afterward doesn't matter. But the true star of the team is the interviewer. She is a priori Famous with a capital F. Even when no one knows her, she's Famous. Because she acts that way. When, after a lot of fuss, everyone's finally ready for the interview, she's disappeared without a trace. She's in the bathroom putting on lipstick and waxing her bikini line. She's had the broadcasting company pay for her plastic Barbie legs and the surgically pointed breasts under her lacy blouse.

When she interviews someone, the interviewee is rarely in the shot. All the cameramen in the country know the rules. And although the questions she asks may sometimes seem naive, everyone knows that the point of the questions is her divine smile when she poses them.

The camera team that unexpectedly made its appearance on the Piazza delle Erbe this evening was only from local TV. You could tell from the stickers. But they ticked all the boxes. The bright red interviewer who was almost as tall as I and, at the most, a quarter of my weight, asked random people on random terraces of random bars questions about their experiences of this or that. I sat quietly writing at my table on Caffè Letterario's terrace; I observed it all from a distance and I have to say, my good friend, that I was amazed they didn't ask me anything. Not disappointed but amazed. That was alright by me, I didn't need them to pay attention to me, but let's face it: a camera crew chancing upon me in the wild and then not immediately pouncing on me, is a bit... let's say, strange. It might sound somewhat arrogant, but that's not how I mean it. I know you understand what I'm trying to say.

And you're right, of course. This is exactly the reason I decided to leave my home country and domicile myself in the labyrinth in all anonymity. Rather than forcing myself to conform to an invented image that media pressure and my celebrity kept forcing upon me in a caricatured way, here in Genoa I've re-earned the freedom to be and become who I am. In my home country, I'm Ilja who knows about the composition of a camera crew; here in the labyrinth, I'm Leonardo, who has taken leave to get lost in his imagination without that immediately having to be coupled with a witty justification in one of the national talk shows. That's the way I wanted it, you're completely right. But then actually being passed over by a camera crew from local television, however desirable that might be, is still an unsettling experience.

This brings me to another matter. I received your money order. Many thanks again for that. It makes me feel good to know that there's someone left back home who understands that temporary financial problems can be solved elegantly. My self-sought loss of status in foreign climes comes with certain material repercussions in the short term. I'm no longer available for commercials and I no longer give readings. And that was exactly enough and I'm grateful for your understanding. You're a true friend.

And something else: I've just learned from my accountant how much the tax authorities in the fatherland want from me despite all the things I did for my former fatherland in the past. There isn't the slightest chance I can meet their obligation. But I don't want to bother you with that.

4.

There are women who go somewhere and sit down, and there are others who make an appearance. This second type can be divided into two categories, too. There are those who make a haughty appearance a chic hour and a half late to splice the world with a glance, and there are those who approach with an expansive display of power and forcefully request with a false smile the place she deserves. Film stars and duchesses, that would be an easy way of summing up the dichotomy. The difference between knock-knees and awe, hope and fear, wet dreams and nightmares. What they have in common is that they are goddesses in the depths of their minds and that every man believes in her because she believes in herself. Whenever she makes her appearance, people stand up spluttering excuses to give her the most comfortable seat, which she'll sit down in with such stunning matter-of-factness without thinking for a second to thank the person who made the sacrifice for her or even deigning to look at him, thereby reducing him to the worm he is while giving the rest of the company ample time to gape at her.

Since the beginning of the summer, there has been a blonde woman who makes an appearance as a duchess almost every day on the terrace of Caffè Letterario on Piazza delle Erbe. Just as Her Majesty's arrival in former times was announced by a chorus of trumpets, her appearance is preceded by her barking lapdog, which isn't on a leash and which runs along ahead of her barking hysterically because it has learned by now that Caffè Letterario's terrace is a place where they serve aperitif snacks that little dogs can cajole for themselves if they look cute enough, or, if that doesn't work, tenaciously make it clear with irritating barking that the only way to shut them up is with a tasty morsel. She follows along at an appropriate distance. She has long, blonde, frizzy curls that stand out quite noticeably among this Mediterranean constellation and wraps herself as a rule in long, loose garments. She's of an indeterminate age above sixty. She walks just a little too slowly, as though suffering from physical discomfort, and along with this, the smile she bestows on everyone who stares at her is a little too forced, as though to show that she's a brave, strong woman who won't be daunted by physical discomfort. But both the painfully slow walk and the fake smile she tries to mask are put-on. She is consummate phoniness. Although there's nothing wrong with her, she plays the role of someone who is smiling bravely to show there's nothing wrong with her.

When she finally reaches the terrace and the dog is jumping up at her barking enthusiastically, her gaze grows fixed. There are actually a few tables free but they don't come up to her strict requirements. As everyone in her duchy ought to know, she drinks dry martini cocktails, and these are served in low wide glasses with a stem and filled up to the brim. That's why it would be impossible for her to sit down at a sloping table. That almost every table on the slightly sloping medieval cobblestones of Piazza delle Erbe is sloping is no excuse in her eyes. And as she stands there in a posture that radiates head-shaking incomprehension at the shocking lack of class awareness in her subjects, one of the waitresses comes running outside to set up a new table especially, while uttering exhaustive apologies. "Thank you, waitress," she says without looking at her, before draping herself over her chair with a sigh.

Her whole attitude doesn't suggest that she has come to Piazza delle Erbe to merely enjoy drinking dry martini cocktails—she is granting an audience. Sitting there the whole evening drinking while her lapdog barks incessantly is a favor she bestows on the people out of kindness and generosity. When no one appears to lap up her wisdom, which sometimes happens for unknown reasons, she reaches for her mobile phone to provide random victims from her almost endless list of contacts with unrequested hours of good advice. She adopts a pained smile when confronted with so much ignorance at the other end of the line and is visibly impressed with herself for not losing her patience while she generously explains for the nth time how the world works, if you look at it objectively. She understands every imaginable topic: politics and spirituality, men and dogs, gastronomy and health, astrology and ethics, interior decorating and exorcism, psychology and the weather—and when anyone else offers a different opinion on these subjects she considers it a waste of her precious time. Worse still, it's a failure to appreciate the inexhaustible well of knowledge she delves into and, in fact, nothing less than an insult to the generosity with which she imparts it to those lucky individuals, but she'll hide her disappointment at so much ungratefulness behind a fake smile that actually means she's hiding her disappointment at so much ungratefulness. She'll never ask a question because she knows all the answers, even to the questions we've never asked ourselves. If it had been up to her, she could have solved everyone else's problems before they even happened. Her thankless vocation is to explain everything, to just keep on explaining everything over and over again to the deaf ears of the blind populace because she is, as we ought to know, a good person.

And as soon as anyone sits down at her table, the true source of her wisdom is revealed. It's her voluminous handbag, along with other objects that she lugs around with her each day that mark her out as a woman of the world, prepared for anything—like a glue gun, mace, a spare wig, a roll of barbed wire, a goldfish bowl, underwear in all sizes, an angle grinder, and a spirit level. And what she fishes out of the bottom of her bag are the Major Arcana.

For a dry martini cocktail or five euros in cash, she'll read your cards. In Italian they are called *tarocchi*—elsewhere, tarot. She has a large pack of cards with the most traditional illustrations and they are well used, anyone can see that from a few feet away. And the people who make use of her services aren't all superstitious old women, who are beyond rescue in any case. A remarkable number of uncertain young women turn up at her table. For them, five euros or the equivalent in martini is a serious amount of money. She shakes her old, wise head of frizzy blonde curls as they drink in her every word, shaking with nerves in the hope of catching a glimmer of good news about their future, or, if that's not possible, an ambiguous phrase that might also be interpreted positively with a bit of good will. Unfortunately, the cards leave no room for doubt. All character failings are visible and mistakes made in the past will be avenged and hope is an expression of naïveté or ignorance. And she can see in the cards that a young man will soon announce himself, but there isn't anything good to be expected from him, either. The witch smiles apologetically. The girl has to understand that she, unlike the many charlatans, doesn't beat about the bush. She tells them what the cards say, even when the message is tough. This is proof of her goodness. The girl goes up to the register, salty tears on her cheeks, to pay for one cocktail. She had hoped for better news, but still, she's grateful. Now at least she knows the truth. And that's worth more than wishful thinking. Isn't it?

I've observed it many times and constantly ask myself why the paying clientele have to be so brutally disappointed. What kind of peculiar take on customer relations is that? The witch sits there with the cards in front of her making everything up, so why not make up something nice, I'd say. Then at least they'd come back. But I've realized that that was a naive thought. People go to her with problems. Her job is to take those problems seriously, to emphasize them and magnify them. Everything is much worse than you thought. That's true customer relations. If she said that it wasn't really all that bad, you'd go home whistling and wouldn't return because the problem would be gone. If, on the other hand, she said with a concerned smile that she was sorry to have to admit that all your concerns were justified and that the situation was even a little worse than you thought, you'd come back a week later with your worsened problems and quiver nervously as you ask whether the cards have something a little more favorable to say now. She'd shake her wise, old head with a smile. Of course she could pretend. But she's not like that. She's a good person. She'll always tell you the truth. And the truth is lying on the table before her. Unfortunately, the cards never lie.

The witch has a name. She's called Fulvia. I hate her. But that was perhaps clear by now.

5.

I went to the theater yesterday. The play wasn't very interesting. It consisted of a succession of three short monologues from the perspectives of three different people who had fled the poverty of early nineteenth-century Italy and emigrated to La Merica, as they consistently called the Promised Land on the other side of the Atlantic. The texts were based on authentic letters and diary extracts. It was interesting material, and the artistic goal of holding up a mirror from the past to the current immigration problems was certainly legitimate, but the construction of three monologues was much too static and the piece devoid of any kind of dramatic tension.

I went because I'd been invited by the play's director, Walter, a very young man I met a few weeks ago in Zaccharia, the café next to the Mandragola, on the minuscule, well hidden square in front of the old Roman church of San Cosimo and San Damiano. The bar was frequented by all kinds of arty folks, mainly actors and actresses, and that was exactly why I didn't go there very often. Put a couple of dozen, in their eyes very talented and scandalously underappreciated, thespians in one room and before long the atmosphere will be somewhat fraught and hysterical. What's more, they all know I'm a writer and conveniently assume that I'm just as underappreciated as they are. Why else would I be in the Zaccharia? Right. That's the question I ask myself.

But Walter is a decent guy. At least he doesn't complain. He's a foreigner and that has something to do with it. Like me, he comes from the north. He is, if I remember correctly, half Danish and half French, born in Switzerland, and he's worked all over the place, mainly in England, Germany, and Spain. Thanks to his northern European background, he is characterized by a measure of sobriety and refreshing realism. Or you could say that the fact he lacks Italian genes deprives him of the talent to wallow melodramatically in typical Italian self-pity, deriving from a paradoxical mix of conceitedness and an inferiority complex. Instead of drowning his frustrations, bitterness, and anger at the disgusting, degenerate world in which there is apparently no place left for high art amid grimly nodding like-minded people, he does something about it. Instead of waiting next to his telephone with a perpetually gloomy expression for the big job that never comes, he organizes small performances with actors he's friendly with. Bits and pieces. An adaptation of Kafka short stories in the cellars of Bar Il Conte in exchange for free drinks; improvised cabaret in Anna's nightclub for a hundred euros a night; an outdoor performance on the square after which the prettiest actress goes around with a hat—that kind of thing. They aren't particularly impressive productions that will give a good gloss to his CV, but in any case he's doing something.

And so now it's that play with the three monologues about Italian emigration in a tiny theater on Piazza Cambiaso in the red light district close to Via della Maddalena. It wasn't his own idea, he was asked to stage it. And he was the first person to agree with me that it lacked dramatic development and was actually a complete failure as a play. He'd played around a bit with the letters and diary fragments the actors had given him, but he wasn't a writer, he admitted it outright. Maybe I'd be able to take a look at it? The material was indeed interesting, wasn't it? There had to be a lot more to be had from it? I nodded. Maybe.

But the play wasn't the main reason he'd invited me. It was the theater. He gave me a tour after the show. It was a modest but exquisite renaissance palazzo with marble columns and frescoes by a pupil of Michelangelo. It had recently been wonderfully restored. A majestic marble staircase led to the upstairs floor where there was a tastefully furnished bar and small restaurant. The hall with columns and Gothic vaults on the ground floor gave access to the theater. It was intimate, no more than a hundred seats. But it was ultramodern, completely decked out in the technical sense and maximally flexible with a completely collapsible stage, state-of-the-art audio equipment, and an arsenal of lights that many a technician from a big theater would find delectable. It was a polished pearl, a brilliant jewel, hidden in the deepest depths of the labyrinth.

"And do you know what the most remarkable thing is?" Walter said. "They hardly do anything with it. The current owners don't have a clue how to run a theater. They want to get rid of it. They've put it up for sale and already asked me if I might be interested. Of course I'm interested. It'd be a dream. But it's impossible for me to organize it all on my own. And that's why I thought of you, Ilja. How would you like to buy this theater with me?"

6.

I was honored that Walter clearly had that much faith in me, but of course I wasn't going to buy a theater. I'd never wanted to do that, so why would I suddenly want to do it now? Apart from that, I didn't have any money. So it was an easy decision.

I was charmed by the idea of doing something with the witness accounts of the great Italian emigration. Walter was right. It was fine material. And there was undoubtedly a lot more in the archives than these few letters and diary fragments he'd worked into his play. It had all happened a relatively short time ago. The two major emigration waves of Italians leaving for the United States or Latin America were at the end of the nineteenth and the beginning of the twentieth centuries. It was a movement of unprecedented scale, a true mass migration. I'd googled the figures and was shocked by them. The various sources I could quickly put my hands on were more or less in agreement that between 1860 and the beginning of the Second World War, a total of around twenty million Italians risked the crossing to the Promised Land on the other side of the Atlantic. Pause and let the magnitude of that sink in, my friend. Twenty million. That's almost a third of the current population of Italy. That's twenty-five percent more than the total population of my home country, infants and the elderly included. I know you can't use the figures like that because those twenty million Italians emigrated over a period of eighty years, but still, to get an idea of the gigantic dimensions; imagine if a third of the population moved somewhere else, or in the case of my home country, more than the total population. The entire country would be left empty. No one would live there anymore. Everyone gone to America. And then us in Europe worrying when a few hundred Senegalese get washed up on Lampedusa.

What's more, I began to realize that the story of the mass Italian emigration was enormously connected to this city. The Genoese and other inhabitants of Liguria were pretty much the pioneers. They were overrepresented in the first wave of emigration. Their favorite destination on the paradisiacal continent La Merica was the mysterious Land of Silver. They settled in large numbers in a district of Buenos Aires they called Boca, after their beloved fishing port, Boccadasse, which by now has been swallowed up by the city and is part of the Genoa Sturla area, but has lost none of its idyllic pull. Supporters of Boca Juniors, one of the big famous football clubs from that part of Buenos Aires, still called themselves "Zeneisi"—Genoese in Genoa dialect. The famous song

"*Ma se ghe pensu,*" the nostalgia-drenched anthem of all Italian emigrants, is sung in Genoese dialect. The story goes that the Genoese immigrants in Buenos Aires invented jeans. That's why they are called jeans—a bastardization of the word "Zeneise." I'd heard that story before and naturally I'd never believed it, but it seems it's true. I've found various reliable sources that confirm this.

But later, too, when the Genoese were less inclined to leave and when the emigrants from other parts of Italy arrived, their story remained linked to this city. Almost two thirds of all Italian emigrants set sail from Genoa for the journey of their lives, the passage from poverty to the promise of a new and better existence. Each day, thousands of desperate people waited on the quaysides at this city's port for a chance to board one of the large ocean steamers that were called passenger ships but more closely resembled freight ships with human cargo. The stench and the sanitary conditions in third class were notorious. Concerned physicians wrote alarming articles about it at the time. Passengers contracted terrible illnesses during the weeks-long crossing. Many didn't survive it.

And for all those thousands on the quays, it was the ultimate dream to gain access to this hell in the belief that the hellish journey would culminate in the paradise called La Merica. They stood, sat, and lay down here to wait, sometimes for days on end. Farmers, artisans, beggars, rogues. Their few paltry belongings with them. They spent the nights on their duffel bags or simply on the ground among the rats. Some of them could afford a place in one of the long, underground dormitories or in an attic without light or fresh air. They were hungry. They'd been hungry all their lives anyway, but here at the Port of Genoa the prices for even the simplest foods reached astronomical heights due to the enormous demand. The Genoese are good but they are not crazy. If you have that many hungry, poor wretches lying on your streets, of course you're going to ask a pretty price for your bread. You have to feed yourself at the end of the day. *A Zena a prende ma a non rende*, as the old saying goes. Genoa takes and gives nothing for free.

They arrived in the new world, destitute and broken, where they had to fight for their lives afresh against the gangsters, Mafiosi, slumlords, brothel keepers, high and lowlifes who were waiting to take advantage of them again with a big smile on their lips. The official website of the research institute for Italian emigration to both Americas emphasizes that the Italian emigrant was character-ized by pride in his fatherland and an unwavering belief in human progress based on work and a strong awareness of civilian virtues and religious piety. It's actually there in black and white. This is comparable with the things I've sometimes heard right-wing Italian politicians say: the Italian emigrants went in order to work, while the African rabble flooding Europe have only come to steal. And then to think that the research institute is financed by the province, which since time immemorial has been in left-wing hands, you can just imagine.

I feel more and more like spending time in the archives excavating letters and diaries that reveal how things actually were, which not one Italian institute would dare put on its website. I don't know if it's going to result in a new play, like Walter wants, but perhaps it might, who knows, why not? In any case the material could be useful when I rework these notes I'm regularly sending you into a novel in which immigration and emigration need to be the major themes.

7.

Yet Walter's proposition kept bugging me. I mean, of course it was too ridiculous for words. As an ambition, it was a long way from anything I'd ever envisioned for myself and was, in practical terms, completely unrealistic. Where was I supposed to find the money to buy a theater? My financial situation in general wasn't rosy and at the moment it might even be called dire. And Walter didn't have any hidden reserves, either; I didn't even have to ask him to be very certain of that. I'd paid for his beer in Zaccharia.

But Walter was a professional optimist and he told me not to look at it all that way. Money wasn't the problem. We'd find a solution for that. "It's a rare opportunity, Ilja. Have you seen how that theater's outfitted? I've worked in big theaters in Germany, England, and Spain that had less than half the resources. You have to imagine all the things we could do there, you and me, with our different backgrounds and talents. We'd quickly become the most talked about theater in Genoa—we'd make sure of that, right?" He slapped my shoulder with a broad grin.

"And yet we can't completely ignore the question of the money, Walter."

"No, of course not. But you don't understand a thing. We'll actually make money from it. I figured that all out long ago. Otherwise I never would have gotten you involved. It's a goldmine. Just think. Open seven days a week, and everything's possible: not just plays, but music, cabaret, jazz, cinema, you name it. And at the end of the night, away with the chairs and the stage and BOOM—dance parties with the best DJs! And all that time the restaurant will stay open. Not to mention the bar. Ha! We'll cover the acquisition costs one way or another. If necessary we'll borrow. It's only a temporary investment. We'll have it paid back within half a year. And then we'll be talking. We're going to be rich, Ilja, you and me, in this fantastic place, with our talents."

"Or we'll find someone to invest on our behalf."

"Or we'll find someone. Exactly. We just need to put together a good business plan. Anyone with a bit of sense in their heads will see immediately that with the right artistic management, this could be a gigantic success. So you're in? Let's agree on this. Let's in any case go and talk to the owners and see what they are actually asking for it. Then we'll see. Alright? I have to go now. Can you pay for my beer? I'll talk to you later."

I had my doubts about the guaranteed riches that would rain down on us as soon as we had the keys to the joint, but I had to admit that I didn't entirely disagree with Walter. There was potential for a successful commercial operation. I could see that. It would be hard work, certainly at the beginning. But as soon as we'd built up a name, we'd grow automatically as long as we continued to deliver quality. I could use my connections back home. I counted among my friends some of the most excellent actors, musicians, and composers in Europe. I'd worked with them. That would be possible here too. They'd be happy to come to Genoa. And Walter had a wealth of international contacts. We'd be able to exploit that fact and our international orientation would make us stand out from the other theaters in the city.

I had to admit that the idea of having a source of income here in my new fatherland, especially over the long term, wasn't unattractive, certainly in light of my precarious financial situation. And there was another matter. Working here would mean putting down roots. Instead of just staying here, living off pen, paper, and my imagination, which in principle would be possible in any other place in the world, I'd have a role and a mission that were directly connected to this city. The idea pleased me. I was also receptive to the thought of being able to give something back to the city that I had so much to thank for. Of meaning something to the one who meant so much to me. And apart from that, there was another thought that I tried to suppress but that kept raising its head—I'd be a theater director. The idea alone appealed to my vanity. They'd be impressed by that back home. And all those failed thesps in Zaccharia would finally take me seriously.

Later that day I ran into Cinzia. We had an aperitif in the Bar of Mirrors. I asked her whether she knew the theater. She shook her head. There you go, I thought, the current owners are charlatans. People don't even know the theater exists. We'd be sure to be much better at that. I described the place at length and told Cinzia about our plans. She listened attentively. I also said that all of this information was highly confidential, obviously; I don't know why, but it sounded kind of professional. She nodded. She wouldn't say a single word to anybody.

"The only thing that worries me is the investment. I'm hesitant to get into debt for this."

"What you need," Cinzia said, "is a rich mistress."

I found that hilarious. But she wasn't laughing.

8.

The theater was closed. We rang the bell. No answer. We looked through the window. It was dark inside. Our appointment was at three, wasn't it? It was already a quarter past. We rang again. Nobody. The door was padlocked on the outside, so there was no way there was anyone inside. We waited. In the meantime, Walter tried to telephone to confirm that our appointment was at three o'clock. No one picked up. We decided to wait a bit longer. And just as we were about to give up and leave, he showed up. It was almost four.

"Where did you get to? I was inside. I've been waiting for you for an hour. Did you ring the bell? Then I didn't hear it. No, and my telephone doesn't have any signal inside. I was just about to leave in fact. But fine. I'm glad I finally found you."

"But how did you get in?" Walter asked. "The door's padlocked. When we saw that, we stopped ringing the bell."

"That's why? But I went in through the back entrance."

"There's a back entrance? I had no idea. Can we see it?"

"Another time. Come."

His name was Pierluigi Parodi. He was one of the two owners, and rather young for a theater director—somewhere in his late twenties, I guessed. He was a textbook case of what they call a *fighetto* in Italian—someone who acts the handsome young man and is the first to believe he's a handsome young man. He had clearly spent much of his life in front of the bathroom window. Blow-drying such a studiously nonchalant coiffure and trimming that ostensibly unkempt goatee would take hours. He wore expensive designer clothes and box-fresh sneakers, and naturally he had Ray Bans perched on top of his head. He was a poor little rich kid and went to no trouble to hide it. His manner of speech and his gestures also betrayed the mentality of a person who considered himself privileged and superior because everything always landed on his lap. He was terribly smug.

"Shall we sit down outside here? It's hot."

"It's cooler inside," Pierluigi said. "And we don't want the neighbors eavesdropping. You're too trusting, you foreigners. Lesson one in doing business in Italy—what you don't know doesn't hurt you. The fewer ears that hear, the fewer eyes that see, the more chance of earning money. So. Now you know that. Nothing is free, but Pierluigi is giving you this important lesson for absolutely nothing." He laughed.

We went upstairs to the bar. He turned on the coffee machine and made three espressos. He placed a large heavy marble ashtray on the table, got a wooden box out from behind the bar, and offered us cigars. He took one himself, sat down at the head of the table, leaned back, and looked at us with a smile.

"It's actually very straightforward," he said. "The asking price is two forty. Half of that can be paid in installments—we'd have to figure out interest, of course. But that's a simple sum. And then we'd have to talk about the takeover costs for the furnishings and fittings: the lights, the sound system, furniture, restaurant crockery and cutlery, kitchen equipment, coffee machine, ice machine, terrace heating, that kind of thing. We'd have to make an inventory of all that, at the end, then you'd decide what you wanted to take and you'd make an offer. We can come to an arrangement. Well?"

"Two forty?"

"Two hundred and forty thousand euros. I can't go any lower than that, I'm sorry. That's an absolute rock-bottom price. Just think. Do you know what an apartment around here costs? You don't know because you're foreigners. But I'll tell you because I'm honest. You'll pay three times that for just a hole in the wall. And what we have here is a blooming, profitable theater with catering facilities. Don't ask me to lower the price. We're friends. Don't embarrass me."

"Why do you want to sell it, Pierluigi?"

"I'm sitting pretty, here. I don't want to sell it at all. I mean, I'm not in a hurry. It's a personal favor. I like you two. I trust you. You want a theater, and I happen to have one. In any case, I wanted to venture out and expand my business. Import and export. I have an extensive network abroad. Do you know that the greater part of what Italy produces goes abroad? You didn't know because you're not Italians. But those are the facts. And you have to know the facts in Italy if you want to do business."

The situation seemed clear to me. As Pierluigi had correctly stated, it was all about the facts. And the most important fact was that I didn't see a single way that I could cough up the asking price, not even in installments, and let's not even mention the additional costs. The adventure ended there as far as I was concerned. But because we hadn't finished the cigars, I decided to ask something else, out of curiosity. "Pierlugi," I began, "could you perhaps give us an indication of the monthly costs?"

He made a dismissive gesture. "That's a stupid question," he said. "Electricity is the only expense. Because of the lights. But that's up to you. I've always been able to keep it to a minimum. I mean, a bit less light in a play only makes it more atmospheric. I can show you the bills. Gas and water are normal. And apart from that the rent is extremely low."

"The council rent?"

"Less than seven hundred a month. A pittance. That's their form of cultural subsidy."

"But why should you pay rent on a building you own?"

"You're foreigners. But let me explain. That's the way it works in Italy. There's a nine-year license. But you don't have to worry about that, it'll be extended automatically."

"But the building is officially owned by the council?"

"That's not the way you should look at it."

"How then?"

"Two twenty. I can't go any lower than that."

9.

We held a crisis meeting in La Lepre, a hip, successful bar just a stone's throw from the theater. The bar was named after the minuscule square in front of it where there was enough room for an intimate terrace. It is one of the best-hidden oases in one of the darkest parts of the labyrinth, between the church of Santa Maria delle Vigne and Via della Maddalena. Not long after I'd arrived in Genoa, I happened upon it one evening. Although I'd actively tried to find the square, I couldn't find it again for a month, when I chanced upon it for a second time.

Walter knew the owners, or in any case, one of them—Raimondo, an energetic young manager who had made it into a success in a short space of time, together with his companion. Since Walter knew him, we were given a discount. And later in the evening, it might be interesting to exchange thoughts with him, if the opportunity arose. In terms of the catering industry, he'd be our neighbor, after all. There might be a possibility to work together in some way. Everything was about the right connections, at the end of the day—that much we'd learned, even if was just through the discount on our drinks bill.

We sat outside on the terrace. Suddenly all hell broke loose. I mean, we all know more or less what it sounds like when a glass breaks on the floor. The sound is more spectacular than the actual damage. Sometimes a full tray goes crashing down. People can talk about that for days. This sounded many times worse.

We got to our feet to see what was going on. Two fellows were smashing the whole damn bar to smithereens. The table next to the entrance was in splinters. Meanwhile, they were using bar stools to hack away at the mirrored wall behind the bar in front of which all the bottles were arranged. Within a minute they had reduced La Lepre to debris. Raimondo and his companion were nowhere to be seen. The other guests fled through the door. And in the meantime, the young men continued their mission with destructive efficiency. Not a single person took it upon themselves to intervene. This was too serious. This wasn't a picturesque Italian row that had gotten out of hand. These were two professionals at work who knew exactly what they were doing. The situation was downright threatening. Walter and I made a quick getaway too.

We went to Gloglo on Piazza Lavagna to recover from the shock. We told Samir, Gloglo's Iranian owner, what we'd just seen.

He nodded. He went inside and came back with three grappas. "On the house," he said. "To recover." He sat down at our table, picked up the third glass, and raised it. "Do you know what?" he said, "Those two boys want too much. Raimondo and that other one. What's he called again? I mean, don't get me wrong. They're fantastic barmen with phenomenal dedication and in a short time they've really made something of the place. It's full almost every evening. Their turnover is excellent. Better than us. Ha-ha! But that's not the point. Cheers!"

He got up to help another couple of customers who'd just arrived. When he returned to our table, he'd brought another three glasses. "And then to think..." he said. "Yes, cheers. Here's to you. And then to think that just a couple of years ago it was a stink hole. Really. Scum went there. And the word 'scum' means quite something in this neighborhood. If you call someone here in the Maddelena scum, you have to—how can I say it?" Samir laughed. "Anyhow. You get my point. But that's exactly those two boys' problem. What's the other one called again? One's called Raimondo. But anyway." He took a sip of his grappa. "You know the toilets in La Lepre? With those big steel doors? Major dealing used to go on there. They had enough of it and cleaned up the place. But this is the payback. Unfortunately, that's how things work in this city."

"But what do you mean, Samir?" Walter asked. "It was Mafia revenge?"

Samir held his index finger to his lips. "That word doesn't exist," he said. "I mean, they exist, but the word doesn't. You have to have very powerful friends to be able to say that word, make sure you remember that." He stared ahead pensively. His voice changed. He began to speak slowly and softly. "This city is a porcelain grotto," he said, "a labyrinth of interests. And if you have any interests yourself, you soon find yourself clashing with others' interests. And then it's the law of the jungle. It's been like that for centuries and it will always be like that. The statutory powers—the police, the judges, the politicians—are nothing more or less than individuals with their own interests who arm themselves with penal codes and truncheons before joining the power struggle. They aren't above taking sides—they're partisan. And that's why you can't get anything done in this city without the right allies. And even with the right allies, you don't get anything done. Change is by definition a threat to other people's business. It's in everyone's interest for things to stay the same. Well, I don't want to discourage you. But that's how it is. I have to go now. The drinks are all covered, alright. Reflect on it."

Samir walked off. Walter and I stayed sitting there for a while. We didn't speak. We thought about what Samir had said. Neither of us wanted to come across as naive by being amazed at his words. We pretended to each other that what he said wasn't new and that we'd known for ages that it worked like that here. And in a certain sense, that was true. But I was genuinely shocked. Genoa had always seemed like a civilized northern Italian city to me. Well, civilized might be the wrong word. But in any case, northern. The Mafia were part of the south. But of course Samir was right. Although, it still remained to be seen. What did that Iranian know?

Walter nudged me. "See them?" Two boys walked into the pizzeria I Calabresi opposite Gloglo. It was them. These were the boys who had just smashed La Lepre to smithereens. "What should we do?" Walter asked. "I know. I'll call the pizzeria and tell them what those two just did." He looked up the number on his smartphone and called. He told his story, but the answer, which I couldn't hear, made him look gloomy.

"What did they say?"

Walter gave me a meaningful look. "They said, 'But those two are our friends.'"

"And so?"

"And so, nothing."

"They're not calling the police?"

"I know what I'll do," Walter said. "I'll call Raimondo. I have his mobile number."

Raimondo picked up. Walter told him that the boys were in I Calabresi at the moment. Raimondo said something. "You're welcome, you're welcome," Walter replied. He hung up.

"And?"

"Do you know what he said?" Walter asked. "He said, 'Thanks. But if they're friends of the Calabresis, we won't report it.'"

10.

One of my favorite television programs back in my home country used to be called, if I remember correctly, *A Place in the Sun*. Do you know it? I think what I saw was a Dutch version of a BBC show of which they'd made several foreign rip-offs. It was a simple formula. Over the course of a number of weekly episodes, you followed a number of northern Europeans, usually couples, who had one dream in their life, and that dream was to start over in the balmy south. What they all had in common was that they'd had enough of the mist and drizzle and all that other dreariness and they were actually going to do something about it. They decided to up and set off in search of a house in Italy, Spain, Portugal, Greece, or some other Mediterranean paradise with palm trees and perma-blue skies. A discreet camera crew would be set up there and do nothing other than regularly turn up for months on end to cold-bloodedly register how their quest for light and warmth was coming along and how they slowly but surely were getting lost in their fantasy of a new and better life in the sun.

Naturally it was nearly always about people of a certain age, who after a long and difficult but relatively successful life as company advisor, interior designer, or environmentalist had saved up enough to seriously think about a modest, dilapidated, but oh-so-idyllic farm in the Algarve, on Mykonos, or in Tuscany.

The camera crew was there when, after having driven around the region they wanted to rediscover their lost youth in, they were introduced to a reliable local real estate agent, a respectable man who, unlike all the other men in the area, had the decency to dress in a suit and tie despite the heat, and who, thank God, also appeared to speak reasonably good English. He had, as he said himself, a reputation to maintain, particularly among foreigners, whom he'd always been able to accommodate perfectly because he understood the way they thought and what they wanted. And he told a couple of horror stories about the malpractices of the men who, to his embarrassment, shared the same profession and who, ultimately, were only in it for financial gain, although he was sorry he had to say that.

Unfortunately, that was how things worked in Italy, Spain, Portugal, or wherever they were. But at the same time it was such a beautiful country, he stressed. And he congratulated the northern Europeans for having found him. Because he was different. He loved his country. And as they whizzed along in his four-wheel drive to the first idyllic heap of rubble that he'd selected for them to visit with all his knowledge of human nature, they were already sold. In the back seat of the car they congratulated each other in their mother tongue for having had so much luck and having found the right real estate agent. Someone they could trust at least. Someone who spoke English. They should count their lucky stars.

A week later we see the same couple again. The third ruin they visited is possibly their favorite. Alright, it didn't have a roof. And all in all, there weren't really any walls. But they'd always fancied rebuilding to completely fit their own taste, with Ligurian slate and marble from Carrara. And just look at that view. Yes, they dare say this in front of the camera—it was the place of their dreams. They'd fallen in love. They dared to say that out loud for the first time, too. Wasn't this a lovely start to a new life? Let's face it. The asking price of three hundred thou' was a little over their budget, but you might never get a chance like this again. As their friend the real estate agent had said, "You only live once." As far as they were concerned that was spot on.

Meanwhile, they showed footage of them sitting in their terraced house in the drizzly north, doing sums at the kitchen table. Whichever way they add things up, three hundred thousand is still too much. And then you have the building costs on top. He tells her it would be an irresponsible move. She tells him he's doing the sums wrong because he also has to add on her own ceramics studio and factor in that she can sell to the local inhabitants. And they'll turn the scullery with the large terrace into a trattoria. Their friend the real estate agent told them last time that there was nothing at all for miles and miles in that region. So there's a gap in the market for a trattoria, certainly in combination with her studio. You'll be able to serve your own local dishes on self-designed, self-fired plates. "And of course my designs will be totally inspired by the local surroundings. Did you see the look on the real estate agent's face when I said that? Run through the numbers again, love, we're talking about our dreams here. I mean, love, look out of the window. It's raining. It's been raining for weeks. It's been raining all our lives. It's now or never. We've been talking about it for so long, you know that."

In the next episode we've moved on a few months. The trucks full of Ligurian slate are arriving. But it's a different kind than they ordered. The man and the woman say in individual in-depth interviews that they consider this a personal failure. They'd made clear arrangements and now everything is going to have to be re-delivered. This means a delay of a fortnight, maybe even a month. And what are they going to do about the limestone ornaments? They're supposed to be arriving in two weeks. Are they going to have to put them in storage somewhere? They can't afford that. They couldn't afford any delays, either. This had already cost much more than they'd ever intended. The trattoria had to open this summer. But if it carried on like this, they wouldn't be ready until after the peak season.

And when the bill arrives for the wrong slate that was delivered, the shit hits the fan. Of course they're not paying it. But there seems to be some kind of clause in the contract that makes them obliged, according to national laws, which have to do with recently changed legislation concerning the use of certain registered sustainable materials, to pay for the wrongly delivered slate. Their hands are in their hair. The friend, the real estate agent, hasn't been answering the phone for days. The trucks with marble from Carrara are expected tomorrow. But there's also been a potential miscommunication there because, unlike they'd agreed, the delivery date hasn't been confirmed by telephone, and it's so damn difficult to make arrangements in this fucking country where no one speaks a goddamn word of English.

Next there are problems with the sewerage permit, but they can't read the local regulations. And while the neighbor claims right of way across their idyllic terrace, there's a reassessment of the property taxes. There's also a problem with the permit for the water pipes. They'd chosen the cheapest option but hadn't realized that the more expensive company had a certain edge in the region, by ill-gotten means. The mayor of the village refuses to understand their problem. They suspect he's being paid by the more expensive company. They live for months with designer copper taps that they had shipped from France but that don't work. The opening of the trattoria has to be put back by a year as a result. They will go on to win their court case, but it will take months. Their attorney is talking years. But that would mean even higher legal costs than they'd already feared.

The only thing missing is for the two of them to fall out. This is covered in detail in the final episode. We see him back in his drizzle-drenched house in the north. Unpaid bills lie on the kitchen table in front of him. As he talks about everything that has happened, his eyes fill with tears. She is still there. She fiddles forlornly with a stunted vine. She uses her skinny sandaled foot to spin her pottery wheel. She doesn't have any contact with the locals. The trattoria never opened. "He was scared and backed out," she says. "And now he's refusing to pay even my maintenance allowance. How am I supposed to survive? From my pots? He has to be kidding."

II.

There are two kinds of women: those who are just there, and others who make a grand entrance. And the second kind can also be divided into two categories: those who set foot on the terrace to conquer it, and those who haughtily beg to be conquered. She fell into this last category.

She was unbelievable. I sat there gawking at her, open-mouthed, my friend, I swear, and I swear I wasn't the only one. It was outside the Bar of Mirrors. At first I didn't notice much around me; I was beetling away at these notes that I send you with some regularity to keep you up to date on my trials and tribulations in my new home country. It's a ritual I've become highly attached to because even intense experiences stick better in the mind when you share them with a dear friend. I can only be grateful to you for that.

But she was unbelievable. Or did I already say that? She gave flamboyancy a bad name. She was tall, almost taller than I, had long dark hair, hot pants, and legs, that added together would, amount to several meters. She was sitting on her own at a table, smoking strong cigarettes and drinking cocktails. And she was old. Certainly over fifty. And that meant something. Anyone dressing so shamelessly at that age had done so deliberately. She was up for anything. She reeked of availability. She was suffused with desperation between her thighs. And squeezed under her elegant silk designer blouse were the two biggest tits you or I have ever seen. I'm not kidding. Footballs. It was almost vulgar. It was more than vulgar. And she smiled along so innocently, like a schoolgirl. But she was fifty. At least. Fifty-five was also a possibility.

I drank my Negroni at another table and cast salacious looks at her from time to time. When she looked back, I pretended to be busy writing this letter to you. And when I looked again, she looked away haughtily. And when she nevertheless had another look, I described her haughtily.

But that's how things often go. I'd never be telling you this story if there weren't a sequel. You know that. You know me. Brace yourself.

A few days later I saw her again at the Bar of Mirrors. She was in the company of the signora, what's her name again, the signora from Part One who explained to me that appearances don't matter in Genoa and that it was regrettable that women in these parts had traditionally ruled the roost. What's her name again? Franca. Exactly. Thank you. Franca Mancinelli. I hadn't seen her for ages. I greeted her. She invited me to sit with them and introduced me.

Her name turned out to be Monia. A strange, unusual name I didn't understand at first because I'd never heard it before. Maybe I'd even made it up. Since she looked like someone who had invented herself, the name suited her well. Out of admiration, I introduced myself as Ilja rather than Leonardo, which induced some confusion in the signora. Monia smiled.

While they continued their conversation, I could observe both of them close up under the pretext of being interested in the topic of conversation. It was fascinating to realize that, objectively seen, both of them were approximately the same age but had totally different ideas about it. The signora was wearing a long white linen dress, too, but that was only because it was August and unbearably hot. She looked well-groomed and elegant, no one could take offense at her, but the dress didn't suit her one bit. She had the body of a potato. But the time she worried about such trivialities was decades behind her. She was an authentic potato. She was the ideal granny. She would never forget a birthday and would always find an appropriate, original, and sensible gift. She was direct in speech, didn't mince her words, and in her carefree, uninhibited way of formulating things, she was sometimes very amusing.

Monia happened to be wearing a long white linen dress too, but the cut was so elegantly and exaggeratedly simple that it was clear it must have been so elegantly and exaggeratedly simply designed by someone with a name, and that it had probably cost a fortune. It fell perfectly over her scandalous body. A nonchalant slit displayed the long arabesque of her climbable legs. She kept herself nipped in with memories of her perfect figure. And her décolleté was downright criminal. You could see from the wrinkles on her breasts that they were real, although many a porn actress would furiously call the plastic surgeon at the sight of her.

She had a very unusual way of talking. She formulated her

sentences with exaggerated care, like someone who was trying too hard to hide the fact that she were drunk. That was probably the case. She tried to sip her cocktails chicly, but sometimes she forgot and accidentally downed her glass in one gulp, after which she ordered a new one, not forgetting all the forms of politeness Italian is so rich in. And all this time she kept her eyes as wide open as possible, as though she wanted to insinuate a facelift.

"Ilja Leonardo," she said, "I have always wanted to meet a famous poet. And this, itself already invaluable, privilege comes at not an inopportune moment for me, as tomorrow I have the great pleasure of having been invited to a simple dinner by two acquaintances whose lifestyle is characterized by a fervent interest in art and poetry. Consequently it would be rather felicitous to find myself in a position of being able to boost my dubious reputation by making a good impression with an artistic dining companion."

She got up and wandered haughtily into the labyrinth with the exaggerated firm tread of a person trying to hide her drunkenness. The signora shook her head. Though I thought I had a dinner date, I wasn't a hundred percent sure of it.

12.

Monia's friends lived right next to Palazzo Spinola. It's one of those places where old and new Genoa overlap in an improbable manner. Centuries ago, this was one of the most aristocratic neighborhoods of the city, where noble ladies lay sighing under high ceilings, hoping feverishly that Genoa might finally lose a war and that the invasion of brutal soldiers with bayonets and barbaric passions would arrive. Some of them are still lying there behind their exquisite paneling. Some of them still sigh in the shimmering heat of the midday hour that brings old spirits back to life. Meanwhile, the neighborhood has been flooded with Moroccan scum, whores, and human traffickers. But history melts away in the heat. What was still the future five centuries ago is now the memory of yesterday's dreams. Everything has changed but nothing has changed. The sharks and fallen women of yesteryear are still here. The streets sweat. The age-old walls drip with damp. High heels click on the cobblestones. Rats dart away. The night groans.

Monia's friends were almost irritatingly civilized. We were received in the drawing room, where we were invited to sit on antique furniture that was so conspicuously antique that you didn't dare settle your full weight on it. Fortunately, we were expected to stand up again almost immediately to admire the collection of paintings. This was an examination. I was lucky enough to recognize a Flemish master. I was rewarded with a minuscule aperitif of something pricelessly exclusive. Once we'd savored that, we were directed to the dining room, where there were more paintings to admire, as well as the table silver. I felt more and more uncomfortable, as though I were trapped in a porcelain grotto. But Monia seemed to feel at home in this environment, even though she gave the impression during the starters of trying to hide the fact that she was well on her way to being drunk. I seemed to be the only one who noticed.

"My friend Ilja Leonardo is a poet," Monia said.

"What kinds of things does he write, then?" the lady of the house asked.

"Poems," Monia said.

The main course was Ligurian-style rabbit with potatoes and olives. An exclusive red wine was served with it. And I had reached my limit with the whole show. Controverting all the rules of etiquette, I grabbed the bottle of red from the table to top off my glass. It meant I'd never be invited here again, but all the better. Unfortunately, it had the opposite effect. They enjoyed my uncouth behavior. I was probably the first person in five centuries to break the iron laws of courtesy in their house. I was a poet, wasn't I? I'd nicely proved it with this sudden act. Laughing, they put six bottles on the table. Monia seemed even more delighted about this than I was.

And gradually the mood changed, but in a way that made me feel increasingly uneasy. The conversation became unmistakably less formal and soon reached a level that almost made me miss the earlier formalities. The word "libertine" occurred to me, and that's not a word that ever occurs to me. Because let's face it, what does that word mean to us—seasoned modern perverts that we are, grunting pigs wallowing voluptuously in the filth of a degenerate world. "Libertine" is to us what "naughty" is to a spent streetwalker. But I was in a different world than the one you and I feel at home in. Here the decline of morals was a traditional and pre-planned part of a successful soiree. And that was why there was an unsettling charge to it.

The lady of the house began to turn more and more emphatically toward her husband even before the dessert, whereby Monia and I automatically became a kind of couple. I didn't know how to handle the situation. After dessert we were invited to partake of a digestif in the study. It was a room that had been closed up to that point and which turned out to house a wonderful collection of pornography. Rare nineteenth-century picture books, antique figurines of Priapus, a Greek vase with a representation of a symposium, and an impressive collection of stereoscopic photographs and viewers. The lady of the house went to slip into something more comfortable for the digestif. She came back wearing exquisite lingerie.

Monia involuntarily saved the day. She was so drunk by now that denial was pointless. She took off her shoes with a lot of wiggling, fell over, but landed by chance, more or less, on the chaise lounge, upon which she immediately fell asleep. When the lady of the house shook her awake, she grabbed one of her pumps, groaning, and began to vomit into it. This was a signal to me that it was time to leave.

But that was a whole song and dance, too. Although I was prepared to take to my heels in a scandalously cowardly fashion, I still had just enough decency left to realize that I was expected to take Monia home. I managed, with the help of the gentleman of the house, to get both her empty shoe as well as her puked-in shoe onto her fishnetted feet. We hoisted her upright and pushed her into the lift. In the meantime, I said my goodbyes to the lady and gentleman of the house. "Well," they said, "we'll be seeing a lot more of each other."

13.

And the worst was yet to come. Because now we were standing on the street. I asked Monia where she lived. She didn't answer. I asked her again. She looked at me with large, staring eyes. Then it occurred to me that she could no longer remember her own address. She fell over. I helped her get up again. Moroccan gang members had noticed us and began to take an interest. We had to get out of here. I slapped Monia in the face. "Where do you live?" She opened her eyes even wider. "That way," she said. Alright, that way. I gave her a shove and she ricocheted through the narrow alleyways like a pinball. In any case, we were on our way. In any case, we'd gotten away.

At last it turned out she lived in Via Chiabrera, just next to Piazza San Lorenzo. All things considered, as the crow flies, from Palazzo Spinola to there, if you know the way—and I most certainly do know the way—the easiest way, Via San Luca to Piazza Banchi and then Via Canneto Il Curto and then up a bit along Via San Lorenzo and then turn right about halfway, all things considered, at a casual walking speed, it's five minutes at the most. It took us two hours. When things were going well, she walked four paces ahead of me with one clacking and one squelching shoe, and when things weren't going well, I had to scrape her off the gray pavement over and over again.

But when we finally reached her front door, we weren't home free yet. She said she lived on the top floor, that there was no lift, and handed me her keys. The moment for me to say my polite farewells hadn't yet arrived. She clearly wouldn't have stood a chance on all those marble stairs without me. I had to support her, watch out for stumbles, and sometimes actually carry her.

And all that time, I was filled with strange, evil thoughts. It had frequently occurred to me how easy it would be to rob her. She seemed rich. She dressed rich. She trusted me at least in so much as she had been entrusted to me. No one would ever know. She couldn't even remember her own address, let alone be capable of telling the police the next day who had brought her home. Of course I didn't rob her, but the idea was exciting.

It was long way up. After I'd unlocked the front door with her keys, we encountered another three cast-iron portcullises. I wondered whether they were intended to keep thieves out or her inside and prevent her from disgracing herself in the city.

When we finally got inside, she began to French kiss me frantically. I tasted the sour flavor of her vomit. She collapsed onto her bed. "Undress me, Ilja Leonardo. I can't undress myself. I'm too in love with you to undress myself. Or maybe I'm not. Hang on." She hiccupped. She began to screech with laughter. Then she began to cry. And all of a sudden she seemed wide awake. She stared at me, eyes wide open. "I want you," she said. She swallowed something. "I want you to fuck me like a dirty, filthy, stinking whore because I am a dirty, filthy, stinking whore." And before I could thank her for her hospitality, she said, "Shove your fat, filthy cock between my tits. I beg you, I beg you, let me be your whore, please." She began to cry again. And then she began to laugh again. She tugged at my fly so violently, I had to open it myself. "Fuck me," she said. This was easier said than done. "I'm a filthy, dirty, stinking, smelly whore," she said. Well, with all due respect, that was the problem. "Spread your legs," I said to gain time. Groaning, she spread her legs. It looked so disgusting my dick shriveled. To conceal my discomfort, I began to lick her. That was a mistake. She tasted of sour piss and rotting fish. I almost threw up. But she screamed with pleasure. She sounded as erotic as a burglar alarm. When I was at the point of vomiting, I jerked off as quickly as

I could over her enormous tits. Before she'd finished trying to lick it off, I had my clothes back on. "Ilja Leonardo," she called, "I want all your cocks between all my tits and in all my asses and cunts forevermore. Come back!"

I threw up on the street. The fishmonger's was already open.

14.

But I may have found an investor.

"Then she'll guarantee a hundred," Walter said. "And she can pay off the other half in installments if she wants. With two hundred we're in because I reckon Pierluigi's hopeless. If we want to open after the summer, we have to act now. Then we'll open with your new play about Italian emigrants. With her money, we can make it really spectacular, with a real ship's forecastle on the stage. I saw something like that in Heidelberg once. With real water, too. There's some kind of chemical salt solution. Then it really smells of the sea. And we'll invite your musicians and put them on a raft. And we'll have it sink in the final scene, not really of course, but you can suggest that really well with smoke machines, together with those special lights you have sunk into the stage. Alright, it'll cost a bit, mainly because you have to make everything waterproof. But I know a technician in Madrid who is specializes in that. We'll fly him in. I could give him a call. I'll call him right away."

"Walter."

"Alright. I know, I'm getting ahead of myself. But that's just my enthusiasm talking. It's how I've always managed to get things done. But you're right. Let's do some realistic math. How much has she promised you?"

"She wasn't in any state to say anything, let alone promise anything."

"But you said she's rich. That's the point. If you just do your work and keep on ploughing and spraying that fertile vegetable plot…"

"Don't talk like that, Walter."

"Why not?"

"I don't like it."

"Just keep on digging away at it, you know, and in a month we'll be raising the curtains on our first premiere."

"Maybe we should talk to the council first, Walter."

"Why?"

"Because I've got the impression that Pierluigi is trying to sell us something that doesn't belong to him."

"Of course he is. I'm not stupid, Ilja. We're in Italy. But we'll pay with her money, won't we? What's her name again? Nadia?"

"Monia."

"What difference does it make? Everyone screws everyone else here. How long have you been here? I've been here long enough to know more than you that everyone here screws everyone else. Are you really that naive, or are you trying to weasel your way out of it? Be honest with me. I have to know. Either I can go further with you or I can't. Either we get a theater or we don't. Say the word. Our friendship won't be affected. Yes or no?"

"I'm not trying to weasel my way out of anything, Walter."

"See."

15.

Monia kept calling me. She also sent text messages the whole time with all kinds of suggestive X's. When I returned her calls, she invited me to the opera. I had to go out shopping with her first, though. She insisted on it. She said it ten times. I had to dress properly for the opera. She'd do that, too, but she couldn't show her face with a person dressed like some old bumpkin from the Low Countries, naturally I'd understand that. Even my summer suit, which I'd bought right in all my recklessness after arriving in Genoa when I was still under the illusion that I had money, was too casual for the opera and certainly too shabby for the company of a women who over-dressed flamboyantly even to just drink an aperitif in a bar. And it was a great opportunity to obtain a really handsome Italian suit at her expense. I'd been wanting one for a long time.

It was a boiling hot day. She took me to a chic shop on Via XX Settembre. She consulted the shop assistant. I could hardly understand a lick of the details they were discussing. Finally they chose something together from the rack. It was a stunning Mafia suit with wide lapels that could also be worn as a tuxedo. I had to try that on. It was important to get an idea of whether it would suit me. I didn't have to worry about the exact fit. Everything would be properly fitted later, of course.

Monia came into the cubicle with me. This was quite normal, apparently. The shop assistant didn't bat an eyelid or blush. "Cubicle" is actually quite a modest description. It was a spacious changing room with tasteful, dark red carpet and a sofa upholstered in the same colored velvet. There was a large, antique mirror with a gilt frame. Monia sat down on the sofa and looked at me. It was a rather strange moment. Now I was supposed to get undressed in front of her. OK, whatever, I'd just have to do it. I made a game of it, acting as though I was a woman doing a striptease. I accompanied it with a sensual dance. I teased her with my tits and my ass in the big mirror. She smiled. And then I stood there before her in my underpants with a nice big "ta-da."

She stood up and handed me the jacket. Then she changed her mind. She put the jacket back on the hanger and the hanger on a hook. She copied my dance and slowly unbuttoned her blouse. It wasn't quite what I'd intended. "Monia," I said, "your life lesson should be that everything will turn out alright as long as you don't do what I do." She had to laugh. She clicked open her bra behind her back.

"Do you need to try on something too?"

"Look at me."

Of course I'd already seen her tits. But at the time it was all late and dark and drunken. Now I saw them in real life, in daylight in a changing room on Via XX Settembre. They were scandalous. Enormous tits like that are immoral. Or at the least, you'd have to pay a fortune in tax for them. And apart from that, I didn't think it was such a good idea to be studying them in the changing room of a chic menswear store.

"Wait," she said. "Don't move." She wasn't concerned with her tits but with her bra. She very slowly and attentively put it on me.

"Now you're a proper pretty girl at last. Dance for me." As she said this, she took my cock out of my underpants. "Look at yourself in the mirror," she said. "You're the most beautiful girl in Genoa. I'd like to comb your hair." She worked my penis. "You could be as pretty as a doll. Look in the mirror. I want you to come for me. It's alright, I have a tab here. Or am I not doing it right? Let me bite your nipples. Let me play with your stiff, hard cunt. I know you get a lot more turned on by young girls with little titties than by me. Admit it. Admit that you're thinking of someone else right now. A girl like that waitress who used to work at the Bar of Mirrors. Say it. Tell the truth. Look at yourself in the mirror. You're wearing my bra, you slut. It's much too big for your little titties. Look at yourself. Your titties are as small as hers. You look like her. You are her. Watch me fingering her for you until she comes." And as she came for me, I came at the same time as she in the mirror.

Monia licked her fingers. All of a sudden she was all decent and dressed again. She stood there fiddling with my lapel. I was very hot. She grunted in approval. "We'll make a man of you, Leonardo, a real Italian man. Just leave that to me."

I was still confused when I got to the register. The August heat was making me feel dizzy. "Leonardo's a poet," Monia said. "And he's a friend of mine. Give him a good price." Ten percent was taken off and the amount rounded down. I had to pay twelve hundred euros. But the amount wouldn't really sink in until an hour later. Monia was walking haughtily out of the shop ahead of me. I gave the shop assistant a kind of apologetic nod.

"It wouldn't be the first time," he said quietly.

16.

What the hell? I was furious the next day. I'd been hoodwinked into buying a suit for twelve hundred euros, about as much as your money order, while the whole idea was that her credit card was supposed to be on the ebony counter, not mine. Investment, you say. Let's fucking hope so.

"But are you sure…" Walter asked.

"Yes."

"I mean, do you know how much money that is? She's investing that in us then, in our project."

"I think I was the one paying, Walter."

"But you have to learn to think like the Genoese. She let you spend that much which means she owes us now. More important than that—it's a sign that she trusts us and that she'll certainly want to invest more in us in the future."

"With my credit card?"

"That's not the point."

"What is the point, then?"

"It's about the network. Everything in this city revolves around knowing the right people. That's how we need to think, Ilja. If we still want to get our theater off the ground this summer, we have to think like that. And you know it."

I nodded, although I didn't agree with him. I nodded because I had made a decision. I was going to get my revenge. I was going to take revenge on Monia. I was going to do everything I could to extort from her the fortune we needed to take over the theater. I nodded grimly.

"What are you thinking about?"

"Alessandro De Santis."

"Is he that actor?"

"No. He was on the *Andrea Doria*. He boarded the 24th of May, 1894, and on June 25th, he arrived at Ellis Island, the newly opened immigration center for New York. He'd contracted whooping cough on board, but he still managed to be admitted, mainly because during the journey he'd learned a booklet by heart containing the best answers to give to the authorities in English. He'd never seen any authorities before and never heard any English. He was a farmer's son, born in a village in Piemonte. What did he know? He knew nothing."

"What's this got to do with Monia?"

"I'll come to that. Listen. Just imagine it. Alessandro arrives in New York. He had no other possessions than the things his family could do without—a woolen blanket, a chicken, which he ate during the crossing, a photo of his mother, and a letter with the address of a distant cousin who'd emigrated years earlier."

"What was she called?"

"That doesn't matter. Elena. She was called Elena."

"And then?"

"Alessandro couldn't find any work, even though they'd promised him that he'd automatically get rich if he managed to reach La Merica and be admitted. But he didn't look for his distant cousin. He didn't want any help. He was an Italian. He had his dignity. He finally got a job as a day laborer on the railways. He and a large group of other Italians were put to work building a new track outside the city. It was incredibly demanding and dangerous work, paid a pittance, and the foremen didn't like foreigners. They were treated like scum. They were sworn at, spat on, and hit. One day a railway sleeper fell on his foot. He could no longer walk. He was fired.

"After that he had various little jobs around the city as a newspaper seller, garbage man, road worker, and warehouse assistant. None of it added up to much. He could barely survive. The worst thing was that he was ashamed. His mother back in Italy was under the impression that her son was a rich, successful man by now in the Promised Land, where everyone got rich and successful without even trying. He sent the small amounts of money he could do without to her so as not to spoil the fairy tale. But he never wrote to her. He couldn't bring himself to tell the truth and write that sometimes he had to resort to stealing to stay alive, but neither could he bring himself to lie to her."

"Did you make this all up?"

"No. Listen."

"I'm convinced you made this all up."

"I went to the archives, Walter."

"Carry on."

"Years went by in this way. And one day the news reached Alessandro that his mother was dying. He had to go back to Italy. He wanted to go back. He wanted nothing more than to be with her. He hoped he'd be in time. But he didn't want to disappoint his mother on her deathbed. He wanted her to die with the dream that her son had become a rich, successful man in New York.

"He decided to set aside his pride and ask for help. There was nothing else to do. He managed to trace his distant cousin."

"Elena."

"Elena, yes. And he borrowed a large sum of money from her. Part of it was for the crossing and with the rest he bought the most beautiful, expensive, chicest suit he could find.

"He was just in time. His mother was incredibly ill and weak but she was still alive. She was overjoyed to see him. And she was overjoyed to see him looking so good. 'I've missed you terribly all these years,' she said in a weak voice, tears in her eyes. 'But my one consolation has been knowing that you've become rich and successful. You wrote so nicely about your new life. Thank you for writing faithfully every week to tell me about it. Since you left, your letters have been the most important thing in my life. Thank you.' With a happy smile on her face, she breathed her last breath."

"His father."

"Yes. It turned out that his father had been writing letters every week on his behalf and making up excuses to go into the city every week to post them."

"And then?"

"That's where the story ends."

"You did make it up, didn't you?"

"Yes. But knowing that it was true."

"You're right. I'm sure it happened like that. It must have happened like that at least once, even though he might not have been called Alessandro. I think I saw a film once with almost the same story, only it wasn't about an Italian in New York but a different kind of immigrant."

"It still happens. People still lose their way in their dreams. And people still do everything they can to keep the fairy tale alive."

"But it's a wonderful story. We'll definitely have to use it in our play. But better still would be if we could work in the story of Monia and your suit in some kind of way. That would give a nice contrast. The upscale immigrant, the expat who buys an expensive suit so he can go to the opera with his rich, older mistress…"

"And the poor sod who gets himself into debt trying to make his mother happy with a dream. And then to think that whole business with the opera suit was only to make our own dreams come true of getting a theater in which we can put on the play about the painful contrast."

"Self-referential theater."

"Yep. We're sure to make a splash."

17.

But it didn't sit well with me, that whole story about the nine-year license and paying rent to the council—and of course it didn't sit well. I decided to investigate. I could go to City Hall and simply ask for the relevant documents, couldn't I? If it was a matter of a license and rental, it meant it was a public case and therefore the contract necessarily had to be public. And if it wasn't, it was something else and then we were a bit further. But Pierluigi himself had said this was the situation, so those documents were probably available.

Genoa's City Hall is a charming palazzo halfway along Via Garibaldi, opposite Vico del Duca. It has prominent neighbors, like museums and the fancy head offices of foreign banks. Via Garibaldi, which used to be called Strada Nuova, is the jewel in Genoa's crown, built to astonish and amaze—a milestone in classical architecture. Rubens walked around making sketches of it. Many Genoese who live outside of the center perceive that street as the edge of the abyss. They dare venture this far and no farther into the labyrinth. The side alleys lead straight into the jungle in their eyes, a place where, within a hundred meters, you'll fall prey to prostitutes, pimps, and knife fighters. And it's not even totally untrue. Incidentally, our future theater was positioned right there in the jungle where no decent Genoese dared to go. That was something else to consider, I realized. But I would concern myself with that later.

I went and stood at the counter in City Hall. But that wasn't the way it worked. I was given to understand that I had to take a numbered ticket and wait my turn. I apologized. I hadn't noticed the ticket machine. I took number 814. I looked at the display. The number at that moment was 409. I waited to see how quickly the line moved. There was only one window open and after fifteen minutes, number 409 was still involved in a number of very special and particularly time-consuming transactions. Number 410 took about a quarter of an hour, too. I began to add up. In any case, I had plenty of time to go outside and smoke a cigarette in the street and come up with a plan.

As I stood outside smoking, a tramp spoke to me. I tried to ignore him. But he was persistent. "Thank you," I said. He reached into his trouser pocket and pulled out a small piece of paper. Number 430. "Ten euros," he said. I decided to pay him. "And your number?" he asked. "Swap." I gave him number 814. "That'll be the day after tomorrow," he said. "If we're lucky. Give me an extra five euros and we'll stay friends."

Two hours later, it was my turn. I explained why I'd come. Although my Italian was quite good by now, I had to explain my request three times in different ways and even then she didn't understand me. On my insistence, on my firm insistence, as number 431 behind me began to break out in a rash, she fetched her manager. I explained it all once again. He asked for my ID. I was prepared for that. I laid my passport on the counter with a triumphant gesture. He picked it up as though it was a rare incunabulum and began to study it at length. He shook his head.

"The information you are requesting is unfortunately not authorized."

"You mean that you're not authorized to give me the requested information."

"You said it."

"So what now?"

He shrugged and turned to walk away.

"Come back, you bastard!" Behind me, number 431 held his breath. It was starting to get interesting. "I'm a citizen of the European Union and I know my rights. Allow me access to the documents I want to see or I'll drag you to the Strasbourg courts."

That made an impression. He humbly retraced his steps. He fished a document out of a drawer and stamped it with great pomposity. He handed it to me.

"What is this?"

"You are hereby authorized to present your request to the other office."

"Which other office?"

"Matitone."

"And that's where they keep the documentation?"

He smiled apologetically. "I've done my best, sir. I've done more for you than is actually allowed. Thank you. Perhaps I could be of further service with a lottery scratch card?" With a compassionate smile that expressed sympathy for my quest, he withdrew to the recesses of his splendid palace.

18.

"*Matitone*" means "giant pencil." And that's what it looks like. A hexagonal block of flats with a pointed roof. The council's pride and joy. Built by the mayor's wife's construction company. But tendered completely transparently and according to the rules, of course. Taller than the famous lighthouse. A new landmark for the modern city. Genoa doing credit to its age-old nickname— La Superba. A skyscraper in the old port. Visible clear across the city. The term "visual pollution" had never had such a golden ring to it. And because there wasn't a single company that wanted to have its offices there, the council moved in themselves. You're either a mayor or you aren't. You do things for the people. You do things for your friends.

I have to say, it's the perfect auxiliary branch to City Hall because it's high and inaccessible. It's Kafka's castle. It is visible everywhere, but just try getting there. In theory it should take an hour to walk there from the center, but were it not for the two motorways you have to cross. You can also try the Metro to Dinegro, but there are rumors about people never coming back.

By now I knew how it worked. I smoked a cigarette outside

and waited patiently until a tramp came to sell me a ticket number. I knew the price. I was prepared to pay fifteen euros. But nobody came. After half an hour, I decided just to go inside. I reported to the counter to ask where I could get a number. The receptionist said it wasn't possible. I asked whether that meant it was my turn. He said it wasn't that simple and I needed special authorization. I said I had that. He shook his head. Practically no one had special authorization. And what's more, it was the lunch break. If I'd come half an hour earlier he might have been able to help me.

"But then I'll come after lunch."

He sighed.

"What time…?"

"Half past three."

In my home country, I only had to give the sign and an alderman would call me back. And in such cases, someone higher up would usually offer help, too. And after that the mayor or the minister would call just to make sure that everything had been satisfactorily settled and to make sure I wasn't going to write a caustic item in the paper about it.

Here, it was with the greatest difficulty that I got to speak to a counter clerk. When I returned at three thirty, there was somebody else there. He refused to look up. I coughed. No reaction. I coughed importantly. He looked up. I produced my stamped document from City Hall on Via Garibaldi. He gave it a fleeting glance and then turned with admirable concentration to a very important, undoubtedly urgent, serious receptionist's task that he had to carry out on his computer. I hit the counter as hard as I could with the flat of my hand. It made even me jump. It clearly happened fairly often during his responsibility-infused workdays. "If you'd like me to call security," he sighed without looking up from his screen, "then I can be of service to you in the blink of an eye."

"If I were you…" I began. I had to bluff my way through this. "If I were you, I'd at least have the courtesy to hear me out before I call someone. I'm a friend of Fulvia's."

It had popped out before I realized. I don't know how I'd come up with it. But he reacted as though he'd been stung by a wasp. "Fulvia Granelli?" he asked.

"Granelli Fulvia," I confirmed.

"My apologies, I thought you were a foreigner. Might I see that document again? And what have you come for if I might ask? Alright, alright, I understand. This is highly irregular. Fourteenth floor. You can take the lift at the end of the corridor on the right."

I was met by a friendly older woman who introduced herself as the secretary to the alderman's personal assistant. I was already beginning to climb the ladder. But the more she began to understand of the reason I was there, the unhappier she looked.

"But it would be impossible for me to give you that information," she said with a pained look on her face which seemed to express genuine disappointment at the fact she couldn't be of service to me.

"Why not?"

"Because it doesn't exist."

"But if you say it's a matter of information you can't give me, that means the information does exist."

"That might be so, but I can't give it to you."

"Why not?"

"I just told you. Because it doesn't exist."

"How can it be possible for something to exist and not to exist simultaneously?"

"In Italy it's very possible."

"Everything exists in as much as it's possible with the right contacts, and nothing exists in so far as nothing is possible without the right contacts."

"You said it. I can neither confirm it nor deny it."

"The Parodis."

"They're a powerful clan in Genoa. They've meant a lot to this city. Could I give you some advice?"

"Advice that does or doesn't exist?"

"Then I won't."

"I understand what you want to say, but I'm not giving up. I want that information that doesn't exist. Where should I go?"

"You could try the City Hall?" she said hopelessly.

"On Via Garibaldi?"

"Yes, City Hall."

"Will I have to get a ticket again?"

"I can reserve a low number for you." The relief in her voice was audible. "I can do that for you. I'd be happy to do that. Thank you. Might I be of further service to you with a scratch card perhaps?"

19.

The heat was relentless. The sun hung above the city like a vibrating copper gong. Its sound still echoed deafeningly along the alleyways. Salty sweat dripped from the gray walls. The pavement sighed under each sporadic sighing footstep. It was about to burst open.

The pus from the swamp under the stones was searching for egress. The stench could already be smelled. Drunken Moroccans hung about on the street corners. It was too hot to mug anyone. Senegalese squatted in the shade of their run-down, overpopulated palazzi. It was too hot to pursue their war against the Moroccans. The sighing of all those afflicted hung like a clammy mist over the dark alleyways. This was the *macaia*, roaming the city like a ghost made of wet bed sheets.

It was, to cut to the chase, much too hot to wear a suit. When I'd put it on at home in front of the mirror, I'd been happy with it. It suited me, in as much as any clothes suit me. But once I was outside amid the half-naked tourists and copper girls in fluttering little nothings, it felt like a ridiculously over-the-top Mardi Gras costume in which I'd sweat to death, like someone wearing a lion suit on the beach, hopping around among the beachgoers for some ridiculous ad.

I'd arranged to meet Monia for an aperitif in the Bar of Mirrors. She wasn't there yet. No doubt she wanted to make sure she arrived later than I so that she could make a grand entrance in her evening gown. And that's what she did. And how. She came swirling around the corner in a gigantic bright yellow confection with a train and a wide, tall collar that fanned out behind her head, and which was so low-cut at the front that there was hardly anything of her scandalous breasts left to the imagination. I was really shocked when I saw her. It was all a bit too—which word should I use for it?—ostentatious. Yes, we were going to the opera and people were expected to dress up. But that doesn't mean to say you should dress as though you were going on stage to perform the role of the Empress-whore of Babylon in the extravagant costume design of a director famous for his provocations. How could I in all decency show my face with a person like that? In my much-too-hot and much-too-expensive Mafia suit? The prospect was mortifying. What's more, I noticed that she wasn't entirely steady on her legs. But that might be due to the exorbitant high heels she was wearing.

She sat down at my table and ordered a Negroni. "Are you going to a masquerade ball?" the waitress asked. She could hardly control her giggles. Monia considered it all totally normal. She explained patiently that we were going to the opera and that her good friend Leonardo the poet was gallant enough to accompany her. I blushed, but luckily it wasn't very noticeable as my face was already bright red from the heat.

I decided to strike while the iron was hot. I brought up the theater. I explained the situation at length to her. I described what it looked like and how wonderfully equipped it was. I gave her an in-depth account of the artistic and commercial potential. I dropped the words "exceptional opportunity" several times. I told her about our chat with Pierluigi Parodi and my attempts to shine a light on the agreement with the council. I asked her what she thought of all this. She gazed at me wide-eyed. But that didn't mean anything. It was the way she always looked.

"But what do you think, Monia?"

It was as though she hadn't heard the question. She continued to look at me, smiling. Then she downed her Negroni in one gulp. "Can I have a kiss?" she asked. "You're so sexy when you talk about business." She leaned forward. Her tits rolled out of her décolleté onto the table. I gave her a quick peck on the mouth. She tried to worm her tongue into my mouth, but I didn't let that happen.

"But to start with," I said to distract her. "To start with, we have to find a way to get access to the contract with the council." She ordered another Negroni. "But I don't have the right contacts. That's logical. I haven't been here for long. Do you know a way of getting that information?"

"That's not a problem," she said. I was incredibly relieved that she responded to my question rather than continuing her attempts to rape me in public. "My good friend Alfonso has excellent contacts at City Hall. Alfonso Gioia. I think he knows the alderman personally. I'll give him a call. If you'll give me another kiss. But now a real one."

Her tongue churned around in my mouth like a wet piece of cloth in the drum of a washing machine. I felt like a prostitute letting herself be penetrated for business reasons. Out of the corner of my eye, I saw the waitress avert her gaze in embarrassment.

"We have to go," she said. "If you pay for the aperitif and buy the tickets at the theater, I'll treat you to dinner. I've reserved a table at my favorite restaurant for us afterward. Chichibio, it's called. In Via Chiossone. Do you know who Chichibio is?"

"Yes."

"Is there anything you don't know?" she asked, laughing.

"I don't know."

20.

Chichibio is a character from one of the stories in Boccaccio's *Decameron*. It's befitting to name a restaurant after him because he was a cook. He worked at the royal court. In Boccaccio's version it's a bit different, but I'll tell you the story the way I heard it. When the king gave a festive banquet one day, Chichibio prepared an exquisite dish of roasted crane. But the king noticed that each bird that was served only had one leg. That old rogue Chichibio had kept a leg from each crane to sell himself. Cranes went for a good price in those days. The king summoned him.

"But your majesty," Chichibio said, "cranes only have one leg. I'm amazed you didn't know that."

"You're a liar, Chichibio."

"I swear I am telling the truth."

"Then tomorrow we are going to investigate. But I'm telling you now, your punishment won't be light if it turns out I'm right."

When they arrived at the lake the next day, all the cranes were standing on one leg. "See, your majesty, I was right. Cranes only have one leg." The king clapped his hands a few times. The flock flew up. It was clear to see that each bird had two legs.

"What do you say about that, Chichibio?"

"But your majesty, that doesn't count because last night you didn't clap for my dish."

Even during the short walk from the Bar of Mirrors to the Carlo Felice opera, this story gained an unexpected relevance. Monia was so unsteady she seemed to be walking on one leg. All things considered, she was blotto. I tried to support her and prop her up but it still went wrong on the incline of Salita Pollaiuoli. She tripped, tore the train of her dress, and broke the heel off her right shoe. Then she really did start walking on one leg, while the full weight of her limp, drunken body hung on my arm. We made a fine couple.

Her bright yellow torn and dirtied train flapped along after us like a rope with dented tin cans behind the car of a pair of newly-weds off on their honeymoon. Luckily, it wasn't far to the opera.

The tickets cost me an arm and a leg. And the aperitif with all her cocktails had already been quite pricey. But it was an investment, let's say. At some point I'd get it all back in duplicate or triplicate. At least that was the intention. To start with, I resolved to entail considerable costs at the restaurant that evening. I had never been to Chichibio in Via Chiossone but I'd walked past it on occasion and it looked sufficiently chic and expensive for me to rack up a hefty bill if I ordered enough.

During the overture it looked like she'd fallen asleep. That wasn't such a bad idea perhaps. As long as she didn't start snoring. But she didn't fall asleep. She kept staring with wide-open, rolling eyes. And all of a sudden she cried out something. It was at the beginning of the first act. I hadn't understood it but it had been loud. People in the rows in front of us turned around with irritated expressions. I laid my hand on her knee and gestured for her to be quiet. She laid her head on my shoulder. But a minute later she was suddenly bolt upright again. "Vegetarians!" she screamed. "You're all fucking vegetarians!" It was unclear to me what this conclusion was founded upon. Perhaps it had something to do with the first act taking place in the great outdoors and to emphasize this there being a variety of plastic plants and trees on stage. But whatever it was, it didn't seem like a good idea to me to start abusing the singers during an opera in a loud voice because of presumed eating habits. The people around us were in complete agreement with me. We were being given nasty looks. There was hissing.

I froze. She was simply blind drunk. The realization dawned upon me that I was sitting in the opera with a blind drunk older woman who was impossible to keep in check. Feverishly, I began to think of what to do. Luckily, she was quiet for the moment. But if she wanted to interrupt again with her shouting… And just as I was thinking that, she did. On impulse I pressed my hand to her mouth and wormed my other hand under her legs. I picked her up and began to carry her out. She wasn't heavy and thank God we were at the side and not right in the middle of a row. Nevertheless, I still had to carry her past a few other audience members, who stood up horrified from their seats to make space for me. The people in the row behind us began to applaud. I worked her out of the auditorium via a side door. I slapped her face. She collapsed onto a bench there. Then I noticed that she'd lost a shoe on the way, the left one, without the broken heel. But there wasn't a hair on my head that contemplated going back for it. I had to get her out of there. Concerned ushers came over to us. I asked them to call a taxi. It arrived within five minutes. I tried to get her upright to take her to the exit. And as I tried to lift her, she vomited—all over my suit. I managed to get her out of the building with the ushers' help. Getting into the taxi, it went wrong again. She lost her balance, fell, and because I was just in the wrong position, I couldn't catch her. She took me down with her. I fell onto one knee. There was a big tear in my suit trousers and my knee began to bleed. I stuffed her into the taxi, slammed the door shut, gave the driver her address and then twenty euros. "That's to take her upstairs. Good luck."

I went straight to Piazza delle Erbe, sat down at Caffè Letterario and began to drink furiously. I looked at my suit. It was completely ruined. I threw it away that same evening.

2I.

The thing I sometimes worry about is that some of the situations I get myself tangled up in here, and many of the people I really have actually met in this foreign decor, are so colorful, not to say grotesque, that they run the risk of being barely believable as fiction.

If I'm ever to transform these notes, in which I take you into complete confidence about my trials and tribulations, into a novel, I'd be forced to violate the truth to a substantial degree. To start with, I'd naturally have to change all these names pretty damn quick. And perhaps also some of the overly conspicuous characteristics of their appearance or personality. If the Genoese I'm telling you about ever get wind of me telling the truth about them, I won't have a life left here, you do understand? And the Genoese always get wind of talk about other Genoese immediately; it's funny, that's why the book doesn't even have to be translated into Italian. They'd do anything for a choice tidbit of gossip. If necessary, they'd learn another language for it.

But the biggest thing is that I'd be forced to seriously soften the truth, because if I told it exactly as it happened, the way I'm telling it to you, everyone would think I'd made it up. That's often the problem with the truth: it's completely unbelievable. But it seems that that problem keeps cropping up continuously here. This medieval labyrinth appears to be populated exclusively by unbelievable novelistic characters of ever-increasing picturesqueness.

For example, how could I ever introduce Alfonso Gioia into my novel, Monia's acquaintance, with whom I have a meeting due to his putative excellent contacts at City Hall? He was a skinny young man, with a boyish, if not to say almost childish, appearance, with short, black, lank hair and small round glasses. That's all fine, until it dawns on you who he looks like. If you saw him in real life, or if I sent you a picture of him, you'd see it at once: Harry Potter. He's the spitting image of Harry Potter. That's fine, you might say. Alright. But he is him, too. Not because his nickname is the Harry Potter of Genoa, that doesn't say much, that could be purely based on his appearance, too. No, it's much worse. He is a wizard. Not a magician, but a wizard. That's his job. I'm not lying. He told me about it at great length. His own words were that he has an enormous collection of magic objects and books of spells. And he told me at great length how just the night before he'd been to an Autogrill on the motorway toward Savona to exorcise the spirits that had been haunting the place for some time. He'd managed it. He'd solved the problem. The management of the Autogrill chain had paid him handsomely for the service. And that was only fair, he said, because it had taken him a lifetime of study. And he had to live off of it—this was his profession.

He also told me he had a special gift of being able to get in touch with the spirits of dead people, or those people floating on the boundary of life and death. Not so long ago he'd had a good conversation with Michael Jackson on his deathbed. I wondered how that conversation had gone because as far as I knew, Michael Jackson didn't speak any Italian when he was alive, and Alfonso Gioia doesn't speak a word of English. I checked that by making a brief, fake telephone call in his presence, in which I gradually introduced funny jokes about him. He didn't flinch.

And there were more things I was curious about. What had possessed Monia to put me in touch with this clown? How the hell was he going to be able to help us? I asked about his so-called excellent personal contacts with key figures in local politics. He said that, without wanting to be immodest, he was, thanks to all his contacts, one of the most important people in Genoa. He had personally assisted pretty nearly all the politicians with any clout in their election campaigns, whether they were left, right, or in the middle. He was a person who could deliver votes. He showed me a fat folder bursting with papers covered in names, addresses, phone numbers, and e-mail addresses. "This is the membership list of the paintball club I'm president of. That's more than three thousand votes. That's how it works in Italy. Almost every politician owes me a big favor."

But perhaps the most important thing, as he told it, was that he had an important role in the local Freemason's lodge. Naturally, he couldn't say much about it, but in strict confidence, he could let slip that he was the Honorable Grand Master himself. "And anyone who knows anything about the political situation in Italy knows that nothing gets done without the Freemasons' approval. We run this country."

I explained the situation regarding the theater to him and asked whether he would be able to get hold of the agreement between the current owners and the council.

"That's no problem. I can give you that contract tomorrow."

"I'd be very grateful. Thank you. We'll see each other again tomorrow, then."

"But then you'd owe me a favor in return."

"Tell me what I can do."

"You're a writer, aren't you? And you write for various foreign papers, don't you? I'll make sure you get that contract on the condition that you publish the following information abroad."

He handed me a thick document he'd put together himself. I began to read it. It slowly dawned on me what I was holding, and I could hardly believe my eyes. The document aimed to prove that he was the real Harry Potter. The writer J.K. Rowling had supposedly based her world-famous character upon him. The evidence, as one might expect, was very flimsy. In 1991, when he was fourteen, he had been a guest on an Italian television show *I fatti vostri* as the youngest wizard in Italy. That must have been the exact moment Rowling had come up with the idea for her series. The first volume was published six years later. And it wasn't just that he looked like the eponymous hero. No, she had modeled Harry on Alfonso. The similarities in appearance were too staggering to be coincidental. And there were other indications. On the show, Alfonso said that he'd been a student of a man with a long, white beard. And the name of one of the four founders of the school Harry Potter went to was Godric Gryffindor, which means "gilded griffin," a central element in Genoa's coat of arms. That was all the proof he needed. It could no longer be coincidence.

I promised him I would inform the world of his shocking discovery. First, I was keen to see whether he could actually get hold of that contract. I no longer had much faith in that. He was a fool. To be honest, it would surprise me if I ever saw him again. And perhaps it was better that way, too.

But he did actually turn up again the next day for our

appointment. And to my astonishment, he had a copy of the contract. I gave it a fleeting glance, but there was no shadow of a doubt. He'd delivered the goods. This was the right document. This was the very document I'd been fruitlessly chasing after.

So that same day I wrote a short press release in which I did my utmost best to make something of his absurd claims. I e-mailed it to one of the papers in my home country that I regularly contributed to.

The next day I got a phone call from the editor in chief. "What the hell's this, Ilja?"

"I know, Rob. I'm sorry. It's a long story. But please just place it as a favor to me. It's important. If necessary you can put it in an inconspicuous corner somewhere. Please do, in fact. And I don't have to be paid for it. And I'll write my next piece for you for free, too. Just place it, please. And can you send me a copy of the paper?"

A week later the paper lay in my postbox. My piece had been neither cut nor edited. Alfonso Gioia was satisfied. We were even.

22.

"But what it finally comes down to is that not one goddamn thing is true."

Succinctly put, that was exactly my conclusion, too.

"Naturally, I knew the whole time that something wasn't right, but now we've got it in black and white. Do you understand now why I kept on pressing for us to get this document? He was lying through his teeth, Pierluigi Parodi. With his cigars. It was all lies. And I mean all of it. What do you think, Ilja? Don't you see now that I was right?"

"Almost everything, Walter. The only thing that's true is the low rent paid to the council."

"Yes, but that means there's hard evidence that the theater belongs to the council and that he's trying to sell something that's not his."

"He's selling a license to be able to rent it at a low price."

"The nine-year license."

"Seven of which have been used up. And it won't be automatically renewed, not in the slightest. It says very clearly that the council is legally bound to put the new concession out to open tender."

"More than two hundred thousand euros for a two-year permit."

"That's indeed what it comes down to, Walter."

"But no one would fall for that, would they? He'll never find a buyer that way."

"There's surely a reason it was so difficult to get hold of this agreement."

"He used his family's leverage to keep it under wraps at the council."

"And he settled his hopes on us, Walter. Because we're naive foreigners and would never think of trying to track down this contract, and if we did think of it, we wouldn't have the means or the power to actually get hold of it. That's how his mind's working."

"But he could ask for a fee for the contents, of course."

"But then we're only talking about the fixtures and fittings in the bar and the restaurant. Everything that goes with the theater: the lights, the sound system, the removable stage, and whatever else, belongs to the council, too. It's all specified here."

"Really?"

"Take a look. Everything. Even the drum kit. And if we're talking about the restaurant, it's not even the kitchen equipment. Even that is recorded here, too."

"So we're talking about…"

"So all in all, we're actually talking about the plates, cutlery, and glasses."

"Unbelievable."

"And even that's not certain. Because there's another entry here that's not specified—'other'—and I think that can only be those things. I can't imagine it meaning anything else."

"So what does that mean?"

"It means Pierluigi doesn't have anything to sell, Walter."

"But what does that mean?"

"What that means, Walter…" It was precisely what I'd been pondering all this time. "It means…"

"It means we don't even need the two hundred thousand."

"If we can convince the council."

"That they have a problem because their theater isn't being used."

"The theater they spent a few million renovating seven years ago."

"Public money."

"Public money, Walter."

"They've got a problem."

"The trick is going to be to get them to see that, too."

"Can we do that?"

"Alfonso."

"Your wizard?"

"I'll call him tomorrow. If necessary, we'll offer him a partnership."

"A what?"

"A partnership."

"What does that mean, Ilja?"

"We can figure that out later."

"I like you, you know that?"

"Cheers, Walter."

"Cheers, my good friend. Here's to our theater. Let's hurry up and get the ball rolling. How's your play coming along?"

23.

I've spent the past few days in the archives of the Ligurian Institute for Emigration near La Commenda at the end of Via di Pré, and just by the Galata Museo del Mare. The quantity of material is overwhelming, both in terms of the primary sources and the secondary literature. It would take months to study it all systematically. I'm not going do that, of course. I don't need to write a scholarly account. Those days have gone. So I just read and flicked through a few things at random. But it did give me quite a reasonable impression of what things had been like. Enough of one, in any case, to be able to invent the truth.

One of the things that struck me was that many Italians who decided to emigrate weren't really that bad off. Of course there was poverty and few ways of escaping it, but at least they had food and a roof above their heads. The character I intended to invent would be a farmer, a simple man, uneducated and illiterate. He owned a small plot of land and had built his own house on it. He lived as his parents had lived and the parents of his parents before them and their grandparents before that. And his children would have lived like that, too, if he hadn't happened to hear of La Merica, a country further away than he could imagine, which everyone was talking about. Many men from the region had gone there. It's important to show how unrealistic their idea of this far-off world was. I'll have him fantasize at length about this paradise where you would get rich automatically if you were prepared to work. The streets were paved with gold, and the houses were as tall as mountains. You could eat your fill every day.

And then a recruiter comes to visit him on his farm, a stooge from one of the large emigration agencies in Genoa who signed up emigrants from the countryside on a commission basis, which the agency in turn, for a commission fee, would accommodate on one of the shipping lines crossing the ocean. I would find a way of making it clear how a complete subeconomy came into existence that revolved around exploiting and extorting money from simple souls with the dream of a better life. In fact, it was pure human trafficking. The recruiter promised our farmer golden mountains, pretty much literally, in the sense that he promised mountains of gold. He would have to sell his house and his land to pay for the crossing but it would be a small investment compared to the enormous fortune awaiting him at the other end. He'd be able to buy the whole village with it, if he wanted, and there would still be enough left to spend the rest of his days in opulence, without ever having to work again.

The next scene would have to show the dire situation on the quays. There he'd sit, our farmer, completely penniless and totally disoriented. He'd been able to arrange the necessary paperwork through the agency and all he had to do was wait until he could board. But there were lots of additional bills from the agency for things he didn't understand but which were undoubtedly necessary. Or so they'd emphatically made clear to him. He didn't have any lire left for a place to sleep or a hunk of bread. The prices were astronomical anyway. He felt frightened and insecure. He'd never seen that many people in one place in his life. But at the same time he felt invigorated by his dream—he would change his life and the lives of his children. He knew he was going to become a wealthy man. Everyone at the agency had assured him of that.

The Genoese observed with mixed feelings the crowds that gathered on the quays day in and day out. Some saw them as a source of income, others felt sorry for them. There was also fear. There were so many of them and the sanitary conditions were abominable. They were dirty, too. Backwards farmers from the backwoods who clearly had never learned to wash. There could be outbreaks of disease. This had happened before. In Naples, the emigrants at the port had caused a cholera epidemic that had cost the lives of many inhabitants of the city.

This is all much easier to recount in a novel than to give dramatic form as a play. I'd have to find a way to suggest the massive scale onstage and make tangible the intensity of all those conflicting feelings. To start with, I'd have to show how little space there actually was onboard. Naturally our farmer would travel third class, down below, in the ship's hold. There was officially room for seven hundred passengers, but there were at least twelve hundred. The leading role could go and sit in a corner, on the floor next to the stairs, clutching a tin plate of paltry food between his knees. He'd sleep in his clothes and shoes on a narrow bunk among screaming children and fellow passengers so seasick they hung vomiting over the edges of their beds. It was a piece of luck getting the top bunk. The stench was unbearable. There were regular outbreaks of disease.

And then there was that continuous angst onboard that everyone tried to keep to themselves, but which gnawed away at all their bellies. It was far from certain they'd ever reach the other side of the ocean. Everyone had heard about a boat sinking on the way. I found a list in the archives and copied it. Perhaps you could simply project it onto the backdrop: March 17, 1891, *Utopia* shipwrecked near the Port of Gibraltar, 576 dead; July 4, 1898, *Bourgogne* shipwrecked near Nova Scotia, 549 dead; July 25, 1901, the first *Lusitania* shipwrecked near Newfoundland and May 7, 1915, when the second *Lusitania* was sunk by a German submarine, in total 1,198 dead; August 4, 1906, *Sirio* shipwrecked near the Spanish coast, 55 dead; many Italians among the 1,523 dead at the shipwreck of the *Titanic* on April 15, 1912; November 7, 1915, an Austrian submarine sinks the *Ancona*, 206 dead; October 25, 1927, *Principessa Mafalda* shipwrecked off the Brazilian coast, 314 dead; July 2, 1940, *Arandora Star* sunk by a German submarine, 446 dead. And I don't even know if the list is complete.

And even if the ship made a safe crossing, there was no guarantee that all the passengers would still be alive when it docked. The journey lasted at least a month or, if you were unlucky, longer. Many didn't survive the terrible conditions in third class. They died of cholera, dysentery, or other illnesses, or simply of hunger, sometimes in the hundreds. There are lists of those, too. I think I copied them as well but I can't put my hands on them.

But perhaps they don't matter. The lists aren't important. I want to see the fear in the face of a man who danced and sang at home. I don't want icebergs or German submarines on the stage, nor crowd scenes with dying passengers. I want to see a person who is afraid. And who clings to hope. I want to see how beautiful that hope is and how unjustified. I want to hear him have whispered nighttime conversations with fellow sufferers, complete strangers, about all the plans they have for the mountains of gold that will fall into their laps at the other end. Those whispered dreams exorcise the fear that can't be exorcised. The sound of waves. Sound of waves.

24.

And then the arrival. The decor could be Argentina, Brazil, or the United States. I'd certainly choose New York if only because I've found the most material about it. But also for dramatic reasons. After more than a month, those who were still alive saw the Statue of Liberty. It was an indescribable sight for our farmer from Piemonte. This was what they'd told him about. In La Merica the women were as tall as mountains and they meant freedom. He hadn't been able to imagine that. But now he could. Now he could see it. Now he could see it with his own eyes. He actually began to cry, I'll be damned if it wasn't true. The crossing had been hellish, but it was all worth it. Everything they'd promised him was true. From a distance he could see the gold shining in the streets. His children would have a better life than he.

And then a hard cut to Ellis Island. In 1892, the Americans had set up an island to process the flow of immigrants from Italy. The first- and second-class passengers were allowed to disembark at the port. Third-class was put into quarantine first, which, given the epidemics onboard ship, could hardly be considered unreasonable. And then the humiliation. The interrogations in English and the medical examination. "Pants off!" Trembling naked bodies in a row who have no idea what is expected of them but who have resolved to do everything expected of them. Single women, even if they were engaged, weren't allowed into the United States, unless they got married on the spot on Ellis Island. Those Americans had a country to run, and the last thing they needed was a decline in morals; unmarried women would lead to just one thing—prostitution.

I picture a wonderful scene here. A young farmer's daughter from Lombardy or Emilia-Romagna doesn't know about the rule. Her fiancé left for New York over a year ago. But to be allowed into the country and be reunited with him, by law she has to marry someone on Ellis Island. She asks our main character. He understands the situation, he gets that it's just a formality, they marry according to American law, give each other a quick kiss, and then he falls in love with her. The only other woman he'd ever kissed was his wife. No, he'd never even kissed her. They had three children, it was true, but love didn't count in the village. That was something that belonged to the New World.

And in the final scene, I'd really rub it in. With an oily rag. As greasy as possible. Those mountains of gold that had been promised to him would turn out to be a fata morgana. He would struggle to find work in a steel factory, on the railways, in a mine. He'd work until his vertebrae were worn and his knees broken, he'd earn dollars not lire, but have less to eat than back home in Italy, in his village, yeah, his village, where the bones of his ancestors were buried and his family was waiting. And he wouldn't be able to forget the woman he'd married for the form on Ellis Island ,either. He'd like to buy a gold ring for her if he had any money and knew where to find her.

And at that very moment, someone knocks on his door. A friend. An Italian who speaks the same regional dialect and who says he understands everything. He can help him. He promises mountains of gold.

I think the play should end there, with the renewal of false hope. His initiation into the gang, the crimes, and, finally, the prison sentence would follow accordingly—people get that. It's a story that never grows old.

25.

Monia kept on calling and texting me. I didn't answer. I resolutely ignored her. But at a certain moment, in the middle of the day, I had an incoming call from a number that wasn't recognized. It was a man. "Emergency," he said. "Emergency. Can you come as quickly as possible? Via Chiabrera. You know. You're the only person I know who has the keys."

"Can I ask how you got my number?"

"Your girlfriend, my upstairs neighbor, gave it to me today by coincidence. For emergencies, she said. But an emergency arose right away. I swear, I'd never have dared call you if that wasn't the case."

I didn't much feel like an emergency. And certainly not an

obviously staged emergency. And certainly not in Via Chiabrera.
I called Monia to find out what was going on. But her phone was
answered by a little girl.

"Can I speak to your mother?"

"I don't have a mother." The little girl began to cry and hung up.
I called back. "Please come, Leonardo," she said. "Leonardo, please
come. I'm drowning here. If you don't come, I'll die. I'm drowning."

What the fuck? What would you do in that situation, my friend?
Exactly. I went to check out what was going on in Via Chiabrera.
Not out of compassion for what Monia might have come up with
to attract my attention, but more as a disaster tourist. I'm your
reporter, aren't I? And if she distorted her voice to imitate a little
girl and even called as the neighbor, there could be something picturesque going down that I wouldn't like to deprive either of us of.

Indeed, I did have a set of her spare keys. I'd wheedled them out
of her the previous time. Maybe I didn't tell you. But you never
know, I'd thought then. The downstairs neighbor was waiting for
me in front of her door, up the marble staircase after the first gate.
He was pulling his hair out. That's a stupid expression, which I'd
never use, only in this case it was literally true.

"Oi, oi," he said. "Oi oi."

I understood why he was saying that. Water was gushing down
the marble staircase. I waded upstairs. The neighbor followed at
a polite distance, as he prayed to various saints as well as the Holy
Virgin herself. The last gate was open by default. And after a bit
of fumbling, I found the right key to the front door.

"Monia?"

She didn't reply. I went inside. The neighbor shuffled along quietly behind me. She was in the bath. With all her clothes on. Well, clothes. She was wearing some kind of wedding dress, a white lacy ensemble with a veil. She had on heavy golden rings and necklaces. Her head was safely above water but she was already unconscious. The bath tap was running full force. The flooding had taken on Old Testament proportions.

I turned off the tap and lifted her out of the bath. I pulled out the plug and put her on her bed. She had come to her senses, slightly. "Undress me, Leonardo. I'm your bride. See how pretty I am." I undressed her. "Oi, oi," the neighbor muttered. "Fuck me, Leonardo. This is our wedding night."

Instead of that I went into her study to look for her cleaner's number. "Emergency?" "Emergency." As I waited for her, I had a better look around the study. I noticed that I couldn't see a single piece of mail or any documents that related to any kind of work whatsoever. There was a pile of fashion magazines, a big pile of brochures advertising long-distance travel to exotic places, and an even larger pile of unopened envelopes. I took the liberty of opening a couple. It was an emergency, after all. They were all unpaid bills—with some court injunctions among them. Some already a year old.

The woman had arrived within half an hour, and half an hour later she'd mopped everything up. Monia was already asleep by then. "Sorry," I said to the cleaner.

"I never say sorry to anybody," she said. "Life is as life does."

"How much do I owe you? I hired you to do the job, after all. How much does Monia pay you?"

"Nothing."

"What do you mean?"

"You might have thought you'd found yourself a rich, older mistress. I know your type. You're an artist, aren't you? We have to work for our money. But I won't hold it against you, don't get me wrong. But she isn't rich. And she's not your mistress anymore, if I can give you one piece of good advice, though it's probably no longer necessary. Goodbye."

"Oi, oi," the neighbor said. He prayed to a few more saints, then he, too, figured it was time to go home.

26.

She came and sat down opposite me, uninvited—Fulvia, the witch—and said this: "I've been hearing a lot of things about you recently, Leonardo. My grandmother always said, 'Leave the wheat growing when it's growing and break glasses in November.' My grandmother was a wise woman, she knew things people today have forgotten. I don't blame them. In every lunar cycle in history you see the same shifts. It goes from Venus to Mars and vice versa. That's how it progresses from the Major to the Minor Arcana." She smiled omnisciently. "The magnetic field under this city was designed many cycles ago as a kind of blueprint for the new era. But we have to interpret it ourselves, a lot of people forget that. We have to learn to think in meridians. From north to south. Like lines on a hand. Let me see your hand. No, your left hand. You see. Do you know what I can see? If you don't die of illness or an accident, you'll live a long life."

Naturally, I was happy with this news. But I kept wondering

whether there were any other causes of death aside from illnesses and accidents. Old age perhaps?

"Thanks." I thought about the different ways a man could die. A tortoise fell on Aeschylus' head. But that falls into the accidents category. And apart from accidents or illness, what's left? Murder?

"You mustn't be so negative, Leonardo. That karma will turn against you. The earth goddess only embraces those who see the pendulum move." She smiled triumphantly.

"Lay down some cards," I said.

"That's not how it works, Leonardo."

"How does it work, then?"

She smiled. Alright. I got it. I went inside to order her a dry martini cocktail.

She smiled. That was how it worked. She began to lay the cards on the table.

"These are all the things you already know."

"What then?"

"You're from Germany."

"Holland."

"You're a painter."

"Writer."

"Exactly, but your mother worries about you."

"Why?"

"Because you're at a spiritual stage in your life where you listen to fairies not elves."

"What does that mean?"

"Don't interrupt. I'm just beginning to make contact with your spiritual underbelly. No, really, there's a lot of resonance there. Do you know what, Leonardo, tell me honestly—do you have that thing that sometimes you feel really good and sometimes you feel really bad and sometimes in the middle? Yes? I can feel it. I understand it."

She lay a few more cards. As she did this, she made a dismissive gesture. That upside down king of swords in combination with the fool didn't tell her anything new. In fact, that's what she'd been trying to tell me the whole time.

"What?"

That I was a man who lived with my heart but also with my head. I was a sensitive person but intelligent, too, unfortunately. I liked love but I also needed my own space. I was strange and typical at the same time. Although I thought I'd found something, I was searching. Although I thought I understood something, I was questioning. Although I thought I could deny the truth of the cards, my future was extremely uncertain.

She laid three more cards. The king of cups, a scythe cutting hay, and an upside down seven of wands.

"Look," she said. "On the basis of these three cards, what would you conclude about my opinion of you?"

"You despise me."

"That's pretty much the first time you've said anything truthful."

"But your pebble-dash opinion is uninformed and will turn against you like the tides against the position of the moon and the rocks against the sea during the equinox."

I was tired of her. I stopped talking.

"You don't understand a thing, Leonardo. Write that down in your little book."

"Ach."

"What, ach?"

"What, ach? What do you want to know? What's your name again? Fulvia. I find you—thank you for having the courage to ask me—a thoroughly reprehensible person."

"Could you explain that, Leonardo?"

"Yes." I went inside to pay for everything, both my drinks and hers, as well as everyone who had sat at her table before me. I put the receipt in my back pocket. Then I ordered another bottle of Prosecco in an ice bucket. I paid for that, too. I took the order to her table personally, took the bottle from the ice bucket, put it on the table and said, "Fulvia, do you know what my grandmother always said? 'You have to keep a cool head.' My grandmother was a wise woman."

27.

I didn't know exactly what he knew or how he had found me, but he knew things and he'd been able to find me. I don't know his real name, but everyone called him Il Varese. That was how he introduced himself to me. I'd seen him before, only I couldn't remember where. He turned out to be the exclusive brewer of Bryton, an authentic Ligurian beer that was undrinkable, but brewed using a method based on well documented archeological findings. Yeah, well, exactly. That was what it tasted like, too. He was a large, broad, fat man who looked like a beer drinker, like someone who sweated and stank and pissed liters of clear piss out of his shriveled fire hose that hung under a massive belly that blocked all view of what, in his wet dreams, was still the instrument of his futile ambition. Misery led him to try to become a successful businessman instead, in the hope that supplicating nymphets might be prepared to suckle on his sorry little pee-pee on the basis of his commercial success. But it hadn't completely worked, that ingenious master plan, and he didn't really know what exactly had gone wrong, either. Somewhere on the way to becoming rich and famous, he'd missed both boats. Since then, sighing with arrogance and condescension, he'd been permanently clamped to his mobile phone filled with important contacts who for incomprehensible reasons kept failing to call him the whole time. But he wasn't going to give up. After all, he could still sell his own beer. He called Berlusconi on his private number in Portofino, but for some unknown reason he didn't pick up. That was definitely the work of the communists. They had special gadgets to prevent honest businessmen from doing business with honest politicians who understood that the country needed honest businessmen. What Italy needed was modern entrepreneurship, of which he himself was a shining example. An archeologist finds a few traces of scummy beer in an earthenware pot almost two thousand years old and sees a business opportunity. That was his skill. That was his genius. With a sigh, he scratched his musty crotch again.

Perhaps I'm not describing him with complete objectivity, I know, but I simply don't like the man. He rudely sat down opposite me.

"So," he said.

And suddenly I knew where I'd seen him before. Right here, on the Bar of Mirrors' terrace. I'd even written about him, I think. Sometime early on. When I'd just arrived in Genoa and was happy and naive, when I described how an Italian greeted another man he clearly had arranged to meet. That was him. But don't look it up, it's not important.

"So you want to buy my theater."

I gave him a confused look.

"You talked to my partner."

"Who?"

"My partner, Pierluigi."

I nodded.

"I've come to warn you about him. How much was he asking? Two ten? Two twenty?" He saw from my expression that he was somewhere close. "What a rogue. The cheeky devil. That guy is even more untrustworthy than I thought. Shall I tell you something? He doesn't have anything at all to sell."

"I know."

"Because I bought it. That's to say—two years ago I bought it for about that amount. He's only a partner on paper since it was handy for administrative reasons. But the theater's mine." He looked at me triumphantly. "So. Now you know just in time. You should thank me. I've just saved you from being conned out of more than two hundred thousand euros. You have to be on your guard if you want to do business here in Italy."

He took a sip of his disgusting beer. The Bar of Mirrors was the only place in the city that sold Bryton beer, somewhat out of pity since he'd been a regular for so long. He was the only person who actually ordered it, but they didn't dare tell him. And what they dared tell him even less was that they regularly had to jettison bottles of it because it was past its sell-by date.

"Therefore," he began, "if you want to talk about taking over the theater, you need to talk to me. But the good news for you is that I'm prepared to discuss it. I'm in no hurry, but I would part with it for the right amount. It's always been more of a hobby for me, really. But I simply don't have enough time for it. I'm too busy with other things, import-export, that kind of work. So tell me, what are you offering? We don't have to come to an agreement right now, but maybe we can scope out the possibilities."

"But you don't have anything to sell, either."

He didn't understand. "What are you saying?"

"I said you don't have anything to sell, either. The theater doesn't belong to you. It belongs to the council."

First he gave me a look of total astonishment, then he roared with laughter.

"I'm not joking. The theater belongs to the council. I don't know how much Pierluigi made you pay, but he's sold you something that didn't belong to him. It's all there in black and white in the contract."

Now he looked a little concerned. "What contract?"

"I happen to have it on me. See for yourself."

And over the next five minutes a spectacle unfurled nearly beyond description. He put on his reading glasses and began to read indifferently. But he soon paled. His hands began to shake. Sweat pearled on his forehead. Then he turned bright red. And he looked even more distended than he already was. Finally he exploded. He banged his hand on the table, swearing. "I'll murder him," he screamed. He got up and stormed off.

28.

"*Vaffanculo.*"

"*Pronto?*"

"I'll hang you from the highest tree on the highest mountain I can find, Leonardo. My father will fuck you so hard up the ass with all his contacts that you'll wish chairs hadn't been invented. We'll strip you so bare you'll wish you were still in your shirt tails. We'll shit on you, crap on you, and defecate on you, Leonardo. And given the belly rot you've given us, it won't be a pretty sight, I can tell you that now."

"Who is this?"

"Who is this? Who is this? I'll tell you who this is. You're talking to the person who is going to break both your legs, pull out your nails one by one, and then punch all of your teeth out before hanging you publicly on the square by your shriveled balls."

"Sorry, I didn't recognize your voice. Hello, Pierluigi. How's it going?"

"It's not going, you dirty foreigner. Think you can come here to my country, my city, ruin my business with your cocky, northern, bulging potato head full of soggy noodles? You're the barbarians who plundered Rome and now you're coming here in person for a pathetic replay in my back garden. I've spent years building something out of crystal glass and you come along with your big, fat, soft, pale body and stamp on it with your clumsy feet. But I can tell you one thing—crystal glass is expensive, and I'll recover every last cent back from you to cover damages."

"I thought we were friends, Pierluigi."

"Right. So did I."

"So?"

"Tomorrow at eleven at my father's office. And please realize this is your last chance to come up with a proposal that will convince us to delay our legal proceedings against you. And that final proposal has five zeros, I can assure you of that."

"Where's your father's office?"

"Find out for yourself. You always know best."

"That's not how it works, Pierluigi."

"Piazza della Vittoria 68/24."

"Look forward to it."

"You shouldn't."

29.

Walter and I were on time. Piazza della Vittoria 68 turned out to be a stately marble building once designed to impress that still fulfilled its function with verve. Next to the main entrance were copper plates with the names of lawyers, judges, and notaries, each one grander than the last. We were expected. We had an appointment. Number 24 housed Parodi's office on the fifth floor. At the end of the corridor on the left. Two lifts. The left one didn't always work. Better take the right.

Walter was visibly intimidated by our surroundings. His nonchalant thespian appearance clashed with the strict patrician marble. He felt uneasy in these palaces of power, probably because he was a director and accustomed to situations where he held the reins in shabby practice rooms in abandoned squats.

"The name's Parodi," Pierluigi's father said. He was sitting at the head of a relatively modest oval table in a spacious, bright office at the front of the palazzo overlooking Piazza della Vittoria. Pierluigi was there, too, but he wasn't allowed to talk. His father was doing the talking.

"The name's important. Sit down please. My son Pierluigi here is an absolute idiot, of course. You don't need me to tell you that. That's why I arranged the theater for him, to keep him off the streets, and because he can do relatively little harm there. But he's a Parodi, too. Do you know what I mean? He might be a prick, but he's my prick. If you'll excuse my French, but I'm trying to make something clear to you.

"That is to say that as soon as you try to put a spoke in that retard's wheel, I am compelled to protect that mongoloid. He's my son. He bears my name. My name is my most important asset in this city. I'd defend my name to the last. I know that you're an intelligent man. And I know you've been in this city for long enough to understand me.

"You're from northern Europe, which is why you think in legal terms. You think that the contract I arranged for my son for that theater is a public matter. I'll have to admit you're right, in essence. And I'd also like to compliment you on the way you managed to get hold of the document. I honestly thought it was sufficiently protected. But clearly you have contacts I didn't take into account.

"All of this makes you a sizeable opponent. But an opponent. By showing that document to my son's partner, you've caused my son substantial financial damage. And you'll understand that I'm left with no option but to collect those damages from you in the Parodi name.

"You still look quite unmoved, sitting there at my table. I know what you're thinking. You believe in Europe and in the idea that Italy is a democratic constitutional state and the fantasy that Genoa is part of Italy. You believe in your democratic rights and in the protection of law. Part of me would like nothing more than for you to be right.

"When you came in, did you see the copper nameplates of all the people with offices in this palazzo? Do you have any idea of my network? You might stand a chance in Strasbourg, Brussels, or at the international court in The Hague—if you had enough money for substantive proceedings against our legal team. But in Genoa you don't stand the slightest chance. Not against me. I seldom lose cases, and I've never lost a case when my good name was at stake."

"What do you want from us?" I asked.

"Two forty."

"We'd already reached two twenty with your son."

"My son's an idiot and I've already initiated proceedings to impound all of your possessions."

"Why should I be afraid of you, Mr. Parodi?"

"I don't want to insult you. You're undoubtedly a respected person in your home country. You're a writer, aren't you? A poet even, look at that. Has your poetry been translated into Italian? I'd like to peruse some of your verses sometime, when I have nothing better to do. No? There you go, we're back to that. It's exactly what I'm trying to make clear to you. You are in Genoa, where my friends and friends of my friends have been calling the shots for centuries, and although I'd like to compliment you once again on the way you attempted to adopt our way of thinking, you will always remain an outsider to us. Worse still, a foreigner. We can tolerate your presence in our city up to a certain degree, and even welcome it as long as you stick to your own business. But as soon as you start stepping into our territory, you're worth little more than your average Moroccan or Senegalese fellow—an irritating but relatively minor problem we can easily rid the world of—we have plenty of experience in that.

"That leaves me to thank you for a fruitful discussion. If you'll allow me to summarize the conclusion we have mutually reached, I'll look forward to your transfer of two hundred and forty thousand euros within, let's say, a fortnight. Is that reasonable enough for you? And if you fail to fulfill the obligation, which naturally seems highly unlikely to me, I will, in accordance with our mutual understanding, be charging you for breaches you never even dreamed existed."

30.

Although I understood that the situation was worse than I'd thought, I wasn't worried. I had my magical contact after all. Harry Potter himself was on my side. I called him immediately. He didn't pick up. The next day I tried again and a few more times the day after.

The day after, I bumped into him by chance on Via Canneto Il Lungo. He was walking his dog and tried to ignore me. I invited him for a coffee. He couldn't refuse.

"Well?"

"Well what?"

"Are we friends or not?"

He stared ahead, silently.

"Alright, I get you, Alfonso. We're quits. You don't owe me anything. But I need your advice again."

"On the Parodi matter?"

"Have you already heard about it?"

"Of course."

"And what do you think?"

He shrugged and looked away.

"But can you help me, Alfonso?"

"Do you know what, Leonardo? You screwed up."

"I know, Alfonso. That's exactly why I sought out your illustrious presence, if you'll forgive me the expression."

He didn't smile.

"I'm a foreigner, after all."

He still didn't smile.

"I'll make you an offer, Alfonso, by way of a return service for the favor I'm asking you now. Parodi threatened me, but together we are stronger than he. Listen, Alfonso. I'm offering you a partnership."

"What does that mean?"

"Whatever you want it to mean, Alfonso. We'll figure something out. We'll get rich, you and me, with Walter. But first you have to help me neutralize this old family. You and all your contacts, Alfonso. Are you listening?"

Alfonso wasn't listening.

"Show me your hand, Alfonso."

"Funny joke."

"What's the matter? Tell me, please."

"You made a mistake, Leonardo, a big mistake."

"I know. But I've already admitted it. I never should have shown that contract to Il Varese. But I've learned my lesson."

"That's not the problem."

"What is then?"

"You're a foreigner, Leonardo. You don't understand where the power lies."

"I'll admit to that, too. But that's why I'm talking to you. I want to learn. Tell me what you think."

He stared at me thoughtfully. His dog started barking at another dog going by. He had to get up to calm the situation. After that he sat down again.

"Do you remember what I told you during our last conversation about the root of my own power?"

"The Freemasons?"

"She's the second highest in the organization, after me."

"Who?"

"She's exceptionally well-connected. She's the personal advisor and a friend of the mayor. The mayor doesn't do anything without consulting with her first."

"Who are you talking about, Alfonso?"

"And you insulted her. She's a personal friend of mine. I still owe her a few favors. And you insulted her to the core. You emptied a bucket of ice over her head quite publicly."

I had to laugh at the recollection.

"Don't laugh, Leonardo. You've made an enemy of one of the

most powerful women in Genoa. And you've made an enemy of one of my most faithful political allies and one of my very dearest friends. I can no longer help you. More than that, you are now my enemy. This isn't Amsterdam or Berlin. This is Genoa. Good luck living the dream."

31.

I met up with Walter in La Lepre for a crisis meeting. His triumphant optimism had evaporated. He was afraid. He loved Genoa like I did but could no longer see a future for himself in the city. The only thing he could see were damage claims.

"But don't leave me here on my own, Walter. The fight has only just begun."

"I'll never leave you alone," he said. But his eyes told a different story.

"One day we'll conquer this city. The city needs us."

"Do you have your credit card on you, Ilja?"

"Yes, why?"

"Maybe we can go to the Piazza delle Erbe. You can have another drink on the terrace and I'll pop into the Internet café for a sec. I'll pay you back, don't worry."

After half an hour he came back out. He gave me back my credit card.

"I owe you eighty euros."

"Come and sit down. We'll have another drink and chat some more."

"I don't have time right now. I'll see you later."

"What did you actually do in the Internet café?"

"I had to book something." He kissed me on the cheek. "See you soon." It looked like he had tears in his eyes.

That evening he sent me a text message. "Pisa. Airport. Sorry." And the next day another from a foreign number. "Good luck living the dream. Genoa will always be in my heart."

Fatou Yo

I.

I met Djiby the first time in Via di Pré, where else? In the daytime, it is possibly Genoa's most beautiful street. "Daytime" is a rather vague word that I only use as a contrast to the night. Via di Pré is at its prettiest in the early evening on a summer's day, when balmy twilight descends on the dark alleyway. This is the hour when everyone has just woken up from their siesta and goes to have a look on the street corner, yawning, at how others are getting on with their work. And others are getting on with their work. Halal butchers work with a great racket under the arches. Next door, loud squabbling as the Afro hair of hurricane-proof black women is straightened—women who gossip in Africa's great multitude of languages about the people who had their hair straightened the day before, joking about how fat the asses in question were and how lazy their husbands. Fruit swells in the shops. Here, just about everything is for sale for nearly nothing. This is Africa.

Women in large, flapping, traditional robes sit on the street selling paper handkerchiefs and toothpicks. But they aren't selling paper handkerchiefs and toothpicks—they are voodoo witches with the power, for the right price, to make a rival impotent or cause an unfaithful mistress to lose a leg. There are white witches and black witches—those who help and those who cause damage, but the difference is invisible to a northerner. They have another function apart from that. They usually sit in front of the door of the palazzo they live in, and for good reason. They are keeping watch. They share their houses with family members, sons and nephews, who deal drugs and get up to all kinds of other shady business, so it's important to keep an eye on who is going into the building. And they're all rolling in it. All you need is for one badly fitted stove gas bottle to explode and the witch's quivering coven turns up in a Mercedes to deliver her to safety, her suitcases filled with gold on the back seat.

At night, when the butchers, hairdressers, and fruit merchants have let down their shutters and closed them with at least four padlocks, the Via di Pré becomes a warzone. Footsteps echo hollowly as you walk between the trenches, sounding just as suspicious to everybody else. The Senegalese are at war with the Moroccans, the South Americans with the Senegalese and the Moroccans, and the Moroccans with everyone. They use stones and bottles as ammunition. Sometimes they use ammunition as ammunition. There are sometimes fatalities, though you seldom read about them in the papers since the victims are illegals, and so officially don't exist, and to prevent further problems, are whisked away as quickly as possible by their fellow countrymen. The police are of no help. They settle scores in their own way.

The only thing protecting you from being hit in the crossfire is your white skin. You're irrelevant in the war between immigrants. To them, you're just a stupid, weak, white outsider who doesn't understand a thing. The gang members allow you, quietly and ignorantly, to trudge through a no-man's-land armed in ways you have no knowledge of. But there are pickpockets in no-man's-land and they set their sights on your unsteady walk, your mobile phone, and the five euros you have left in your trouser pocket. The police are not players here. They avoid Via di Pré after sunset because it's simply too dangerous.

2.

Cinzia lives there, just by the Commenda, on the top floor of a palazzo that's been dilapidated since the Middle Ages. The stairs are so worn you could cook soup in them. She no longer has any neighbors, not really. She does have cracks in the wall from a gas bottle that exploded in the adjacent building. But she has the prettiest terrace in Genoa. You can see everything from her roof: the despairing labyrinth, the badly planned motorway, the lighthouse, and the port. The view of the port is magical. Slowly drifting skyscrapers like the MSC *Fantasia* and the MSC *Poesia* greet the city with three low hoots of their horns, while ferries leave for Sardinia, Sicily, Barcelona, and Africa. All of the boats together form a poignantly slow ballet of dreams of other places where it will be just as bad as it is here, but at least it won't be here.

I was sitting with Cinzia on her terrace, thinking all these things, when he came in, carrying something heavy. He smiled happily. White teeth shone in his black face.

"Hey, Djiby," Cinzia said. "What's today's gift?"

"I know exactly what it is," he said. "Something heavy." He

found that terribly funny. "You know that's my job—carrying heavy loads. Francesco has someone else for light loads. But he earns even less than me." He set down his large bag in a corner of the terrace, giggling.

She introduced him to me. "Leonardo's a foreigner as well, like you."

"He might be a foreigner but he's not like me. He doesn't have to carry heavy loads. He's allowed things I'm not allowed because his ears are translucent and his teeth are blacker than his face." Grinning, he said goodbye. He began to sing on his way down the stairs. It sounded like "*Fatou yo*." It sounded melancholy. The sound died away as he descended to street level.

"He has keys to your house?"

Cinzia shrugged. "He's a good boy. He's one of Francesco's, my landlord's, slaves."

"Do you rent?"

"He's the owner of the entire palazzo. And I've heard he has dozens of buildings, mainly here in Via di Pré."

"So he mainly rents them to Senegalese?"

"But he's a good person. I think he has political ambitions, too, so he can't allow himself to get a bad name as yet another slumlord exploiting illegal immigrants. And he loves Via di Pré. He wants more white people here and is really doing his best about that. That's how I got this apartment."

"So that his buildings will be worth more. If this weren't such a black neighborhood."

"But at least he's doing something about it. The thing he had Djiby bring over is a sack of cement to repair the cracks in the wall made by the gas explosion. Many of them here on the terrace. See that crack there? Other landlords put fifteen Senegalese in an apartment and let the lot rot away."

"And your friend Djiby, where does he live then?"

"I can see what you're getting at, Leonardo, but it's complicated."

3.

I saw Djiby often in the days that followed, and in my neighborhood, Molo, too—a long way from Africa. Sometimes in the early mornings, Oscar had him put out the Gradisca's tables, chairs, and umbrellas. After that he went to the fruit shops and fishmongers on Via Canneto Il Lungo to deliver heavy boxes or take empty ones to the trash. He rang on various bells to assist the helpless old ladies without a lift that he worked for, carrying bottles of water and other heavy things upstairs. I'd probably seen him before, before we'd been introduced to each other, but he hadn't stood out. Now that I knew him, I always greeted him amicably. He chuckled as he greeted me back.

And then when I saw him once in the evening with some bracelets and other trinkets he was trying to sell, I invited him to join me at my table.

"What will you have? Are you a Muslim?"

"A beer's good."

"Small or large?"

"Depends on how much you've got to tell me."

"Actually, I wanted to ask you something. You're doing the telling."

"In that case, a *very* large beer."

The beer was brought. We clinked glasses. He began to laugh.

"Why are you laughing, Djiby?"

"At you, Leonardo. Because you're funny. Because you have such a funny name."

"Djiby's an even funnier name."

"Like Leonardo DiCaprio with his arms outstretched and then blub, blub, blub."

"Actually my real name's Ilja."

He found that hilarious. "That's a girl's name." He roared with laughter. "Would you like to be a girl, Ilja? Can I be the first one to fuck you if you do?"

"I wanted to ask you a serious question, Djiby."

This made him laugh even more. "Blub, blub," he said. He downed his beer in one. "I'll be serious again tomorrow."

"Serious?"

He slapped my shoulder. "I like you, girly Leonardo."

4.

His full name was Djiby P. Souley. I asked him what the P. stood for. Laughing, he said he didn't know. He'd thought of the P. himself because he wanted to have three initials: DPS, it looked chic, for later, when he was a rich, successful businessman.

"Is that what you want to be, a rich, successful businessman?"

"I am that already to my family back home in Senegal. It might be the biggest joke of the century."

"Did you tell them you were?"

"No, but they know I'm in Europe and everyone in Europe

gets rich and successful without trying. Every African knows that."

"But they know better by now?"

"Well, no, they don't. Not really. Do you know what they told me about Europe? Back home in Senegal, before I went away? They said that Europe is a fortress. That its borders are so well guarded it's almost impossible to get in. But that's understandable because everyone inside can get free money. You can go to a counter and they arrange a wage for you that you can come and collect each month without having to do anything for it. Everyone in Europe wears expensive designer suits and gold watches, which they check the whole time because everything in Europe happens punctually. They sell sunglasses there that cost more than a month's salary in Dakar, but everyone wears them, even though no one really needs them because there's less sun than in Africa. Everyone can easily afford them. And if you want to, you can work as well. And then you become a millionaire. And the jobs are just there for the taking, and in Europe there aren't any really exhausting physical jobs, like farming or working in a factory. Robots do that kind of work. All the people work in banks where they look after the money the robots earn for them. All you have to do is sit at an office desk in a suit and do nothing but stare at a computer screen that says how much money is flowing in. The banks also give free debit cards to anyone who wants them and you can use them to get money from a wall if you need it. At home, too, all the work is done by computers and machines. Nobody has to do the laundry, or clean, or cook. There are appliances for that. That's why the people have plenty of time to go and watch football matches on televisions as big as cinema screens. And everyone drives lovely big cars, like Mercedes or Jaguars, and most people buy a new one as soon as the ashtray is full. The buildings are made of silver and glass. They've invented a special kind of glass that's made of silver and reflects light like a mirror. They cover palaces as high as mountains with it. And there is so much gold that some people put it in their teeth, not even for decoration, because nobody sees it, but simply because they can. And there's always as much food as you can eat because they've developed scientific techniques that can make tomatoes as big as apples and apples as big as melons, and the cows are even fatter than hippos. Europeans don't only eat meat on public holidays, but every day, for breakfast, lunch, and dinner. They have so much water they shower every day. And they shower with perfume as well. Beer doesn't come in bottles but out of a tap like water. Anyone who gets ill can go to a laboratory for free, where they cure them. They can do everything there. They can even give you new body parts if you need them. And you can have as much sex as you want because all European men have tiny dicks and their women long for a real one. And you don't even have to marry them because they're emancipated, which means it's only about the sex."

"You're exaggerating, Djiby."

"I know by now that the reality is a bit different." He laughed. "But these are the kinds of stories going around in Africa. And if you hear them often enough, while day in day out you have just enough francs in your pocket to buy some bread, sooner or later you get the idea of maybe making the trip. And if you don't come up with that plan yourself, there are family members or friends who suggest it and as a small favor in return for their suggestion, they ask only that you don't forget them once you've settled in the Promised Land. In Africa, it's considered a scandal for a young man to be poor and there are a lot of friends and family members who'll remind you of that."

"I'd love to hear the story of your travels."

"I knew it. Are you going to write it down in your book?"

"Does it bother you?"

"On the contrary. I've always wanted to be a character in a novel. And if I can't be rich and successful, at least I might become famous in that way. It's something at least. Will you make sure you spell my name correctly? Djiby P. Souley. The P. in particular is very important."

"I understood that."

"But seriously, I think it's important that my story be told to the people in the north. It's the story of my people. I'll tell it to you." A broad grin appeared on his face. "On the condition you pay for my beer. And I'll need a lot of beer because it's a long, thirst-inducing story since it mainly takes place in the desert and onboard ships under a scorching sun."

5.

"I was the chosen one. My two younger brothers might be physically stronger, although everyone thought that only because they themselves kept saying it the whole time. But I'm cleverer, and even they couldn't deny that. I'm good at languages. I probably inherited that from my mother. My Italian's already quite good, isn't it?" He laughed. "Don't say yes or no. But languages are important for a trip like that. Maybe even the most important thing. Because you have to negotiate stuff the whole time. But I didn't know that at the time. Muscles are important for a black man once you're in Europe so you can earn a few euros carrying heavy things, but you need a set of totally different skills to get into Europe. You need to know which way the wind blows on your third day. To do this, you have to speak the tongues that cool the desert and part the waves.

"The old route had been made impassable. They used to all come to us. From Kenya or Nigeria they came all the way to Senegal to cross the sea to the Canary Islands. That had always been a dangerous route, but since 2006 it's actually been closed. Too many checks, too much navy about, no one does it anymore. The experts said that the Morocco route to the Spanish enclaves of Ceuta and Melilla was also no longer navigable. When I left, everyone agreed that the most promising route was via Libya. I think that's still the case.

"Family and friends had rustled together the money. I gave my mother a kiss and shook my father's hand and left. 'I'm proud of you,' my mother said. 'Make me proud,' my father said. My brothers didn't say a thing.

"The first part of the journey was the easiest. I had to go to the city of Agadez in the north of Niger. I could take a bus with the money from my family and friends, and then another one and another one, and all of that together took more than a week, but then I arrived, and then it started for real."

He took a sip of his beer. "I'm keeping it short because there's still a lot to come."

"Tell me everything, Djiby, please."

"The bit I'd just cut out for simplicity was the way we crossed the Mali border and after that the Mali-Niger border. It's not really a matter of getting a simple stamp. Even if you had enough money to bribe the officials, it wasn't going to be easy. And I didn't have the money so that wasn't an option anyway.

"So what happened was that we were dropped a few kilometers from the border. We had to wait there until it got dark. At a certain point, trucks were supposed to come past, they said. They'd stop at the place we were waiting. You had to give the driver a small fee. After that you had to hold on to the shaft at the back and crawl under the truck until you could put your legs over the axles. It would be hard, they said, but we only had to stay like that for a couple of hours. Until we were safely over the border.

"And that's how I crossed the Mali border, lying on the axles underneath a truck. I got cramps in my hands after just ten minutes. At that point, there was still a whole night to go. And it wasn't exactly the A7 from Milan to the Riviera. We drove along a dirt road full of bumps and potholes. Everything jolted and shook. A few times, the truck jerked so much I almost lost my grip. It was incredibly dangerous, really. It's not difficult to imagine what would happen if you let go. And then taking the Mali-Niger border in the same way. The truck hit a rock and almost tipped over. I lost my grip but by some miracle, managed to grab onto something to get back in place. But the boy lying next to me was less lucky. He was catapulted forwards, fell on the ground, and one of the wheels drove over his head. Fortunately for him, it all happened really quickly. And fortunately for me, it was dark so I couldn't see what was left of his head."

6.

"It's difficult to describe Agadez. In some ways, it's a beautiful town. Or in any case, it once was. It's one of the few places in Africa where history is tangible. A lot of tourists used to come, they told me. But the town fell into the hands of petty criminals, Touareg rebels and dubious characters with links to Al Qaeda, and fell into decline. The tourists no longer come. Instead, the city is flooded with emigrants like me. The town stands at the crossroads of various routes to the Promised Land. They arrive from all four corners of Africa, not just from Senegal but also from Sierra Leone, Ghana, Nigeria, Cameroon, Chad, and more. The two most important routes to the north start at Agadez: the one via Tamanrasset in Algeria to the Spanish enclave Mellila or to the Tunisian coast, and the one to Libya. Agadez has always been a smugglers' den. Its inhabitants know the mountains of the border area with Algeria and Libya like the back of their hands. They used to smuggle cigarettes and weapons. Now it's black men. 'And that's better business,' one of the many smugglers I met there said. 'Cigarettes and weapons don't have legs.'

"Most emigrants are completely broke when they arrive in Agadez. They're put up in the Ghetto, where dozens sleep in rows on the floors of unfurnished sheds or in enclosed yards. In total, there are tens of thousands of penniless black men in that small area of the town, continuously. There's no running water. The sanitary conditions are awful. Many suffer from malaria. There are regular outbreaks of other illnesses. They told me it was better a few years ago because there were western aid workers in Agadez, but the town became too dangerous for them, too. And most of the emigrants are forced to stay because they don't have any money for the second half of their journey. They try to find work. I spoke to a couple of men from my home country who'd been there for longer than a year.

"Compared to them, I was a privileged person. I still had some money left from my friends and family, and in theory it was enough to be able to continue directly on to Libya. But I had to operate carefully, that much was clear to me. To start with I had to try to avoid running into police officers. I was taken down to the station on my very first day in Agadez. I got away with a twenty-dollar fine. Later I found out I could thank my lucky stars.

"It wasn't easy to find someone willing to smuggle me over the Libyan border. On the contrary, I was continuously pounced on by a wide array of figures with a wide array of arrangements, each more expensive than the other. I decided to spend a few dollars on a sleeping place in the Ghetto to give me time to gather information. The Ghetto was dirty but cheap and safe. The police didn't go there because it was run by Mohammed, a Touareg whom everyone called the Boss.

"I spoke to as many of my countrymen as I could and all I heard were horror stories. A Nigerian had paid five hundred dollars to an Arab with a car who had promised to take him to Tamanrasset, but the Arab stopped at a police station, ran away with the money, and the man was locked up. The driver of a large truck had dumped eighty-five passengers in the desert. They'd all died of thirst. Another convoy had been ambushed by armed Touareg rebels. They'd forced everyone to undress, confiscated everything of value, and taken six Senegalese and three Nigerian women into the desert. There were army checkpoints all over the place. And Niger's northern border was littered with land-mines. It was important to find a driver who actually knew the area. But they cost more. And the Ténéré desert was merciless. Travelers often died of simple thirst on the road because they hadn't bought enough water before they left, which was understandable because a five-liter jerry can of water cost six dollars in Agadez."

7.

"This story's making me thirsty. I did warn you. Will you order me another beer?"

"It's making me thirsty, too."

"That doesn't interest me." Djiby began to laugh. "If you're writing a story about thirst, you're not interested in whether it makes your readers thirsty, too, are you?"

"Actually I am, Djiby. To be honest, that's the only thing that interests me."

"Maybe you're right. Cheers, then. Here's to your thirsty readers. So I'm doing a good job?"

"Spectacular. I don't need to do anything to it."

"Ha ha ha. I'm only telling it like it was. The truth."

"Carry on, Djiby."

"Alright. The next day I decided to give it a go. I went through the Boss, Mohammed, the Touareg. He put me in contact with a *tchagga*. That's what they call the human traffickers in Agadez.

This one was a friend of his. That made him more expensive but it seemed to me that a friend of the Boss's would be trustworthy at least. I was sorely mistaken.

"He charged three hundred and fifty dollars for the journey to Sabha in Libya, which was about sixteen hundred kilometers away. I managed to get him down to three hundred. Twenty of us set off in the back of his four-wheel drive pickup. He took us to a cabin, thirty kilometers to the north of Agadez. He picked us up again the next evening. We drove northwards in the dark. We were about seventy kilometers from the border when the engine began to splutter and then stopped. He said we were out of gasoline and that he'd go fetch some. We were near a village, he said. It wasn't far. But perhaps we could contribute something. He got together around two hundred dollars and went off. It was too dangerous to go with him, he said, because of all the checkpoints.

"When he hadn't returned by sunrise, we realized he was never coming back. We decided to continue on foot. But after two days without food or drink we realized it was pointless. A trade convoy from the north passed us on the road we were walking along. They offered to take us back to Agadez. We said we didn't have any money and needed to go north. They said we shouldn't be so stupid, we'd die if we did that, we should get in immediately and we didn't have to pay anything. Four of the group decided to carry on, despite their warnings. I was taken back to Agadez along with fifteen others."

8.

"But then I was just as broke as all the rest of them. And I couldn't even go and punch Mohammed the Touareg for his friend's betrayal because I needed his protection and his contacts even more than ever.

"I had to find work. I got myself various insignificant jobs that paid practically nothing. And there, too, I was conned and ripped off many times, but that's only logical and I don't need to bore you with that. But I became more clever and more wily. I learned to think like them, however much I hated their way of thinking. I ended up in Agadez for just under six months. Damned city. Then I'd earned enough to have another go.

"This time we traveled in a large truck. More than ninety blacks in an open flatbed. That was cheaper. One hundred and fifty dollars per person. And it also felt safer because there were so many of us. The jerry cans full of water dangled from either side of the truck. And we only fit in if everybody stood. There's wasn't enough space to sit or lie down. We slept upright, sandwiched between others who may or may not be sleeping, so we hardly slept. Anyone on the outside had to take extra care not to be accidentally pushed overboard by the sleeping people leaning on them.

"At a certain point, the driver drove off the road to avoid a checkpoint. And then it happened. We drove over a landmine. It exploded at the front right corner of the truck. Luckily it was a small one and luckily I was at the back on the left. I was alright. But there were maybe seven dead and a few wounded. And maybe even worse was that we had a flat tire.

"The driver began to change the tire with our help. In the meantime, the question was what to do with the dead and the wounded. The driver was a good person. He said he could ask for help via satellite telephone. But that would mean us being taken back to Agadez. No one was up for that. There was almost an uprising. Punches were thrown. And then we just left them behind. We took the walking wounded with us, but we laid the hopeless cases next to the dead bodies in the sand and went on our way. Do you know what the worse thing was, Ilja?"

He took a sip of his beer.

"That night, in those circumstances, I completely agreed with the decision."

He began to laugh. Then he stared ahead. He looked at me and began to laugh again.

"Why are you laughing, Djiby?"

"I don't know. Because I made it. Because I reached the Libyan coast, where I was politely handed over to the sadists who stole my money and kicked and punched me for weeks on end because there was no money left to take from me. Because I'm in the Promised Land now, drinking beer with you, a writer, who is interested in my tale of woe. That's why I'm laughing. Because I'm too thirsty to cry."

9.

"We were kicked awake by Libyans in the middle of the night. They said our boat was ready and we had to leave as fast as possible. They said we still had to pay. We'd already paid. It was for our accommodation, they said." He began to laugh. "Can you imagine how funny I found that? They'd locked us up in a tiny barracks without any ventilation under the burning sun of the Libyan coast for weeks. They'd exploited us, hit us, and tortured us. They'd raped the women. Sometimes several times on the same day, six or seven of them at a time. And now they were telling us, as cool as you please, that the hotel costs for our luxurious stay at the welcoming Libyan seaside were going to be deducted from the advance we had paid and that we owed them a new fee for the crossing.

"But the fact I found that funny was something they didn't find funny at all. They hit me and spit in my face. It was their way of making it clear that they weren't joking. They lack a sense of humor, the Libyans. We managed to scrape a bit of money together as a group. They wanted more but when they realized it was all we had, they were happy to take it. They took us to the tideline in the pitch dark. And that's where our ship would be waiting, the lily-white ship of our dreams that would take us to Europe, its proud prow cleaving the water. Our journey had been difficult but finally we had reached our goal. Once we were finally onboard our ship, reaching paradise would be a breeze."

He took a sip of his beer. "And there was our ship. They shined their torches at it." He laughed. "It was a rubber dinghy. One of those simple orange things. About as long as from you to the next table there. I swear it, no bigger than that. Seven meters, max. And there were fifty-one of us. Men, women, two of them pregnant. There was even a little girl, Julia she was called, a sweet little kid, we all adored her. Most of them were Senegalese like me, but there were also a couple of Eritreans, two boys from Mali, and an Egyptian. Well, that isn't really important. What's important is that there were fifty-one people and that boat was hardly bigger than a bathtub.

But the Libyans meant it. They herded us aboard. They gave us a jerry can of gasoline for the outboard motor and two bottles of water. We asked whether that was enough. They said we shouldn't complain, Lampedusa was close by and Lampedusa was Italy and Italy was Europe. We asked how far it was. A couple of hours sailing, they said. We asked which way it was. North, they said, you can't miss it. They disappeared into the night. We managed to pour the gasoline into the tank in the dark without spilling too much and get the motor started. We sailed off, onto the open sea, on our way to the promised land where we would get rich without even trying."

10.

"At first we were overjoyed. A feeling of euphoria came over us—do you get that, Ilja? The sea was black and smooth under a black, smooth night sky. We were on our way. The light from the barracks where we'd been abused for weeks soon disappeared from view. We were free. Do you get what I'm saying, Ilja? We were free.

"We were sitting on each other's laps. I got cramp in my left leg, but I couldn't change my position, there wasn't enough space. But it wouldn't be long. Africa was a long way behind us. Europe was shining on the horizon. We began to sing. Not '*Fatou yo*' but happy songs. The Egyptians told jokes in Arabic that we only half understood.

But we laughed loudly all the same. We were happy. We were so happy, Ilja."

He took another sip of his beer. He didn't carry on.

"What are you thinking about, Djiby?"

"Julia."

"That little girl?"

"But you have to imagine, Ilja. Once we'd lost sight of the Libyan coast, we couldn't see anything anymore. Then we stopped singing. There was no moon. You couldn't see whether we were going backwards or forwards. We drifted on an inky sea under inky heavens. How much black ink do you need to write down our dreams on black paper? And who will read them? Do you understand, Ilja? You have a pen and a name."

"Carry on with the story."

"After that it got really frightening. The sea that had seemed so smooth when we left began to swell dangerously. The waves were sometimes meters high. The women screamed. Julia had her hands in front of her face, too scared to cry. And it's almost unimaginable if you've just left the suffocating heat of Africa behind, but it was cold at sea. There was a persistent, strong, icy wind. Most of us were wearing nothing more than T-shirts and shorts. Luckily it wasn't far. Not long now and we'd be there. But how did we know whether we were going in the right direction? One of the Malians said he could navigate by the stars. He'd learned that in the desert, but were the stars above the sea the same stars? There was uncertainty in his voice. He tried to reassure us and himself by saying that we simply had to go north and that was the easiest of all directions.

"We began to take on water because we were too overloaded. But we didn't really worry about that because we were nearly there. We emptied two bottles of water into the sea and cut them in half to make cups to use for bailing. It was nighttime. We had to survive the night. If we survived the night we'd land on one of Europe's golden beaches."

"Do you want another beer, Djiby?"

He laughed. "You know what was funny? Yes, I do want another beer. What's really funny is that we were happy when the sun came up."

"Why was that funny?"

"I've laughed enough today, Ilja. I'm going to drink my beer and…"

He choked. I slapped his back. "Thank you," he said. "See you tomorrow."

11.

"Why was it funny that the sun came up?"

Djiby had to laugh at my question. "But Ilja, you've got to be kidding. It's always funny when the sun comes up. Then you think your nightmares are over, just because a new day is starting. It makes me laugh."

"And then?"

"We were happy to see the sea. The sea looks a lot less scary by daylight than when you're at its mercy in the pitch dark. It was calm and blue. It was transparent and glistened. This was the Mediterranean Sea we'd been taught to dream of, just as the same can be said of you. For us, it was the topaz highway to our dreams."

"What went wrong?"

"What went wrong, what went wrong? Ilja, you're such a terrible interviewer. Let me just tell it. It'll save us both a lot of bother." He laughed. "But the funniest thing was that the sunlight wasn't our friend."

He took a sip of his beer. Bare legs walked past. He reached his arm up past his face, made a mouth with his hand in the air and sang, "*O mami sera boutuo mbele, o mami casse boutou mbele.*"

"What does that mean, Djiby?"

"It's from my song, from '*Fatou yo,*' the song my mother always sang to me when I was a child. I always sang that song when I was frightened. It's kept me alive, really. But I don't know exactly what it means. Something about giraffes. Everyone speaks Wolof in my region. But the song isn't in Wolof. My mother came from the southeast. It's probably in her native language, though I don't know what that was. Balanta maybe. Or maybe Jolaa or Soceh. My mother never taught me her language." He nodded in the direction the bare legs had gone. "We're lucky, you and me, that we can live in this country full of giraffes."

"Are there giraffes in Senegal?"

"And in your home country?"

"Sorry, Djiby."

"Do you have beautiful women in your homeland, too?"

"I've already said sorry, Djiby."

"In the light of the rising sun we saw that we had truly left Africa behind. The continent was no longer visible. Can you imagine the feeling, Ilja? Europe was not yet in sight, but we were almost there. We thought we could see the golden glow of its streets.

"And then it began to get hot. I had Julia on my lap. The men took turns to bail out with the cut-up plastic bottles. The sun glowed. There was no shadow in our boat. It was forty degrees around midday. We didn't have any water left, but that didn't matter, we were almost there. In half an hour we'd see Europe. Perhaps even sooner. We were in high spirits.

"And then the engine cut out. We were out of fuel. That was all the Libyans had given us. We stopped moving. There we were, floating on the open sea, fifty-one of us in an orange inflatable dinghy. A few men began to paddle with their hands, but soon realized it was pointless. There was nothing else to do but wait and see if anyone rescued us."

"And how long did that take?"

"What do you mean?"

"You're sitting here with me, so you must have been rescued. How long did it take?"

"Twelve days."

12.

"Twelve days?"

"Twelve days."

"But no one can survive that long."

"We survived, all of us, even little Julia. It was a miracle. Twelve burning hot days and twelve bitterly cold nights without food or water with fifty-one people in a boat seven meters long at the most.

It was hell, but I don't need to tell you that. We kept ourselves alive by drinking our own piss from the cups we'd made from the plastic bottles, the ones for bailing. Fights regularly broke out when someone tried to steal someone else's cup of piss. In the meantime, I tried to look after Julia. I gave her my piss to drink. Right from my dick, so that no one could steal it. It might have looked a bit weird to anyone not involved, but I didn't care." He laughed. "I'm so proud that Julia survived."

"And then they took you to Lampedusa?"

"If only. From time to time, a ship would pass in the distance. At the risk of falling overboard, the men stood up and screamed while waving their arms frantically. But they didn't see us. Or they didn't want to see us. Finally we were rescued by a Spanish fishing boat. The *Francisco Catalina*, I still remember it well. They'd set off twenty days earlier from Alicante to fish for crab and shrimp in the international waters between Libya and Sicily. The captain told me that. He was called José Durante Lopez. I talked to him a lot because I was the only person in our group who could speak a bit of Spanish. He told me we were one hundred and thirteen nautical miles from the coast of Libya and that Lampedusa was just as far again. The Libyans had given us exactly enough gasoline for half the journey. Typical Libyan humor, let's say."

He took a sip of his beer and looked at me with a broad smile.

"We were lucky, Ilja. Captain José was a brave man, do you realize that? Other captains have gotten into big trouble helping poor wretches like us. To start with, it's quite a big deal to take fifty-one starving and dehydrated people onboard your own ship. You'd have to really want to, let's say. And that while you set off from your home port with totally different plans, like catching shrimp and crab for example, you have to keep the wolf from the door, you have a wife and children to keep, and the same goes for the twelve-man crew. Reeling in black men isn't very profitable. On the contrary, it only costs you, because you have to give them food and drink and you lose valuable time. I'm only too aware of all this.

"And then there's a much bigger problem than that. Do you know what they did two years previously with the captain of the *Cap Anamur* when he rescued thirty-seven outcasts from the open sea and took them to Lampedusa? Don't laugh. They arrested him on the charge of assisting illegal immigration. Captain José wasn't the one to tell me that. I heard it later, when I was already here. But then I suddenly realized why so many boats had gone past preferring not to notice. And that's exactly why Captain José is a brave man."

13.

"As soon as we were all onboard the ship and had been provided with food and water, he broadcast a call on the international distress frequency, channel sixteen, asking what he should do. The Italian authorities replied that he should take us to Malta. But as soon as we entered Maltese waters, we were stopped by their coast guard. They told Captain José to go away. They said he'd picked us up in international waters and therefore there was no legal reason for Malta to accept us. He got into contact with the Italian coast guard to ask whether he could take us to Lampedusa, but they used the exact same argument.

"The deadlock lasted seven days. We could see the coast of Malta in the distance. Europe was there. The Promised Land was there. But we weren't welcome. In the meantime, the situation onboard became more acute. The *Francisco Catalina* was a ship of twenty-five meters, significantly more comfortable than our seven-meter orange dinghy, but built for twelve Spanish crew-members and a captain, not for thirteen Spaniards and fifty-one Africans. There was little space on deck because there were *nassa* everywhere—the cages they use to catch shrimp and crabs. The happiest of all of us was Julia. She and her mother were allowed to sleep in one of the three cabins for the crew. She'd just turned twenty, Julia's mother. The rest of us just had to make do in the open air. During the day we had shade, and at night, blankets; we had food and drink, so all in all we couldn't complain. But some did anyway. We were tired. Arguments broke out. The Egyptian threatened to jump overboard at one point. Then Captain José decided it was no longer possible to go on like that and something had to give.

"A compromise was reached with the authorities in La Valletta. The two pregnant women, Julia, and her mother, were allowed off the boat. The coast guard sent a boat to pick them up and take them to Malta. The rest of us would be taken somewhere else by Captain José."

"To Lampedusa?"

"Captain José confided in me. He said there was nothing else for it. And he said not to tell the others otherwise a mutiny would break out. I understood. '*Fatou yo*,' I sang. '*Fatou yo*.'

"After a day and a half's sailing, we reached the coast. Everyone was over the moon. We were being dropped off in Europe. Captain José dropped the anchor close to the shore. Everyone jumped overboard and ran onto the beach cheering. I walked along behind them, singing softly. Captain José waved to me apologetically and sailed away."

He took a sip of his beer. He began to laugh. "It's really quite funny if you think about it."

"Where were you? In Sicily?"

"In Libya."

14.

"It wouldn't be long before the Libyan militia or the human traffickers who worked with them noticed us and everything would begin all over again—the hitting, the kicking, the spitting, the torture, and the rapes. And it would only be worse than the previous time because none of us had any money left—to compensate our hosts for the inconvenience, let's say.

"We had to hide. I was just about to shout to the others, who were running on ahead of me, that this wasn't Europe, but then I changed my mind. There were still forty-seven of us and it would be impossible to hide as such a large group. And how long would we be able to keep that up? And what would our plan be? I realized I only stood a chance if I was on my own. I decided not to warn the others. I let them go. That hurt, Ilja. It hurt a lot because I know they were walking right into the arms of their torturers.

"I went off to look for a hiding place. It wasn't easy. I was on a wide beach that turned almost seamlessly into desert. There was hardly any vegetation. I instinctively continued to follow the tide-line. I didn't want to get too far from the sea because although I didn't have the slightest notion of how I was going to manage to get away from here, the sea was my only prospect for salvation, the only route to freedom. After a while, I spotted something on the beach, about a hundred meters inland. It was an empty, rusty barrel. Probably had contained oil or gasoline. At least, it smelled like it had. I dug it out a bit and climbed in. After that I swept the sand back until there was just an opening left that was big enough for me to breathe and see what was happening on the beach.

"Night became day and I soon realized that my hiding place was far from comfortable. It was cramped, it stank, and long before noon, it became unbearably hot. Luckily, I'd brought a bottle of water and some bread from the Spanish fishing boat. But it became clear I wasn't going to be able to stay here for long. At the same time, leaving my hiding place wasn't a real alternative because Libyan militias were driving along the beach in their jeeps on After I while a regular basis. It was a rather comical situation. For fear of being taken prisoner, I'd made myself a prisoner and I didn't have a clue how to escape my self-imposed captivity."

He laughed. "Will you order another beer for me, Ilja? A big one, because I get incredibly thirsty remembering all this."

"How long were you there in that oil barrel?"

"I was very lucky. During the third night, I was jolted out of my sleep by shouting. I wasn't really sleeping, that was impossible in my awkward position, but I had dozed off. I saw a group of men walking over the beach. Around twenty-five black men and four armed Libyans swearing at them. They were walking toward the tideline.

I recognized the ritual. They were being taken to a boat. I couldn't see the boat from my position but there had to be a boat, nothing else was possible. My heart began to thud so loudly, I was almost worried they could hear it.

"The Libyans left. I heard the sound of attempts to get an outboard motor started. This was my chance. I didn't hesitate for a second. I crawled out of my barrel and began to run as fast as I could. I'd never run that fast in my life. I got to the boat at the exact same moment the engine began to purr. I jumped onboard. The Libyans had seen me. They came running up. But they were too late. The boat was already moving. But the others weren't very happy that I'd jumped in with them, uninvited and without a valid ticket. They tried to throw me into the sea. 'You need me,' I shouted. 'I know the way.' With some reluctance, they decided to believe me. And so I set off on the journey to the Promised Land for a second time."

15.

"It was a terrible experience. The others were just as excited about their newly regained freedom and the fact that their big dream was finally coming true as I'd been the previous time. Only I knew what was coming next. I saw the jerry can of gasoline. It wasn't any bigger than the one the Libyans had given us last time. I saw that we only had two bottles of water again. I told them we had to use it sparingly. They thought I was just a worrier. I said that Lampedusa was much further than they thought. They didn't believe me. It was nearby, the Libyans had said so. We were probably nearly there.

As they joked and laughed, I quietly sang '*Fatou yo.*'

"The boat was just as big—just as small, I mean—as the last one. But there were fewer of us. Twenty-seven in total, all of us men, all of us about my age. Almost all Senegalese like me, but there were also two Nigerians, and a boy from the Ivory Coast. And because we weren't as overloaded as last time, we hardly took on any water. We didn't need to bail. So, luckily, there was something positive to say."

Djiby laughed.

"You tell it all in such a happy way."

"How do you think I should tell it, then? It was bad enough, the way it went, so it's better we laugh about it."

"And did the engine fail halfway?"

"Of course. Everything was exactly the same as the first time. The original elation made way for fear and the cold of the night and the original relief at dawn melted under the burning heat of the sun and when the gasoline ran out. It was all just as bad as the first time, apart from that, then it got much worse."

"How long was it before you were rescued this time?"

"Twenty days."

"But twenty days without food and water—no one can survive that."

"That's right. You've hit the nail on the head, Ilja. More than half of us didn't survive. When we were finally intercepted by the *Sibilla*, an Italian navy boat that had sailed out for us after a small Sicilian fishing boat, the *Pindaro*, had spotted us and raised the alarm, there were only thirteen of us. Fourteen strong young men had died by then. We'd thrown their bodies into the sea. What else could we do? We no longer had the strength for the fourteenth.

We just left him lying there and that was lucky because he wasn't completely dead, he was in a coma.

"But all of us were practically comatose. We were in a truly pitiful state. We were all severely dehydrated and malnourished. When the Italian navy came, it was really difficult just gesturing with my hands for them to help us. Most of the others couldn't even do that. Our lips were swollen and had burst from the sun and the salt. Our eyes were empty and hollow. We were ghosts. Moussa, a Senegalese boy, was the only one who could still speak. He was holding a necklace with a cross and said he was a Christian. He just kept repeating it.

"The captain of the *Sibilla* called for an air ambulance. The worst cases were taken to Palermo hospital. Along with six others, I was taken onboard the *Sibilla* and nursed there. At sunset, we sailed into the port of Lampedusa. I was in Europe at last."

16.

"But Europe wasn't what I'd imagined. It looked like Africa. All blacks. And I didn't get very far with getting rich without trying. I'd never seen so many poverty-stricken black people in one place, not even in Africa. The only difference with Dakar was that the policemen were white. But they were just as bastardly in Dakar.

"The fact was Lampedusa was one big concentration camp. Big isn't the right word. It was a small island. A rock in the sea. It was a small concentration camp. Too small. There wasn't enough room for that many prisoners. And every day new ones arrived, while no one left the island because that wasn't allowed. They needed papers for that and clearly that posed a major logistical problem to the Italian authorities—bringing papers to Lampedusa.

"Once upon a time, in the not-so-distant past, they'd built facilities to accommodate Africans like me. A grass plot with a barbed wire fence around it. Two barracks, hundreds of tents, and a soup kitchen. Piss in the woods and wash in the sea. You could probably piss in the sea, too. In any case, there was no active policy of checking what we were doing. But that reception center was full, so they let us roam the island. We slept on the streets. Three times a day we were allowed to fetch water and some food, but a Mercedes and an income weren't provided, though they were just what we had all come for. Food and drink was something we had in Africa. And it was better. And there was more of it. And at least we had a roof over our heads there. But without papers you were forbidden from becoming rich and the papers didn't arrive. I spoke to fellow Senegalese who had been on Lampedusa for a year. A year. Do you know how long a year lasts, Ilja? Do you know how long a year lasts if you can't remember how long it has been since you set off?

"There were frequent uprisings. There were just too many angry, frustrated black men sitting on a rock. I saw other men setting fire to a shop because you had to pay with real money there. I didn't join in but I understood. I understood only too well."

"But you're in Genoa now."

Djiby found this very funny. "You have such great observation skills, Ilja." He roared with laughter. "Give me another beer."

"But I meant…"

"How did I get here?"

"Yes, that's what I wanted to ask."

"Ha ha ha, Ilja. Don't you read the papers? That was because of that excellent joke that... What's his name? The last one? The last Italian prime minister."

"Berlusconi."

Djiby roared again. "Yes, exactly. Handsome man, that. With his bunga bunga. He could have been an African. Berlusconi. I'll never forget that name. He came to Lampedusa in his private helicopter to solve the problem. He liked that, solving problems. Especially when there were TV cameras pointing at him. And when they were pointing at him, when his hair was all combed and they'd finished his makeup, he said he'd give us all a temporary residence permit."

"I read about that."

"It was brilliant. In fact, he was telling the rest of Europe, if you don't help us by sending army ships to the Sicilian Channel to stop those dehydrated, starving black men and send them back to Libya, I'll give them a permit so that they can come to you."

"And he knew..."

"He knew they all wanted to go to France. The Senegalese in any case. We spoke French and most of us have a second cousin or a friend in Paris. Berlusconi chartered a few ferries to Genoa that would drop us off handily at the ferry dock that just so happened to be near the international train station on Palazzo Principe, where we could get the intercity to the French border at Ventimiglia. The French wouldn't be able to stop us since we had residence permits for the European Union and Berlusconi had solved the problem."

"So why didn't you go to Paris?"

"I don't know anyone there. When we sailed into the port of Genoa at sunrise, I was standing on deck. Pink light fell on the pink city. I held my breath. It was such a beautiful sight. Do you know what they call Genoa?"

"La Superba."

"Exactly. And that morning, as the ship maneuvered in the harbor and I saw the play of light on the houses, the towers, the city, I fell in love. I don't know any better way of saying it. You know, Ilja, there's no history in Africa. And from the boat, I saw nothing but history. In Africa there is no other beauty than the overwhelming beauty of the golden light on green trees growing from red earth. Everything people have built there is hideous. And that morning on the boat's deck, I saw a living landscape of centuries-old buildings sandwiched between the blue bay and the hazy blue mountains, a manmade jungle in improbably warm pastel tints, and for the first time in my life I saw how a city could be beautiful. Now I was in Europe at last. My eyes filled with tears."

17.

"But my infatuation didn't last long. Or let's say: my love will last forever; I'll cherish that moment on deck until I die. I love Genoa. But the city doesn't love me. It spat me out like a rat. That's not a very good expression because you don't normally want to swallow rats, but you get my meaning."

"Don't worry, Djiby. I'll puzzle over the metaphors. That's my job."

He laughed. "Horses for courses. We both came to this city because of a dream, you from the north and me from the south, and we make a perfect combination. While it's my job to carry heavy things and survive, it's your job to think what the best comparison is for that. And you earn a hundred times more than me for that."

"Do you consider that a laughing matter?"

"Hilarious." He let out a belly laugh. "Are you also going to have me speak beautiful Italian without any mistakes?"

"I'll go one better, you'll speak my mother tongue."

He doubled over at this. "Can I apply for a residence permit for your country, then, too?"

"I'll make sure you pass the language test with flying colors in any case."

"On paper then."

"But on paper is the only way that counts."

"Ha ha ha. You're quite right about that, Ilja. Paper is the only thing that counts. Anyone who exists on paper has the right to exist. If you don't have any papers, or you have the wrong papers, or not that one specific piece of paper, you're not a legitimate person. Your existence is illegal. Do you know how that feels when someone forbids your existence? You don't know. You've never experienced that. They've made my existence a punishable offense. I can go to prison if they find out I'm alive. The only advantage is that I'm barely alive. Anyone who looks as black as me is not licensed to see the daylight. He wears the camouflage of the night and won't laugh so that his shining teeth don't betray him."

"But you have a residence permit, don't you?"

"On to that already, are we? Do you want me to show you my ID? I've got it with me, you know. Do you want to take my fingerprints? Here, put some of that ink from your pen on my thumb, I'll press it into your notebook. Fuck you."

"Sorry, Djiby."

"It's alright. By now I know that your lot think like that. I know how things work in Europe by now. And this is your country. What right do I have to talk about it? You have laws and you're proud of them. We don't have any laws in Africa and we're not proud that we don't have them, but at least you don't have to have an ID card to exist.

"And yes, I do have that card. The temporary permit I got from Berlusconi. Valid for one year. See. It's written here. I have just over six months left. My existence isn't a punishable offense for the next six months. And then what?

"But the real problem is something else. My life in the Promised Land has now been legally permitted for almost six months, and I have just a little more than the same again before I can be arrested for existing. I thought just getting here would be enough to automatically get rich. That's what everyone told me. Once I was in Europe, I could go to the counter where they'd give me my pay and I could choose which Mercedes I wanted. I'd be able to send home a thousand francs a month for my family and friends, and then I'd still have thousands of euros left to buy a watch and sunglasses that would reflect the sun proudly when I returned to my home country for a well earned holiday.

"In the meantime, I share a run-down two-room apartment with eleven compatriots for a hundred euros per person a month, while the rats are allowed to eat there for free and I have to stay on the right side of my landlord because he lets me carry heavy things from time to time for ten euros. But instead of paying me, he always thinks of some debt or other—gas, electricity, water, service costs—which are deducted from my wages. And he's a good person. I should be grateful to him.

"And even though I'm legal for now, I'm still careful not to go out after a certain time of night. A black man on the loose after nine p.m., the *carabinieri* get very nervous about that, I can tell you. There's a sticker on my house that says:

> *derattizzazione in corso*
>
> *non tocare le esche*

"Do you know what that means? I've looked it up in my dictionary. It's the joke of the century. It means that pest control is underway and it's inadvisable to touch the bait. While the rats inside the building clearly aren't put off by the sticker, or maybe they are, in the sense that they take more care not to touch the bait, I'm personally more and more inclined to a metaphorical interpretation of the text. Since if the real rats aren't being exterminated, it must mean something else, mustn't it? You're a writer, you know that kind of thing. That's how metaphors work, isn't it? And who lives in the tumbledown buildings with the stickers on them, aside from the rats? Exactly. And that's exactly how I feel in this Promised Land called Europe: like the rat the stickers on my house warn people about. And the bait that brought me here—the guaranteed riches, the Mercedes, watches, and sunglasses—can't be touched. I feel like a pest that should be exterminated in this city I once fell in love with from the deck of a ship. The truth is that I'm a rat to everybody in this city, even to you, Ilja."

18.

I denied this most emphatically.

"Can you maybe lend me fifty euros, Ilja?"

"Why don't you go back, Djiby?"

"Are you listening to what you're saying?"

"That's not the way I meant it. I…"

"I know you didn't mean it that way. No one who says that kind of thing really means it. That's the problem with us black people. The whole time everyone keeps saying stuff about us that they don't mean. But they do say it. And you're a good person, Ilja, I'm sure you know it. You're not a racist, no more than those hundreds of shop, bar, and restaurant owners I've asked for a job are racists. They simply don't have any work for me. And you're paying for my beers because I'm telling you my story, but you'd never lend me fifty euros. We'll never be real friends. You're too afraid for that, you think I'll ask you for another fifty euros then and you won't be able to refuse because we're friends. Some people are afraid of me because I'm black, but there aren't actually that many of them. Most are afraid of me because I'm poor. They can tell because of my black skin. And if a person's poor, you're better off keeping your distance. Everyone knows that, even in Africa. It doesn't have anything to do with racism, even though the fact you're rich or poor has everything to do with the color of your skin. But it's the same in Africa. The way a white in our country is rich by definition, a black man here is by definition poor."

"Do you really want to borrow fifty euros?"

"I know you're only asking so you can write down that you've asked me. That's the only reason you're talking to me anyway, so you can write me down. And as soon as you have enough material, we'll smile for the camera one more time and after that, we'll never see each other again. You won't avoid me, but you won't look for me, either, or invite me to your table. But don't feel guilty. It's fine. I want my story to be told."

He smiled. "Order me another beer. Make it a big one because all this talking has made me thirsty. What did you ask again? Why I don't go back? To Senegal? Are you kidding me? I'll tell you exactly why, but first more beer."

19.

"Do you know how much it cost to get me to Europe? And by that I don't mean everything I went through and the fact it nearly cost me my life several times. What I'm talking about here is money. I worked it out. Everything added up would be about three thousand euros in your currency. Three thousand. Do you know how much money that is? For a boy in Africa? For a boy in Africa with his family? My uncle has a good job. He works in a steel factory just outside of Dakar. It works out to about a hundred euros a month. In Senegalese terms, that's a good income. He's the richest in my family, anyway. My father has a barbershop and my mother works as a seamstress. Maybe combined they make it to a hundred euros a month. And my mother's work is drying up because the Chinese do it even cheaper. A good friend of mine runs a shop for used mobile telephones and spare parts, but he doesn't have many customers and the margins are narrow.

Apart from that, there's nobody in my family with a regular income. I didn't have any work myself and neither did my two brothers. From time to time, I helped in my friend's shop and occasionally I had temporary work. The same goes for most of my good friends. Can you imagine how big a sacrifice it was for my family and friends to get together the three thousand euros necessary for my journey? And they all contributed. My father even took out a loan and two of my friends did the same. They got into debt for me, Ilja. But they did it with conviction. They saw it was an investment that would pay out ten or a hundred times. It was guaranteed I was going to be rich, after all. By contributing to the costs of my travel, they bought the right to a share of my immeasurable riches.

"And then you just coolly ask me why I don't return to Senegal? Do you think I'd still have friends? Do you think my family would welcome me into their arms like a prodigal son? They'd see me coming, their mega investment for whom they'd gotten themselves into major debt, returning penniless, empty-handed, without cars, gold bars, washing machines, luxury yachts, smartphones, diamonds, or even a dishwasher, come to explain that alas, nothing worked out, that he slept surrounded by rats, with eleven fellow countrymen, was able to find no other work than carrying heavy things from time to time, and that the whole idea that you automatically get rich in Europe was a misunderstanding as far as he was concerned."

"But…"

"Hang on Ilja, I'm still talking. Because on top of that, I'd be the first."

"What do you mean?"

"Everyone in Senegal knows that it's a long way to Europe, fraught with danger, which only the strongest survive, making it an investment accompanied with large risks, so the family has to choose the best candidate to undertake the journey. But everyone also knows that every Senegalese who has actually managed to reach Europe has become rich. If I were to admit I hadn't managed it, I'd be the first one not to manage it. Can you imagine what kind of shame it would bring upon me?"

"And the eleven other Senegalese sleeping among the rats with you? And all the others on the Via di Pré? It's a fairy tale."

"It's a fairy tale everyone in my home country continues to believe because none of us has had the courage to be the first to admit that it's a fairy tale."

"But sooner or later they'll realize that their investment hasn't paid out?"

"What do you mean, Ilja?"

"That no money's coming."

"But of course money's coming."

"How then?"

"I send a couple hundred euros a month. Through Western Union. I have to."

"And that's how you sustain the fairy tale."

"I don't have a choice. That was the deal."

"How do you get the money?"

"I borrow it. We all do."

"And how are you ever going to pay it back?"

"I came here with a dream of a better life. In the meantime,

I got lost in that fantasy. That's my story. That's what I had to say. Funny, isn't it?"

20.

A few months later, I was sitting on Caffè Letterario's terrace on my own, thinking about things I've already forgotten, when I saw my Senegalese friend again. He saw me, too, and came over. It seemed like he'd been looking for me. It worried me because it could only mean he wanted something from me. What was his name again? I should be more careful about making friends with those kinds of people. At the end of the day, they all expect you to help them. Of course, I hadn't really made friends with him, don't worry. I was simply curious about his past. Let's call it research. My interest was less in him than his horror stories about his hellish journey to the Promised Land, Europe, which I hope I'll be able to use in my novel, where discrimination against immigrants will be a major theme. But professional interest is all too often confused with friendship in those cultures. He had a desperate look on his face. What was his name again? Djiby. What does it matter. But, well, I think it was Djiby. He always looked desperate, but now more than usual. I prepared myself for the worst and resolved to be nice to him but not to give him money under any circumstances.

"I don't need anything today, Djiby." I shook his hand. I'd have been better off not doing so because it gave him permission to sit down at my table.

"You have to help me, Ilja." There we had it already. I tried to put on my strict but fair face.

"I'm sorry, Djiby. These are difficult times for everyone. I mean…"

"I mean…Ilja, listen. Do you know what happened?"

"It's terrible, Djiby, but I really can't help you."

"There were four of them. It was about one in the morning. Maybe a bit later. I was on my way home. I was walking along just near here, there, on Salita del Prione. They cut me off. A car with bright headlights. Slamming doors. They forced me to the ground."

"*Carabinieri?*"

"Four Italians. Not in uniform. They said they were from the police. One of them showed me his ID. But I didn't see anything, it all happened so fast. They asked for my papers. They took them from me. After that, they searched my pockets. They stole everything. Even the six hundred euros I had on me."

"Six hundred euros? How did you get hold of six hundred euros?"

"And the four of them kicked me all over. In my belly, in my face, in my…I had to go to hospital, Ilja. I was lucky it wasn't a lot worse."

"You were attacked on the street and beaten and robbed by Italian policemen?"

"You don't get it, Ilja. They pretend to be police. They show you a fake ID and then they rob you and beat you up. And sometimes they don't even do that. This happens in Genoa if you have a black face."

"Did you report it?"

"Yes."

"And?"

Djiby sighed. He stared into the distance, right through the centuries-old houses, across the sea to a continent where he'd never
been free, either, but where the authorities that had mistreated
him had been just as black as he, although that didn't necessarily
mean it was any better. If you're beaten up because the color of
your skin is different, at least there's some kind of reason. But what
does it matter? These are my thoughts, not his. I'd have looked
right through the houses in a northerly direction, in any case, just
as I'd once daydreamed myself away from my home country with
its dark gathering clouds when I still skulked around there, as he'd
once daydreamed himself away from Africa to the north where
everyone got rich without trying. It's all the same romanticism.
Djiby probably wasn't gazing at a meaningful horizon like me, but
just taking a brief pause to reflect on the best way to get money
out of me with his wretched story.

"They asked for my papers. I'll have to tell it a different way.
I was sent from one police station to the next. When I got to the
police head office and was finally able to tell my story, they asked
me whether I knew the four men. Of course not. But did I want
to report it anyway? Of course I did. They asked for my ID to
do so. But my papers had been stolen, that's exactly what I'd just
explained. They gave me a look of reproof. And do you know
what they said then?"

"What?"

"If you don't have any papers, you're an illegal. Being an illegal
is a crime in Italy. If you disappear now, we can pretend we never
saw you. Otherwise we'll be forced to arrest you."

"But why did you have six hundred euros on you?"

"What it comes down to is that the Italian law allows you to assault and rob a black man as long as you remember to steal his papers. Then he can't report you."

"I don't believe your story, Djiby."

"It wasn't my six hundred euros. It was my friends' money. I was supposed to give it to the man who arranged their travel and our accommodation. He's a businessman. He has little patience with clients who don't meet their financial obligations. He won't believe my story. And neither will my friends. I'm fucked, Ilja. I'm fuckeder than fucked. But I'm not asking you for money. I just want you to tell my story. Because you were such a good listener last time when I told you about my journey. For your book. I want you to tell it to the people in the north. That's the only thing I'm asking. Promise me you'll do that, Ilja?"

He didn't wait for my reply. He stood up and walked away. Then he changed his mind. He came back and said, "Do you know what the best thing was? It was my birthday. But it seems like every day's my birthday in this beautiful city in the fairyland of Europe." He laughed. He kissed my forehead and left. "*Fatou yo*," he sang quietly as he went. It was the last time I saw him.

PART THREE

The Most Beautiful Girl in Genoa (Reprise)

I.

How wafer-thin must it be, the difference between everything and nothing? Mere centimeters of cracking, sodden wood separate the sailor from his grave. A couple of steel plates make up the difference between hope and despair for tens of thousands on their way to the New World. Something improvised out of plastic brings Africans to Europe or it doesn't.

I can't live anywhere. I'm only fooling myself with pavings, walls, and names, places that have something to do with happiness. It's as thin as tracing paper. When winter comes, I won't know how I'll cope because the places you're allowed to smoke indoors aren't exactly happy-making. In my home country, everything would be much worse. I drink too much. I need warm, beautiful places where I can drink too much and smoke too much and easily meet friends who admire, worship, cherish, admire, worship, and cherish me. Naked girls who coo when faced with the heft of my celebrity. Frothy girls who automatically plop themselves in my lap because of all of the capital letters in my name.

I can't live anywhere. I think it's about places but instead it's about smoking in bars and restaurants and the time the pub shuts.

Everywhere. Doesn't matter where. Should I go farther south, then? No one will know me there for sure. And how will I get girls, then? What's there to do in Genoa when it's raining? What's there to do in Casablanca when it's raining? What's there to do in Cape Town when it's raining? Tell me how to live and I'll laugh in your face. Forget it. I'd rather wait for the waiter. And a clean ashtray.

And meanwhile, you spend a while in a city you think you discovered yourself. Genoa—ooh, you think you're seriously different from your eternal writer friends with their eternal Venice, Florence, or Rome?—real and authentic, with a port, immigration, a labyrinth you can get lost in, problems, transvestites. Fuck that. Do you believe it yourself? Mere centimeters of creaking, sodden wood.

By now I no longer find dying such a bad idea. I used to panic at the thought. Now I understand that it doesn't matter much how far south I travel. It'll be the same everywhere. You can do something or not. You can find a city, friends to drink with, and cafés to make your own with renewed, unsuspected passion, but you know that one day you'll betray it all for a new illusion. And then you'll write about it. That's the biggest illusion of all. I only write thanks to the lack of women and drinking pals keeping me, protesting, from my work. If Genoa really were as great as I say it is, you wouldn't hear anything about it, my friend. Everything I write is fake because I don't write when I'm myself. It's an escape from reality on a rickety raft of language, like the boats that went to La Merica, the same as those poor suckers come to Europe, the Promised Land.

The only place I can live is elsewhere. I'm going south, she's going north. It probably won't really matter if we die—she of hunger, me of boredom and thirst. It would save us a lot of futile dreams.

2.

There's no winter in Italy. By that I mean that in the two or three months that it's genuinely cold, Italy no longer exists, in the sense that it stops functioning. Yesterday a thin layer of snow fell on Genoa. A millimeter that melted away in no time. Normal life was completely disrupted. The buses crawled along Via XX Settembre with snow chains on their wheels. Schools were closed. Shops, bars, and restaurants shut earlier than usual because the suppliers could no longer reach them. The only people still out on the street are weirdos or foreigners. A homeless person or a Senegalese tried in vain to sell umbrellas for five euros to nonexistent tourists. A cold, wet wind drives through the abandoned streets. I notice I've switched to the present tense for no reason. It's because I'm so fucking cold. I'm writing this in the smoking room of the Britannia, a tasteless English pub I only come to for its smoking room. It's the only place I can go to since the upstairs room at Bar Berto was closed down by the police because the fume extraction system didn't meet safety regulations. But the owner of the Britannia is a stingy old miser who has never given me a discount and makes a profit by turning off the heating to save on fuel costs. See him standing there behind the bar in two thick jumpers selling cocktails and beer over his reading glasses at extortionate prices. I hate him. Yet I still come here because I don't know of any better place to go in the winter. Or I'd have to stop smoking, but that would be the other extreme, I'm sure you'd agree with me, my friend. Then they'd have won. The others. Our enemies.

In the meantime, the Genoese shut themselves away in their palazzi. They have their own rituals. They turn their backs on the city before ostensibly dedicating themselves voluntarily to demanding members of their family. For them too, Italy ceases to exist for a couple of months. Or they leave for their lodges in the mountains where there's supposed to be snow, where each year they ski for an hour between lunch and the aperitif, with similarly minded people who are all dressed in the latest ski fashions.

And so the labyrinth becomes a grim and impassible place. The smooth, pitch-black, threatening paving stones gleam in the darkness that has descended early. A short walk is a survival trek past closed doors and shuttered windows. It's like in Dickens or those Anton Pieck Christmas cards, but then not picturesque. The snow isn't warm, white, and fluffy but dirty and wet and gray. And the friendly, smiling beggars in their special Christmas tatters who tap hopefully on the windows receive no alms. They can fuck off.

Yesterday a homeless man froze to death in the passage under the Carlo Felice opera. It was in the papers today. The story is all the more cruel because there was a grand opening ceremony taking place for the opera's symphonic winter season five meters above his head, with the mayor and all the Genoese magistrates in attendance. His name was Babu. I knew him. An African boy. He often came past the terraces begging. I never gave him anything. Today I walked to the passage under the opera. His fellow homeless had set up an altar for him in the alcove where he perished. Genoese wearing fur coats came by to leave offerings and assuage

their guilty feelings. The alcove was full of flowers, packets of cigarettes, and bottles of gin. And so Babu got everything from his
new fatherland he had ever desired.

3.

The flowers were still there today. The packets of cigarettes and
bottles of gin had gone. Babu's homeless friends were nowhere to
be seen, either. Mediagenic tragedy and strokes of luck have often
made uneasy bedfellows.

That last line will have to be cut when I rework these notes into
a novel. Much too pretentious. One of those sentences where you,
as a vain writer, openly stand there posing with your unique ability
to grasp reality with a telling analogy. Linking the concrete to the
abstract. Normal people don't see those deep kinds of connections.
The momentary pleasure of a cigarette is a reconciliation with
the transient nature of life. Those kinds of profundities. X=y. I can
just toss them off. Perhaps my pen's hesitation above the paper
was a harbinger of the slowly dawning realization that I was on
the wrong track. Pleasure is nothing more than forgetting everything ahead of us after the moment of pleasure is gone. There was
another paradox in that, did you spot it? And another, I'll make
one with rum and Coke. Rum and Coke is the music of the night
that sounds like a cacophony in the morning. And do you know
that really happens, too? I'm actually drinking rum and Coke as
I write this, and right away an Italian girl comes over to ask what
I'm writing. I say I'm writing about her. She doesn't believe me.

If I turned this into a book, I'd have to delete the whole of that last paragraph. If I ever wanted to turn it into a book. Sometimes you ask yourself whether it's worth all the effort. People don't read anymore. And they're right. They have better things to do. Like surviving, buying Christmas presents for their in-laws, keeping their mistresses a secret, or assuaging their guilt by giving gin and cigarettes to the friends of a tramp who froze to death. People already know how everything is and should be. They don't need a book to teach them. I've always thought that our role as literati was to shake things up. To unsettle fixed values. Even if just for a moment. But now I realize that people don't need that at all. Their daily lives are already challenging and unsettling enough. Thanks to their obligation to continuously fulfill all their obligations, they are continuously on unstable ground. They look for stability in their rituals and routines. They look for consolation, for someone to pin them down and tell them that things always run their course and that it's not their fault that a tramp froze to death in a passageway under the opera, because they are decent people who after a hard day's work for their boss use up their last strength getting to the right shop just before closing time to buy the right kind of *panettone* for their mother-in-law. What more can you do? Read a disturbing book about immigration? *Per carità.* They already have their hands full with their own problems. Do you know how difficult it is to find a garage in this city? And do you know what happens when you simply park your car on the street? The Moroccan and Senegalese rabble know what to do with it, I can tell you. But we're good folks, we vote for the left and take cigarettes and gin to the Moroccan and Senegalese friends of Babu.

And they weren't even his friends. I never saw them together.

Those so-called homeless friends of the homeless Babu live in Via di Pré or the Maddalena quarter. They're burglars and pickpockets. They have to survive, too. They read it in the paper, just like me and all the other Genoese. They understood the rare opportunity, put on their filthiest clothes, chased away the real tramps, and lit candles in the passageway under the opera. They're not there anymore today. Of course they aren't. They'll never be there again, unless there's something new to be had. And you come along with literature? Like a world traveler musing in the hotel lobby? You have to feel the despair of the wet gray snow and lose yourself in a dream that gets watered down under your increasingly unsteady tread to understand anything at all. You don't need to read books, you need to try to survive outside where you get screwed, fucked over, and robbed.

X is never y since it depends completely on what you want to achieve with x and y. The abstract is always concrete. Friendship is always about fifty euros. Mourning a so-called friend who froze to death reaps multiple rewards. Everyone cons everyone else, that's what it comes down to. That's what I've learned, my friend. Tomorrow I'll write something more cheerful again.

4.

Sometimes, in the dark pit of the night after closing time at the end of that thieves' alley San Bernardo, at the furthest tip of the labyrinth, in the neglected and forgotten part after Via delle Grazie, where you can smell the fish market and the rotting waters of the port, there's a nightclub. Sometimes. Because just as often it's closed or you can't find it. It's where there's a drain for the dregs of the night: actors, transvestites, Moroccans, and the clientele they have to accompany to the toilets every five minutes in order to snort drugs, suck cocks, or both. It smells of smoke, piss, vomit, and hash, and those smells are freshly produced all around you continuously. Fights regularly break out, arising from conflicts that none of those involved can remember the next day, and mostly ending with someone slipping in a pool of vomit, smacking his chin on the bar, and being carted off.

The proprietor, Pasquale, is just standing there mixing cocktails in plastic cups; if requested, he'll explain that he has a permit to run an arts club. Cocaine is sold in his toilets, kilos at a time, but Pasquale pretends not to notice. He avoids trouble that way. Both the Mafia and the Moroccans protect him because they need him, or at least his arts club, or at least its toilets.

That's the mistake Fabio made with his bar in the same neighborhood. He tried to keep it clean. He got the police involved and threw the Moroccans out. They smashed his bar to bits and since then Fabio's been missing an eye and his walking has gotten a lot worse. And they also seem to have found out where he parks his car and where he lives.

Pasquale, on the other hand, has been in business for nearly twenty years—if you can call it a business, getting the drunken outcasts of the night even drunker while pretending not to notice a thing and never cleaning your toilets, no matter how encrusted the shit gets on the walls. I go there sometimes. I like to go there. Being lonely among other lonely people is a sublimated form of loneliness. I sit there at the sticky bar like a silhouette of a midnight cowboy, nursing a much too strong Negroni in my wisdom-clenched fists, and conduct laconic one-line conversations with actors who can no longer get their words out, and maybe because of this or for other reasons they can't determine, get tears in their eyes and, assuming they've made a new friend, sycophantically offer me another Negroni with their last pennies.

And one evening, I kissed the dangerous transvestite Penelope Please with my thirsty tongue, which put up a minutes-long fight against her drunken tongue while I protected the wallet in my back pocket with one hand, and proof that indeed she was no woman took on ever more convincing forms in the other. Not for any particular reason, just because I felt like it. Because the place compels you to do things you wouldn't do elsewhere. If you've sunk so low as to find yourself there, there are no more appearances to keep up and you might as well descend to dissipation and ruin for good.

And that evening, content with the poetry of my existence, as I wandered along the Via San Bernardo like a giant, lonely wraith, I was mugged. I had always thought that I looked too big and strong to be robbed. Muggers don't want trouble; they look for easy prey, like an unsuspecting tourist or a drunk Erasmus student. I'm almost two meters tall, weigh more than a hundred kilos, have a black belt in aikido, and can look very threatening, even when I'm drunk. But there were two of them and they were professionals. Of course they were Moroccans. I think I'd even seen them earlier in the nightclub. They'd watched me and followed me. They knew exactly which pocket my wallet was in. I managed to throw one of them to the ground, but in doing so I lost my balance, and by then the other had grabbed my wallet. They ran away and disappeared into the dark labyrinth. The whole skirmish had lasted no more than a few seconds. And I hadn't stood a chance. I didn't even try to go after them. Hard, intent, and stoic, I went on my way. I was in Genoa. I was no longer a virgin. And I'll be damned if a smile didn't appear on my face.

5.

Today, right at the end of Via San Vincenzo, just by Brignole station, I discovered a porn cinema. I must have walked past it hundreds of times, but I'd never noticed it before. There weren't any suggestive photos in the window, no screaming advertisements for forbidden pleasures. But today my gaze fell upon an amateurish poster, made in a print shop, with the English words "nonstop show." I had to choose between screen 1 and screen 2. I asked what the difference was. I didn't understand the answer. Then I asked which show was cheaper. I was intending to choose the more expensive. The price was the same, so I ended up in screen 1.

It was a real cinema with a large screen, rows of tip-up seats, and a balcony with boxes and seating at the sides. It was dark inside. I needed the flesh-colored light of the screen to see that I wasn't alone. The silhouettes of twenty or thirty men were as widely spread around the room as possible. When we had tests at school, we had to sit a ways apart so that we couldn't copy each other. Everyone was sitting separately here, too. No cheating.

The show consisted of a French porn film, I guessed from around the mid-1980s. Its dialogue had been dubbed into Italian.

They'd left the original sounds intact in the sex scenes. This confirmed my fantasy that Italian girls only acted like they spoke Italian until you stuffed something into them. The film was actually quite good. There were pretty girls with small tits. The scenes proceeded smoothly, without a surplus of soporific gymnastics in close up. There was even a kind of storyline: the man with the long coat and sunglasses commissioned various girls to make their fantasies come true. And they did that. That was what the film was about. And so it might happen that a girl was masturbating in a graveyard at night before being taken by two supposed tramps, until the man with the long coat and sunglasses appeared on the scene to finish things off properly. There was also a remote controlled car that had special hooks that could steal the panties of girls who just happened to have taken off their panties in a public place.

I sat as far apart from the others as I could and wondered whether there was anything like this in my home country. I knew we used to have them, sure. On the day of my eighteenth birthday I'd been to the legendary Cinema Rex. Those were the days. But the whole porn business had been so Youtubed and Youporned and Redtubed over the past few years. A real cinema with tip-up seats and popcorn, velvet, and a silver screen, a counter where you had to pay to be allowed inside, the emotion shared with a room full of like-minded people in the darkness of hidden fantasies that the city didn't want to know about. And when it was over, stepping blinking out into a daylight filled with shoppers while inside your head you were still in the film. I was grateful to have found a real porn cinema.

But it didn't really excite me all that much. At least, that's what I'd decided in advance. The problem with such a lovely old-fashioned porn cinema is, of course, that, despite the relative gloom and spread-out seating strategy, you hardly have any privacy. In some ways, it's still a public building. That's why you can't smoke there, for example. And it's not really the perfect spot to have a nice long wank. At least that was the way I tended to think about it. But when I took a look around in the skin-colored gleam of the big screen, I saw that pretty much all the paying customers differed from me in that respect.

First I became aware of a jerking off kind of a movement diagonally behind me. I turned my head in such a way as to be able to check out my suspicions. And I was right. It stood out, to give a graphic description, like a sore thumb. An old, dirty Genoese man sat in the seat diagonally behind me unmistakably, convincingly jerking off with ever more frantic gestures.

As you'll understand, my friend, I was shocked. I was convinced that he was a notorious pervert who, somewhere between now and the next five minutes, would be thrown out of the auditorium for the umpteenth time. A gentleman doesn't behave like that in a place of public entertainment. But when I very discreetly turned my head to give the corner of my right eye a good view, I saw that the fat man sitting four seats away on the same row as I had his whole fucking trousers around his ankles including his dirty underpants and was sitting there with his stinking, wrinkly member in his fists. I could see the tip of his cock and his scrotum. When I went on and had a less discreet look around, I realized that I was the exception, not them. And not only because I was by far the youngest. All those filthy, squalid phantoms of men were wanking before my very eyes. And then I saw that if they were watching the film, it was only out of the corners of their eyes. From time to time, someone would turn his face to the screen to get some inspiration or to feign artistic interest. But everyone was mainly looking at everyone else. And the privileged ones in the boxes had a fantastic view of the room in its entirety.

My first instinct was to make a quick getaway, but I had to get out on the right side of the row, and how do you ask someone to get up and make way for you when he has his trousers around his ankles and he's holding his cock? I decided to wait politely until he'd come. But once that had happened, he started all over again. He looked at me with eyes that glistened like a false tooth in the night.

I'm not telling you the entire truth, my friend, but you've guessed that already. My first instinct wasn't to make a quick getaway. As the youngest and, in all modesty, most attractive visitor at the time, I felt I was being stared at. Something was expected of me. I was an object of fantasy. I could feel it in my veins. My first instinct wasn't to get away as quickly as possible, but to unbutton my fly as slowly as possible. Glittering eyes gazed at me like wolves in the night. I've seldom felt so turned on. And by the time I had slipped down my underpants agonizingly slowly, I found myself the owner of a monumental erection that gleamed in the light of twenty, thirty, or forty pairs of eyes. I was blind to the film now. Nice and slow like a woman, I began to play with my cock as though it were a pussy. My own imaginary breasts turned me on like a transvestite. I took off my top and played with the world like I was fucking myself in my thoughts. If a horny old pervert had come up to me that moment waving his festering member, I would have sucked him off like I was wearing lipstick. I was La Superba. La Superba was me. I almost ejaculated at the thought, but delayed it a little for sake of the show, and instead, something quite different happened.

All things considered, it's a terrible story—embarrassing, filthy, and humiliating for me. Naturally, I would never put something like that in my book. Or I'd invent another character who did it. And even then. I'm only telling you, my friend, because I trust you and I want to make something clear to you in this unusual fashion. That afternoon I was a victim of my own imagination. I felt sexy, but I was just a fat writer behaving scandalously in a public place in Genoa. Anyway, you get the point. The circumstances were extreme, but the truth of the matter is that I sincerely believe we are all like that. We dream our dreams, feel desired, inspired, and admired until the lights go on.

Because suddenly the lights went on. The French film had finished, clearly. I'd stopped watching it. A new film was put on the reels. It was a nonstop show, after all. But in order to change the film, the light had to go on. Just for a moment. A minute is enough. And there I was. There I was with my titties, my teased-up top, my remotely-removed panties, fondling myself like a girl in a Milo Manara drawing, with a painfully postponed orgasm on the fifth seat from the right of the second to last row of a cinema at the end of Via San Vincenzo, close to Brignole, in front of all of the eyes of Genoa. Somehow, all the dirty old men had suddenly turned into impeccably dressed, fine gentlemen. It was only then that I made a quick getaway.

6.

It was a cold night and had started snowing again. The snow didn't even melt but settled. I was looking for a bar that was still open. It was Sunday, so the options were limited. Even the Britannia was closed. I went to the Piazza delle Erbe but all the shutters had already been rolled down. There was no one out. I pinned my hopes on the historical Bar Barbarossa on Piano Sant'Andrea under the Porta Soprana. I walked uphill along Salita del Prione, my head deep in my collar. I had to watch my step as I climbed. The street was definitely too steep for these weather conditions. I almost fell over twice. But it was too late to change my mind. The journey back downhill would be just as slippery, and what's more, there was nothing to do down there, as I'd already found out.

In the distance I saw the shadow of someone trying to descend the same street from the other side. It was a woman. She didn't seem to have any trouble with the slipperiness of the snow-covered cobblestones. She barely seemed to touch the ground.

We met halfway. She was an old woman, I could see that from her face. But she moved almost weightlessly. She looked almost transparent. She was wearing strange clothes, a long black skirt, and a gray shawl—she seemed to come from another era. In a strange way, she looked older than she looked.

She spoke to me. I didn't understand a word she was saying. She spoke too quietly. I apologized. She apologized in turn and repeated her question. I realized she wanted directions, but she was speaking the Genoese dialect and I could only half understand it. I've heard drunken heating engineers and roadworkers at Paolo's *enoteca* screaming in the dialect at each other that the other has a tiny *belín,* but I'd never heard friendly, polite Genoese. She repeated her question. Vico dei Librai? I'd understood. Vico dei Librai. Did I know where it was? That's where she lived and she couldn't find her house anymore.

I reflected. I knew Centro Storico very well by now, but I couldn't place a Vico dei Librai. Was it in Centro Storico? Yes, it was just near the port, near Porta Soprana. It did sound like the name of an alleyway in Centro Storico, I had to admit. She didn't seem demented or confused. She seemed to know exactly what she was talking about. But I didn't know. I'd never heard of that alleyway.

But at the same time, under these circumstances, I couldn't allow myself to just shrug apologetically. It was cold, snowing. She was an old lady who couldn't find her way home. I couldn't abandon her to her fate at this time of night. I was charmed by the idea that, as a foreigner, I could be the savior of a woman who was so Genoese she didn't even speak Italian. I suggested going to Bar Barbarossa. They'd certainly be able to help us there. And I was on my way there, anyway. She nodded, turned around, and walked along beside me.

The Barbarossa was open but practically empty. I ordered a Negroni for myself and asked what I could get for her. She didn't want anything. I insisted. I said it was cold. I ordered her a hot cup of tea. I said it was the least I could do for her.

We stood at the bar. She didn't touch her tea. I asked the barman whether he might know where Vico dei Librai was. He didn't know, either. I said it had to be in the neighborhood and that it was important because the lady had to get home. He did his best, looked in the phone book, but couldn't find the street in question. How did you spell it again? Dei Librai? Like the booksellers? Strange. Wasn't in the index. The woman was still standing silently next to me. He fetched a colleague. He had a smartphone with navigation. The problem would be solved within two minutes. I ordered another Negroni. She still hadn't touched her tea. But Vico dei Librai didn't exist. His smartphone gave no results. Maybe he didn't have a signal. Maybe it was because of the snow. She thanked us. She laid a banknote on the counter to pay for the tea she hadn't drunk a drop of. I protested. The barmen protested, too. But she was already on her way out. We followed her with the money she'd left behind. She was nowhere to be seen. There weren't any footprints in the fresh snow. What she'd left behind turned out to be a one hundred-lira note from the Kingdom of Italy.

7.

"Your coat smells like a cage of wet, wild animals." It was the signora. "If you want to become a Genoese *gentiluomo*, you'll have to start going to the dry cleaners from time to time. But I'm prepared to forgive you that today on the condition that you give me your dirty arm and accompany me to the Bar of Mirrors. It's slippery for a lady. And I'll thank you with a drink. As long as it's coffee and not the usual shit you drink. What's it called again? Negroni. That's healthier for you and cheaper for me. I have to think of everything, Leonardo. Promise me you'll go to the hairdresser's soon, too?"

"It's such a privilege to be able to keep you company that I insist you allow me to thank you by offering you anything you would like."

She smiled. "You're learning, Leonardo."

We sat down inside, in the porcelain grotto, at the small round table next to the window. I ordered a Negroni and she a hot tea with Cognac.

"If you're the one paying, I'll have one, too. You'll understand that, as a Genoese."

"Thank you, signora. As a Genoese, I understand that you are doing me a service by so unambiguously accepting my hospitality and I can only hope that I will soon find myself in a situation whereby I can pay you back."

"I see that my lessons are starting to bear fruit. You're indebted to me for that, too."

"I was only too aware of that."

"What happened with the theater?"

"How do you know about that? I mean, which theater? I mean…"

"As a Genoese you ought to know that, as a Genoese, I know everything about you."

I nodded to say that I should have known and I shook my head in response to her question.

"Parodi?"

"It didn't go that well."

"I hope you haven't turned them against you. They're powerful in this city."

"I know that now."

"Where is the theater actually?"

"Piazzetta Cambiaso."

She gave me a confused look.

"That little piazza on the crossroads between Vico dietro il Coro di Santa Maria delle Vigne and Vico delle Lepre, opposite Da Francesa, the fish restaurant, between Piazza Soziglia and Via della Maddalena, actually on the corner of Piazza Lavagna."

"I don't know that part."

"De Maddalena."

"I never go there. I never go further than Piazza Soziglia and Via Luccoli."

There you had it again. Maybe it was better that the whole project had ended in disaster. Real Genoese like the signora didn't even dare to set foot in those alleys.

"But you know the rest of Centro Storico."

"I've lived here a lot longer than my youthful appearance might suggest, Leonardo."

"More than twenty years?"

"Don't flatter me. At least, not in such a cheap way. I know every street in this neighborhood, Molo."

"Do you know Vico dei Librai?"

She seemed to freeze. "Why do you ask that?"

"Oh, no reason. It's just…"

"Did somebody ask you the way?"

"Yes, it was…"

"An old woman? Where?"

"Just next to Porta Soprana. On Salita del Prione."

The signora made the sign of the cross.

8.

"You've met her," the signora said, "the old lady of Vico dei Librai." She was speaking softly all of a sudden, as though we were discussing someone who had just died.

"Is she famous?"

"You could say that. Or, rather, you couldn't say that, because to be famous you at least have to exist, which in her case is definitely the question. But that question is famous. She's a myth, but anyone staying in these dark alleys long enough, where the shadows are more skittish than the rats, runs into her sooner or later. What did she look like?"

I told her the whole story. She nodded. "Yes," she said quietly, "that's exactly what the other witnesses said about her. And that hundred-lira note, do you still have it?"

"No, the barman in the Barbarossa kept it. She was using it to pay for a drink, after all. But please tell me who she is."

"Vico dei Librai doesn't exist, at least, not anymore. It was in the area that used to be called Madre di Dio, just near the old Barbarossa city walls, at the foot of Porta Soprana. It was an old working class neighborhood. One night in 1942, the neighborhood was flattened by shelling from the English fleet. And after the war, they built that hideous new Genoa that you know, with new streets and tarmacked squares named after poets who'd have been rendered speechless at the sight of those underground motorways and fly-overs. Piazza Dante, Via D'Annunzio, and the Giardini di Plastica. Vico dei Librai used to be somewhere there. Until one winter's night in 1942.

"The story goes that the old lady of Vico dei Librai was on her way home that evening. She'd taken bread to the orphans and flowers to the church. She was later than usual that night because she'd had to shelter from the bombing. When things finally quieted down, she continued on her way home. She was overcome by the cold somewhere near Campo Pisano. She stopped to rest on the steps of the doorway to a palazzo and passed out. Or died. Or maybe it's the same thing. But when she woke up, her neighborhood didn't exist anymore. Since then she's been roaming the city, particularly on bitter winter nights, asking the way to Vico dei Librai in antiquated Genoese dialect."

9.

In terms of ghosts and spirits, I've had a clear policy all my life. Although there is no scientific evidence for their existence and every checkable and verifiable foundation of modern metaphysics excludes the possibility of their existence, I've always chosen, against my better judgment, to believe in their existence because it's more amusing than justifiably not believing in them. The stories are too wonderful to dismiss as nonsense and then ignore. I've believed in them as I've believed in the characters of novels who have come into my life and whom I understand in so much as they play a part in a story that interests me. And in that way, I can picture them as fully alive.

But you can imagine, dear friend, that it's a rather unsettling experience if ghosts suddenly decide to exist on their own, instead of me beneficently allowing them to exist. That's not what's supposed to happen. Then I lose control. Neither do I want a character in a novel whom I've invented to come and sit down at my table and interfere with my chapter structure and the way I'm depicting him, threatening to inform the trade union for fictional figures about my dubious practices and considering taking that ultimate measure: going on strike. That would be a pretty mess. It happened to me before, with my last book, *Real Life: A Novel*, when the characters, under the leadership of master schemer Drinsky, started a revolt because of what they considered to be disappointing catering, and it turned into a bloodbath. I had to make an example of that Drinsky and execute him. I don't want to have to go through that a second time. So the last thing I need is a ghost who decides to exist.

And I wasn't even drunk that evening. I had been planning to be, but everything was closed and that was exactly why I'd slipped and scrambled uphill to the historical Bar Barbarossa. I really did see her. I really did talk to her. I really did hold that hundred-lira note. I can start doubting all those things retrospectively, but that's just as irrational as believing in ghosts.

The signora gave me a book about Genoa's ghosts, poorly written tourist trash, but she's in there, the old woman of Vico dei Librai, and everything was the same. That was exactly what she'd looked like, exactly how she'd acted, exactly the question she'd asked and that was exactly the way she'd mysteriously vanished. If I'd read the book first, I might have been able to invent that I'd actually met her. But the other way round, no, that doesn't work, there are too many consequences.

I read the whole book as a knee-jerk reaction. Genoa was truly infested with ghosts. And the worst thing is that I'm seeing them everywhere now. I go to Piazza San Matteo and bump into Branca Doria, who shows me his blood-smeared hands. Centuries ago, he used to live in the beautiful palazzo to the left of the church. His good friend and brother-in-law, Michele Zanche, while visiting him, was betrayed and murdered in cold blood by Doria. This led Dante to place Doria in the third zone of the ninth ring of hell, even though he was still alive when Dante was writing. But at that time, people knew that anyone betraying a friend would immediately lose their soul and reside in hell, while their earthly body would be possessed by a demon, until their heart gave out. Doria tried to wipe off his bloodied hands on the second column on the left of the church.

At Porta dei Vacca, I saw the coach driven by a monk who was faceless under his hood, taking the restless victims of violence to a quiet place in the mountains. I heard the prisoners' chains rattling on Campo Pisano. I saw the veiled woman of Vico del Duca, and on Piazza del Amor Perfetto I saw the beautiful prostitute holding a cabbage from a window on the fifth floor, but when I took a better look, I saw that it wasn't a cabbage but the head of a jealous lover.

Just by there, on Piazza Banchi, at night I heard the ethereal music of the composer Alessandro Stradella, who had met with major success in Venice but had fallen in love with the wrong woman there. He'd fled to Genoa and hidden in the labyrinth. But an assassin had been able to find him and stabbed him on the steps as he tried to escape into the church.

On my way home, I sometimes saw a man in a purple tunic leaning against the portico of the San Donato church. That's

Stefano Raggi. He was wrongly accused of betraying the Doge and, to save himself from being disgraced, rammed a crucifix into his heart on the church steps, screaming that he would never leave the city.

And the worst was Via del Campo, in the middle, by the fountain. In the light of the moon, I saw the bloodiest of scenes, like a macabre kind of *son et lumière*. Giulio Cesare Vacchero's house once stood here, a nobleman and putative confidant of the Doge, who conspired against him with Count Carlo Emanuele I of Savoy and then was betrayed in turn. A supposed friend informed the Doge of the plot and Guilio Cesare Vacchero was executed, his possessions confiscated, his sons banished, his house razed to the ground, and now in the place where his house once stood, there's a marble column with a Latin inscription that has immortalized all of this for eternity:

JULIJ CAESARIS VACHERIJ

PERDITISSIMI HOMINIS

INFAMIS MEMORIA

QUI CUM IN REMPUBLICAM CONSPIRASSET

OBTRUNCATO CAPITE PUBLICATIS BONIS

EXPULSIS FILIIS DIRUTAQUE DOMO

DEBITAS POENAS LUIT

A.S. MDCXXVIII

I don't need to translate that for you. Anyone can understand it. And his grandchildren were so ashamed of it they built the fountain to obscure the view of this column.

By now I no longer know whether I can see the apparitions because as a writer I have been occupationally cursed with a great deal of empathy and the old lady of Vico dei Librai has weakened reason's last line of defense, causing me to lose myself in my imagination, or whether I'm really seeing and hearing them and rapidly losing my mind.

10.

I try to imagine it. Every boy born in the known world back then dreamed of it. Every shield-bearer up to his ankles in shit, cleaning the stables, fell asleep with cheeks red with excitement that he saw reflected in the suit of armor he'd polished for his master until it shined. And he'd never forget the day the horses were saddled. The quiet, dull clap of black leather on the back of a gelding as the stirrups tinkled. The flapping of the banners. The heavy thumping footsteps of a knight weighed down with armor. The groaning and squeaking of the pulley that dropped him onto his horse's hollow back. The historical pronouncement that echoed in the cavities of his suit of armor. The dry click of his helmet's visor. The swelling storm. The banners do battle with the wind. You avert your gaze submissively as you pass his shield with its religious insignia. A determined sword snaps into its scabbard. The best sword ever wrought. Thousands of swords snap in response. The best swords ever seen on the surface of this heavy, black, boggy earth: clumped, fertile, black. The order is given in a guttural bark. The horse whinnies at the sharp jab of the brand new shining spurs in its dun flanks. Hundreds of horses whinny.

You ride behind them with the carts of onions and potatoes. It's the happiest day of your life. You're on your way. The adventure is beginning. Your life is beginning. It's beginning at last.

Months later you're standing at the gates, emaciated beneath the dusty, tattered pennants. You saw dozens of good men drown in the first river they had to cross. In the southern expanses it was easy to survive stealing chickens from the farmers and raping their daughters. And that's where the rendezvous with the troops from the islands took place. They were a week later than agreed, but more numerous than the stars in the night sky. Their king had the heart of a lion. He was three hundred feet tall, sat on a golden horse, and radiated light. His cloak bearing the religious insignia flowed behind him like the ocean embracing the continents. He didn't eat onions and potatoes but tiger marrow and dragon's wings, served in the gilded skulls of his enemies.

You crossed the mountains with him and his army. The mountains were higher than anything you'd ever seen in your life or could have imagined. An experienced spear-thrower wouldn't be able to reach any further than the sturdy, indifferent ankle of one of those giants. The army's top archer wouldn't make it to the line where the trees had been eaten away from the top with his lightest, fastest arrow and his heaviest iron bow, which no one other than he could span. You trudged along slippery, frozen mountain passes with thousands of shining knights. Noblemen disappeared into ravines, suits of armor and horses and all. It's a wonder you still have your cart of onions and potatoes and that you're alive. Many froze to death at night in the camps. Many collapsed during the day of exhaustion and were left behind. Some fell prey to wolves in the night, as white as the snow that concealed them. Cutting winds wailed in anticipation of the new victims of a new night. Indifferent mountains stayed silent. The day grinned and the night sliced. Major figures from the known world fell into oblivion with sliding hooves, jingling with skillfully forged precious metals. Dying screams began to seem commonplace.

But things did come to an end, even for those like you who had survived. You no longer knew whether you should be thankful or not. When you saw the sizzling plains of the south, you almost wished you had been torn apart by hot-blooded snow wolves, high up on the roof of the world, shivering with cold. Eye to eye with the heat-cracked mud before you, it seemed like mercy in comparison. And this is where the second rendezvous with the knights of the kingdom took place. Their tents were more elegant than a princess' skirts. Their suits of armor gleamed in the latest fashion. Plumes fanned frivolously on their helmets. The stirrups of their coiffed horses had been gilded. The onions and potatoes were no longer needed. They ate half-drowned songbirds with marbled peacock's tongue and stuffed caviar. Their golden helmets shone next to their golden plates like at home in their white castles on gentle rivers that ran through woods where unicorns grazed that could only be painted in pastel tones. And when, the next morning, the golden king had the bugle blown, it was the loveliest sound you'd ever heard. You buttoned up your trousers, let the onions be, and stumbled determinedly to your deeply desired downfall.

II.

As the mountain mists and the shimmering of the southern plains still clouded your eyes—or perhaps it was tiredness or the drunkenness of adventure or the blinding brilliance of hundreds of thousands of suits of armor in the sun—you imagined you could see the contours of a city on the horizon. Thousands of towers. You heard the bells chiming. Walls as high as castles and palaces as high as mountains. You'd never seen anything like it. A landscape of marble, built by human hand. Behind those smooth, shining, white, inaccessible, high walls that spanned the entire width of the land as far as the eye could see must live a privileged folk who bathe in asses' milk before dressing in purple, it couldn't be otherwise. Where you come from, they scrape onions and potatoes from the black earth; here the most colorful fruits grow on every tree, fat silver fish leap onto the banks to offer themselves to you, and pheasants and birds of paradise fly through the open window and spontaneously chirp into the hissing pans of golden oil. Where you come from, filthy beer is drunk from dirty tankards; here clear wine spurts from every fountain on every square. Perhaps you're exaggerating a little. But the city did make that much of an impression when you saw it in the distance. Her name was Genoa. The other shield-bearers had already been whispering its name for months like a secret prayer. This was the capital of an independent republic, they said: the Serenissima Repubblica di Genova. They said its motto was "*respublica superiorem non recognoscens*." You didn't really understand it, which impressed you all the more.

It was called La Superba, and even though you weren't inside its walls yet, you understood exactly why this was. You stand in front of the Porta Soprana, the tall, elegant city gate flanked by two tall towers. The whole thing is so perfectly in proportion it looks more like the façade of a cathedral than an impregnable bulwark. It is said that the dimensions and proportions of the gate were calculated by a secret order of monks and that the magic of their mathematics protects the gate and paralyzes enemies of the city. Banners bearing the religious insignia flutter from the proud towers, the blood-red cross, as fiery as the burning belief in the holy cause, on lily-white ground, as white as the pale innocence of pure intentions. You are part of the holy army and you've finally reached the holy city, which is the gate to the holy land. The powerful army of crusaders has returned home to the crusade's most powerful city so that it can finally sally forth. In Genoa, it will board thousands of galleons with billowing sails to head east in the name of the one true belief with the flaming swords of the only true God to free Jerusalem from the dark hordes with their scimitars, kneeling before a false prophet. Good will defeat evil. God will triumph over the devil. And you, a simple shield-bearer, will be part of the holy mission to steer the history of the cosmos onto the right path.

The golden king of France and the English king with the heart of a lion line up on their horses between their troops and the closed gate. The golden king recites each of his hundred honorary titles and greets the city. His horn blower gives the signal. His drummers beat their biggest kettledrums. The doors to the mighty gate swing open. The two kings give the order. The biggest army the world has ever seen enters the city.

Hundreds of thousands of knights on horseback, followed by a seething horde of foot soldiers, lancers, archers, chaplains, servants, and shield-bearers goes through Porta Soprana along Via San Lorenzo, past the cathedral, and down toward the port. The sound of hoofbeats, tinkling metal, footsteps, drums, and trumpets echoes between the city's high buildings. You can't believe your eyes. The streets are made of stone. You've never seen anything like it. The towering marble palaces are decorated with the most blinding ornaments. They have large windows of transparent glass. There are banners with the holy insignia all over the place. You can hardly take in the cathedral for all of its beauty. It's the biggest building you've ever seen. It is built of different colors of marble in white and gray stripes. The façade is an overwhelming display of sculptures, columns, mosaics, and ornaments in different colors. A people capable of building a thing like that must be the richest and wisest on earth. The last palace before the port is decorated with a towering mural, so colorful and true to life that you're almost afraid of it. It is of Saint George. He is dressed in a suit of armor and seated on horseback, wearing a cloak, and carrying a shield with the holy insignia. He is the patron saint of the crusaders. His lance pierces the throat of a terrifying dragon, exactly like this army's swords will pierce the black throats of Satan's monster with its hundreds of thousands of heads, the Moors, worshippers of the false god, in Jerusalem.

But the people make the greatest impression, the city folk who have gathered along the route to see the army with their own eyes. You might think that such a large army might instill fear, even with its good intentions. But there's not a trace of fear to be seen in Genoa's eyes. The people exude something impenetrable. They recognize no superior. Dressed in tasteful costumes made of the finest and most expensive fabrics, they look lofty, haughty almost. It is as though they know that the mightiest army the world has ever seen is nothing more than a temporary guest and will have to pay for its sojourn in this eternal city with many chests filled with silver. But the women make the greatest impression. You can see them hanging out of the windows of their palaces or on their marble balconies. The women you have known in your life were farm girls or shepherdesses. They had coarse hands, coarse tongues, and two udders you could squeeze for a farthing. The women of Genoa are aristocratic and as slender as princesses, as finely cut as an ivory trinket, with large knowing eyes, their gazes fiery and arrogant. They know no superior. When they speak, they sing, and when they are silent, they recite poetry.

And then all of a sudden you see her. For the first time in your life you see the sea. A big blue reflective surface that reaches out cool and impenetrable to the horizon. You feel like you are going to faint, but luckily you manage to stay on your feet.

12.

But soon you grow to hate the city. There was no space to erect the tents at the port. The knights slept on satin cushions in the many palaces in the city, while their craggy, silent hosts arranged girls to waft coolness over their well earned resting beds with their rustling fans for a small surcharge. They were in less and less of a hurry to leave. You slept with the foot soldiers on the quayside using your empty knapsack as a pillow. You felt yourself being fileted and pickled by the burning sun. It was an enormous operation, embarking such a large army. Troops were regularly rowed over to the black, heaving galleons in the distance, but there were so many of you. You began to do the math. At this rate, it would take weeks, not to say months, to get everyone onboard. By now you were hungry. But the impenetrable, superior Genoese who had admired your entrance into the city turned out to be even more arrogant and shrewd than you thought. They perceived your hunger as merchandise. With thousands of starving foot soldiers on their doorstep, they raised the price of bread by three cents. Dried fish were sold by auction. By now the sanitation was inadequate. To put it mildly. There were outbreaks of illness. Good men died of coughing or blackfoot. The Genoese implemented a ban on leaving the overheated quays and placed soldiers in the shadows to stop you going into the cool alleys to steal water from the fountains. The warm, salty water at the port didn't taste nice, not even in combination with soup made from shoe soles and horse droppings. The silent Genoese folk didn't even smile. They took no malicious pleasure in this, that much you'd understood. They stood and watched. They silently raised their prices. Rats scratched around your improvised bunk. You began to wonder what they'd taste like. One evening you tasted one and what you vomited up in disgust was greedily scooped up by your bedmate.

It wasn't much better onboard the ship. At least on the Genoan quay you'd had fresh air, however relative that concept was in close proximity to hundreds of thousands of sweating, dying foot soldiers from the biggest army the world had ever seen. The smell of sulfur left by Lucifer himself permeated the galleon's hold. Lucifer, the prince of utter darkness, who tried to suffocate the soldiers of the army of angels with their own breath. Thin shit streamed along the joists. The planks creaked.

13.

The disembarkation in Palestine was coupled with a great display of power. Above deck, the flags were raised and the trumpets blown, while below deck, you lay in your own vomit and shit, green with misery, among the stinking bodies of your comrades-in-arms. Your lord and master was the first to jump ship in his shining suit of armor, just like all the other lords and masters in their shining suits. It wasn't until their empty words had died away in the wind that you could stagger, more dead than alive, up the beach. And while, at a full gallop with a drumroll and a fanfare of trumpets, an immediate advance was made on the holy city of Jerusalem, which had fallen into Muslim hands, the biggest enemies of your God and of civilization, you needed a moment to recover from the journey. There were palm trees and shade. There was a sea breeze. You managed to get away from the others. You needed a little rest before fighting the soldiers of evil and spitting in the face of Satan himself, sword raised. Just a moment. Five minutes of rest. You fell into a deep sleep.

When you woke up, it was quiet. There was no sound of hoof-beats, drums, or trumpets. You cautiously opened your eyes. You looked into the eyes of a black woman. "Black" wasn't the right word. She was as smooth and dark and shiny as an olive. Her skin gleamed with sweat, power, and truth, and her coal-black eyes could turn entire legions to ashes. She was holding a glittering knife to your throat. She said something in her tongue, which you accurately interpreted as a threat. You felt yourself grow moist with fear. And fearfully, because you were in such a panic you might have done anything, you rose slowly to your feet. She kept her knife to your throat but didn't cut. You moved upwards to her lips and kissed her and you were sure you were going to die. But she didn't cut.

"Why?"

She replied in that scraping dry language you didn't understand. She spat in your face, kissed you passionately, hit you, and put you on a mule. "Hee!" she screamed. "Hee!"

Months later you were sitting next to her father in the blue tent. He held the holy scepter tight as he begged the new god and the new prophet to keep you both safe. There were tears in his eyes during the final prayer. She touched your hand for a moment. After the sword dance, you talked in their language about everything she'd taught you. You spoke of water and fire, harmony in mathematical proportions, the philosophy of submission to the truth, and your love of your new wife. The applause bubbled over like water in a desert.

And that night, still enjoying the afterglow of the honey and the lukewarm, salty sea of her unconditional surrender, you heard hoofbeats outside the camp. You pushed aside the books by Arabic philosophers, grabbed your sword, and went outside. But there were many of them. They wore the cursed sign of the flaming red cross of revenge on the off-white ground of hypocrisy. There was nothing you could do with your scimitar. You got yourself and her father to safety. There wasn't a trace of her. The encampment was massacred and burned. The books by the wise men were burned as repellant heresy. The women were raped, time and time again, until someone was merciful enough to ram a sword in their bleeding cunts instead of taking them again. You saw her die that way.

From that night on, your only desire was to stop living. Her father nodded. And so your second desire became to take revenge.

"But the warriors of the blood-red cross are always too great in number."

You nodded. "But they have one weakness."

"What is it?"

"Their city. The city of Saint George and the dragon. I shall wreak revenge for your daughter on that city."

"What's the name of the city, my son? Genoa? I've heard that it's the most beautiful city ever built."

"Genoa," you said, "is the place I hate most on earth. I promise you, Father, I shall return. Allow me to rob myself of my own life and to haunt it as the spirit of vengeance for the victims of the cross."

14.

It was nighttime. But I was having trouble falling asleep. Ghosts from my past popped up in dreams that didn't want to become dreams. Specters from my fatherland appeared. My publisher's flabby face loomed dangerously close and gave me an accusing look. He was silent but I knew exactly what he meant. He drummed his fingers impatiently on the table. I tried to hide from him behind a pile of letters, but for some reason or other, you were loitering there, my good friend, and your face didn't look too friendly. And you were right, too. I'm sorry I still haven't paid back the money I borrowed from you. And I hardly dare to ask, but that whole business with my so-called rich mistress only cost me money. I saw Monia's face before me. I tried to repress it, but then she pushed her scandalously big tits in my face. I jerked awake out of my insomnia because I couldn't breathe. I smelled the sour stench of her cavities. She stank of an amputated woman's leg in a garbage bag. She stuck both her fiery red tongues out and hissed that she was my bride. Her head turned three hundred and sixty degrees. "Is there anything you don't know?" she asked me. "Fuck me. Or are you a vegetarian?" She spread her legs and kicked off one shoe. It was full of vomit. "Oi, oi," the downstairs neighbor said. "Oi, oi." The cast iron portcullis halfway down the stairs clicked shut.

I got up and went to the bathroom to wash my face. I didn't turn on the light so as not to make myself any more awake than I already was. I had to throw up. And then when I looked in the dark mirror, I saw her. She could only be seen in mirrors. I leaned forward cautiously to give her a kiss. She responded to my gesture. My lips touched her cool, glassy lips.

"You're the most beautiful girl in Genoa."

"Do you always say that to your own reflection?"

"What are you doing here?"

"You live in your imagination too much."

"You've always been the only girl I've ever loved."

"Step back. Slowly."

As I slowly distanced myself from the mirror, she did the same, at exactly the same pace, until instead of just her face, I could see her entire body. She was wearing her uniform from the bar. One of her feet was pink with disinfectant. Her trouser leg was rolled up, probably because the seam would rub too much otherwise and irritate her wounds. I couldn't see her other foot.

"What happened?"

Instead of replying, she began to take her trousers off.

"What are you doing?"

"I'm showing you how real you are."

She had already undone her belt. She undid the top button and then the zipper. She held on to her trousers.

"Are you ready?" she asked, and before I could reply she had dropped her trousers and stood naked before me in the mirror. She only had one leg.

15.

I turned on the light. She had disappeared. I washed my face again. I involuntarily stroked the mirror in the way a person strokes an eastern lamp in the hope the story's true. But the only genie that appeared was my own naked reflection telling me I needed to get some sleep.

But I couldn't sleep anymore. My hard little IKEA bed felt like the narrow bunk of the lower deck of a creaking galleon on its way to the holy land or like the third-class sleeping quarters of an ocean steamer on its way to La Merica. "*Fatou yo*," I sang softly. "We all live in a yellow submarine." Outside there was some noise. Someone shouted something in Arabic. He began to kick and hit doors, including mine. I pulled the sheets over my head. Then he shouted in Italian that he wanted revenge. The neighbor on the other side of the street knew what to do. She opened her shutters and threw a flowerpot onto his head from the fifth floor. He disappeared weeping into the labyrinth. But the neighbor stayed there, discussing the incident in a loud voice with my upstairs neighbor, who'd clearly also woken up. And that woke up various other neighbors who found the discussion even more annoying than the thing that had induced it, which set off a kind of chain reaction and led to even angrier discussions that in the end pretty much the entire street took part in. Everyone was leaning out of their open windows, screaming that the others shouldn't scream so much. There were people sleeping here, they screamed, who, unlike all the other screaming freeloaders, had to go to work in the morning to earn their keep, for fuck's sake.

I couldn't take it anymore. I got dressed and went outside. There was nobody left on the street. My footsteps echoed hollowly through the high, peeling house intent, and stoic fronts. Rats shot away into the cracks and crevices between the street and the houses. Dark and forbidding, I walked randomly. Here and there, white teeth shone in murky alcoves. Chances were weighed up. But I wasn't drunk. I was big and angry. I'd have bitten off any thrust knife at the shoulder, arm and all. And they knew it.

I felt like fucking a whore. It was the perfect night for it. But the whores weren't around. They're for lunch, when the Genoese magistrates nervously grip their calf-leather briefcases under their sweaty armpits. But I was determined to find someone. I went on my way, hard, intent and stoical. After Via della Maddalena there was still Via del Campo. Via del Campo *is* a whore. If you want to possess her, all you have to do is take her by the hand. She sells the same rose to everyone. And after Via del Campo there's Via delle Croce Bianca and the Ghetto if necessary.

But even the Ghetto was deserted at this hour. I wandered aimlessly through lifeless alleyways. When there aren't any fat, hairy transvestites to look at, it becomes noticeable how truly dilapidated the alleys are. Entire sections aren't even paved. Plasterwork crumbles under your gaze. You only have to lean against a wall for a little rest to find yourself involuntarily creating a new passageway, a random alley you might name after yourself for a night before it all begins to shift once more.

Sighing, I sat down on some steps up to a door. "And this then?" I asked myself. "Is this just fantasy, too?" The door opened from the inside. I turned around.

"Your fantasy is my profession."

I couldn't see him very well in the darkness but he was certainly well built. He was wearing a wig and a short, tight miniskirt. He was missing a leg. "Come," he said.

"What's your name?" A stupid question, I know, but in my fright I couldn't think of anything else to say. I heard the griffins screech.

"Ornella," he said.

16.

He hopped on his crutches ahead of me into the sex cubicle. It was a seedy cubbyhole, not much more than a small garage with a bed in it, but there was more light there than in the alleyway. Although outside, with a bit of goodwill, sufficient horniness, and perseverance, he had something womanly about him, little of the illusion remained in this electric light. He had shaved his face and leg, put on a wig, a single sexy stocking, and a leopard-print skirt that was quite tight around his belly, and stuffed his bra. But that was the full extent of it. I noticed I couldn't bring myself to use feminine pronouns for him, not even to keep the illusion intact. He looked like a parody of his own fantasies. He wanted it too much. In theory this can be quite a turn on—a person who, despite an evident lack of the necessary talents and physical attributes, is hungry to play the game and knows himself desired—indeed, that's generally a lot more exciting than a sketched body that only has to be touched to arch back, wispily sighing in the knowledge it can induce ecstasy without even having to lift a finger—but you can also overdo an evident lack of the necessary physical attributes.

He leaned his crutches in the corner and sat down on the bed. "Come," he said. He gestured for me to sit down next to him. I stayed standing.

"What's wrong?"

And then there was the matter of that one leg. It wasn't really the problem. It was more the missing leg that was unsettling. Legs usually get in the way, alright, that's one way of looking at it, I got that. But all in all, it was quite a specialist fetish. Something for the rare connoisseur.

"Why do you do this?" I asked.

"And you?"

It was a fair question in return, I had to admit. It was exactly what I was starting to wonder myself. "How long have you had it?"

"What do you mean?"

"Your leg."

"I think the question is more how long I haven't had it."

He was clever, too. But that was something I really didn't need. It was the last thing I'd left my house for in the middle of the night. This was slowly turning into an even bigger nightmare than the nightmares I'd been running away from. Maybe it was best to leave.

"What I've got between my, albeit, no longer existent legs still functions perfectly well, by the way. What's your name? You can invent a name if you like, I don't care."

"I'm sorry."

"Then I'll call you Giulia. What's your greatest desire?"

"I no longer have any desires right this instant."

"Oh yes you do, dear Giulia, you're overflowing with passionate desires, even though I might not be the one who can fulfill them. But your desires are flickering in your eyes. I see that kind of thing."

"Once again, I'm sorry. I sincerely apologize. I made a mistake. But I'll pay you. How much is it?"

"It's nighttime. It's the hour of the wolf. Only you and I are awake in this cursed labyrinth. I'll tell you a story. Take a seat. You don't have to pay anything. All I want is for you to listen."

17.

"You might not think so at first sight, but I used to be a man. Or maybe you would think that at first sight, but I'm perfectly capable of making you forget that at second sight. Love is all about illusions. As a man, I learned that in a painful way, and as a woman I'm applying that lesson now. If you want to be desired, you have to satisfy the image the other has of you. Being yourself and others respecting you for who you are and things like that are just foolish talk by people in relationships and happy about it, without knowing true love: she is a cruel goddess who requires sacrifices. She rends the earth with her eyelashes. She can break strong men with a glance, the way she broke me. She crushes, or worse still, ignores, anyone who thinks they can stay themselves—that they'll even be respected for it.

"As though there is such a thing as being yourself. That's another problem. As though there's even such a thing as yourself. Identity is always a concoction, a construction based on the image that a person has of what others think of them. And that's not a constant. It's as changeable as the shape of a cloud in the wind—now it looks like Scandinavia, and the next moment some ducks, a lady, or sheep and a shepherd.

"What you have to learn, Giulia, is that the highest achievement is to coincide fully with the fantasies of your lover. And you don't have to worry about him doing the same. Or her. Sorry. I know you're not far enough to consider that distinction irrelevant. But the time will come. You have the potential to become a sensible girl. You have to become her. Or him. But I won't make it too difficult for you. You have to become her. You won't begin to love her until you see her face in the mirror. But your real job is to ensure that she sees your face in the mirror. Which is to say that she sees her own face, because that face has become your mirror image. Do you understand that, dear Giulia? It's a dangerous game, you're right about that. You find yourself in a labyrinth of mirrors in which it's easy to lose your way. But that has to be your desire—to lose your way.

"I can see you don't understand. Poor girl. Come and sit down. I'll explain it in a better way."

"I'm not a girl."

"Of course not. Sorry. I've never been one, either. I was a man with both legs firmly planted on the ground. I could plaster walls and chop logs. I've never been afraid of insects, no matter their size. I was big, black, and forbidding. I laughed at rats. If I'd been born in a different century, I've have had a sword on my hip."

"And then what happened?"

"Her name was Moana. That isn't her real name, but it doesn't matter. To me she was the most beautiful girl in Genoa. She was the love of my life. I loved her so much that adoring her like any other would was no longer enough. My greatest desire was to be one with her. I didn't want to possess her, that's banal, that's for normal people who have relationships. I wanted to become her."

"And did you manage?"

"Don't be so cynical, Giulia."

"I apologize. Carry on."

"The story is actually quite short and rather predictable."

"I want to hear it."

"Do you know what it means if you decide to love a woman for once and for all?"

"Don't ask questions, just tell me the story."

"She sat in the highest towers of my longings and writhed under the tentacles of my darkest nights. She was the impregnable plateau I had to conquer and the fertile garden I would lay myself down to rest in afterward. She was the fire that scorched me and

turned me to ashes and she was the fire that gave me warmth
and strength. She was the hissing ice that cooled me down and
reassured me, and she was the hard ice that rejected me."

"Why are you talking like that all of a sudden?"

"Like what? Poetic?"

"You said it."

"Bastard."

"And then?"

"It's a very dramatic, painful story. But given your lack of interest, I'll skip to the heart of the matter—she found someone else.
And at the end of the day, it didn't even matter that much. I'd
learned what I needed to learn."

"Good story. And then you became a transvestite?"

"Watch it, you. I'll read you something I wrote recently. Do
you want to hear it? Hang on, here it is."

"I don't seem to have a choice."

18.

"There are people who say I'm a fiction. But you could say
that about anybody. Just as the man in the real estate agent's suit
I saw walking along the street this morning invented himself in
a real estate agent's suit, and the politician I saw on television yesterday invented, in consultation with his advisors and spin doctors,
his air of authenticity so attractive to voters, I invented myself.
I dreamed myself up and then granted myself the freedom to exist.

"There are other people who say that I'm a man's dream. As
though that's a crime. Since I've allowed myself to walk through

every world imaginable on the haughty legs of sorrow, the echo of my high heels resounds in many people's dreams. I like to be desired, because I'm as much a desirer as the rest of them. Sometimes I'm just like everybody else.

"Do you know that particular story? Pygmalion was his name. He had a funny name because he was an ancient Greek. He was a sculptor, an artist. Let's say he knew what beauty was. And of course he was in love with Aphrodite, the goddess of desire. Men shaped gods in their own image and Aphrodite was lust's incarnate fantasy. Or how do you say that? The fantasy of incarnate lust. Anyone not desiring her hadn't properly envisioned her. And no one was better at envisioning her than the artist Pygmalion. He made a sculpture of her from the whitest, most expensive ivory that was available in those days. It was a work of love. It was a sacrifice to the goddess. It was a sacrifice to his own fantasy. And when the statue was ready, he took her to bed with him. In crude human words, you'd say he made love to her like a pimply computer nerd might fuck a homemade inflatable doll. But those are crude human words. He united himself with his deepest longing. It was the highest form of love. The goddess Aphrodite understood. And to reward him, she brought the statue to life.

"I might not have told the story entirely correctly because now it sounds like there are three characters: Pygmalion, Aphrodite, and the statue brought to life. But that's wrong—all three are one and the same person. It's very important to understand that. Alright, it's not easy, I admit. But people who don't understand it will never understand what love is. That's the tragedy."

That was all, apparently. He shut up. Or paused for a moment.

I reflected. I understood what he wanted to say and it wasn't even that badly formulated. But I wasn't at all thinking about what he'd said. I was thinking about the situation. As far as I was concerned, it was much more interesting. Because imagine this, dear friend: in the dead of the night, in the sketchiest part of a thoroughly corrupt town, the author so celebrated in my home country is perched on a rickety cot next to a disastrous transvestite with one leg reading a story he wrote himself, intended as a valuable lesson. During my countless interviews and public debates back home, I've often been asked for my definition of poetry. This nocturnal scene came closer to the truth than any smart answer I ever gave. I smiled. I was grateful to my new friend. I wrapped my arm around his shoulder. "Thank you."

"Why are you smiling?"

"Because of the situation."

He kissed me gently on the cheek. I allowed him to. "Tell me about your leg."

19.

"What?"

"How it happened."

He sighed. "Do you really want to know? One leg more or less is not that important, certainly in comparison to what I just told you."

"I really want to know. Were you born that way?"

"No."

"When did it happen?"

"Not that long ago. I was the victim of my own success. I know that you see me as a man with a beer belly in a tight dress wearing a wig. In some ways, you're right. I am, too. But I can bewitch men with my availability. In their rough hands, I can change into the woman of their dreams by becoming an empty mirror for their obsessions. Here in the Ghetto your main clients are Moroccan adolescents whose religion forbids them from loving and leads them to perversity. When they're together they act tough and brag but once they're alone in this room, they quiver like children. But if a boy wants me to be a sheep, I'm a sheep. If he wants me to be one of the promised virgins in paradise, I will be. And that's how he falls in love."

"Did he fuck you?"

"He didn't dare. He bought me gifts. Rings and bracelets. Like these ones. Cheap trinkets. But he was sweet. He wanted to lie down next to me and then said he felt small."

"But all of a sudden he did dare."

"Exactly. It could only lead to that. He said he'd asked his parents' permission."

"Really?"

"He was only saying that, of course. It became kissing and stroking. I gave him a good blowjob. But he wanted more. He felt between my legs."

"And then he found…"

"This." He pushed aside his lacey panties. "And I was harder than I am now. Really hard. Can you imagine?"

"Make it really hard."

"For you, Giulia? Do you want that? Will you help me?"

"No."

"Do I have to do it all on my own? You're a cruel girl."

"I'm not a girl. I just want to see what a one-legged transvestite looks like jerking off. I'm interested in a journalistic way."

"In a journalistic way? Are you writing a comparative analysis for a consumer guide? Well? What do you think? Am I doing it well? How many stars do I get?"

"Tell me about your leg."

"He turned up with friends with knives."

"And then?"

"He had a knife, too."

"And then?"

"Then he wanted to cut it off."

"Your cock?"

"Yep."

"And then?"

"And then I said, please, cut off my cock. I want to be a girl."

"You were hoping he wouldn't do it, then."

"He didn't do it. He paused and reflected for a moment and then said he'd only be doing me a favor by cutting off my dick. Then I'd really be a girl. He didn't want to grant me the pleasure."

"And then..."

"And then he took my left leg."

"Have you come?"

"Sorry. Do you want to lick it up?"

"No, thank you."

"It's free."

"That's very kind of you, but no thanks."

20.

"This didn't happen."

"Of course it didn't," I said.

"It's a strange night. I can hear the griffins screeching. Could you pass me a tissue? Thanks. I was lucky. As a matter of fact, I was lying there bleeding to death. But someone saw me and called an ambulance. Code red in the hospital. I can still remember it. I was more or less conscious. They asked for my papers. I didn't have them. They asked who I was. I gave my tranny name. They asked whether I was allergic to antibiotics. Not a clue. They asked so many things. And after that the *carabinieri* came and asked even more. As soon as the wound was a bit better, I left through the back door using two stolen crutches. These two. I still have them."

"Did you press charges?"

"Why kind of funny question is that? Are you a foreigner or something? This is Italy."

"Sorry. It's just I thought…"

"You think too much. That's your problem. Shall I get you off real quick before you go?"

"That's a generous offer. But no thanks. And you're right, it is time I went."

"I feel like licking your little cunt, Giulia."

"They all say that." It was definitely time to go. "One last question."

"Where my leg is?"

"Yes."

"If only I knew."

"Here in the Ghetto?"

He kicked my stomach. "Here?" He laughed loudly. "We rule the Ghetto. A Moroccan with a knife doesn't stand a chance here. We once even went to war against the US Marines. And we won. Have you ever heard that story?"

"Yes."

"Is there anything you don't know?"

"I don't know."

"I do. I know how it works. When my sweet Moroccan fiancé turned up with his pals to settle scores, it wasn't here. They'd never dare. Too many stiletto heels. Too much gravity. Too many alleyways that change direction from one second to the next. Moroccans know that. They're stupid but not backwards. They pick their moments and their strategy. You mustn't underestimate them, Giulia."

"What do you mean?"

"They waited for me in some club, a long way away, under Via San Bernado, the gutter of the night."

"I know the place."

"Of course. I worked there as a tranny under various different names. I also went there to enjoy myself. Under other names."

"Which names?"

"Too many to list. And they grabbed me in the alleyway and mutilated me. On the corner of Via San Bernardo and another alley."

"Vico Vegetti."

"Could be. And you know the strange thing, Giulia? A few weeks later, they found my leg in the burning woods above Arenzano. That's quite bizarre, isn't it? There was an item about it in the paper."

"In *Il Secolo XIX*."

"I've never understood how it got there."

"What was your name again?"

"Ornella. Why?"

21.

Outside, I took a deep breath. It was vertiginous. I had to get out of there as fast as possible. I took the closest exit out of the Ghetto, to Via Lomellini. It felt like returning to the city after a long period in the wilderness—like I was being embraced by civilization. It was already light. The shops and bars were already open. Delivery boys were already pushing handcarts filled with crates of fruits and vegetables. There was a line at the fishmonger's. He was shouting out that morning's special offers in Genoese dialect. The magistrates of Genoa were on their way upwards, to Via Cairoli and Via Garibaldi, to the ancient palazzi of their power. They acted as if they had no knowledge of the dark jungle to their left. The poultryman on Piazza Fossatello was singing as he plucked chickens. Clean laundry fluttered on lines strung across the alleyways. I took another deep breath. The fresh air did me some good.

I went to the historical Bar Cavo on the corner of Via Lomellini, Piazza Fossatello, and Via San Luca for a cup of coffee. Seven *carabinieri* were standing at the bar. I squeezed between them and ordered a coffee. Their uniforms were spotless, I could verify that from close up. All their buttons were gleaming. I've rarely felt so safe drinking my morning coffee.

And in the long, narrow shopping street of San Luca, where it's always busy, it was evidently busy even at this early hour. All the colors and scents, all the bustle, all the excited voices felt like a soothing shower after my nocturnal adventure. The excess of clear normality worked like an antidote to the black syrup of madness that had rendered my thoughts ever stickier. I slowly managed to see the truth without getting into a panic.

It was almost laughable. There was no longer a shadow of a doubt. It was completely clear to me. That woman's leg—which I had passionately stroked, adored, kissed, and adored—had been a man's leg. Simply because of the sexy stocking, I'd imagined the woman of my dreams attached to it. And the truth, the solution to the conundrum, everything the leg had been lacking, everything I'd lustfully added on in my thoughts, had been sitting next to me that night on a rickety stretcher bed in a garage in the Ghetto with cotton wool in his bra. Although you always realize that in some ways you are living in your fantasies, that realization becomes rather more acute when you get a retrospective glimpse into reality. It doesn't happen often. Luckily.

Street musicians played the usual evergreens from the Balkans on their oh so authentically false accordions. "Maestro." It was Salvatore. He whispered in my ear, "Will you promise me to never give them a penny? They aren't really Romanians. They're gypsies. They're richer than you and me put together. They give honest people like me a bad name." I looked at him in astonishment but he didn't return my gaze. He'd already hopped along further on his one good and one supposedly bad leg.

And that the leg—after all my clumsiness with the stocking, the shower, the garbage bag, and the scouring pad I had thrown into the sea at Nervi—had been scooped up by a firefighting plane and found again in the burned out woods above Arenzano is, my friend—I swear to you—a plot twist I never would have come up with myself. It's really too cheap, too improbable, and it doesn't add anything. I mean, you don't really believe it, do you? That, as chance would have it, this actually happened doesn't affect your sense of disbelief? If I were to rework these notes into a novel, it would be the first thing I'd have to scrap, even though it really happened. I can link those thoughts on fantasy to the theme, but that fire plane is too much. It's really not possible.

But how can I get back to establishing that the leg had belonged to Ornella? It's completely dependent on that newspaper item in *Il Secolo XIX* that I chanced upon, since the name Ornella was mentioned there. And that's what really happened last night: when Ornella told me it had happened in a side alley off Via San Bernardo, I'd had strong suspicions, of course, even though I couldn't confirm that Vico Vegetti was actually the alley where I found it. Via San Bernardo has dozens of side alleys. Naturally, they aren't all scattered with amputated legs every day, that's true— that would have been one way of looking at it. But I hadn't. You mustn't forget that until just a short time ago, I'd been convinced that it was a woman's leg and that I would have repressed any association with the handicap of the man sitting beside me. I hadn't known for sure until Ornella said it had been found in the burned woods above Arenzano. That was when everything fell into place. It was all such a unique combination of circumstances that the possibility there were two separate legs could be statistically ruled out.

Perhaps I'd be able to do something with that in terms of the theme: the contrast between a bizarre fantasy and a reality that gained its credibility from the fact that it was so bizarre nobody

could have made it up. The alternative would be to come up
with a completely different story. But that's easier said than done.
That whole leg has to be cut out, you're right. It's all too complicated and, more than that, too unsavory. Instead of that, I'll
write something about the famous aquarium and the wonderfully
restored museums. It'll cause less trouble with my Genoese friends,
too, should my hypothetical novel ever be written and translated.
I might even get a certificate from the tourist office.

When I got home, I found an alarming-looking letter. That was
all I needed. But first—an hour's sleep.

22.

I could almost forgive Walter for running away, the cowardly weasel. They really are doing it. But I won't let them drive me away.
This city is mine as much as it is theirs by now. What are they
thinking? That I was going to surrender fearfully to their southern dirty tricks like a pale mollusk from the flabby north? I can
see their big brown hook-noses being seriously put out of joint.
What's all this? I will fight. I will crush them.

Sorry, my friend, I'll try to explain the situation to you calmly.
The letter I found yesterday at home was an official missive from
Antonio Bentivoglio. He's a famous lawyer in this city, as he never
fails to impress on everyone. I've googled him now. It's true. It's
even an understatement. He is the most expensive, most successful lawyer in Genoa. He is famous for the scale of his network
and his unconventional, aggressive methods. In the forty years
he's been in the profession, he has practically never lost a case.

And there are a few big scandalous cases among them.

Antonio Bentivoglio wrote to me on behalf of his clients Abramo and Pierluigi Parodi. The first one must be the father. I had to read the letter five times before I understood it. I needed a dictionary. It's not written in Italian but in Legalese, the official jargon of bureaucracy, which even native Italian speakers have trouble with. In the end I managed to decipher about ninety percent, enough to understand that he wanted me to believe I was in deep shit.

On behalf of his clients he was seeking two hundred and twenty thousand euros for the breach of a verbal purchase agreement, an amount that would be increased in accordance with interest rates and with two or three offsets. Aside from this he was also demanding more or less the same amount for the fact that I'd leaked confidential information to their business partner. The total reparation would come out to just over six hundred thousand euros, including costs and legal aid fees. On behalf of his client, he suggested a settlement of four and a half within two weeks of the date of this letter. In the case of a failure on my part, a hearing date had been set shortly after that, at which my presence would be very much appreciated.

See. Of course it's just cheap scaremongering. I'm no legal expert but I know enough about the law to see that his claim doesn't stand a chance. I don't know anything about Italian law, but I've enough confidence in the universal principles of law to believe that no judge would find it reasonable for me to have to pay twice for the same theater, one I didn't buy and which therefore isn't in my possession. I mean, let's face it, my friend, even in Italy they couldn't do that. And if they did, I'd go to the

European Court in Strasbourg. And their so-called verbal purchase agreement is nonexistent. But that's their word against mine, it's true. But even if it did exist, there are conditions of termination. Then I might owe them a percentage, but certainly not the entire amount. Let alone twice the entire purchase price.

In short, you don't have to worry, my good friend. We're certain to win this case. I'm worried about just one thing, and that's Antonio Bentivoglio. The two of us on our own can hardly go up against a man of such stature. We don't speak his language. Quick as a flash, he'd have us caught up in some kind of procedural trap. We shouldn't be stupid, my dear friend. We need to get hold of a good lawyer. I know I still owe you money. You'll get it back as soon as possible. But if you could just send me another couple of thousand, I'll get us a good man. And I guarantee you'll get that money back within two weeks, as soon as we've won and they have to pay the litigation costs. Perhaps we'll even be able to get some juicy compensation out of it. See it as an investment, my dear friend.

23.

They were dark days. The winter hung like a gray horsehair blanket over the inhospitable city. Day and night were one in my apartment on the ground floor of the narrow Vico Alabardieri. If I'd closed the shutters, it wouldn't have made the slightest difference. I had to go out. But I didn't want to. I'd go out into the night where the same ghosts roamed as in my darkest thoughts. The alleyways were printed in black on a black background on the map of the city. I would lose my way again, my head sunk deep into the black collar of my long black coat. I would disappear like a crow in a coalmine, like a gravedigger in his own catacombs.

During the nine-month-long summer, the half-light in my house had felt like a pleasant chill. But during the three months of winter, which seemed to last three times as long, it was a tomb. The walls are so thick that my mobile doesn't have a signal inside. I can forget about Internet. I have to go out for all those things. And that's not a problem: in the summer, it's exactly what I want to do. I toddle drowsily in my pajamas into the alleys to drink coffee and read the paper. I shower at the sight of fountains. I clean my teeth with the smiles of random passersby. But in wintertime, I sit there with the knowledge that it isn't much better outside than it is in.

I pressed the buttons on my phone out of boredom. No messages. I was in an isolation cell, an isolation cell whose key was in my own keeping, in a Siberian prison camp without fences. I was my own prison guard. I could free myself whenever I wanted and escape into the vast expanses of the dark winter. After a while, I'd return to my cell on my own, my tail between my legs, if I hadn't succumbed under the weight of the night in the meantime, or been torn apart by the bears and wolves of my doubts.

I had to go out. I put on my coat and pulled my iron door firmly shut behind me and locked it with my big, authentic Genoese key. I had to go some-fucking-where to drink strong fucking coffee. Fuck the winter.

When I was outside, my mobile beeped. I had a message. "*Ciao, grando uomo! Come sta? Io vengo per vistare te presto, nel caso che per tu va bene! Va tutto ben! Sono anche imperanda Italiano! Io desidero stare con tu! A presto alora!*" With a fat blonde smiley. The world record for grammatical mistakes in a single SMS was suddenly hanging on a thread. It was Inge, my German translator. She messaged me a specific time of arrival.

24.

The weather was bleak. The wet snow had melted into a kind of inconstant drizzle that was slapped into your face by the strong wind like a wet tea towel. Deeply unpleasant.

"Maestro." I only had a two-euro coin. I gave it to him anyway. I was in a kind of defeatist mood, if such a mood exists. Water was seeping through the wooden planks. The wood creaked. Sooner or later we'd sink. Two euros more or less wouldn't make any difference.

"Why don't you go back, maestro?"

I looked at him in surprise. "What do you mean, Salvatore?"

"Why don't you return to the north where your friends are?"

"My friends are here."

"Where?"

"Don't be so rude. You're my friend." I smiled.

"Could you lend me fifty euros perhaps?"

"I've just given you two euros."

"Exactly."

"Exactly what? What do you mean, Salvatore?"

"You never give two euros. The fact you're doing it now means something. Because everything has a meaning. Without a meaning, everything would be pointless. And since that would be pointless, it can't be true. *Quod erat demonstrandum.* What do you think of that, maestro?"

"You could be a medieval philosopher, Salvatore."

"I was once."

"When?"

"Are you putting me on? In the Middle Ages."

"How long have you been here, Salvatore?"

"Oh maestro! Time is long and memory is short. For me it's all about what I find in my cap: florins, euros, pieces of silver, emergency currency, francs from the mountains, francs from over the mountains, Vatican scudos, Neapolitan or Sicilian piastras, soldi, denari, sesini, ducati, grana, tornesi, cavalla, Sardinian centesimi, florins from Tuscany, Lombardy, or Venice, quattrini, paoli, Austro-Hungarian guilders, pounds, kreuzers, crowns, and marks, just as long as they're round and shiny. I've been here as long as the rats, and I'll be here until the last rat jumps ship for some better place. Just get used to it, maestro. You're my customer. I will find you wherever you are in every era. But I'll always give you a good price. Because like you said, you're a friend."

"And the fact I just gave you two euros, what do you think that means?"

"But, maestro, it's not that difficult. A question of deduction. In theory it might mean that you're generous, but you're not, because you've never given me that much before. It could mean that I've done you a favor or that I've changed in some way you like, but that's not the case. We hadn't seen each other for a long time until bumping into each other two days ago, and I change more slowly than the centuries. So there's just one possibility left: you have changed. And I've always seen you in this city as a confident, successful man. And because you've necessarily changed, you're no longer that. *Quod erat demonstrandum.* The fact you've given me two euros today means that things are not going well for you. And that's the reason I'm asking why you don't go back north."

"What would I do there? Escape you?"

"You wouldn't be able to, maestro. I'd find you wherever you were. You don't have to go to any trouble. Just call it all part of the service. You're my customer."

25.

I remembered her as a big blonde, not exactly slender, but in her own way impressive and, most of all, present, like a woman with the power to fill silences and cavities with the engorging plumpness of her obvious northern appearance. When I saw her again at the specific time of arrival she'd texted me, I was shocked. It could be that, unlike the previous time she'd arrived, I wasn't really in the mood to be hospitable to luscious forms or forms of any other kind, but she stormed toward my halfhearted welcome hug like a cow toward an open gate. She was enormous. Maybe she'd gotten bigger in the meantime. Or maybe as a result of a summer full of calligraphic, wafer-thin scooter girls I'd forgotten how to see her as an attractive woman. In any case, in my eyes she looked like a blonde mountain with bulges that were in theory in more or less the right places. As she kissed me elaborately in the station, I saw pity in the eyes of my fellow city dwellers. It made me feel embarrassed.

"Ciao," she said, much too loudly. "Are we going to your house or shall we get drunk on your little square first?" She laughed much too exuberantly. "I know already," she said. "First, a few drinks. Come on. I know you. I know what you want. I'll take you to your little square. I think I still know the way."

I needed a stiff drink, she was right about that. But the way she charged through my city on her overly fat and overly confident legs, rolling her wheelie case noisily behind her, deflated my enthusiasm even further. Every paving stone covers an ancient, well hidden secret that we might whisper about one day when the wine is full, the evening quiet, and the stars favorably positioned. Two or three fragile stories lie on every street corner. Anyone with the courage to admit it will meet the tenuous old ghosts. Anyone living here will lay their ear from time to time to one of the gray, crumbling housefronts and focus on the weak echo of voices from the past. They don't always say what we want to hear, that's true. And it's not always easy to understand them. But that's why you listen harder. And when you listen really well, you can hear the old walls creaking as they rearrange the labyrinth bit by bit at night. You can hear alleys twisting and the palazzi sighing if you know how to listen and if you listen to the minimal echo of the almost inaudible footsteps within a porcelain grotto.

And she charged cheerfully through all of that on her fat legs. "Nice weather, though. It's much worse back home. Ooh, I do fancy a Negroni. It's great to see you again. Come here and give me a big kiss."

We walked down from the station to Via di Pré. It wouldn't be the route I'd have chosen in these circumstances at this time of day, but she was leading the way. This was Africa. If I French kissed a blonde mountain of that size in this quarter dominated by black, frustrated, jealous Muslims, I might not make it out alive. "I'm so happy to be back in Genoa, too. It's all so wonderful here." She should be counting her blessings that she hadn't been robbed, raped, and sold as a white slave to the Bey of Tunis by now. A fair amount of money could exchange hands for a woman as massive and blonde as she. "It almost feels a bit dangerous here. I'm glad I'm with you. Give me a kiss. Come on, give me a kiss." I saw the shining teeth in hungry faces. Knives glittered. Someone spat blood. "It's so nice here!"

26.

We reached Piazza delle Erbe. Miraculously, we were still alive and in possession of all of our limbs. She wasn't impressed. She ordered a Negroni. "*Allora!*" she shouted. The barmaid discreetly whispered in my ear, was it OK? I gestured subtly that it was and that I'd pay.

Within half an hour she was blind drunk. "*Va bene!*" she screamed. I cautiously suggested that now might be a good time to go home. She was tired, I suggested. Perhaps she needed to rest after the long journey. After that she could freshen up and we could go for another drink. Or maybe she simply preferred to turn in for the night. That wasn't a problem. Tomorrow was another day, I assured her. "*Va bene!*" she said, ordering another Negroni.

I'd invited a couple of my Genoese friends to add luster to the occasion of her return. They'd been courteous enough to invite us to their house for a simple dinner. I told her this, and asked whether

she was happy with the invitation. She wasn't obliged to go or anything. I'd understand perfectly if she preferred to get an early night.
My friends would also fully understand.

"*Va bene!*"

She asked what time we had to be there. I said they were coming
to pick us up. It would be an honor for them to partake of a little
aperitif with us before going to their house.

"*Va bene!*"

And in the meantime, I'd already bought wine, *fave*, and salami.
My friends were taking care of the main course and the dessert.
She didn't need to worry about a thing.

"*Va bene!*"

But perhaps it was advisable to lie down for an hour beforehand. Recover a bit from the journey. Perhaps sober up a little
before dinner. There was plenty of time for that; she didn't have
to worry in the slightest. And I'd come and fetch her. She didn't
have to think about a thing.

"*Va bene!*"

But she didn't go. And that evening as we carefully peeled the
fave and attractively draped the special salami in delicate, thin slices
on a fragile plate and poured the whispering wine into beautifully
designed goblets, one of my female friends cautiously asked her in
polished English what she thought of the poetry of contradictions
in Genoa's ancient labyrinth.

"*Va bene!*" she cried with a slice of sausage in her mouth. "*Va
molto, molto bene!*"

27.

That night I barely slept a wink. After I'd pushed her, staggering and swaying, wheelie case and all, through the alleyways and
hauled her up Vico Vegetti to my house on Vico Alabardieri,
I was full of hope that in all her enormity she would fall asleep like
a log as soon as her spinning head hit the pillow, after which
I could tranquilly search for a strip, shred, or crack of available
space on the mattress where I could hide with the sheets over
my head. But the opposite was true. As soon as she'd stumblingly,
topplingly undressed and was lying in my bed with her scandalous
blonde thighs and tits, she spotted me next to her and seemed to
awaken. Or some kind of demon awoke in her. She bit my arm, hit
my belly, and grabbed my cock like a builder reaching for his tools.

"Well," she said. "Well. There you are at last. Did I misbehave at
your friends' party? I hope so, I certainly meant to." She began to
laugh hysterically. "Do you know what's so funny? I've suddenly
realized that I'm lying here with a famous poet's cock in my
hand!" She laughed even louder. "At least, one who used to be
famous." She began to kiss me wildly. She tried to ram her tongue
behind my epiglottis. Survival instinct made me fight back with
my tongue. "See! You like it, don't you? Tell me you missed me.
Say it!" Her tongue made it impossible for me to say anything.
"You know what the funniest thing is?" I'd long lost my sense
of humor—there was nothing funny, let alone funn*iest*. "Maybe
you think I misbehaved with your friends this evening, but that
was just the start. Tonight I'm going to show you what real mis-
behavior looks like, you mark my words." She rammed a finger

up my ass. I screamed. "Yes, scream away. I know you like it. My lovely transvestite. Scream away. Yes. Like that. Like that. Yes. Yes."

At last she fell asleep. She turned onto her side, taking all the covers with her. I was cold, and carefully tried to pull back some covers. But that woke her up, and then she began again. When she finally fell asleep a second time and confiscated all of the covers again, I resigned myself, shivering, to my fate. I lay on my back and looked up at the ceiling. I was cold. I tried to move as little as possible for fear of waking her up again. I shivered. It felt like I'd been raped.

28.

"I'm going for a coffee." She was completely blonde, freshly showered, awake and cheerful. I felt shattered. "And after that I'm going to go for a little walk. But you can stay in bed, darling. But will I see you again before I leave? I'll text you where I am."

She slammed the iron door behind her with a loud bang. I was alone at last. Although I was always alone, it felt like a long-awaited liberation. I turned my back to the door, the city, and her and tried to sleep, not only because I was tired but because I didn't feel like existing. I didn't feel like the passing of time. I wanted to cheat. I wanted to skip a stretch of time. Preferably a large stretch. A day or so. In any case, until Inge had safely and, as far as I was concerned, definitively left the city. Perhaps just to be sure I should factor in a safety margin of an extra day.

Hibernation. I muttered the word as a silent prayer. My lips tasted it like the first word, the *logos* from the beginning. Before the beginning even. That timeless, blissful state the universe was in before it had to go and begin. Everything was perfect until someone rolled over onto their other side and, because he took the covers with him, accidentally awakened a divinity. That was the start of all that crap with time and specific arrival times that had to be texted. That was the start of the misery of consciousness and the consciousness of misery. That was the start of fantasies about belief, hope, and love. That was the start of the fantasy of a better life elsewhere, because it could hardly be worse anywhere else than it was here. *Utinam ne in nemore.* If only that first tree had never been felled in the holy forest before being deprived of its bark and hollowed out as a vessel to sail to another, better place. All our unhappiness springs from that. But you can't blame us for any of it, because staying put isn't an option, either. We can't remain safely at mama's side because we've been cursed with curiosity and longings. It would have been better off for all concerned if they'd just left us to have a nice sleep. What's wrong with sleep? According to statistical analysis, the majority of crimes committed in the world are perpetrated by people who were awake, while the contribution of sleepers to the crime figures is negligible. And is the person sleeping unhappy? What kind of longings, failings, complications, or insurance claims from lawyers does he experience in his sleep? Does the sleeper long to awaken so that he can toil away in the frustrated wakeful world among others who are also complaining about having been awoken by such shrill sounds?

The divine being who set off the alarm clock should be immediately arrested and tried at the International Criminal Court. He should be accused of serious crimes against humanity, on behalf of humanity. We have numerous millennia of irrefutable witnesses.

He will be given a fair trial, but there's no other imaginable outcome than that he'll be given the heaviest sentence. And on that day, delirious crowds will gather on the world's squares and jubilantly burn their alarm clocks.

29.

I was awoken by her text message. She was in the Bar of Mirrors. I ached all over. I didn't want to see her again. I wanted to float away in my black gondola along the black river of the black winter.

But I was a knight, too. My suit of armor shone in the corner of the room. I'd sworn an oath of allegiance, though I couldn't remember to whom or what it involved. But I realized it was my duty to be a good man. I rose creaking from my creaking bed. I splashed my face clean with the little bit of firewater I had left, did up the buckles on my armor, and clattered downstairs.

She was inside the porcelain grotto. I saw her from a distance through the window. I faltered. She sat there so enormous and self-assured that I became embarrassed I was on my way to her, that she was a so-called friend, and that I would have to sit down at her table. She'd seen me, she waved.

She was drinking Prosecco. "Ciao!" she said, much too loudly. I whisperingly ordered myself a Prosecco, too. There she was then. She sat there striking a false note. With everything. With the fragile, elegant people in the bar and with the bar itself, this sacred place where I'd met the most beautiful girl in Genoa and I'd kissed her in the little cubbyhole where they make the *stuzzichini*. The blonde colossus wouldn't even fit in there. And she had no idea.

That's what bothered me the most. She thought it was good to be herself, and she hadn't the faintest inkling of the politely restrained, quivering discomfort around her or my suppressed embarrassment. There she sat, inconsiderate, legs spread, in one of the most sacred places on earth without even wondering where she was.

Some people don't belong in some places. That's what they say here about the Moroccans and the Senegalese, I know. But in this case, I can say it, can't I? If I want to deny a big blonde woman from my very own fatherland access to my new, old, fragile city because she doesn't understand how old and fragile it is and she doesn't understand how gentle, slender, and petite she has to be to be allowed to stay here, that doesn't make me a racist, does it?

I took her to the nearest taxi stand, gave her a peck on the cheek, and said, "See you soon." I was lying. As far as I was concerned it was a lie. When I went back to the Bar of Mirrors I noticed a large crack in the porcelain-tiled ceiling.

30.

Dear friend, I have good news and bad news. I'll start with the good news. No, naturally, I should start by thanking you first. The amount you sent me didn't leave much room for maneuver, but after asking around among friends and with a good bit of negotiating, it turned out to be enough to get us represented by a respectable lawyer. Her name is Stefania Volpedo. She's young and doesn't have that much experience, but she works at a reputable office. To be honest, this is her first case. But she was ready to take it on, she assured me. I think it makes her even more motivated to prove herself. And a more experienced lawyer is simply too expensive for us. Essentially this is a simple case. We don't need a chic hotshot to be able to win it. Stefania made this point several times herself. She described Parodi's claim as ridiculous, grotesque, and without a hope in hell of succeeding. Exactly like I told you. She said that the judge would probably rule it as inadmissible at the preliminary sitting. In any case, that's what she'd be aiming for with her plea. In fact, she was amazed that the great Antonio Bentivoglio had even made himself available for such a hopeless case. She was also honored that her first court appearance was going to be against such a renowned criminal lawyer and she was looking forward to inflicting on him one of his rare defeats. It would help her career enormously. It would be a dream start. She thanked me for finding her. She almost kissed me.

The hearing was today. I didn't have to be there myself, she assured me. It was in fact little more than a pro forma sitting. I wouldn't be asked to do anything. She would represent us and ensure it didn't get any further than this one sitting. It has just finished. I just spoke to her. Naturally you're the first one I'm telling the news to, pronto.

The good news is that we won. The judge ruled in our favor on all the points. The strategy of Stefania Volpedo, Attorney at Law, J.D., worked perfectly. The claim was ruled inadmissible. The great Antonio Bentivoglio hadn't even prepared a rebuttal. He waived his right to plead his own case. He simply smiled. It was almost too easy, Stefania said. It was too easy.

Just before the sitting was adjourned, he spoke. For two seconds. He announced that he would be appealing against this ruling on behalf of his client.

I asked her what it meant. She is convinced that any court of appeal would endorse the verdict. The Parodis can litigate their way to the Supreme Court or the European Court with their star lawyer if they want, but this first judge's line of reasoning will be adopted everywhere. Stefania is completely sure of this. And I believe her. We will win.

I asked her whether it meant that the Parodis will have to pay the litigation costs. So here comes the bad news. Stefania explained to me that if the case goes to appeal there's no definitive ruling. And without a definitive ruling, there's no winner or loser. And without a winner and a loser, there's no certainty about who is going to be responsible for the costs. We'll definitely win, but we haven't won yet. I asked her how long it might take in her professional opinion. She reflected. "A week or two?" I asked. "Three weeks, perhaps?"

She looked uncomfortable. "Maybe a bit longer," she said.

"How much longer?"

"You have to understand that Italy is a constitutional state. Lawsuits take time."

"How much time? A month?"

"About seven years."

"Seven years?"

"If we don't have to go to the Supreme Court. We'll leave the European Court aside. But don't worry. We'll definitely win."

"And how much will that cost?"

"I'll charge the same hourly rate to the bitter end, I promise you. I'm grateful to you for giving me this case. I owe you one."

31.

In October of the year 1347, twelve merchant ships sailed into
Messina harbor in Sicily bearing the white flag with the red cross.
They were part of the Genoese fleet that regularly used this harbor. But the spectators ashore soon noticed that this was no routine visit. The ships were behaving oddly. They were sailing more
slowly than usual. The oars were moving irregularly. Some of
them weren't being used at all, and because the number of oars
being used on port and starboard wasn't the same, some of the
ships continuously seemed to be drifting off course. They were
swerving dangerously to one side until the helmsman compen-
sated with the rudder. They swayed into the harbor like twelve
drunkards. A few times they only just managed not to crash into
each other. The Sicilians grew suspicious. Genoa had the best
fleet in the Mediterranean. The discipline of the Genoese crew
was legendary. Something very strange was going on. To be on
the safe side, they drafted in halberdiers to wait for the ships and
their crews on the quayside.

When the ships had finally managed to dock and the Sicilian
soldiers boarded them to find out what was going on, they found
a situation much worse than their grave suspicions. Most of the
crew were critically ill. They had black lumps in their armpits and
groins, some as big as an egg, some even as big as an apple. Blood
and pus seeped from them. The stench was unbearable. Many of
them had black spots on their skin. They had a fever and were
suffering terribly. Several dozen seamen had already died. They
hung lifelessly over their oars.

They came from Caffa, one of the captains said, coughing up blood. It was one of the most important trading posts for the Genoese. The city was in the Crimea, on the Black Sea, and was the end station of the Silk Road. A few months previously the city had been besieged by Kipchaks, Tatar soldiers from the Golden Horde's Khanate. At a certain point, they'd begun to catapult the dead bodies of their own men over the city wall. They had died of a horrible sickness. They were covered in lumps and black spots. It didn't take long for the inhabitants of Caffa to begin to show the same symptoms. The illness spread rapidly; within a few days half of the city was sick. Most of the people who were infected were dead within five days. There was hardly any time to burn the bodies. There were rumors of doctors who became infected visiting a patient and died first. People going to bed healthy could be dead the next morning from the boils and bruises. When the first soldiers in the Genoese garrison died, they fled with these twelve ships.

The Sicilians disembarked the survivors and put them in quarantine. The doctors could do little more than provide them with brandy, willow bark, dried myrtle leaves, and other painkillers. Within a few days, they'd all died. They burned the bodies and disinfected the ships with sulfur and smoldering sage branches. They'd have preferred to sink them but messengers from the north had already announced that the Genoese wanted their ships back. And Genoa was a powerful ally. They couldn't ignore her requests.

The ships sailed into Genoa harbor a week later with Sicilian crews. They were suitably rewarded and spread across various ships with different trade missions so they could return to Messina. None of them showed any symptoms of the mysterious illness.

The crisis seemed to have been averted.

But no one saw a black rat emerge from the hold of one of the ships and run along the black cable with which the ship was moored to the quay, in search of food. And no one saw a second rat follow it, and after that dozens of others from the other ships. The quayside always provided for scavengers. It was covered in fishing waste and other garbage. And from the harbor they disappeared into the caverns of the city.

A few days later, the first Genoese began to display lumps in their armpits and groins, as big as an egg or an apple, oozing pus and blood. Their skin turned black. The illness spread rapidly. Within no time, half the city was sick. Some were dead within five days. There was hardly any time to bury the bodies. And from Genoa, the sickness spread across Liguria, Piemonte, and the rest of Europe. The Black Death would be responsible for millions of victims in the fourteenth century and decimated Europe's population.

32.

And the letter you were so kind as to forward to me didn't contain good news, either, but I suspect you already knew that, if only because of the emphatic "open immediately" printed on the reassuringly lavender-colored envelope. It was an official notification from the tax authorities back home. They refer to arrears built up over the previous years. There's also the matter of a new tax assessment for the past calendar year. This all adds up to a sum I couldn't cover even if they impounded my belongings. If I were still back home, this tax bill would make me technically bankrupt.

I'm busy preparing my response. Every writer of repute has written a long letter to the Inspector of Direct Taxes at some point in their lives. I will explain at length why I merit special status. I will address my contributions to the cultural climate in my fatherland and in a hilarious manner I will calculate to the last cent the various ways in which the bureaucracy is doing me, culture, and humanity a disservice. I will compose an anticipatory ode to the inspector, immortalizing him. I will praise his literary taste and compare him favorably to his fellow inspectors from other districts who, unlike him, are only interested in the banality of bookkeeping and the wheel trims on their company cars, while I will ascribe to him alone the power of discernment that will allow him to write history.

Perhaps, if I do my utter best, my letter to the Inspector of Direct Taxes will please my publisher. Perhaps he will publish it in a small edition. Perhaps I could wheedle a nice advance for it. Because just like my illustrious predecessors in the genre, I am under no illusion that, aside from an eventual publication and the obligatory chapter in an eventual biography, I will make any profit. In the most likely scenario, I can count myself lucky if I can sell my letter to the Inspector of Direct Taxes, the truest and most autobiographical document that I have ever written, as a curiosity to a literary magazine like *The Lying Dog* or *The Barren Rabbit*. After which my belongings will be impounded.

Unfortunately, my fatherland is not like Italy. Back home your belongings are packed up, while here a calm conversation is possible. Back home there are laws, while you don't necessarily have to see things like that here. Back home the system works, while here it would be out of the question to have a system that transcended an individual approach to individual cases and that was still valid the next day. Back home there are payment terms of seven days, while here, with a bit of ingenuity, enough can be invented to make them last seven years.

As soon as I'd read the letter you forwarded, I secured my possessions back home. In concrete terms, I emptied my account at the post office, not hesitating to get maximally overdrawn. Take what's for the picking. Don't ask questions, take advantage. A bald chicken can't be plucked. Eleven hundred euros. I have eleven hundred euros in the inside pocket of my jacket now. If I'm frugal, it'll be just enough for a month. It probably won't be. And with that, I'm five thousand in the red and hiding from a tax bill that's ten times that. With a mixture of alienation and relief, I realized that I had cut off my return route home. I can't go back, even if I wanted to, or in any case not until by some miracle I've become rich enough to pay my debts there.

I'll be safe here in the labyrinth. The Dutch tax authorities won't be able to find me here. But, at the same time, objectively seen, it wouldn't be that foolish to escape this city because of the Parodis' case against me. Of course, in theory I will win in the long run. But I'm not stupid. I've gotten the point. They're smoking me out with their fortune. They have all the time in the world. It will be impossible for me to hold out as long as they. I don't stand a chance. But I don't want to leave at all. This is my city. My life's here.

My last eleven hundred euros in my pocket and without a plan, I'm signing off here in the realization that I can neither stay nor return. But have a drink on me. I'll think of something.

33.

A strange sound woke me up. When I looked out of the window, I saw men in hermetic silver suits proceeding silently along my alleyway. They were spraying a bilious green liquid into all the cracks and holes in the old city. They moved like robots. I got dressed and went outside to ask what they were doing. I addressed someone wearing a glass oxygen mask carrying a spray gun. He didn't even see me. I tapped him on the shoulder. He didn't react. So I tapped a little harder, and then on the visor covering his face. He gestured no with the index finger of his right hand and carried on working. Green steam rose upwards. His colleague stuck stickers on the walls:

> *derattizzazione in corso*
> *non toccare le esche*

I went back to bed and dreamed about the sun. When I was a boy and a long way from here and my knees were bare, there was sun every Sunday at grandma and granddad's house. Ants crawled secretively between the paving stones. But I knew what to do about that. I'd poke their nests open very carefully with sticks. Grinning like an omniscient god, I'd survey their panic. I'd spit on the columns of refugees a bit for fun. I didn't discriminate between enemy troops and civilians. And when I'd had enough, I'd take my pee-pee out of my shorts and annihilate their entire habitat with my piss-yellow Agent Orange.

I wonder how Djiby's doing. And Rashid. The European Court employs methods that are as slow as gas. The first thing to evaporate is the fake Rolex on your wrist. Afterward, hope evaporates.

And after that, green clouds rise up. You try to tap on the glass of the mask of authority, but they ignore you or gesture no with their finger.

A magical finger. And where's your magic, Rashid? Where are the dry, lucid, razor-sharp mathematical harmonies of your old, tawny-skinned folk? And Djiby, where is the magic of your bubbling laugh in the face of every inferno? And where is your magic, Leonardo, Ilja, Ilja Leonard, the magic of your splashing words that surge higher than any of the seven seas? All of our magic has become beached on a sandbank of procedures, paperwork, and problems.

The white ship sounded its horn just once. It was a porcelain ship that sailed to every country that everyone on board had ever dreamed of. Two blasts of the horn warned of the danger of incoming reality. In the meantime, in the harbor, a slow ballet could be observed of bone-white, floating palaces that avoided each other in their determination to dream in every direction at once.

And you, Leonardo, Ilja Leonard, are you going to stay onshore with the rats, or are you going to join the rats on the ships heading south where everything will be even more of the same than it already is? A fresh, cheerful crusade would do you good. Up against the Moors wearing a hip suit of armor. Every scratch that you can inflict on the black, stinking leather of a savage with your expensive designer saber will make the annals of history. Singers will sing of the heroic deeds of Don Leonardo at the walls of Aleppo, the walls of Sanaa, the walls of the Holy City, for all eternity.

Three blasts of the horn meant nothing. Or, better said, it meant everything, but even the oldest mariners in the city could no longer remember what. They'd last heard that signal when their grandparents were children and they'd heard from their grandparents that nobody remembered what three blasts of the horn meant.

You want to embrace someone so you embrace your own arm. Until the cramp starts to hurt. You allow yourself to cry. But even that doesn't work. When nobody's watching, the black ship with lowered black sails sails silently into the black night.

34.

Around midday I walked along Via della Maddalena. It seemed like midnight. Pitch-black whores leaned against the gray walls of dark alleyways in black thigh-high boots. They hissed between their shining white teeth. They said words like "*amore*." They said they wanted to run their fingers through my long hair. I was on my way to the theater. I was hoping Pierluigi would be there. Since he and his father had launched a court case against me, he'd stopped answering his phone. He'd probably even changed his number, because I'd also tried calling on the mobile phone of a friend he couldn't possibly know and many times from Caffè Letterario's landline. I had to speak to him. Maybe I could persuade him to have some sense. Maybe I could even convince him that their exhaustion strategy would only cost them money, too, as I could never comply with their demands because I simply didn't have that much money. I was even prepared to offer my excuses. Maybe I could suggest working together. I would write plays for them and help them put together the program. If necessary, unpaid. I'd offer them access to my contacts abroad. I was prepared to do anything if this absurd court case was dropped.

But Pierluigi wasn't there. The theater was closed, just like yesterday, the day before yesterday, and the days before that. There were no shows or events advertised. I wandered aimlessly through the streets. In Vico Angeli my eye fell upon a whore who was different from the rest: she was white. That itself was highly unusual. And she was slender and attractive. She wasn't flaunting all kinds of showy bulbous wares. She even looked pretty, and that was truly unique in these parts. She was a little hidden in an alcove, almost timid, as though she wanted to attract as little attention as possible from potential customers. She was wearing a strange red wig that reinforced the impression of shyness. It seemed as though she wanted to hide her face while she reluctantly showed off her slender body.

She fascinated me. I tried to look her in the eye. For a short moment our gazes met. She let out a shriek and ran away. I followed her. During the half second she'd looked at me, I'd seen something familiar in her eyes. I had to know what that was. I had to know who she was.

When I reached the corner of Via della Maddalena she was nowhere to be seen. She was quicker than I. She'd probably run farther downhill to Vico dei Corrieri or Vico Lavagna. But perhaps that was too simple. I hazarded a guess that she'd count on me being that simple. In that case she would have gone upward to the parallel alleyway, Vico del Duca, and then she'd probably hide in that narrow alley called Vico Trogoletto that crosses it, out of sight of Via della Maddalena. I went up to the next alley that ran parallel to Vico Angeli, Vico Salaghi, but I didn't see her in Vico Trogoletto. I walked down along Vico del Duca, and when I came out on

Via della Maddalena, I saw her peering around the corner from Vico Angeli. She saw me and fled along Via della Maddalena. She took the first left. I ran as fast as I could in pursuit. She'd committed an error. Obviously she didn't know the alleys in this neighborhood as well as I did. The first left was Vico Malone and that was a dead end.

35.

She stood with her back to the alley against the fence blocking her exit. "Please," she whispered. "Go away." She hid her face in her hands. "Please go away. I beg you. It'll be better for everyone."

"I'm not going to hurt you."

"Yes you will. You'll hurt me. And you'll hurt yourself, too." Her shoulders shook. She was crying. I cautiously laid a hand on her back. "Don't touch me!" I pulled my hand back in shock. There had been something strangely familiar about that touch.

"I don't want anything from you," I said gently. "I just want to see your face. I want to know who you are. And then I'll go. I promise you. If you want, I can even pay for it."

When I said that, her crying increased dramatically in volume. She crumpled. Her whole body shuddered. I was overwhelmed by a warm, salty flood of pity. I had an almost irresistible urge to softly take her in my arms, but I didn't dare touch her again. I didn't know what to do. I rocked on my heels. What should I do? Perhaps she was right. Maybe I should just go away. What was I doing? I'd cornered a slender white prostitute wearing a red wig in a dead-end alley off Via della Maddalena. All that was missing was a pimp coughing politely with a knife to my back and asking why I was scaring the wits out of his herd. And then there was still the possibility, however improbable it might be in this neighborhood, of police patrols and being charged with harassment or worse. As if I wasn't in enough trouble already. Perhaps I really should leave her alone. But something was stronger than I. I had to know who she was. It couldn't be a crime to want to see her face, could it?

"You'll be making the biggest mistake of your life," she whispered, "if you don't go away immediately."

"I don't believe you. But if it is so, I'm prepared. And what kind of damage can seeing your face cause to us? Unless you're so pretty I'll never get you out of my mind, which is a possibility I'm not ruling out, I don't think we're really capable of causing each other pain."

"You don't know what you're saying."

"Wouldn't be the first time," I said. But she didn't laugh.

"I've warned you, Leonardo."

"How do you know my name?"

She didn't reply. She straightened up proudly, still facing the fence, and pulled off her red wig. Long black hair flowed down her back. And then she turned around.

36.

Processions of penitents marched through the depopulated cities. Anyone still strong enough to knead dough or work the bellows for the blacksmith's fire abandoned their ovens and anvils to dress in camelhair and walk barefoot, praying and wailing, through the streets among the stinking bodies covered in suppurating boils and black blotches. In some cities, people were so desperate to suffer sufficiently and pay penance that the streets were scattered with thorns, shards of glass, and glowing coals, replenished on a daily basis by the authorities. Anyone discovering a swelling or a black patch on their skin threw themselves screaming onto one of the many man-sized funeral pyres, the name of the one true God on their lips. Young widows smeared their young breasts with the fresh ash of their husbands, fathers, sons, and lovers. The sound of every city in Europe was of lamentations directed at the heavens. The smell was the odor of putrefaction and burning human remains.

Processions of penitents marched across the depopulated countryside. Long corteges of penitents dressed in jute and ash proceeded through fields of corn that were no longer harvested, cows that were no longer milked, and sheep that were no longer tended. They walked under cloudless skies across blistering hot gravel in the scorching midday sun and slept under open skies on bare rocks in the cutting cold of the night. They trampled every flower. At every blackberry bush, fights broke out over who was the greatest sinner, who then would be first to be allowed to wallow in the sharp thorns. They carried whips with heavy knots in the ropes with which, sobbing, they flailed their own backs until they bled. They pulled their own hair out with their bare hands. They broke the bones in their hands and feet with sharp, abrasive rocks. If an occasional villager offered them alms or a morsel of bread out of pity, they'd angrily kick him lame for having wanted to lessen their suffering.

All Europe had fallen prey to despair, desperation, apathy, and, most of all, a crippling sense of guilt. The Black Death testing all the Christian kingdoms couldn't be anything other than God's punishment. And that punishment was so unimaginably heavy that immense sins must have been committed for the Almighty to bring down such devastating wrath on mankind. If the epidemic was God's punishment, the only remedy was to pay penance. And given the severity of the punishment, penance couldn't be severe enough. And it didn't help. On the contrary. Ironically enough, the processions just helped to spread the illness farther afield. And because they didn't help, the self-castigations became more and more extreme, the processions of penitents longer, their journeys farther, until there was nothing left but a pure, undiluted, silent sense of guilt, that, although it was unbearable, could only be borne.

37.

That's pretty much how I felt when I saw her tear-stained face. She was right. It might be the biggest mistake of my life, wanting to know who she was. It hurt more than I can say to see her in this situation, and I could see that it hurt her immensely to be seen here in this situation. The circumstances completely unnerved me. Thoughts and feelings tumbled over each other like shards of a large mirror that had been smashed to smithereens with the brutal blow of a sledgehammer. If I'd come across her somewhere else after all this time, in a quiet, innocent place, I would have become unsteady on my legs. But seeing her here again in a dead-end side street off Via della Maddalena and realizing that she was no chance passerby but was working the neighborhood with her suggestive, slightly-too-short miniskirt and her torturously attractive legs clothed in the kind of stockings questionable men find exciting, and seeing how she looked at me with tears in her eyes, beyond pride or embarrassment, as though she were standing naked before me, showing me her suppurating wounds because I had insisted as much, set off a cacophony of overwhelming emotions inside me that rendered thought impossible. And all those squeaking and creaking emotions that tried to crowd each other out of the foreground were drowned out by a single loud keynote that swelled increasingly until I could hear nothing else—and that was guilt. Although, objectively, at a different place and a different time, one might come up with a few sensible arguments to put that feeling in perspective, there, at that moment, in Vico Malone, I was overwhelmed by the feeling that it was my fault I was here, that she was here, that everything was like this, and that it was my monstrous fault that the most beautiful girl in Genoa, who was made of different stuff than what girls are usually made of, found herself forced to offer her fragile body to every slobbering old letch who had an itchy cock in his trousers and a fifty in his pocket. I broke.

"You're the only person I've ever loved," I said quietly.

She looked over her shoulder, past me. Her gaze hardened. "It's alright, Khalid." She took my hand. "Come on." Her heels clicking professionally, she strode out haughtily ahead of me onto Vico Angeli.

"Was that your pimp?"

"That was Khalid."

"But is he your pimp?"

"Why do you want to use ugly words like that? Isn't it bad enough already? You have to realize that I just did you a huge favor, even though I'm not sure you deserved it. Pretend to be a nice, normal customer now, otherwise Khalid might cause you some trouble. And he has a whole hell of a lot more experience with trouble than you, believe me."

She opened the door. I went inside. It was a small, square-shaped, windowless cubicle with a bed, a chair, and a sink. She locked the door behind us and went to sit on the bed.

"Are you happy now, Leonardo? Now you've seen my face? My true face. Would you have ever believed me capable of this? I know you're too shocked to be able to answer so I'll speak for you. No, you'd never have thought me capable. Me neither. And spare me your predictable questions. Why? It's not exactly what I planned to do myself. It just happened. After you betrayed me, things didn't go well with my boyfriend, either. I just couldn't believe in anything anymore. But that turned into a really big deal. I'll spare you the details. At a certain moment I actually had to run away. I didn't even have time to pack a suitcase, I reckoned. I owned half the house. I could whistle for that money, of course. But I reconciled myself to it. It's not important. And where could I go? My mother died when I was sixteen and my father has spent his life criticizing everything I do. He got remarried, to a witch who hates me because I'm the only reminder of his previous marriage. I don't have any other family. I stayed with various friends for a bit and then I met Khalid. That's why. Is he forcing me to do this? That's a stupid, predictable question by a person who doesn't understand a thing. Just as love can be a form of coercion, so can coercion be a form of love. Got any more questions? If not, quickly fill me in on your own sorry state of affairs, then we'll be all up to date. Then you can go, and after that I hope I never see you again."

38.

"I'm sorry," I said, gasping for breath.

"What are you sorry about exactly?"

"Everything. I should never have come here."

"I'm glad we've finally understood each other."

"Did you ever... How can I say it?"

"Love you? I was prepared to give up everything for you, even though I didn't have much. I wanted you to take me with you to the north where we'd start a new, quiet life together in a civilized country where everything runs smoothly and people don't scream and shout when it doesn't. I wanted to learn your language so I could read your poems. That was my big dream."

"Maybe it's not too late," I said softly.

"What do you mean?"

"I'll have to solve a couple of problems first. There are debts to be paid. But financial problems can always be solved. It won't be easy, but I'll think of something. Maybe with my publisher's help."

"What are you talking about?"

"Sorry. I only wanted to say that it might take a while, but after that I can take you with me to the north. And in the meantime, we could start teaching you my language."

She began to laugh. "What world are you in, Leonardo? In your dreams? Maybe women in your home country are cold-blooded and fainthearted enough to allow people to walk all over them for financial gain and a stable future, but I'm a southern girl, born in the froth of the Mediterranean, daughter of the Serenissima Repubblica di Genova, which knows no superior, and I believe in love. I loved you but you betrayed me for a fat blonde tart from your own tribe. How could I ever trust you again? How could I ever believe in you again? I despise you. And apart from that, I'm with Khalid now. I know you'll never understand but I love him."

"The way you loved that man who threw you down the stairs."

"Exactly."

"I'll never throw you down the stairs or force you to prostitute yourself."

"Exactly. You're different. You don't get it. You'd have to be a southern girl to understand."

"But what, then? What can I do? How am I going to live in Genoa now that I've seen you here today and understood that you despise me?"

"Why don't you go back?"

"It's not possible."

"You've just said that the financial problems that are stopping you can be solved."

"That might be so. But there are more important hindrances. I'd be the first. I mean, I'm a famous poet in my home country, at least, I was. Too many people know that I emigrated with great fanfare to slake my thirst with *la dolce vita italiana*. I was and am envied for it. But to return home with my tail between my legs like the next nitwit on my favorite television program, *A Place in the Sun*, who can't read the local sewer regulations, and to admit that it all went a little bit differently than planned, and that, to be honest, it was rather disappointing, would be a huge loss of face. I'd be the laughing stock among my cultural friends. In some ways, I got lost in my fantasy of a more beautiful, truer, and more romantic life elsewhere."

"But you just said you'd be happy to take me with you."

"But that would be completely different. If I returned to my fatherland with the most beautiful girl in Genoa at my side, it would be seen as a major triumph."

"The most beautiful girl in Genoa?"

"That's what I've always called you."

"That's actually quite sweet of you."

"Sorry."

She stood up and straightened her skirt. "I'm sorry I can't fulfill the role you came up with for me—the spoils of war for your triumphal return. Before you go, just one last thing. Khalid is waiting outside. I give the money I earn immediately to him. It's safer that way. If you want him to keep on thinking you're a regular customer, and you do, you'll have to pay me."

Of course. That was safer. I asked her how much it was.

"Forty euros." I gave them to her. She didn't thank me. "Of course, in theory, you have the right to fuck me for that amount. Do you want to?"

39.

And that's how I underwent the ultimate humiliation, my dear friend. Of course I should have looked at her with a deep, dark haughty look before stepping wordlessly out into the dark night:

hard, intent, stoic. But I was weak. I was confused. I was over-whelmed. I could produce hundreds of excuses and explanations for it, but they're irrelevant. And when she saw that I was hesitat-ing, she began to undress in a practiced manner. Before I knew it she was standing before me naked like a breathtaking statue of exceptionally soft, fragile marble wearing high heels and stockings, and from that moment on, it was out of my hands. She coerced me with the professionalism of her gaze. She was La Superba.

"Get undressed. You can put your clothes on the chair. Do you want me to put my wig on? Or would you rather have me like this?"

She took a tube of lubricant, smeared a generous dollop between her thighs and lay down on the bed, her legs spread. "Come," she said. She tore open a condom packet with her teeth. I lay down next to her—soft, small, fragile. There were tears in my eyes. She paid no attention to them. She stroked my cock with her long, sacred fingers. "Good boy," she said. The condom was already on. She was experienced. She lay back again and pulled me toward her. Her hand led my cock to the entrance of her Vaseline-filled cunt. "Go on, sweetheart," she said in a strange, high-pitched voice.

She didn't look at me as I penetrated her. She wasn't there. I was only fucking her body. I was nothing more than a customer. I burst into tears and came at the same time.

"Well," she began, "now on your triumphant return to your cultural friends in your fatherland at least you can say you fucked the most beautiful girl in Genoa."

You understand, dear friend, that I'm telling you this with the greatest possible reluctance. I've always taken a great deal of satisfaction from regularly keeping you up to date with my trials and tribulations in my new country. But I never thought I'd lose my way so badly.

I have just one final request, but it won't come as a surprise. I'll never rework these notes into a novel. They're too painful for that. I don't want anyone in our home country to ever know where I am and what happened to me, and I'm begging you—destroy everything I sent you. I know you'll understand and that I can count on you. My thanks.

40.

I made the necessary purchases en route, in Via Canneto Il Curto, Via San Luca, and Via del Campo. Although I didn't have any interest in bartering or trying to get discounts, no one overcharged me.

Ornella stood smoking on her one leg in the alleyway in front of her sex cubicle in the Ghetto. "I knew you'd come back, Giulia." She kissed me. "Come in. Let's have a look at what you've got. I'll help you." She got her crutches and extinguished her cigarette with her one blood-red pump.

She picked up my bag. "Let's see what we've got here. Oh, you got that blue dress from that shop. I almost bought that one. But it's a bit too respectable, don't you think? This black one is good, not just because it's a bit shorter but because of the cut-out sides. I think that'll look lovely on you. And the black has a slimming effect. What kind of a wig do you have? Long black hair. That's really lovely. Where did you find it? Did it take a long time to find? But it will go perfectly with the black dress. First we'll have to shave you. Get undressed. I'll do it for you. It's important that it's done properly. Can you just fetch that silver razor from the bathroom for me? I'm a little unsteady on my leg. And the shaving foam. And a towel. Yes, the red one is good. Come and lie down. It won't hurt. See? All fixed. Now we'll get you nicely dressed. The room next door is free, actually. Well, that's actually a relative concept in the Ghetto, but you can use it for the time being anyway. I have the key. No, that blue dress isn't good at all. Try the black one. And what kind of stockings do you have? No! Those are much too thin. A single snag from a fingernail and you'll have a ladder. You're a professional now, remember that. I'll lend you some. Shoes? Wow. That's courageous. Almost no one here has heels that high. And you're already so tall. Let me give you a tip. If you're standing in the alleyway, you have to stand on the ball of your foot and support most of your weight on the wall by leaning back against it. That way you can lift your other leg up sexily if someone walks past. Got any lubricant, by the way? You're going to need it, believe you me. Otherwise I can lend it to you for tonight. I'm sorry I'm so stingy, but on a busy Friday or Saturday night you can get through entire tubes of the stuff, and it's quite pricey. Sit down. I'll do your makeup. Why don't you fill your bra in the meantime? Don't hold back, a bit more. Do you want to earn money or not? And now your wig. Oh that's lovely. It looks like real hair. So soft. And it looks stunning on you. Ready. Come, take a look in the mirror. What do you see?"

"Giulia," I said in a strange, high-pitched voice.

"The most beautiful girl in Genoa."

Thank you all
for your support.
We do this for you,
and could not do
it without you.

DEEP
VELLUM

DEAR READERS,

Deep Vellum Publishing is a 501c3 nonprofit literary arts organization founded in 2013 with the threefold mission to publish international literature in English translation; to foster the art and craft of translation; and to build a more vibrant book culture in Dallas and beyond. We seek out literary works of lasting cultural value that both build bridges with foreign cultures and expand our understanding of what literature is and what meaningful impact literature can have in our lives.

Operating as a nonprofit means that we rely on the generosity of tax-deductible donations from individual donors, cultural organizations, government institutions, and foundations to provide a of our operational budget in addition to book sales. Deep Vellum offers multiple donor levels, including the LIGA DE ORO and the LIGA DEL SIGLO. The generosity of donors at every level allows us to pursue an ambitious growth strategy to connect readers with the best works of literature and increase our understanding of the world. Donors at various levels receive customized benefits for their donations, including books and Deep Vellum merchandise, invitations to special events, and named recognition in each book and on our website.

We also rely on subscriptions from readers like you to provide an invaluable ongoing investment in Deep Vellum that demonstrates a commitment to our editorial vision and mission. Subscribers are the bedrock of our support as we grow the readership for these amazing works of literature from every corner of the world. The more subscribers we have, the more we can demonstrate to potential donors and bookstores alike the diverse support we receive and how we use it to grow our mission in ever-new, ever-innovative ways.

From our offices and event space in the historic cultural district of Deep Ellum in central Dallas, we organize and host literary programming such as author readings, translator workshops, creative writing classes, spoken word performances, and interdisciplinary arts events for writers, translators, and artists from across the world. Our goal is to enrich and connect the world through the power of the written and spoken word, and we have been recognized for our efforts by being named one of the "Five Small Presses Changing the Face of the Industry" by Flavorwire and honored as Dallas's Best Publisher by *D Magazine*.

If you would like to get involved with Deep Vellum as a donor, subscriber, or volunteer, please contact us at deepvellum.org. We would love to hear from you.

Thank you all. Enjoy reading.

Will Evans
Founder & Publisher
Deep Vellum Publishing

LIGA DE ORO ($5,000+)

Anonymous (2)

LIGA DEL SIGLO ($1,000+)

Allred Capital Management
Ben & Sharon Fountain
Judy Pollock
Life in Deep Ellum
Loretta Siciliano
Lori Feathers
Mary Ann Thompson-Frenk
   & Joshua Frenk
Matthew Rittmayer
Meriwether Evans
Pixel and Texel
Nick Storch
Social Venture Partners Dallas
Stephen Bullock

DONORS

Adam Rekerdres
Alan Shockley
Amrit Dhir
Anonymous
Andrew Yorke
Anthony Messenger
Bob Appel
Bob & Katherine Penn
Brandon Childress
Brandon Kennedy
Caroline Casey
Charles Dee Mitchell
Charley Mitcherson
Cheryl Thompson
Christie Tull
Daniel J. Hale

Ed Nawotka
Rev. Elizabeth
   & Neil Moseley
Ester & Matt Harrison
Grace Kenney
Greg McConeghy
Jeff Waxman
JJ Italiano
Justin Childress
Kay Cattarulla
Kelly Falconer
Linda Nell Evans
Lissa Dunlay
Marian Schwartz
   & Reid Minot
Mark Haber

Mary Cline
Maynard Thomson
Michael Reklis
Mike Kaminsky
Mokhtar Ramadan
Nikki & Dennis Gibson
Olga Kislova
Patrick Kukucka
Richard Meyer
Steve Bullock
Suejean Kim
Susan Carp
Susan Ernst
Theater Jones
Tim Perttula
Tony Thomson

SUBSCRIBERS

Adrian Mitchell

Aimee Kramer

Alan Shockley

Albert Alexander

Amber Appel

Amrit Dhir

Andrea Passwater

Anonymous

Antonia Lloyd-Jones

Ashley Coursey Bull

Barbara Graettinger

Ben Fountain

Ben Nichols

Bill Fisher

Bob Appel

Bradford Pearson

Caroline West

Charles Dee Mitchell

Cheryl Thompson

Chris Fischbach

Chris Sweet

Cody Ross

Colin Winnette

Colleen Dunkel

Cory Howard

Courtney Marie

Courtney Sheedy

David Weinberger

Ed Tallent

Elizabeth Caplice

Frank Merlino

Greg McConeghy

Horatiu Matei

Ines ter Horst

James Tierney

Jeanie Mortensen

Jeanne Milazzo

Jennifer Marquart

Jeremy Hughes

Jill Kelly

Joe Milazzo

Joel Garza

John Schmerein

John Winkelman

Jonathan Hope

Joshua Edwin

Julie Janicke Muhsmann

Justin Childress

Kaleigh Emerson

Kenneth McClain

Kimberly Alexander

Lissa Dunlay

Lori Feathers

Lucy Moffatt

Lytton Smith

Marcia Lynx Qualey

Margaret Terwey

Maria de Vries

Mark Shockley

Martha Gifford

Mary Costello

Matt Bull

Meaghan Corwin

Michael Elliott

Michael Holtmann

Mike Kaminsky

Naomi Firestone-Teeter

Neal Chuang

Nhan Ho

Nick Oxford

Nikki Gibson

Owen Rowe

Patrick Brown

Rainer Schulte

Rebecca Ramos

Richard Thurston

Scot Roberts

Steven Kornajcik

Steven Norton

Susan Ernst

Tara Cheesman-Olmsted

Theater Jones

Tim Kindseth

Todd Jailer

Todd Mostrog

Tom Bowden

Will Pepple

AVAILABLE NOW FROM DEEP VELLUM

CARMEN BOULLOSA · *Texas: The Great Theft*
translated by Samantha Schnee · MEXICO

LEILA S. CHUDORI · *Home*
translated by John H. McGlynn · INDONESIA

ALISA GANIEVA · *The Mountain and the Wall*
translated by Carol Apollonio · RUSSIA

ANNE GARRÉTA · *Sphinx*
translated by Emma Ramadan · FRANCE

JÓN GNARR · *The Indian* · *The Pirate*
translated by Lytton Smith · ICELAND

LINA MERUANE · *Seeing Red*
translated by Megan McDowell · CHILE

FISTON MWANZA MUJILA · *Tram 83*
translated by Roland Glasser · DEMOCRATIC REPUBLIC OF CONGO

ILJA LEONARD PFEIJFFER · *La Superba*
translated by Michele Hutchison · NETHERLANDS

RICARDO PIGLIA · *Target in the Night*
translated by Sergio Waisman · ARGENTINA

SERGIO PITOL · *The Art of Flight* · *The Journey*
translated by George Henson · MEXICO

MIKHAIL SHISHKIN · *Calligraphy Lesson: The Collected Stories*
translated by Marian Schwartz, Leo Shtutin,
Mariya Bashkatova, Sylvia Maizell · RUSSIA

COMING SPRING 2016

MICHÈLE AUDIN · *One Hundred Twenty-One Days*
translated by Christiana Hills · FRANCE

CARMEN BOULLOSA · *Before*
translated by Peter Bush · MEXICO

NOEMI JAFFE · *What are the Blind Men Dreaming?*
translated by Julia Sanches & Ellen Elias-Bursac · BRAZIL

FOUAD LAROUI · *The Curious Case of Dassoukine's Trousers*
translated by Emma Ramadan · MOROCCO

JUNG YOUNG MOON · *Vaseline Buddha*
translated by Yewon Jung · SOUTH KOREA

SERHIY ZHADAN · *Voroshilovgrad*
translated by Reilly Costigan-Humes & Isaac Wheeler · UKRAINE